Jenny B.

d.a. gregory

Jenny B.
A World War II Diary

d.a. gregory

For Dwain, who made dancers of us

This Story's Story

When I moved here from Chicago in October 2008 and bought this old house just off Dreier Boulevard, I had no idea how much work it would be restoring it to livable condition, but neither had I any idea of the treasures I would find. The house hadn't been lived in for years and most of the things belonging to the previous owner and the owner before that had just been left. I was told that Mrs. Leyton, the most recent resident, was in her late eighties when she moved in and that she hadn't changed a thing. I guess she liked the place the way it was. This diary was found in an old tin that once held cookies from a bakery that went out of business in the early fifties. It was in a prominent place on the living room fireplace mantle, right next to the Leyton family Bible, and wrapped in waxed paper as though it had been an important keepsake for someone. I doubt if Mrs. Leyton ever bothered opening the tin that looked like it belonged right where I found it.

  I haven't met anyone who remembers Virginia Brewster, but I haven't tried very hard to find people who knew her either. I want those who might read this diary to get to know her the way I did, from what was written, not from things said about her by people with long faded memories. The diary reveals clearly who she was and at times I feel I know her better than I knew my own sister. There are several Brewsters in Evansville and from public records I know that Jenny and her family once lived in this neighborhood in the house five doors down the street toward Dreier from here. Yearbooks from Centennial Elementary School and F.J. Reitz Junior High and High

School provided me with pictures, but from the diary I already knew what she looked like much better than pictures could reveal. Mrs. Chandler had been the youngest teacher at Centennial according to the diary; I'm sure she would remember Jenny if she were still living and I would have liked to talk with her. She was the only teacher I attempted to track down. She died in 1984 though and the other teachers are likely long gone too. Jenny had classmates who are probably still alive who would remember her, but none of their memories are really important for the story, as it's not a piece of family history or genealogy. My task has been simple: to transcribe the diary as accurately and as literally as I could. The title is mine, because of course the diary didn't have one, and since a great deal of what's written is about Jenny, her name seemed fitting. The story's a glimpse into what real life was like for two children—becoming young adults—beginning just before and continuing through the duration of World War II. It was a time when every boy and girl would have been given a diary by a parent or grandparent and encouraged to write in it often. Few did and most regretted it later in life as memories of the war years began to fade.

In a quiet Evansville turned upside down by a booming war economy, hardly anyone noticed the two best friends becoming much more than that and the story of their love would never have been written if not for the daring of the young author. This story being set during the 1940s is what makes it worth reading. At the time, many of the adventures and situations casually narrated by our young writer weren't spoken of in polite social circles and were certainly not put to paper.

The day I found the diary, I spent hours reading it and I've read it several times since. I laugh and cry as much now as I did when reading it for the first time. I have a feeling that, in her time, Jenny was an extraordinary woman and it has been a privilege getting to know her. She and most of the characters in this story don't fit well into the Hollywood history of that time and the only reason younger readers will believe these diary entries to be credible is because they were not intended to be read by anyone other than their author. It was a different, almost unimaginable time—not simple as some would have us think—and there was nothing magical about a war that consumed youth and threatened to destroy the world. The war was real and touched the lives of every family across America, sometimes in horrible ways.

The diary is reproduced substantially as it was written with only minor grammatical changes made for readability; most involved picking out quotes and attributing them to the right speaker. The author was a good writer, even at eleven, and I hesitated making any corrections at all. The diary is what it is and speaks for itself, free of pretense and self-promotion as only a young writer can be.

Kathleen Reinhard Sparks
Evansville, Indiana

Chapter One

1940
Monday, October 7, 1940
Night

Mom gave me this diary for my sixth birthday and told me to write down important things in my life, but I never had anything to write about even when I learned how. It must have a million pages and all of them were blank until today. Nothing much ever happened worth writing about until Jenny showed up and now that she's my best friend, maybe I'll write about her. I'm only eleven, but my teacher says the tests we took last year showed that I might be a writer someday. I think I'd like that.

Virginia Lee Brewster's the prettiest girl in fifth grade; everyone says so. Her shoulder length brown hair, curled by her mother every morning, and her pretty blue eyes make the boys in my class crazy and the girls jealous. When she smiles in my direction for no reason as I walk with her to school every morning, that makes me feel really special. Jenny, or Jenny B. as I sometimes call her, moved here with her family two summers ago from somewhere out west; I forget the town. She was like any other girl in the neighborhood then, and now she's my best friend in the world. Her father was looking for a job and found one at the Missouri Valley Bridge and Ironworks where my father works. Dad says that soon they're going to start building ships, called LSTs, for carrying tanks across the ocean in case there's a war. He calls them 'Large Slow Targets,' although I'm pretty sure that's not what LST is supposed to stand for. Evansville, Indiana is a long way from any ocean and why they want to build ships here, I have no idea, but almost everyone at our school has a parent who works at the Ironworks. It's huge. They even have their own newspaper, *The Invader*. I guess, after so many years of no one having a job, the government deciding to build boats—or ships—here sounded like a good idea. Now, there are new families moving into our neighborhood almost weekly but the Brewsters were one of the first to arrive.

My birthday was in the summer, June sixth, and Jenny's birthday was the day before. She likes reminding me she's older than me even if it's only by one day. She lives five houses away on the same block and our families sometime get together for cookouts and stuff. I think I was the first person in Evansville her own age Jenny met. It's always a big deal when a new family moves into our neighborhood and soon everyone on the block knew the Brewsters. I especially like her mom. She's smart and nice and really young to be someone's mother, although I guess she's older than Mom. I don't really know Jenny's dad very well. He works all the time like mine. I have one older sister in high school and Jenny has one older brother who's in the Army somewhere in England. He joined as soon as he graduated high school. I would love to go to England someday.

Thursday October 10, 1940
Night

School is school. There are ten boys and twelve girls in my class this year at Centennial Elementary. Most of us started school when we were seven. My parents could have enrolled me at six but a lot chose to wait a year. They're the same kids that were in my class last year, except for Marston. He failed the fifth grade and is having to repeat it. He thinks he knows everything just because he's a year older than the rest of us. He announced on the first day of class when Mrs. Winston wasn't in the room that he really likes how Jenny has filled out since last school year; like he was describing an ear of corn or something. Filled out what? It's such a stupid thing when he just stares at Jenny. I've seen him do it and I'm pretty sure what he's staring at. She pretends not to notice, but she has to. Though I'd never say it out loud, I hate him.

Jenny and I went to the neighborhood pool almost every day during the summer and I was the first to see what was different about her, before Marston, and I had the politeness not to say anything. I guess I still look every day but I don't stare; that would be, I don't know, rude or something.

Jenny and I talk about things, lots of things and yesterday she told me she knows Marston stares at her chest and that now some of the other boys in our class are doing it too.

"Why don't they stare at the other girls?" she asked me. "Some of them have boobies bigger than mine. He's such a crud and if he doesn't stop, I'm going to tell Mrs. Winston."

Her saying that sort of shocked me. We talk a lot, although we've never talked about things like that before and I've never heard anyone call breasts 'boobies.' Mrs. Winston's our teacher and she was my mother's teacher. For me, telling her anything like that would be like telling my grandmother, but not for Jenny. I thought for a minute what to say and told her that Marston's behavior was just vulgar. That was the best word I could come up with. The important thing is that she told me something very personal she didn't have to and I thought about that a lot last night.

Since the weather's turned cool, Mrs. Winston says we're having gym inside tomorrow and we have to bring our gym clothes. I hope I can find mine.

Friday October 11, 1940
Afternoon

I just got home from school after stopping at Jenny's for a few minutes. Jenny's mother is painting their living room and I offered to help, although I could tell she really didn't want anyone helping her. Today we played volleyball, boys versus girls. My gym clothes from last year fit me just fine; Jenny's are much too small. Her shorts are a lot shorter than everyone else's and her T-shirt didn't hide anything. All the boys noticed of course, especially Marston, but the girls were looking too. I think she looks great in shorts and a T-shirt and that all the other girls are just jealous. She told me on the way home that she was given a note for her mother by Mrs. Winston after school. Naturally we read it. The note said Jenny needed to get new gym clothes before dressing out for gym again.

"I was expecting this," Jenny told me as I read the note. "She looked at me funny during gym today. I guess I've outgrown my gym clothes from last year."

I didn't say anything.

Tuesday October 15, 1940
Night

Fifth grade is the year boys and girls are shown the film, *Our Developing Bodies*—separately of course, and we've all heard stories about how stupid the movie is, but I'm sort of looking forward to it. Mrs. Winston announced it to the class today by saying that tomorrow after recess we'll be shown what she called 'a very important movie' and that all the boys are to meet in Mr. Mitchell's room and all the girls are to meet in Mrs. Chandler's room. Mr. Mitchell teaches sixth grade and coaches basketball. Mrs. Chandler is the third grade teacher and the youngest teacher in the school. We all know what very important movie we're going to see; they always show it to fifth graders within the first month or so of school. Maybe I'll learn something.

Jenny and I met today as we always do at recess under the big oak tree in front of the lunchroom and shared a Popsicle. My favorite flavor is banana and hers is grape, so today I bought grape. We talked about the film some.

"I'm glad it's going to be in Mrs. Chandler's room. I like her. I might just talk to her about Marston instead of Mrs. Winston. Maybe she can tell him to stop staring at me."

I didn't say anything to that, but earlier this morning when we were walking to school, I noticed that the blouse she was wearing would occasionally open up between the second and third buttons and that I could see a lot if I walked half a step behind her, so I walked half a step behind her. Maybe I should have told her about the blouse right away, but I didn't want to admit that I'd looked.

Sitting on the grass under the oak tree, I waited until I was sure I would get a good look and I looked. Her starched and ironed white blouse was puckered out between the two buttons and I saw everything. It wouldn't be right for anyone else to see what I'd seen, especially Marston, so I told her.

"Jenny, I think you should do something about your blouse; it's sort of open between two of the buttons…I mean, when you move just right I can see clean through."

She just kept talking about the movie as if what I'd told her didn't matter.

"I'll get a pin from Mrs. Winston after recess and fix it," she finally said. "Thanks for telling me."

We sat there, eating our Popsicle halves and talking, and I looked whenever I could without her noticing, but I think she caught me a couple of times. Maybe she didn't mind me looking; after all, we are best friends. When the bell rang we got up and started back to class. On the way she had something to tell me.

"I'll have a surprise for you tomorrow. My mom and I are going shopping today after school for some new clothes and you'd better notice."

I have to remember to say something nice about her new clothes tomorrow.

Wednesday October 16, 1940
Night

Jenny must think I'm the biggest dunce in town. On our way to school this morning, I tried to think of something to say about her new clothes, but I know every skirt and blouse she ever wears and this morning she was wearing the yellow skirt with the light blue blouse I'd seen her wear lots of times. She looked really pretty, although nothing she was wearing was new. I thought maybe something had come up and she and her mother hadn't gone shopping after all. She didn't say anything about her clothes and neither did I. There was something different though; I just didn't say anything.

Sitting under the oak tree again at recess, far away from the others, she leaned over and whispered to me:

"Want to see what my mom bought me yesterday?"

Before I could answer she unbuttoned two of her buttons and I caught a glimpse of the new white bra she was wearing.

"It's not exactly what I had in mind when Mom said we were going clothes shopping. I hate it, but she says I have to wear it to school anyway. As soon as I get home, I'm taking it off. I wanted a black one or any color but white. As I expected though, Mom wouldn't hear of it."

I sort of like it and hate it. It makes her look more like a real woman for sure, but I won't be getting any more looks either. I hate it mostly. Jenny and I are close and we talk about things with each other we wouldn't dream of talking about with anyone else. Before today we've never talked about underwear though. She knows I think she's pretty whatever she wears or doesn't wear. I've told her often enough and I don't say it only to be nice.

After recess, the boys and girls split up and went to see the movie. It was as boring as everyone said, although I did learn some things and it'll give Jenny and me a lot more stuff to talk about. I wonder if the boys and girls saw the same movie. I didn't ask anyone.

Friday October 18, 1940
Night

Today after school I helped Jenny carry her poster home that she did for geography class. It was a map of South America on heavy cardboard and she glued on little things representing the major exports of each region. She got an A on it and wanted to show her parents. When we got to her house, her mother wasn't home, which is unusual. She's always on the front porch waiting for us. The note on the door said she'd gone down the street a few blocks to visit Mrs. Wilkerson—she has a new baby—and that she would be home by five. I brought the poster into the house for her and leaned it against the wall in the living room. Then Jenny had an idea.

"Let me change out of my school clothes and we can catch the matinee at the Rosedale if it's okay with your mom."

It was only a minute running to my house and Mom said it would be fine if I went as long as I was home by dinner. We had plenty of time. I raced back to Jenny's, called out for her, and heard her answer from upstairs, but she'd turned the radio on and I couldn't understand what she said. I knew which was her room and went up the stairs. When I got to her room, the door was open just a crack. The right thing to do would have been to make some noise to let her know I was there. I didn't. Instead, I stood along the wall beside the door and peeked inside. I watched as she undressed and carefully placed her clothes on hangers. She was soon wearing nothing but her new bra and a pair of pink panties as she searched through her everyday clothes for something to wear. When she found something, she hesitated for a moment as if thinking what to do next and then took off her bra and panties and placed them in a basket to be washed separately from other clothes. I guess the panties were new too. She stood there and looked at herself for a minute in the full length mirror on the wall.

Today I got an eyeful of what Jenny looks like and she's even more beautiful without her clothes. I look more like the eight year olds in the film we saw the day before yesterday. She found a pair of plain white panties and put them on and then pulled on a white T-shirt that was too small and grabbed a long sleeved shirt that looked too big. That was when I decided it was time for me to get downstairs before she finished dressing. I feel so like a Peeping Tom for spying on her.

I was waiting for her at the landing and tried not to stare. I like how she looks in a T-shirt with nothing on underneath, but I won't be telling her that. She put on the long sleeved shirt as she walked down the stairs. It's pretty cold out today. As she ran past me out the door with her coat, she yelled back, "Okay, let's go. I have no idea what's playing, but I guess we can see it anyway."

It was *Pride and Prejudice*. Jenny's read Jane Austen's book; I haven't. It didn't matter. I got to sit next to the girl I'd just seen naked. The story was hard for me to follow, but Jenny knew every turn, and during one of the love scenes, she reached for my hand. I was in Heaven for the next hour and forgot all about the movie. On the way home, she held my hand again as she talked about wanting to fall in love someday. Maybe I'm already in love. She's all I think about and after this afternoon, I'll have a lot more to think about.

Sunday October 20, 1940
Night

I didn't see Jenny yesterday and it was a terrible day, but then I got to sit next to her in church today. Our families usually sit together and we sit in the same pew every Sunday. Last night I dreamed about kissing her. I want her to be my first kiss. They say you always remember your first kiss and I want that memory to be of her. I don't even know how to kiss and what if she doesn't kiss me back? She might let me kiss her just because she's nice and all, but would she kiss me back? That's a stupid thing for me to think about. Why would she want to kiss me anyway? Maybe I'll ask her if she's ever been kissed. But what if she has? Then I won't be the first for her. I'm not going to ask. I don't want to know.

Thursday October 24, 1940
Night

Daddy says we'll be in the war any day now. It's been going on since last year, but so far we haven't gotten involved. The Germans are bombing England every day and he says we won't stand for it. Our teachers at school talk about it a lot, too. Jenny's worried about her brother. He's in England and if we do get into the war, he'll be one of the first shipped out. Jenny and I talk every day, and every night I think of how I might kiss her. Should it be a simple kiss on the cheek or should I go for it all and kiss her on the lips and hope for the best? I think of her all the time and dream of being close to her. I want to read this diary to her when we're old so she'll know how long I've loved her. New Year's! That's when I'll kiss her. Everyone kisses on New Year's. That's my resolution. I'll kiss her on New Year's Eve at the stroke of midnight at the very latest.

Daddy and Mr. Brewster are going to someplace in Pennsylvania along with a lot of other men to help build an air raid shelter. Maybe we should have one in Evansville. Daddy says it'll be the first shelter built in the United States. Does he think the Germans will bomb us like they do the British? I have to talk to Jenny about this. She knows a lot about the war.

Wednesday October 30, 1940
Morning

Our class has been planning a Halloween party for the last two weeks. Jenny and I are supposed to work in the haunted house and do our best to scare the life out of the younger children. Admission is only for students under eight so we might just be able to pull it off. Jenny's mother has been working for a week on a Dracula costume for her and I'm supposed to be one of her, or his, victims. My parents weren't so crazy about the idea to begin with, but since it's a fundraiser for the school, they've agreed to let me play a part. My dad even built Dracula's coffin for us. We've rehearsed our roles half a dozen times and we're pretty scary, especially in the dark. I'm looking forward to being in the dark with Jenny. She's one vampire I wouldn't mind being bitten by.

Friday November 1, 1940
Early morning

Last night was too much and I couldn't write about it when I got home. I had to think for a while. It was great having Jenny's mouth on my neck every ten minutes and a few times I managed to slip my arm around her in the dark, accidentally of course. Everything was going great until about nine when we were ready to close the haunted house. Most of the younger children had already gone through a couple of times and the parents running the event started letting some of the older students in, even though they weren't supposed to. That's when the trouble started. Marston and some of his gang got in and when I heard Jenny scream a real scream, I ran over in the dark with my flashlight to find him holding her and each of his buddies pretending to bite her on the neck. I'm pretty proud of myself for stepping in and chasing them out, although they could've picked me up and thrown me through a wall if they'd wanted to. Jenny's screams also brought Mr. Mitchell and he's probably the real reason they left. We closed the haunted house after that. Jenny was quiet as we started walking for home, but about half way, she stopped and turned toward me, put her arms around me and hugged me. She was crying and trying to talk.

"They pinched my boobies hard and it really hurt. They still hurt."

She started rubbing her breasts with her hands.

"Why did they do that? I'm going to tell Mrs. Chandler on Monday. I hate them all."

We took a little detour and sat side by side on a bench under the big tree in Mr. Brock's front yard. It was pitch black and there were no lights on in the house. I held her in my arms as she cried. She was shaking she was so upset. I've never seen her cry before, not even when she scraped her knee at the pool and had to wear a bandage for a week.

"I don't know what I would've done if you hadn't been there."

I didn't exactly know what to do so I just held her—and with my other hand, I reached under her coat and put my arm around her waist. For some crazy reason, I thought it would be okay and that it would make her feel better. She didn't move my hand and I didn't stop hugging her. I just wanted to do something and it must've worked because in a few minutes she stopped crying.

New Year's came early this year. I pulled my hand from underneath her coat and raised her chin, pulled her close and kissed her, like in the movies; maybe not exactly like in the movies. She didn't try to pull away and I felt her arm move behind me and pull me closer to her. When she leaned back against the bench I kissed her again, moved my hand back under her coat and held her close. I thought about sliding my hand under her blouse, but the light from a flashlight along the sidewalk put a stop to everything. Neither of us said anything as we walked the rest of the way to her house. The porch light was on, and so I said goodbye like I had so many times before. As she opened the screen door, she turned to me and I read her lips; she said 'thank you.'

I did it. I kissed her. I don't know if I did it right, but it must have been okay because she kissed me back. I still hate Marston, even though he and his gang's horrible behavior got me my first kiss and more. It was a crazy night. I definitely love her.

Saturday November 2, 1940
Late afternoon

I walked past Jenny's house about a dozen times this morning before she finally came out and walked down to the sidewalk. She said she'd been watching me from her bedroom window. We walked together to the bench we'd sat on just a few hours earlier. We sat together, but not nearly as close as we had before. Her look was serious and I was afraid something was wrong; that maybe I shouldn't have kissed her last night.

"You know our parents would kill us if they knew what happened last night."

I was terrified until the big smile she was hiding escaped.

"Mine would probably send me away to a reform school on the east coast somewhere," I said with just as big a smile.

"Come with me back to the house. Mom's making lunch and she asked me to invite you."

So I went. I sat next to Jenny and her mother sat across the table from us. I always like eating Saturday lunch at Jenny's house. Her mother makes some pretty unusual things on Saturdays and she likes to try them out on us. They're always good and today we had crépes. I didn't know what they were. They tasted sort of like pancakes, but really thin and buttery with lots of syrup. I could have eaten about a million of them. Jenny held my hand under the table whenever her mother would get up to do something. When we finished eating, we helped Mrs. Brewster clear the table and wash the dishes. Then Jenny told her mother she wanted me to help her move the bed in her room closer to the window. We went upstairs to her room and had the bed moved in a few minutes. I turned toward the door to leave, but Jenny turned me back around to face her and then she kissed me. She really kissed me. I wasn't expecting that and we just stood there kissing until I heard the squeaking of the stairs. We walked out and met Mrs. Brewster in the hall. She wanted to inspect the job we'd done. Eventually, we moved the bed twice more before she and Jenny were happy.

Right after the Brewsters moved into the neighborhood, Mom told me I was to ask Mrs. Brewster every day after school if there was anything I could help her do. I don't mind; it gives me more time with Jenny. So I ask every day and almost every day, she gives Jenny and me a little job to do. My mom has my older sister and me to help around the house, but Mrs. Brewster doesn't have anyone other than Jenny. I might be kinda scrawny but I'm strong and between Jenny and me, we can do almost anything that needs doing. Our fathers work every day except Sunday and sometimes they work on Sunday too, so they're mostly not around to help with things. When they are home, they sleep a lot. Their work must be terribly hard.

I'm thinking about asking Jenny to ask her mom if she would cut my hair. She cuts Jenny's and her father's and it looks really good. Mom cuts mine and Daddy's and she did a good job when I was a little kid, but she always cuts it too short. She says that's the only way she knows how, so last time I asked her not to cut it at all and she didn't. Now it's too long. My sister gets one of her friend's moms to cut her hair. Sometimes it turns out okay.

Monday November 4, 1940
Night

Yesterday after church, Jenny and I went for a long walk in the park. It was a cold day but we didn't care; we were together. Maybe this is what flirting is. We sat on one of the benches at the lake and talked most of the afternoon. It was too cold for anyone else to be out so we had the lake to ourselves. We sat close—not too close—and held hands.

"You're a really good kisser," she told me out of the blue.

When I told her I'd never kissed anyone before, she smiled and gave me a quick kiss on the lips and told me she'd never kissed anyone either. So it was perfect. Jenny's perfect. And I can close my eyes and relive every kiss and every touch. I just had a terrible thought—maybe this is all just practice for her for when she starts dating or gets married or something. I've heard that some girls do that with boys or even each other. Is that what this is? Is it just practice? I wish I'd never thought of that. If she's only practicing with me, I don't think I could stand it. But if I ask her, she might stop and that would be worse. Maybe I shouldn't even care, but I do. I'm going to ask her; not just yet though.

Thursday November 7, 1940
Night

The idea that when Jenny and I kiss, it's only practice for her bothered me a lot today. I spent yesterday rehearsing what I would say to her; how I would ask her. I had to know, so today on our way home after school I just asked.

"When we kiss, Jenny, is it just practice? I mean, do you kiss me so you'll know what to do when you go out, when you get older and start dating?"

"Well, when you kiss me, is it just practice for you?"

I wasn't expecting that. I'd never even thought such a thing. I had an answer though; it just came to me.

"Yes it is practice…for when I can kiss you whenever I want."

"And what makes you think I'll let you kiss me whenever you want?"

If she hadn't been smiling when she said that, I probably would have died. We smiled at each other a lot the rest of the way home. I think she loves me too.

There's a new movie playing at the Rosedale this weekend and I'm going to ask her to come with me. It's called *Dance, Girl, Dance* and it has Lucille Ball in it. She's probably Jenny's favorite actress so I know she'll want to go. I wish I knew how to dance. Jenny knows how; her mother taught her and Mr. Brewster. I wonder if she would teach me.

Jenny says her mom will be happy to cut my hair if I come by tomorrow after lunch.

Saturday November 9, 1940
Late

I love my new haircut. Jenny's mom knows what she's doing. My hair is thin, like my sister's. Maybe it's because our hair is so light colored. Jenny's hair is thick and dark brown and there's enough of it that Mrs. Brewster can style it any way she wants. She says the style she did for me is something between Louise Brooks and Freddie Bartholomew. I don't know who Louise Brooks is but Freddie Bartholomew was great in *Captains Courageous*. I saw it about a dozen times.

We went to the movies tonight and it was really crowded. I didn't get to kiss Jenny even once through the whole movie, but we did hold hands under our coats. She has nice hands. On the way home I asked her if it would be all right if I asked her mother to teach me how to dance. There's always a Thanksgiving dance sponsored by the Ironworks and I want Jenny to go with me. I go with my parents every year and mostly I don't like it, but I do like watching the couples dance, at least the ones that really know how. Jenny thought it would be a great idea if I asked her mother to teach me and she was sure she would say yes. Jenny didn't give me the chance to ask though. She was so excited, she asked for me as soon as we got back to her house after the movie. Mrs. Brewster was in the middle of mopping the kitchen floor and she just stopped what she was doing. It was like we'd rescued her from a prison or something. Her eyes lit up as she dropped the mop where she stood and went in search of records.

We began with a simple waltz. The music was slow and I was able to learn the steps quickly. It's the kind of dance I see the parents do every year at Thanksgiving and I like it, but I want to learn how to swing dance. I don't really know what it is, but everyone talks about it. Mrs. Brewster knows how and she said she'll teach me if I can stay for a lesson every day after school—and I have to get Mom's permission. I'll ask her Monday morning. She's always in a good mood in the mornings after getting Daddy off to work. Poor Daddy, he has to work on Veterans Day, but we're out of school.

Monday November 11, 1940
After dinner

I did it. I asked Mom about Mrs. Brewster teaching me how to dance and she said yes. She thinks it would be a good thing for me to learn how to waltz, that it was a sign of proper upbringing. I didn't exactly tell her what kind of dance I really want to learn. No matter, I can learn to waltz too. I had my first real lesson today and it was great. Maybe I'll like the waltz after all. Having a good reason to hold Jenny close is nice. Thanksgiving is November 21 this year and the dance is always the Saturday night before, so I have a week to learn everything I can. Mrs. Brewster had to practically chase me away this afternoon and I can't wait until tomorrow's lesson: she promised it would be all swing.

Saturday November 16, 1940
Late

Jenny's parents came by and picked me up for the dance early. Mr. Brewster was drafted to be the ticket taker at the door and Jenny wanted me to ride with them. Even though the dance is free, you have to be an employee of the Ironworks or their guest to get in. Everyone was dressed in their very best. Jenny was dressed to the nines, wearing a dress I didn't recognize, and I would have remembered it. Later she told me it was her mom's favorite dance dress from when she was her age. It was beautiful and it fit like it was made for her. It was yellow, my favorite color, with big puffy sleeves and a neckline that made her look at least seventeen. I'm sure Jenny's father didn't approve, but she was just so beautiful wearing that dress he couldn't possibly have said no. I didn't have anything special to wear, so I wore my normal church clothes. Jenny told me I looked nice anyway. When we arrived I heard one of the men tell Mr. Brewster that he would have to beat the young boys off with a stick. I found out later that the man was Mr. Cohen, the plant manager.

Since we were early, we had the dance floor to ourselves. It was so much bigger than the Brewster's living room. Jenny and I got a quick lesson from her mom before too many people showed up, then she and the other women tended to the buffet. I hoped she would get to dance some and not be stuck serving food all night. She's a good dancer, much better than any I've seen at this dance before.

Jenny and I sat at a table together, away from her parent's, and ate things I don't remember as the crowd arrived. When Mom and Dad got there, they sat with Jenny's dad. My sister didn't show up. I guess this was a little too boring for her and her friends. There were a few people my age that came with their parents though. They were mostly from my school, but there weren't any I wanted to dance with. There was a real live band and when the music started, I recognized the first number as a waltz. Jenny's father came over and asked her to dance. The two of them looked wonderful together and it was obvious her dad had learned a lot about dancing from her mom. When she came back to our table, Jenny was not happy.

"He always does that. He likes to show off that his daughter's a good dancer; now none of the boys will ask me. Boys don't like to dance with girls who are better than they are and I bet there aren't three of them here tonight who know how to dance at all."

She was right; the boys were too shy to ask her to dance and I was sort of glad. Pretty soon most of the older boys were standing up against one wall and most of the older girls were standing against the opposite wall. It's like they were daring each other to walk across the dance floor. One young boy, he couldn't have been more than eight, finally came over to our table. He said that his mother told him to ask Jenny to dance. Jenny was a foot taller than him, but she danced with him anyway and then thanked him for asking when he brought her back to our table. Mrs. Winston had let us know yesterday, in no uncertain terms, that she wanted to see all of us dancing tonight and that it would be perfectly fine for a girl to ask a boy, that it was a tradition at this event. I guess I'd never noticed that before, but I was never this interested in dancing before either. It didn't matter, because no one was asking anyone to dance. Mrs. Winston dragged a few of the boys out on the floor, and they didn't look too happy about it. She might be old, but she's a good dancer too. I remember seeing her and her husband dancing at this event last year.

My dad and mom don't know how to dance at all. It didn't matter; there they were on the floor holding each other close and moving to the music. A lot of the parents were dancing or pretending to, but when Jenny's parents stepped onto the floor, they stole the show. They danced for about six songs in a row and I didn't recognize most of the steps. They looked good together though and seemed to enjoy showing off a little. I wanted so much to ask Jenny to dance—it was different with so many people watching. She could ask me, I thought, but maybe she felt the same way. Mrs. Winston wasn't happy with the participation she was seeing and began pushing the girls toward the boys, across the floor. It was funny when she dragged one of the bigger boys out on the floor, paired him up with a partner and just stood there waiting for them to dance. No one wanted that, so some of the boys and a few of the girls began walking across the floor for partners, although no one came for Jenny and me. Maybe Mrs. Winston didn't see us. It was pretty dark in there. The trips across the dance floor lasted for about half an hour, then the boys and girls went back to their walls. Some of the girls danced with each other after that, but I didn't see any boys dancing with girls. Jenny danced with her father a couple more times and with that kid once more—or it could have been a different kid.

"I didn't come tonight to dance with my father or some kid," Jenny announced after dancing with yet another boy sent by his mother. "We've practiced together enough. It's time we danced, so if you're not going to ask me, I'll ask you. May I have this waltz?"

I was so nervous; God was I nervous. I was sure I'd forgotten everything Mrs. Brewster had taught me. It was a slow waltz and when we started moving, I remembered the steps. We danced close, but not so close anyone would notice. It felt good having her arms around me and mine around her and soon I didn't care who was watching. It was a wonderful feeling, being that close to her, moving to the music with all the multi-colored lights around us. I didn't want the song to end. We sat out the next song but when the band started playing a Tommy Dorsey song we'd practiced to, I got up my courage.

"Miss Brewster, may I have the honor of this dance?"

We both laughed as we walked back out onto the dance floor. People were watching us this time; or rather they were watching Jenny. Anyone would look good dancing with her, even me.

When the band took a break, I saw Mrs. Winston talking to the band leader and when they started back up, it was all swing music. Jenny and I didn't wait for anyone to ask us to dance and we danced like we were the only ones on the floor; at times we were. For the last song they played a waltz and by that time almost everyone, including my parents, had gone home. The people left were all on the dance floor so there was no one watching us and the lights had been turned down real low. At the end of the song, I made sure no one was looking and I kissed her. It was my best kiss yet I think because she almost collapsed in my arms.

On the way home, Jenny's parents talked on and on about how well we danced. They didn't mention that mostly we danced with each other. At the dance Mrs. Brewster insisted I keep up the lessons after school, and it was easy for me to promise I would. It's been the most wonderful night of my life. If I tell Jenny I love her, will she tell me back? I do love her. I know it.

Friday November 22, 1940
Morning

Yesterday was Thanksgiving and since the Brewsters don't have any family around here, my parents invited them to our house. Mom and Mrs. Brewster had this all planned and the two of them put together a dinner like I've never seen. That was the biggest turkey we've ever had and the desserts Mrs. Brewster made were so good. Some of them I recognized from her Saturday experiments she tries out on Jenny and me. It was a good day. We ate our dinner early and afterward Jenny and I helped with clearing the table and dividing the leftovers. My sister even helped with the cleanup before stalking back to her room upstairs. Our house must have been built by the same people who built the Brewster's because they are practically identical. My room is exactly where Jenny's is in her house and my sister's is directly across the hall.

Jenny brought some records with her and I asked Mom if she and I could go up to my room and play them. First I had to borrow my sister's portable record player and she's very particular with it. It was an expensive birthday present. Of course she said no when I asked, but Mom told her she had to share just for today. She brought it into my room and set it up for us and put on one of the records Jenny brought. I had to promise I wouldn't touch it except to change the volume. When she was finally satisfied we weren't going to break it, she went back to her room. Glenn Miller's my favorite and Jenny brought four of his records. Neither of us can just sit and listen to "In the Mood". That's swing dance music, so we rearranged the furniture a little, took off our shoes, and went through every move we know. Mom only had to come up once and tell us to hold down the noise. After getting my sister to come change the record for us every five minutes for half an hour, she finally agreed to let me change it. It's not hard and I don't know how she thought I could hurt her precious record player by simply changing the record.

Jenny and I were pretty exhausted after an hour of swing so I put on a waltz. We were alone, although my bedroom door was open. I looked and made sure my sister's door was closed and then took Jenny in my arms and held her close as we danced to "Imagination." It's a perfect waltz; not too slow and easy to make the steps fit. It was the first time we've danced alone to a waltz and it felt good being able to hold her as close as I wanted. It's one thing to see the curves of her body and something else to be able to feel them. Kissing while dancing that close seemed for both of us like the right thing to do. By the end of the song, we weren't really dancing anymore, just sort of moving to the music and kissing. Jenny chose the next song. I didn't know it.

"This one I picked out just for you," she said as the music started.

We didn't even pretend to do any of the steps anymore. My hands moved farther down her back and hers moved farther down mine. When the music stopped, our hips were together and our hands were even lower. I hadn't realized just how hot it was in my room until then.

"Like the title of the song, 'Body and Soul,'" she whispered in my ear, and then she kissed me like she'd never kissed me before, with her mouth open a little. Our tongues touched and we were one body and one soul for a moment. It was a little scary for both of us I guess, because we backed away from each other without intending to. I wonder if the look in my eyes matched what I saw in hers. It must have because we were soon wrapped in each others arms again. We're not children anymore.

Dad yelled upstairs that the Brewsters were leaving and I walked downstairs with Jenny and told everyone good night. It was a good evening up to then. It was getting late so I went back upstairs and started getting ready for bed. I'd just gotten my pajamas on when my sister came through the door without knocking.

"I saw you and Jenny. I saw you kissing and your hands on her ass."
That shook me for a moment, but something came to mind right away.

"You didn't see anything; just like I didn't see anything last summer."

She knew what I was talking about and if looks could kill, I wouldn't be writing this right now. She walked out of my room and slammed the door behind her. What I didn't see last summer was completely accidental. I wasn't spying on her. It was a hot night and our doors were open so the attic fan could circulate a little air in our rooms. It was late and all the big lights were out. I was asleep until I heard a strange sound. When I looked out my bedroom door, I saw that there was a dim light coming from her room. She sometimes falls asleep with her nightstand lamp on while reading trashy romance books. That's what everyone calls them. Anyway, there was this sort of moaning sound coming from her room so I had to investigate. I stood in the doorway and saw her naked with her knees in the air. Her hands were out of sight—but now I have a pretty good idea where they were and what she was doing. I hadn't seen her naked since we were kids. She has really small breasts, no bigger than Jenny's even though she's almost six years older. She didn't get her period until she was fourteen and she made such a big deal out of it. I was maybe eight and had no idea what she was talking about or why she was telling me, but I do remember Mom saying to me something like, "Your sister's a woman now." Yeah, right. She still doesn't look as much like a woman as Jenny.

I just stood there in the doorway watching for a while. When she turned toward me and opened her eyes, there I was. She threatened to kill me if I told anyone. I didn't, although I knew at the time it was something I should remember. She won't be telling anyone about Jenny and me.

Sunday December 1, 1940
Night

Jenny told me today after church that Mr. Cohen has asked her father if Mrs. Brewster could teach his son to dance. Her parents talked it over and the boy's first lesson is next week. I guess they couldn't say no, with Mr. Cohen being the plant manager, but at least Mrs. Brewster will get paid for the lessons. I'm not too crazy about this because I'm sure Jenny'll be expected to help. The Cohen's are about the richest family in all of Evansville. Their children don't go to public school. Jenny says they go to a private school on the other side of town.

At lunch today I happened to mention the dance lessons Mrs. Brewster will soon be giving the Cohen boy. Dad had a cold disapproving look on his face when I finished my story.

"I would never let any wife or daughter of mine dance with a Jew, even if they were paying for it. They see all Gentile women as nothing more than practice."

My sister and I looked at each other and at Mom. We knew what he was talking about. I've heard those kinds of stories about Jews before and I guess I've never realized that the Cohens are Jews. I have to talk to Jenny about this tomorrow.

Monday December 2, 1940
Late afternoon

Jenny told me on the way home today that she's expected to help her mother with the Cohen boy's lessons. I knew it. She said there will only be one a week, on Wednesdays, and that I can still come over every other afternoon for a lesson just like always. Jenny wasn't happy about the whole thing.

"I don't like it and neither do my parents, but we can use the money and Mr. Cohen is Daddy's boss, so we have to do it."

"Then I'm sure your father wouldn't mind an extra chaperone," I added.

She smiled that smile I look forward to seeing every morning.

"You could just sit and watch. I think that's a great idea and I'm sure Daddy would like you being there. I'd kiss you if old Mr. Brock weren't watching us from his front porch. He sits out there every afternoon and I know he watches us. I think he knows we sit on his bench at night sometimes."

Then I told her what my father had said about Jews only liking Gentile women for practice. She laughed and told me her father had said the same thing.

The Christmas parade is next Sunday and we were told today that the city schools get out of class Friday to help with the decorations. We have all new ones this year furnished by the government's WPA—the Work Projects Administration. We learned about President Roosevelt's plan to give people jobs last year in school, but this is the first time I've heard about anything the workers do. I'm glad Jenny and I weren't picked to march in the parade for our school. I'd much rather watch it than be in it; that way we get to see the whole thing.

Wednesday December 4, 1940
Night

Martin. The Cohen boy's name is Martin. He's in high school and not at all interested in learning how to dance. His parents are making him take lessons. That's a relief. This afternoon he mostly watched Mrs. Brewster dance with Jenny and me. He doesn't look old enough to be in high school. I have to think of a Christmas present for Jenny soon. It has to be something special and something I can afford.

I would like to never get hungry and never have to work. I'm happiest when I'm writing in this diary…well, except for the times I'm with Jenny and then I have even more to write about.

Wednesday December 18, 1940
Afternoon

We're out of school until January second next year and I know what I want to get Jenny for Christmas. I put the order in on Monday at Roger's Jewelry. It's a silver ring, just a plain band really with "Merry Christmas, 1940" engraved in pretty script, but on the inside, I had the jeweler inscribe BAS for "Body and Soul". She'll know what the inscription means and no one else will. I thought about getting her earrings. She's the only girl in fifth grade with pierced ears, but I like the ring better. It's more personal. It's beautiful and I know it'll fit the ring finger of her right hand. I read that the wedding band was traditionally silver and worn on the right ring finger in Europe. Jenny'll know that too. Maybe I'll tell her I love her on Christmas Eve—or New Year's Eve—or maybe she'll tell me first. I know she loves me or I think I know she loves me.

Tuesday December 24, 1940
Very late

She loves me! It's freezing even under the covers as I'm trying to write this by flashlight. I could wait till morning, but I'm afraid I'll forget something. Jenny and I decided yesterday we would exchange gifts tonight at the stroke of midnight. I went to bed at ten wearing all my clothes and a flannel shirt of Dad's and sneaked out of the house with my flashlight at eleven-forty. I've never done that before, but I know my sister has lots of times. Once, two summers ago, she didn't get home until four in the morning. She doesn't know I know about that, and I know the boy she was with too, Roger Simpson. He graduated last year and is married now with a baby. It was one of those miracle babies that only took five months.

It was snowing hard when I left the house headed for the park. It was a crazy plan, but I knew Jenny would be there. She was sitting on our favorite bench when I arrived and she brought a huge quilt with her. We huddled under the quilt with our coats on. I don't know what anyone would have thought if we'd been seen, but it's Christmas Eve and there wasn't a soul out anywhere. We sat there wrapped in each other's arms for the longest time, trying to get warm, until I managed to whisper, "Merry Christmas Jenny" in her ear. She kissed me and my face didn't seem so cold anymore.

"I hope you like what I got you," she said with a little uncertainty. "I wanted to find something you could keep with you every day and think of me when you look at it."

Her gift was elegantly wrapped and I was almost ashamed of mine. I should have let the man at Roger's wrap it for me, but I wanted to do it. We couldn't decide who should open their gift first.

"I know," she said as she reached under my coat.

I could feel her ice cold hands on my back and her touch sent shivers through me. I unbuttoned her coat and slid my hands up her back. Neither of us could keep that up for very long. This has become sort of a game for us to see who will back away first. I lose most of the time. I was freezing and I had to pee so it wasn't much of a contest.

"I win," she said with a smile. "You have to go first."

I unwrapped her present and had no idea what was in the flat rectangular box until I opened it.

"You have to write your first book with it."

I took the silver pen out of the box and shined my flashlight on it. I had never seen anything like it before. It didn't look like a fountain pen at all.

"It's a Biro pen. I saw an ad for one in a magazine last summer and knew that was what I wanted to get you. They're made in England so I tore the ad out and sent it with some money to my brother. He bought it and sent it to me. I've had it since Thanksgiving and I've been dying to give it to you."

It was engraved, "Merry Christmas, 1940 BAS"

"I just thought of what I wanted engraved on it last week: "Body and Soul," remember? It's funny, but the man at Roger's said he'd just engraved a ring with the same initials."

I handed her my present and could barely keep a straight face as she unwrapped the ring box.

"It's beautiful and it says the same thing as your pen, "Merry Christmas, 1940"."

I handed her my flashlight, "Look on the inside."

A single tear rolled down each cheek.

"I'll always remember our first kiss and I'll always remember where we were when I first told you this. With my body and soul, I love you Jenny B."

She sniffled but didn't say anything. I was petrified. It was so quiet, I heard the clock at Reitz chime eleven times and on the twelfth, she leaned over and whispered in my ear, "And I love you, body and soul."

I slid the ring on her finger and tilted her chin up a little to kiss her; she turned away.

"Don't want you to see me cry. You don't know how much I've wanted to say those three little words to you, but I was afraid you didn't feel the same way. I mean, this is not how I thought it would be when I was a little girl."

"We're not exactly Clark Gable and Joan Crawford are we?"

That brought a faint smile to her face. We wrapped the quilt around us and walked back toward home. All the lights were out at Jenny's house and I watched her as she slipped inside. She turned and blew me a kiss just before she closed the door. I made it back home and into my room without waking anyone. So what if we're not Clark Gable and Joan Crawford. I love her and she loves me.

Tuesday December 31, 1940
Early morning

I can smell breakfast. It's so nice not having to get up early and go to school. Today's the last day of 1940. I'm writing this with the pen Jenny gave me. It has a thin metal tube inside that holds the ink and you don't refill it like a fountain pen. It came with a pack of six extra tubes for when this one runs dry. I think I'll only use it for writing important things, like in this diary. Jenny and her family left the day after Christmas for Lincoln, Nebraska. Mrs. Brewster's sister and her husband live there. I hope I get a postcard. I miss her already. They left the key to their house with Mom and we promised to check on things while they're gone. She sent me over yesterday afternoon to make sure everything was all right. It was sort of creepy going into the house alone. Mom and I went together Friday and that wasn't so bad, but yesterday she was busy and sent me. I walked through the house like we had before and didn't see anything out of place and then went upstairs. Walking into Jenny's room, I could smell her. She always smells nice. Her brother sent her some French perfume last summer and it's the best thing I've ever smelled in my life. Jenny's dad told her it smells too much like the wrong kind of woman, but he lets her wear it sometimes anyway. Looking around in her room, I saw that she'd left some dirty clothes in her hamper and I took out one of her T-shirts she wears under her blouse when it's cold out. That was really her smell, all mixed with the perfume, and I missed her so much right then.

She hadn't made her bed before they left and I sat down on it with Jenny's shirt to my face. The craziest idea then came to my mind and I pulled on Jenny's shirt and climbed into her bed under the covers. I don't know why I did that. I just miss her and wanted to be close to something that had been close to her I guess. I lay still with my eyes closed and thought of Jenny and wished she were there with me.

Chapter Two

1941
Monday January 6, 1941
Night

Jenny and her parents got home Saturday night and I saw her yesterday at church. It seemed like we'd been apart for months. We sat together and it was horrible not being able to even hold her hand. It was freezing cold and there was more snow yesterday but that didn't matter, Jenny and I still spent the afternoon sitting on our bench at the park. At least I could hold her hand under our coats.

"I thought about you a lot while I was gone," she said after a while. "My aunt kept asking me if I had a boyfriend and finally, when there was no one around but the two of us, I told her about you—maybe not every little detail, but I liked doing that, talking about you. Then she had to know if you'd ever kissed me. I missed you so much."

I told her about lying in her bed under the covers wearing her T-shirt, but I didn't tell her what I was thinking about at the time. She looked around and made sure there was no one in sight and gave me a quick kiss.

"Which T-shirt?"

"The light blue one with the red design around the sleeves, why?"

"Because I'm going to wear it to bed tonight and every night and think about you."

Being in love with Jenny is the most wonderful thing in the world.

Tuesday January 14, 1941

Late afternoon

My dance lessons with Jenny over the past week have been the best so far. Who knew there were so many waltzes? Her mother taught us a new one beginning last Tuesday. It's called the Viennese waltz and we like it even better than swing. When Jenny's mom told us it was a particularly difficult dance and that we would have to hold each other close, I knew I wanted to learn. Now we can hold each other as close as we want every afternoon, as long as we're dancing. I have a feeling we'll become experts at this Viennese waltz thing. The "Blue Danube" has become my favorite song. I think it's the most beautiful waltz ever written and I get to dance it with the most beautiful girl in the world. Mrs. Brewster has two records of it. One is only about four minutes long, but the other one must be three or four times that. I like both of them.

Monday January 20, 1941
Night

School today was horrible. There's a rumor going around about my sister. Centennial Elementary and Francis Joseph Reitz Junior High and High School aren't that far from each other and anything that happens eventually makes its way down to us. We had boys versus girls volleyball today (we won) and one of the girls told me she heard my sister was doing it with Mark Boetcher, the captain of the Reitz High School basketball team—I know who he is—and she said it loud enough for everyone to hear. I didn't know what to do. I wanted to punch her and I still might. I talked to Jenny on our way home about it and she told me she'd heard the same thing.

"Why haven't you told me, Jenny? And I had to hear it in front of everyone today? I thought we told each other everything."

"I thought you probably knew. Anyway, it's just a rumor and tomorrow there'll be a different one."

"It's not just a rumor. She's my sister."

I walked faster and left her behind. I didn't want to talk to her anymore. My sister's been sneaking out at night again; I've seen her and it's going to stop. Mom and Dad are asleep and I'm going across the hall.

Tuesday January 21, 1941
Early morning

Things did not go well last night. I was upset and just barged into her room without knocking.

"Are you doing it with Mark? I want to know if what everyone's saying is true."

"Doing what?" she said all innocent like.

"Fucking him."

I surprised myself saying that word. I'd never said it out loud in my life. I hadn't planned it. It just came out.

"What if I am? What business is it of yours? Are you fucking your little girlfriend yet? Don't forget what I've got on you. Now get out and leave me the Hell alone."

I could have killed her, but I heard Dad yell something from downstairs. I just turned around and slammed the door on my way out.

My sister's a whore. I have to apologize to Jenny today for being so hateful yesterday. It's not her fault. I'm not going to eat breakfast this morning. There's no way I'm going to pretend everything is fine. If only Mom or Dad could catch her sneaking out of the house. I'm so glad she's graduating this year. Maybe she'll get a job and move out or maybe she'll marry that stupid Mark. I don't care. I hope

Jenny's right, that there'll be a different rumor today at school.

Saturday January 25, 1941
Night

Everything's fine between Jenny and me. I apologized for what I said and she apologized for not telling me what she'd heard, and then we went roller skating. I could understand her not wanting to tell me. How could I tell someone I love that their sister's a slut?

When they had a couples-only skate tonight, I asked Jenny to skate with me. We turned it into a sort of waltz on wheels, but I'm a much better dancer than skater.

Friday January 31, 1941
Late night

I heard her leave a few minutes ago. I know the routine. There'll be a car start up just down the block in another minute and my sister will be gone again, for the second time this week. She'll be back in about two hours. Is that how long it takes? The rumors have died down at school. Now everyone just knows she's doing it with Mark whenever he wants. If this gets out of school into the community, it'll kill Mom and Dad.

Thursday February 6, 1941
Night

Martin had his dance lesson yesterday and Jenny told me something this morning that sort of bothers me. She said that he asked her mom if it would be all right if he took

Jenny to the Valentine dance at his school. He didn't even ask her. It didn't matter, her mom told him yes anyway. He's fifteen and will be sixteen next month. Why couldn't he find a girl his own age at his school to go with? I know I shouldn't be jealous but I am. It's her first date and it's not with me. Jenny says it's not a real date and that she's not going to tell anyone at school. I hope she doesn't. If they find out she is going dancing with a Jew, it'll ruin her reputation.

"You won't Viennese waltz with him will you?" I asked on our way home.

"He barely knows how to foxtrot and do a simple waltz. He would never even try a Viennese waltz. Besides, that's our dance."

"You're not going to kiss him, are you?"

"Daddy's not going to let me go unless he drives us and I can guarantee Martin won't try anything with him around. If he does, I'll punch him. I'm sure he only asked me to the dance because his parents made him. I bet they even have some Jewish girl picked out for him to marry already. If I know Daddy, he'll sit in the car during the whole dance and then take Martin straight home."

I like Jenny's dad.

Thursday February 13, 1941
Night

I bought Jenny a Valentine card today. The front is all red and in little tiny white letters at the bottom it says, "Do you know how much I love you?" And inside in huge red letters on a white background it says, "To the depth and breadth and height my soul can reach."

This is from Mom's favorite poem. She knows it by heart and she used to recite it to me every night in bed when I was little. I remember every word. It's perfect for

Jenny. We write each other letters and poems all the time. I sign mine with the left side of a heart and she signs hers with the right. Sometimes one of us will start a poem and the other will finish it, then we sign it with a complete heart. She's a good writer and I love reading her letters and poems over and over again. I keep them hidden separate from this diary, although if anyone found them, they couldn't read them anyway. We have a code. Instead of writing a word normally, we use the letter before the letter we mean and A wraps around backwards to Z, so H KNUD XNT is I LOVE YOU, but mostly we just abbreviate it as HKX. Lately we've begun just running all the letters together. That makes it even harder for anyone to figure out what we've written. This line is from a poem she wrote for me while she was in Lincoln:
"ZMGNTQVHSGXNTHRLNQDSGZMRHWSXLHMTS DRENQLDSNBGDQHRG".

Saturday February 15, 1941
Late night

Her dad didn't sit in the car at the dance; he went in with her and Martin. They danced exactly two waltzes and that was it. He ate and talked with his friends and ignored Jenny completely. What a crumb, just a crud. He thinks he's so much better than Jenny. He's a twit who deserves to be married to some fat ugly Jewish dame he has to sleep with every night. I hate him.

I realize how stupid that sounds. I'm glad he ignored her, but he's still a twit.

Jenny and I went to a movie this afternoon. It was *Charlie Chan at the Wax Museum*. It was a pretty stupid movie, but we liked it. There weren't many people there for the matinee so we sat in the back row and kissed a lot. I can never tell her I love her enough.

Wednesday February 19, 1941
Night

No more dance lessons for Mr. Martin Cohen. The man who always drives him to Jenny's house came alone today and told Mrs. Brewster that her services would no longer be needed by the Cohens—like she was their maid or something. He gave her a check for the unused lessons and left. She told Jenny and me about it this afternoon.

"No matter," Mrs. Brewster said with a smile after telling us what happened. "In ten years I couldn't have taught that boy to dance."

The three of us sort of celebrated with something special she made on Saturday. She wouldn't let us have any then because she said it had to age for at least three days. Jenny and I helped her make it and it took all afternoon. I cracked black walnuts with a hammer and Jenny picked out the insides and ground them. We collected the walnuts last fall from under the tree in their backyard and Jenny's mom told us then she would make a special pastry for us with them. It's called Baklava or something like that and I think I could have eaten the entire pan.

"I was prepared to teach a dance lesson this afternoon," Mrs. Brewster announced with a smile as everyone licked the honey from their fingers, "so let's see how your Viennese waltz is coming along."

She put on the "Blue Danube" and Jenny and I did our best Viennese waltz yet. We've practiced a lot and we were graceful, or as graceful as we could be in our school clothes. When the music ended Mrs. Brewster hugged us and I think I saw tears welling up in her eyes.

"It's the most beautiful dance in the world and the two of you do it as if you were one person. One leads and the other follows, then you switch roles without breaking time. How do you do that? I didn't teach you and it has to be the first time I've ever seen it done. It was beautiful. Do it again."

She put the music back on and this time she followed our every move, like she was studying us or something. I held Jenny close and we moved like we could read each other's thoughts. I never realized we were doing that, switching roles like Mrs. Brewster said. It just seems to work for us.

After the third time through the short version of the "Blue Danube", Mrs. Brewster had a very serious look on her face.

"I've decided something. The two of you are going to dance competitively and you're going to win. We start tomorrow on your routine."

I wanted to kiss Jenny so bad it hurt.

Friday February 28, 1941
Very early

Mrs. Brewster has been talking to Mom about Jenny and me maybe competing in a ballroom dance contest in Chicago. It's on April 19 and Mrs. Brewster says we can be ready by then. My mom's not so crazy about the idea, but Mrs. Brewster talked her into coming to see us practice this afternoon and I'm so nervous about it I could hardly sleep last night. I've never been to Chicago. I've never been anywhere.

Mrs. Brewster has arranged for us to be able to practice in the gym after school today. The basketball team has an away game and the place will be empty. The school has a nice record player and Mrs. Winston got permission for us to use it as long as she operates it. I don't think I'm going to be able to eat any breakfast. I have to remember to take my dance clothes with me this morning. I wish I had something better to dance in. Jenny's going to wear the dress she wore to the Ironworks dance.

Late night

I can hardly write. Jenny and I are going to Chicago! I can't believe it and we're getting real dance shoes too. I'm so excited—and the batteries are dying in my flashlight.

After school Jenny and I changed into our dance clothes and went to the gym. Mrs. Winston was just setting up the record player. Then we had to wait for our moms to show up with our music. Jenny said she was so nervous she couldn't pee when she went to the bathroom. The school was practically empty, so while we waited, we walked the halls and held hands. Whenever we turned a corner and there was no one in front or behind us, we stopped and kissed. By the time we made it all the way back around to the gym, everything was set up. There was no audience except for our moms and Mrs. Winston. The gym floor seemed a lot bigger than it had during volleyball. We had the short routine Mrs. Brewster taught us down cold and we took our places at opposite corners of an imaginary square. When the "Blue Danube" started, we walked gracefully toward the center of the square. I held out my hand inviting Jenny to dance. She turned away and then she held out her hand inviting me to dance and I turned away, just like we'd rehearsed. We took three steps toward our corners, and on cue with the music; we turned at the same time, ran toward each other and threw ourselves into each others arms and began dancing. It was like magic. We made every spin turn in perfect time with the music and switched leads after each bridge, changing to the opposite spin direction without breaking time. The cross leads, hesitations, and fleckerls were the best we've ever done. The dance ended just as the music did, with our noses touching in a dance pose at the center of the square.

Breathing like we'd just run a mile race, we walked hand in hand over to our moms and Mrs. Winston. The two of them were hugging and it looked like they were both going to cry. My mom spoke up first.

"Mrs. Brewster and I have decided that if we have to sell cookies on street corners, the two of you are going to Chicago."

Jenny screamed and hugged me.

"That won't be necessary," Mrs. Winston interrupted. "I don't see why the school can't sponsor this trip. The football, baseball, and basketball teams aren't the only things at this school we can be proud of now. Watching the two of you dance is like something from the movies and maybe it'll be an inspiration for other students to get involved. What we need is a dance club and I know the right officers to lead it. For Chicago, you'll both need true ballroom dance shoes as well and the school will pay for them as part of your uniforms, just like the other sports teams. The athletes pay for their uniforms and we pay for the shoes. Bring us back a trophy from Chicago."

I won't ever go to sleep tonight.

Monday April 7, 1941
Night

Jenny and I are practicing for two hours every day now and we'll keep it up until the competition. I'm so tired. I think I even practice in my sleep because I wake up tired. Our mothers are feeding us like we're getting ready for the Olympics. Mom learned somewhere that pasta is good food for athletes in training for the marathon and decided that's what I needed. She told Jenny's mom and now both our houses have turned into Italian restaurants. Soon we'll look like weightlifters. Our new dance shoes came in yesterday. They're beautiful, with suede soles that let us just float over any smooth floor. We had to order them from Mason's downtown. No one in town has ballroom dance shoes in stock. Mrs. Brewster picked them out for us. Jenny wanted high heels until her mother reminded her what she would be doing in them. I just went along with Mrs. Brewster's choice for me and I like them a lot. They cost more than my last three pairs of regular shoes, but she told the man at Mason's to send the bill to the school.

With the new shoes, Mrs. Brewster taught us something called the canter pivot. We can't do it very well yet but I like it. Our legs are between each others all the way to the hips as we rotate right or left, depending on who's leading. This is not a move you would ever do with a stranger and I'm sure Mrs. Brewster noticed our beet red faces the first time we tried it.

Jenny keeps asking her mom what we're going to wear. Right now, I don't care. I just want to sleep.

Wednesday April 16, 1941
Afternoon

Today when Jenny and I got to her house Mrs. Brewster was grinning like the cat that ate the canary.

"No rehearsal today," she announced.

We had no idea what she was talking about and when she pointed toward a large box on the sofa, Jenny screamed. Honestly, sometimes she's such a girl. Maybe I was a little excited too, but only because I recognized the name on the box. It was from Hoffman's, probably the best clothing store in town, but it's a men and boys' store.

"You have one at your house too," she said to me. "Go home and open it. Jenny and I will meet you there in half an hour. Your mother and I have pictures to make of our dancers.

I was out the door before she finished talking. Mom met me on our porch with the box. I wanted to tear into it right away, but she made me sit and listen to the story behind the costumes.

"You and Jenny now have real matching ballroom dance costumes that were ordered from New York City by Mr. Hoffman himself. Mrs. Brewster and I went to his store the day after you danced for us in the gym. No one in town had any idea where we could go to order dance clothes, then we heard that someone at Hoffman's might be able to help. None of the salesmen there knew what we were talking about when we described what we were looking for, so one of them sent for Mr. Hoffman. He invited us into his office and when we told him about the Chicago dance competition and what we needed, you should have seen his face light up. He pointed to an old photograph on his wall of him and his late wife in a dance pose. He asked what dance you and Jenny would be doing and when we told him the Viennese waltz, I thought that old man was going to cry.

'Give me the measurements,' he said. 'The finest dancewear in the world is found in New York City and if you'll trust me, I guarantee your children will outshine all those bums in Chicago.'

When I asked him what the costumes would cost, he just smiled for a long time before answering.

'Did I mention a price? I don't think I did and when Sal Hoffman doesn't mention a price, there's not one. Now you ladies leave this up to me. All I ask is a photograph to put on my wall here. It's about time someone in this town showed a little interest in culture. Cultured people dance and the most cultured learn the Viennese waltz.'

We gave your and Jenny's measurements to Mr. Hoffman's assistant and left. I hope we got them right."

I went upstairs and opened the box. It took a while to figure out where everything went.

It was black—thin, shiny, satiny, flowing black and I felt completely naked when I first put everything on; then I found the skintight black body suit in the box that's supposed to be worn underneath, so I took everything off and started over. The black jacket with puffy sleeves looked good with the black gloves and the wide white sequined belt that tied at the side. By the time I got everything back on, Jenny and her mom had arrived. When I saw Jenny, it was like I was looking at a negative of myself. Everywhere I had black, she had white. Her dress was like a shimmering white cloud and I could just make out the white bodysuit underneath. Her jacket was white, her gloves were white and her belt was black with sequins that looked just like mine. We were a perfect contrast in black and white, like some old photograph before Kodachrome.

Mrs. Brewster took about a million photographs while we posed in our best dance positions. We look so good together and I love her more every day.

Friday April 18, 1941
Very late

We had our last rehearsal this afternoon and we were supposed to get to bed early, but I can't sleep. We leave for Chicago tomorrow morning at five, or maybe it's this morning now. The competition starts at eight in the evening at the Drake Hotel. Mr. Brewster has to work, so Daddy's driving us. That means my sister will have the house to herself. I can only imagine what she has planned. Jenny and I are as good as we're going to get. The canter pivots still make her blush bright red every time—and I probably do the same thing.

Sunday April 20, 1941
Late night

I can't believe I'm writing this... *We won.* We actually won. We got first place in our division and sixth overall. The last two days have been the best of my whole life.

It was a long drive to Chicago. Mrs. Brewster sat in the back seat with Jenny and me and retold us stories of when she was our age and competed in the very same event. She and her mother rode a bus for eighteen hours to get there. I think she was as excited as Jenny and me. The hotel was magnificent and huge with fancy woodwork everywhere. Mom, Dad, and I had a room to ourselves and Jenny shared a room with her mom. The bed was twice the size of mine here at home. After a short nap, we all went downstairs to register for the competition. Mrs. Brewster sort of knew her way around competitions and made sure we got everything done correctly. Our number was fifty-six. Jenny said it was lucky because her birthday is the fifth and mine is the sixth, but that also meant there were already fifty-five other couples registered. I had no idea there would be that many. There were four divisions: under thirteen, thirteen to eighteen, the adults, and the seniors. Mrs. Brewster found out there were nine couples registered in our division so far including Jenny and me. I hoped there wouldn't be any more.

There was a meeting at four o'clock for all contestants and when we walked into the room designated for our division, I almost fainted. It was packed. I guess Mom saw I was really nervous because she hugged me and pointed out that all the parents and probably some grandparents were there too. Jenny and I waited as the roll was called and each couple waded through the crowd to the front of the room. I quickly counted when we were all lined up. There were fourteen total couples and some of them didn't look to me like they were under thirteen years old, not at all. Several of them looked to be a foot taller than Jenny and me. Girl-girl couples were allowed in our division as well, and I counted five of them. I guess I wasn't expecting that many and when Jenny caught me staring, she whispered something to me that made me laugh.

"They're not real. They all have their bras stuffed with cotton balls."

We were given a short lecture on the rules and then led into the ballroom. It was the most wonderful room I've ever seen. The dance floor was oval and made of perfectly sculptured wood and there were seats for spectators all around it. There were bright white spotlights everywhere and they swept the floor in random patterns. The judges' box was on the side opposite the area roped off for contestants. We weren't allowed onto the dance floor, but I could tell it would be a very fast surface, almost like our gym floor. I told Jenny that our canter pivots would be easy.

"If we can keep from falling on our butts," she answered with a smile.

If Jenny and I hadn't been so nervous, we would have enjoyed the early dinner. Mom and Dad and Mrs. Brewster said it was the best meal they'd ever had. I ate a little, just to get Jenny to eat something. The schedule had the under thirteen division going first. There would be an individual dance with only one couple on the floor followed by a group dance with everyone on the floor at the same time. Mrs. Brewster said that couples would mainly be dancing for the judges and would stay close to their box. She told us weeks ago that only two minutes were allotted for the individual couple dance. Jenny and I would be doing the same routine we did in the gym. It was the only one we knew and we'd practiced with the first two minutes of the "Blue Danube," but I didn't know how we would be able to spend more time in front of the judges' box. When I asked Mrs. Brewster about that, she told us she had a plan.

"These are professional judges and they know couples will try to impress them by dancing most of their time in front of them. That's not what the two of you are going to do. I want you to do your routine just as you've always done it and cover the entire dance floor if you can. You're going to dance for the crowd. That's what will impress these judges. That's what will separate you from the rest."

After dinner, we went back to our rooms and tried to rest. I couldn't do anything but go over the routine again and again in my head. At seven, I got dressed, making sure everything was perfect. With all the bright lights, I could see the reason for the bodysuit. I like the way it feels anyway. Mom inspected me when I finished dressing and decided I needed a little color in my face. She got out her makeup and started to work. I have to admit, it did make me look older.

We met Jenny and her mom at the roped off contestants area. I couldn't believe it was Jenny. She looked gorgeous and her mother had gone all out with the makeup. She looked eighteen.

"They're not cotton balls," she whispered in my ear. "Mom sewed some padding into my costume to make them look bigger. Do they look all right?"

All I could manage was a nod. She looked fantastic.

The lady in charge of our group drew numbers from a hat to determine our order. We were twelfth. Jenny's mom said that was a good number, that you never wanted to be first or last and that it was better to be near the end. She also reminded us to smile. Each couple in turn was first introduced at the center of the floor and after the applause, all the house lights went down and it was completely dark until the spotlights came up shining on the dancers. At the end of the dance, the house lights came back up and everyone applauded again. I was glad we hadn't been first so we could see the routine to follow. I did notice that, like Mrs. Brewster had told us, couples danced mostly for the judges.

When the house lights went down just before our dance, Jenny grabbed my hand and squeezed. I turned and kissed her. We were on. Walking to the center of the floor seemed to take an hour. The place was packed, but I heard Jenny's mom yell out something to us while everyone was applauding after we were introduced. Jenny and I knew where our imaginary square was and we walked to opposite corners and waited for our music. The house lights went down and I thought my heart would explode. The spotlights came on, one on me and one on Jenny. The music started and we walked gracefully to the center of the square. Just like we'd rehearsed, I held out my hand inviting her to dance and she turned away; she did the same thing and I turned away. The crowd was deathly silent as we took the three steps toward our corners. This all took place during the first part of the music where it's really soft and slow and you're not really sure what it is. We knew every note and when the violins and horns crashed in with the melody everyone recognizes, we ran toward each other. The next thing I remember is our noses touching and hearing all the applause.

We did it. I held Jenny's hand as we walked back to the contestants' area. She was breathing so hard she couldn't speak. The lights went down for the next contestants and she grabbed me and kissed me. She then turned my head and whispered in my ear.

"I can never love you more than I do right now."

The spotlights came up and the next dance started. We held hands and didn't care who was watching.

After the final dance, it was time for the group dance. Jenny and I didn't dance for the judges; we danced like we were the only ones on the floor. We were happy and we'd done our very best. It was all up to the judges now.

There was a short break while the judges added up their scores and our parents came down to congratulate us. Mom and Mrs. Brewster didn't try to hide their tears and I think Dad might have had one or two roll down his face as they told us how proud they were.

"The judges have never seen anything like the two of you," Mrs. Brewster finally managed to say, "and how on Earth did you manage to do a lead reversal in the middle of that string of canter pivots. It wasn't in the routine."

Neither Jenny nor I remembered doing that but I guess it worked.

Everyone went back to their seats when the room lights blinked. The master of ceremonies stood in the center of the floor with a microphone ready to announce the winners. The top four places would receive a trophy and money, a hundred dollars cash for first place. When the fourth place winners were announced, all the spotlights followed them as they walked to get their trophy. I knew we didn't have a chance of getting a trophy after that. Fourth place was the best I'd hoped for. The third and second place winners I remembered. They were really good; one was a girl-girl couple, but neither couple looked too happy about not being first.

I don't remember our names being called, I just remember Jenny grabbing me and jerking me up from my seat and hugging me. I could barely walk onto the floor. Then Jenny took me in her arms and we did advanced left and right turns all the way to the center of the floor. The crowd came to its feet; the applause was deafening. We held the trophy above our heads as we walked back to our seats. I was in shock I guess, because Jenny had to remind me to breathe.

The next division competition began as soon as we could clear out of our seats. We wandered around in the hotel lobby looking for our parents. When they found us, I thought they would squeeze us to death. Dad announced that he had a table reserved for us in the hotel dining room. We'd already eaten, so I didn't know what that was all about. We sat down at the table and by the look on his face, I could tell that he'd been planning something. Two waiters came with a cart and on top of the cart was a silver bucket full of ice surrounding a bottle of something. We were all given glasses and the waiter poured them full of a bubbly almost clear liquid I read on the label was champagne. Dad then stood up.

"To the best dancers in all of Chicago and the pride of Evansville, Indiana."

We all took a sip. It was sweet and bubbly and I liked the taste a lot. When we finished our glasses, Dad filled them again. Our parents were treating us like adults for the first time in our lives. We drank the entire bottle and I felt all warm inside. Neither Jenny nor I had ever seen any of our parents drink, but this was a very special occasion and I could see how proud they were of us.

I was a little woozy as I changed out of my costume. We had to be back downstairs for the overall awards at eleven. Mrs. Brewster said they would mostly go to couples in the adult and senior divisions, but that all dancers were expected to be there to congratulate them. We arrived in the ballroom early and got good seats. I was so tired I could hardly hold my eyes open, or maybe it was the champagne. The top ten couples would receive trophies and the top four would get money as well, two hundred dollars for first place. When Jenny and I were announced as sixth place winners, I couldn't believe it. There were over a hundred couples in the competition and we got sixth overall. It was too much to be true. We dragged Mom and Dad and Mrs. Brewster out to the center of the floor with us to accept the trophy. I carried it back and whispered something to Jenny along the way and she nodded. When we sat down, I handed the trophy to Mrs. Brewster.

"Jenny and I want you to have this. None of this would have ever been possible without you."

She tried to speak, but she couldn't get the words out so she just hugged us and cried.

We slept until almost noon today and had a nice lunch before we left Chicago. Everyone talked at the same time on the way home. It's been a wild couple of days. I'm glad we won but I'm sorry it's over. I wonder if Jenny's still awake.

Tuesday April 29, 1941
Night

Last night there was a big argument downstairs between Mom and Dad. They never argue or if they do, I never hear them. My sister's name was mentioned several times, but I couldn't figure out what the argument was all about until this morning. Mom told me at breakfast that my sister's moving to Little Rock right after graduation; that she's going to live there with Aunt Doris' family, Mom's sister, and look for work. I know why she's going. She's probably pregnant and that bastard won't marry her. Funny, I just called him a bastard and my sister will be having one herself in a few months. That's not very funny, but I won't be sorry to see her go.

My and Jenny's first place trophy looks good in the trophy case at school. Mom and Mrs. Brewster delivered a picture of us to Mr. Hoffman yesterday that was taken at the competition and he hung it on the wall in his office. I would like to go back to that hotel in Chicago someday and spend a week there with Jenny. We haven't had any time alone together lately and it's driving me crazy.

Mrs. Brewster got a nice surprise in the mail yesterday. It was a package from the organizers of the dance competition. There were more really good pictures of Jenny and me. My favorite is the one right at the end of the dance where our noses are touching. Maybe I'll ask Mom if we can have copies made.

Wednesday May 7, 1941
Late night

My sister and Mark did it in my bed while we were in Chicago and they've done it in my bed lots of times. That's just disgusting. I don't know if they really have, or if she just told me that because she wants my bed. We had a terrible fight tonight. I'm glad Mom and Dad weren't home to hear it. They went out to dinner and didn't get home until about an hour ago. She just burst into my room without knocking and announced that she was taking my bed when she moves out because it's nicer than hers. I think she was drunk. I told her that just because she's knocked up doesn't give her the right to any of my stuff. We had never talked about her being pregnant, although I know she is, and she knows I know.

"Well maybe I got knocked up in your bed. You ever think about that? Well think about it tonight before you go to sleep. You want me to explain where that spot on your bedspread came from?"

She pointed to a white stain on my brown bedspread I hadn't noticed before.

"You wouldn't know about things like that would you? Because you're just a kid. Your little girlfriend Jenny ever get all hot and bothered when you dance with her? I've seen you with your legs all wrapped around hers. Don't tell me the two of you aren't doing it. She's gonna spread her legs for a real man someday and kick your ass to the curb."

I'd had enough. She was not going to talk about Jenny like that and get away with it.

"Get out, you whore. You're not getting my bed. I'll be glad when you move out; then you can fuck anyone you want anywhere you want. Jenny's more woman than you'll ever be and I'm exactly what she wants. You think Mark's a real man? A real man would marry you."

We said a lot of other things I don't want to write down. I pushed her out of my room and slammed the door, then pulled the bedspread off without looking at the stain and put it in my hamper. I won't have it back on my bed. I hate her.

Sunday May 11, 1941
Night

Today was Mother's Day and my sister and I sort of called a truce for the day. Dad got Mom a pretty bouquet of flowers and my sister and I gave her a card with two movie tickets in it for tonight. *The Philadelphia Story* is playing. It's pretty good and I thought she would like it. Mom and Dad deserve more nights out together without us. When they left, Mom yelled at us not to wait up for them. The truce with my sister ended as soon as they were gone.

Thursday May 22, 1941
Afternoon

Graduation at Reitz is this Saturday and we're taking my sister to Little Rock on Monday. She already has everything packed and she's not getting my bed. It'll be a quick trip because Dad can't get off more than two days from work. I don't really want to go, but Mom doesn't want me staying here by myself.

The weather's warm and I still walk with Jenny in the park, even though we're never alone. I wonder if she's as frustrated as I am. It seems like months since I've kissed her, really kissed her.

Wednesday June 4, 1941
Night

The trip to Little Rock was hurried and we didn't get to spend much time with Aunt Doris before getting back on the road.

Jenny's birthday is tomorrow and mine's the day after. I've got a present for her and I've had it a couple of weeks. It's not much, but I had no money to spend. When I told Mom I wanted to get Jenny something, she gave me two dollars and told me that was all she could spare. I found a little silver charm for her charm bracelet. It's a pair of dance shoes. They're really ballet slippers, but that's okay. One good thing though: when Mrs. Brewster suggested we have our birthday dinners at the same time, Mom agreed. It'll be tomorrow night at our house.

I'm so glad my sister's gone. Mom and Dad seem to be much happier and I know I am. I just hope Aunt Doris can put up with her, at least until after the baby's born. Maybe she'll find a job or a husband in Little Rock and never come back. It was good seeing Aunt Doris and my uncle again. They have two boys, Mike and Harry, but we didn't stay long enough for me to get to know them again.

Saturday June 7, 1941
Late afternoon

It's been a wonderful day. Jenny and I had our birthday dinners together on Thursday night and Mrs. Brewster made the cake—coconut, my favorite. She put twenty-four candles on it, twelve for each of us. We blew out all the candles at the same time. I made a wish and it was that Jenny and I could be alone together soon. I've about forgotten what she feels like. Sometimes at night I think about things I probably shouldn't and sometimes I get carried away and can't stop myself. I wonder if she does that. Maybe it's like peeing in the shower: everyone does it but no one talks about it. We talk about everything—but we haven't talked about that.

Jenny liked the charm I got for her. She has a story for every one on her bracelet and now she has one from me. She got me the best present though. She gave me the picture I like of the two of us from the dance competition, the one with our noses touching. It's in a pretty frame and I have it hanging on my wall right now. I didn't ask for it. I thought we could have a copy made, but the man at the drugstore said that since we didn't have the negative, it would be terribly expensive and might not turn out right, but it did. She always knows what to get me, although she shouldn't have spent so much money.

Today Mrs. Brewster made strawberry tarts in little individual pie crusts. She's such a good cook and I think Jenny and I could have eaten a dozen of them. Afterward we walked over to Bosse Field and watched the Bees play. I've never paid too much attention to baseball before, but Jenny loves it and I got to see my first ever home run. Everyone stood and yelled. It was great.

Friday June 13, 1941
Night

We went to the pool this afternoon for the first time this summer. Jenny's mom bought her a new swimsuit this week after having a look at her in the one she wore last summer. Jenny said her mother thought it was much too small. I'm sure it is. The new one is black and white polka dot and she looks good in it. She got a lot of looks today from the older boys. I guess I wasn't very good at pretending I didn't look too. Sometimes I think about what my slutty sister said, that Jenny will kick me to the curb someday. We stopped at the park on our way home and sat on our bench. We talk about everything, so I just opened up.

"Do you think you'll find a boy someday you like better than me? I see how they look at you, Jenny. You're beautiful and you could have any of them tomorrow if you wanted. I bet a senior would ask you out. I'm as plain as a plowed field I know and I just want to tell you that I would understand if…"

She got a really serious look on her face and lifted my chin up to where we were almost touching noses.

"I never want to talk about this again and I mean it. I love you, body and soul, remember? I can't help it if boys look at me, but you'll never see me looking at them, and you're not plain. You don't notice all the times I look at you when we walk together, do you? You don't know what I think about in my bed every night, do you? I think about you, only you, and if we don't figure out how to be alone together soon, I'm positively going to explode. So I never want to hear you talk like that again, okay?"

"If I could kiss you right now, I would kiss you a thousand times."

"Kiss me once now and I'll remember it a thousand times."

Our lips touched and for the next few seconds, the world disappeared. When I opened my eyes, the world was still there, and there were no lightning bolts from Heaven or anyone taking notice of us at all. Children played at the shore of the lake with their parents nearby and people walked on the sidewalk behind us as if we were invisible. It was a wonderful kiss.

Monday June 23, 1941
Early morning

Yesterday was Father's Day. Mom and I made breakfast for him just the way he likes it. That's what he always asks for as a present. The pork chops were delicious and he ate three. We were late for church and so were a lot of other fathers. Pastor Knott recognized all the fathers in the congregation after his sermon and we applauded. In the afternoon Jenny and I sat on our bench in the park and watched the children play near the lake again.

"Do you ever think about what you want to be when you grow up, Jenny?"

She answered almost before I got the question out.

"Yes I know what I want to be; the same thing I've wanted to be for every minute of the past year…somewhere with you."

Sometimes I feel really lost when talking to her. It's because she thinks so much deeper than I do; I could never come up with something like that and she does it all the time. Maybe I'm just not romantic or maybe I'm still just a kid pretending to be in love.

Tuesday July 1, 1941
Afternoon

Jenny's parents and their next door neighbors, the Millers, are going out to dinner and a movie tonight. Jenny's supposed to babysit the Miller's new baby at her house while they're gone, and after school her mother asked if I would mind keeping Jenny company and helping her watch the baby. I was going to ask anyway. We'll have the house to ourselves for hours. It's been a long time since we were alone together. My hand is shaking so much I can hardly write.

Late night

I got to the Brewsters' just as everyone was leaving and promised to stay until they got home—around eleven, Mr. Brewster said. Mom doesn't like me being up that late, but since I was sort of doing everyone a favor, it was all right. We got instructions for the baby, but he'd just been fed and Mrs. Miller said he would probably sleep the whole time. He's four months old and a really happy baby. Jenny and I have sat for Mrs. Miller several times in the afternoon for an hour or so, however this was the first time she and Mr. Miller have gone out in the evening since little Thomas was born. After everyone left, Jenny put on a record with the volume down low. Thomas was sound asleep on a pallet in the floor and didn't seem to mind the music.

"I'll be back in a minute," she said as she ran up the stairs.

When she came back down, I knew what she had gone upstairs for—my favorite T-shirt, which is much too small now. She didn't say anything but I noticed right away she had nothing on underneath. She hates wearing a bra and takes it off every chance she gets. She changed the record and put on a slow waltz and with a smile asked me to dance. It was so good to get to hold her in my arms again. I could feel her curves through her shorts when I accidentally let my hand go a little too low and I did that a lot. Soon we were too wrapped up in each others' arms to notice that the music had stopped. We stood there kissing and still moving to the music that wasn't playing. She felt good and I had my next move planned. I slid my hands up under the back of her T-shirt and then slipped both into her shorts in a move that was so smooth I thought she hadn't noticed—until I felt her hands do the same thing. I squeezed, she squeezed. I made circles with my hands, she made circles with hers; then Thomas started crying. Jenny and I were practically stuck together, but we pulled our hands from each other and went to see what the problem with him was. He had a dirty diaper and Jenny changed it like an expert while I watched.

"Someday I'll tell him I saw him naked," Jenny said with a laugh, "and you're my witness."

I reached for a diaper, but I was too late. Little Thomas gets sort of excited when you change him and he'll pee even if he's just peed. We learned that lesson the hard way last month and I wasn't quick enough with the diaper this time either. A stream shot straight up from him, but Jenny was fast enough to avoid it and I got him covered before he soaked everything. Last time it went right into her hair.

"I don't think I'll be telling him about that when he grows up."

After we finished changing Thomas, Jenny fed him half a bottle and he went right back to sleep. I turned on the radio to a station that plays a lot of jazz and swing music and we sat sideways together on the sofa, facing each other and talked. Then she remembered something.

"I have a treat for us and I almost forgot it. Mom and I made them and she made me promise I'd share them with you. They're so good."

She left for the kitchen and returned with a plate of little chocolate covered things.

"They're chocolate covered Maraschino cherries and they just melt in your mouth. Here, try one."

She picked up one and put it in my mouth. It's probably the best thing I've ever tasted. I picked up one and started to put it in her mouth, but she held my hand and put two of my fingers in her mouth with the chocolate covered cherry. She sucked on my fingers and the chocolate until it melted, then licked the chocolate off. When she fed me one, I did the same thing. Then when I fed her another one, she pulled me to her and kissed me. Her chocolate covered tongue slid into my mouth. We finished the cherries that way and I felt warm all over.

"Mom had no idea I was planning this while she and I were making them, but I was. It was all I could think about. Do you ever think about me?"

Do I ever think about her? If she only knew.

I pulled her close and answered her question with a kiss as I slipped my hand under that tight T-shirt and around to her back. Just like before, she duplicated my every move and began to lightly tickle my lower back. That drove me crazy and when I did the same thing to her, I felt her shiver. I knew that game and I knew I would lose. The electricity went all the way through me and I think it got passed on to her. I was in Heaven until eleven tonight.

Sunday July 6, 1941
Afternoon

We went over to the Brewster's on Friday for a July Fourth cookout. Neither my dad nor Jenny's had to work. It was great seeing the two of them together. They're best friends but hardly ever see each other except at work. They talked a lot about the war and I listened. Both think we'll have to get into it soon, but they thought that months ago, and so far we've managed to stay out. I heard on the radio last week about Germany invading Russia. Now they're at war with them and England. The Germans have already beaten France and I know Italy and Japan are on their side. Sometimes I get really scared for Jenny's brother. What if Hitler invades England? That's what everyone thinks they'll do next, and now they've invaded Russia. I don't understand. Daddy says we're sending guns and ships to England already and that soon we'll be doing the same thing for Russia. The Germans won't just sit back and let us do that. No one seems to think they'll invade us though. We're too far away, but if they invade England, we'll have to do something. I don't like thinking about it.

I sat with Jenny at church this morning. We wrote notes to each other when no one was watching and exchanged them after the service. Hers read: "VHKKXNTKHBJSGDBGNBNKZSDNEEZMXSGHMF HOTSHSNM?"

Yes, I would and I'll probably think about that all night tonight.

Thursday July 17, 1941
Night

The Millers said Jenny and I took good care of little Thomas last time, and we could use another job or two like that. I like Mrs. Miller, but Jenny told me Mr. Miller has a girlfriend. How could he do that? He's married and has a new baby at home. She says it's the girl at Muir's Drugs. I know who she's talking about. It's Mr. Muir's niece and I heard him call her Hazel when I was in there with Mom last week. She's been working at the drugstore for several months and every time I've seen her, she's been wearing a low cut tight sweater that was much too revealing, like she was trying to be Lana Turner or somebody. I looked. How could I not? I think her bra was stuffed. No one has breasts that big unless they're nursing a baby.

Friday August 1, 1941
Night

A great discovery the whole world should hear about over the radio; I finally have something growing down there—not much, just fuzz really—but it's definitely there. I felt it last night and used a mirror in the bathroom this morning after my shower to get a better look. It's thin and I had to look hard to see it but I don't care; it's there for sure. I know it wasn't there last week. Maybe I'm starting to grow up finally.

Monday August 18, 1941
Night

Mom announced at dinner tonight that she and Dad are going to Little Rock to see my sister. There was no mention of me going. I guess they don't want me to see her pregnant. Her being pregnant has never been mentioned and I've never asked. I guess it's one of those family secrets that really isn't a secret. We just don't talk about it. Jenny and I talk about it. The way we have it figured, the baby should be born in October or November.

"The Brewsters have a spare bedroom and Mrs. Brewster was nice enough to say you can stay with them. I told her you wouldn't be any trouble, so I want you to be on your best behavior."

Best behavior? I'll be right across the hall from Jenny. I'll do their laundry and mop their floors if they want.

Mom and Dad leave early Wednesday morning and won't be back until late Saturday afternoon. I'm supposed to go to the Brewster's right after school on Wednesday. I do that anyway for dance, I just won't go home afterward.

Three nights with Jenny only a few feet away; nothing could possibly be better.

Saturday August 23, 1941
Very late

I was wrong about nothing being better than three nights with Jenny only a few feet away, so very wrong. Jenny and I had our Wednesday dance lesson as usual and then I went home to make sure things were okay and pick up some clothes and my pajamas. Jenny and I helped Mrs. Brewster make dinner and that was fun. Mostly we stayed out of the way, but I'm pretty good at peeling potatoes. She made beef stew. That's Daddy's favorite too, but she makes it different with lots of spices and stuff. It was so good everyone had seconds. After dinner Mrs. Brewster and Jenny took me up to my room and I put my clothes away. It looks like my sister's room except there's a window fan. The bathroom down the hall is in exactly the same place as ours. Everyone listened to the news for half an hour and then *Blondie* for an hour, just like I would've done at home. The news was bad. It looks like the Germans are going to beat the Russians by Christmas, but at least there was no mention of the war during *Blondie*. Afterward, Mrs. Brewster said that Jenny and I could stay up and listen to the radio for another hour if we wanted as long as we kept the volume low. She and Mr. Brewster then went to bed. That's usually when Mom and Dad go to bed since he has to leave for work by five. Jenny switched the station and found some good jazz music at WLS Chicago. We danced some and then sat on the sofa and talked, mostly about *Blondie*. When the clock chimed ten, Jenny said we should be getting to bed. I followed her up the stairs and into my room and she turned on the window fan for me.

Lying in bed all I could think about was coming up with a reason to go across the hall and knock on Jenny's door. We were only a few feet from each other, but it seemed like a mile. It was a restless night and it seemed like I'd only been asleep an hour when I heard the soft knock on my door. My first thought that it was Jenny was right. It was also broad daylight. She was still in her pajamas and when the door opened, I could smell breakfast downstairs.

"Are you going to sleep all day? Mom has breakfast waiting for us and it smells good. Did you sleep well?"

She came over and sat on the bed. She looked good even in the morning, although her hair was sort of a mess. I leaned up and kissed her on the cheek and slid my hand up the back of her pajama top. She backed away and smiled.

"Where were you last night when I wanted you to do that? I waited for you but you never came."

"I was right here waiting for you."

She then kissed me and dragged me out of bed downstairs for breakfast. It was nearly nine. I almost never sleep that late.

A neighbor had given Mrs. Brewster a huge basket of grapes and we spent the day making jelly with only an hour's break for lunch. By the time we finished, it was time to start dinner and Mrs. Brewster chased us out of the kitchen after we helped clean up the jelly making mess. We had twenty-two pint jars and Jenny and I delivered six to the neighbor who had given Mrs. Brewster the grapes. She said that I could take six jars home with me for helping. After delivering the jelly, Jenny and I walked toward town.

"It's Thursday afternoon and Mrs. Miller will be visiting her mother with the baby which means Mr. Miller will be at the drugstore flirting with his girlfriend."

I didn't want to believe her, but when we got to the drugstore, there he was, sitting at the soda counter and there she was, falling out of her sweater for him. Anyone could have walked by. We didn't go in.

"Mom and Dad are very sound sleepers." Jenny said as we walked back toward her house.

I turned and saw her smiling.

The routine that night was the same, just like at my house. Dinner was leftover beef stew, but Mr. Brewster didn't complain. He saw all the jelly we made and said that he couldn't wait for breakfast to sample some of it. That thought had crossed my mind as well.

When Jenny and I went upstairs for our showers, I turned to go into my bedroom and she followed me in. She kissed me and whispered in my ear.

"I'll be back when I finish my shower."

I got into my pajamas and waited for her. In a few minutes she came to my room and slipped into the bed. My shower was finished in two minutes and I was back in the bedroom. In the pitch black, I felt for the bedcovers and slid between the sheets with her. We lay there side by side for a few minutes, neither of us knowing what we were supposed to do. It was one thing to kiss and maybe hold each other, but being in bed together with only our pajamas separating us was something only married people did. If Mrs. Brewster had come upstairs looking for Jenny and found us in bed together, we would both be in reform schools on opposite ends of the country by now. Jenny had to have been thinking the same thing because when she finally did whisper something to me, I could hear the uncertainty in her voice.

"Do you want me to go? I will if you want me to."

"Does your mom ever come up to check on you after you go to bed?"

"Not that I know of, but I'd be asleep probably. I know she didn't last night because I hardly slept."

"I love you Jenny and we may never get to sleep together again. I don't want you to go."

I wrapped my arms around her and pulled her close to me and gave her my best movie star kiss. I could feel her whole body next to mine through her pajamas and for the first time, I really smelled her, no perfume, just her. I think I could pick her out blindfolded in a crowd just by her smell. We were so close, I could feel her heartbeat in my chest. I thought maybe reform school wouldn't be so bad. Until we fell asleep with our arms and legs wrapped around each other, we did our best to make every part of our bodies touch. It was like having a twin of myself I could just melt into.

The stairs in Jenny's house squeaked like ours and at the first sound, we were both wide awake. It was light in the room and the look on my face was probably as terrifying as the one on Jenny's. When I heard the knock on Jenny's door, I stopped breathing. The doorknob turned and the door squeaked as she opened it. Jenny was fast. She was out my door in two seconds and I heard the toilet flush in the bathroom three seconds later. I opened my door a crack just in time to see Jenny coming out of the bathroom and her mother coming from her room.

"Your breakfast is ready Virginia," her mother said as she turned and walked back down the stairs. "See if our guest is awake and the two of you come down and eat before it gets cold. I have to run to Fant's and get some sugar. We used all of ours yesterday."

Jenny waited until she heard the front door close and walked back into my room. She pushed me back on the bed, crawled on top of me and kissed me.

"Was that close enough for you? Tonight I have to remember to get back to my room before daylight."

"Tonight? Are you crazy? We almost got caught."

"Yes, but we didn't. We fell asleep too soon last night, that's all. It won't happen tonight."

I chased her downstairs and was met with the smell of fresh baked biscuits. Biscuits with butter and new grape jelly; Jenny and I ate four each. We were dressed and ready for whatever Mrs. Brewster had in mind for us when she got home from the store. We were immediately sent back upstairs to make our beds. I guess we forgot that the day before too.

Sunday August 24, 1941
Night

I fell asleep last night before I could finish and I want to write everything down before I forget—not that I ever will. I sat next to Jenny this morning in church, but she didn't say much. Mom and Dad got back yesterday afternoon and Mrs. Brewster made a big deal out of how much help I'd been and that I was welcome back anytime. If she only knew.

Friday must be laundry day for everyone on the block. Clotheslines were already full on either side of the Brewsters' by the time we got the first load done. Jenny and I collected dirty laundry from all over the house and took it to what they call the utility room just off the kitchen. That was different from our house. We don't have a utility room but our kitchen is bigger. The Brewsters have a built in Bendix washing machine that's bolted down because it shakes the floor like the house is sitting next to railroad tracks, but it spins the clothes almost dry. We loaded and unloaded while Mrs. Brewster did the hand laundry things. We had everything washed and hanging by noon. After lunch Mrs. Brewster gave Jenny and me fifty cents each and told us to go to the movies while the clothes dried. The Friday matinee is always a bunch of Three Stooges shorts for the children, but I didn't care. I like the Three Stooges. There were about a hundred kids there and all of them sat up front. Jenny and I sat in the very back row alone and held hands. Between each of the shorts, the theater was almost dark for about a minute while the film was changed and that was nice.

We collected all the clothes when we got back and put away everything that didn't have to be ironed. That used to be my sister's job; now I have to do it at home. It was either making dinner or ironing and Mrs. Brewster let us choose. No one complained about the meal we made and we got a lot of help. She already had the roast in the oven, so all we had to do was make the potatoes and we were told we could make them any way we wanted. That was an easy choice. We made French fries and they turned out great. Jenny and I ate almost all of the first fryer full as soon as they were done. We were also having carrots and spinach. They were easy to do too. After we got the carrots washed and scraped and the spinach washed three times, all we had to do was boil them with some spices Mrs. Brewster gave us. The carrots got a little mushy. As if the three of us had rehearsed the ironing and cooking, we had everything done and the table set right before Mr. Brewster got home. He complimented Jenny and me on the meal, although we hadn't done anything special, and he thanked me again and again for helping. It was the least I could do for them letting me stay—and getting to sleep with Jenny.

We followed almost the exact same routine as the previous two nights, except Mr. Brewster let Jenny and me listen to *Time to Smile* with Eddie Cantor. Jenny didn't know that he's the man who recorded "Santa Clause is Coming to Town," my favorite Christmas song for as long as I can remember. After the Brewsters went to bed, Jenny and I played a hand of Rook; I lost.

I'd barely had time to get my pajamas on when Jenny came over.

"Tonight we leave the lamp on so we won't go to sleep. She turned on the small bedside lamp and turned off the overhead light and slid into bed beside me. We both had clean pajamas and I think Mrs. Brewster ironed mine. We were soon intertwined like two snakes and I decided reform school would definitely be worth whatever was coming next.

"Body and soul, remember?"

"Body and soul," I whispered back.

Jenny pulled the sheet up over us and we wrapped our arms around each other again. We were closer than we'd ever been and I could feel the warmth of her body as we tried to crawl inside each other's skin. Jenny rolled over on top and then pushed herself up off me a little. I couldn't figure out what she was doing and then she smiled like she had something planned. When she came back down to me slowly, until I could just feel her lightly touching me through our thin pajama tops, I thought I would pee. There's no other feeling in the world like that.

"I love you and I've thought about this all day, but I can't keep it up. I'll faint or do something crazy."

She then rolled over and pulled me on top of her and I soon understood what she meant. We were hot and covered in sweat. I threw off the sheet and we lay there trying to catch our breath. She snuggled up close to me for a while and I guess she thought I was asleep, but I wasn't.

If she hadn't left the lamp on, we would've slept the rest of the night just as we were. Sometime in the night she slid out of my bed, turned out the lamp and went back to her room. I took off my sweat soaked things and slept on top of the sheets the rest of the night. Jenny didn't come to wake me for breakfast the next morning. I found my way downstairs to an empty house. There was a note on the table from Mrs. Brewster telling me my breakfast was in the oven and that she and Jenny had gone grocery shopping. It was almost ten and I felt like a slacker for having overslept and not being up to go with them. The least I could do was clear the breakfast dishes and collect the laundry, including my pajamas. I went into Jenny's room and found her panties on the floor. They were still damp and I knew why. I started the wash and went back upstairs for a shower. The washing cycle had finished and I was out of the shower and dressed by the time they returned. Jenny had a look on her face I'd never seen before and she was very quiet. Something wasn't right.

Thursday August 28, 1941
Night

Jenny's been different this week. She won't talk to me. Maybe I did something wrong at her house. She's making me crazy. I tried to kiss her yesterday and she wouldn't let me, and she wouldn't tell me why. She has to tell me what's going on.

Tuesday September 2, 1941
Morning

Last night Jenny and I met after dinner at our bench in the park. She hasn't been talking to me much since my stay at her house, but tonight when she started talking, she went nonstop for an hour.

"Friday night we did some things we've never done before and I guess I'm worried about what might happen next."

"Did I do something wrong?"

"No, no, you didn't do anything wrong, I did, something really wrong…while you were asleep and I shouldn't tell you. It's just that it felt so good being that close to you and I didn't want it to end, so I…"

There was no one around so I leaned over and kissed her and this time she let me.

"Like peeing in the shower, only better?"

She smiled. A single tear was stuck in the corner of her eye and I brushed it away.

"Like a home run," she whispered. "You pee in the shower."

We've talked some about that sort of thing, and I really didn't know what else to say. I hadn't been quite asleep when I first felt her roll toward me and her leg go over mine late last Friday night. It was nice; like she was glad she was in bed with me. Her head was on my shoulder and I could hear her breathing. I was afraid to move, afraid she might think I was awake. She lay still beside me, but a few minutes later, I knew she wasn't asleep. When I heard her take a deep breath and then felt her body tremble for a second, I knew for sure. I didn't dare say anything when she got up, turned out the light and went back to her room.

I should have told her I'd been awake, but I felt like such a bluenose, I just couldn't. Maybe she believes me when I tell her I'm pretty sure everyone does it.

Tuesday September 9, 1941
Afternoon

Jenny and I spent the whole morning at the pool. School starts next Monday and yesterday I went clothes shopping with Mom. I'll be so glad when I can shop for clothes by myself. She always picks out things that will last the entire school year without any concern for what they look like. Of course I love my mother, but she has no sense of modern style. Thankfully I've outgrown my church clothes as well, so I was able to get a few nice things.

Jenny hasn't mentioned the thing we talked about a week ago.

Monday September 15, 1941
Night

Today was the first day of school and there were lots of new people in our class, including our teacher. Mrs. Delaney introduced herself and said that she'd taught sixth grade in St. Louis for the past ten years and had come with her husband to Evansville when he got a job at the Ironworks. She seems nice and all, but the class was too excited to listen until she scratched her fingernails along the blackboard from one end to the other. That got our attention in a hurry. All of us have grown a foot since last year and we spent the day getting reacquainted. Marston wasn't in class and I've heard his family moved. I'm glad because he would have been crazy with all the new boobies to look at. There were lots of new clothes and stuffed bras. Mrs. Delaney separated Jenny and me before recess for talking. That was normal. Mrs. Winston did it last year on the first day for the same thing.

Tuesday September 23, 1941
Very late

I don't know what time it is. I went to bed early, but I couldn't sleep. I have to write down some things that happened today. When I stopped by Jenny's this morning, her mother told me she was sick and wouldn't be going to school. Jenny's never sick. I must have looked worried because Mrs. Brewster said I could go up and see her for a minute before going on to school. I knocked on her door and heard her say something so I just walked in. She was in bed and I sat down on the bed next to her. She managed a smile, but I could tell she didn't feel well. I leaned over and kissed her.

"I have cramps, really bad cramps. They started late last night. Mom says that means my period will come soon, probably today, and so I'm staying home from school. I guess that stupid film we saw at the beginning of the year last year was right, but the 'discomfort' they told us about is just wrong. It hurts. It really hurts. It's like when I ate too many green apples when I was six. Mom's getting me a heating pad this morning, although I don't think it'll help."

I made Jenny promise to tell me everything her mother told her. I remember when my sister's period started—it wasn't important to me at the time, but this was Jenny and it was important now.

When she doubled over in pain and tears streamed from her eyes I couldn't stand it. I wanted to crawl into bed with her, hold her and make the pain go away. She rolled over onto her side away from me and curled up into a ball. I slid my hand under the covers, reached around her waist under her pajama top and began to rub her stomach, thinking that might help. Maybe it did because in a few minutes she rolled over onto her back and smiled. I continued to rub her stomach.

"Does that help?" I asked.

"What would I do without you? Can you stay here all day and rub my stomach when it hurts?"

We talked for a while and I didn't stop rubbing her stomach. I would've done that all day if she'd asked. When another cramp came, I could feel her muscles tighten and the expression on her face told me how much it hurt. I rubbed harder, put my face down close to hers and kissed her cheek until the cramp passed. While my hand was on her stomach I sort of explored her navel and she didn't seem to mind. That didn't last nearly long enough. The sound of her mother's footsteps coming up the stairs told me I'd stayed long enough. I met her at Jenny's door and told her I would be back after school with homework assignments. Then she did something I wasn't expecting. She kissed me on the forehead and told me how much she appreciated me being a good friend to Jenny.

I couldn't think of anything but Jenny all day at school today and I couldn't wait to get back to her house. When I arrived, she was on the porch waiting for me. She looked fine and asked if I would like to go for a walk. We walked back to the park to our bench. It was nice out today, although for some reason there was no one else around. When we sat down, she started talking and kept talking.

"Thank you for coming by this morning and rubbing my stomach. Cramps are terrible, but mine didn't last too long. My period started just before lunch today and then the cramps stopped, just like that. You should see this thing I'm wearing. It's like having a pillow between my legs and there are all sorts of straps and things that hold it in place. I haven't bled much so far, but Mom says I should check things every couple of hours. This means I could have a baby now. I could get pregnant anytime... I mean, if I...you know."

That wasn't covered much in the film we saw, although I know what she was talking about. I've heard things and I've seen pregnant women before and I do have a pregnant slut for a sister. I'm not a complete moron.

"Mom says my breasts will start to grow fast now."

I noticed she didn't call them boobies.

"I hope they don't grow too much," she continued. "I like them the way they are, maybe just a little bigger would be okay, but not huge like Mrs. Sanders'. Maybe hers are big because she has a new baby and she's nursing. I think I'd like to nurse a baby someday. It's something every girl thinks about I bet."

She smiled and then added, "I wonder if I could do that...nurse someone's baby for a little while. That sounds really stupid doesn't it?"

It didn't sound stupid to me. I learned a lot from Jenny today, though some I sort of knew. She'll have another period in about a month and she told me that she expects me to rub her stomach again if she has cramps. It's a terrible thing for me to wish, but I hope she does; not really bad ones like this time though.

Monday September 29, 1941
Night

Jenny's period only lasted three days and she feels fine now, especially since she no longer has to wear that pillow, as she called it, between her legs. I know she's only a week older than she was before her period came, but she seems more grown up now and it's like she's joined a club or something at school. Jenny says the girls who have gotten their periods all talk about it and they act like it's some big secret that others aren't allowed in on. Thanks to Jenny I know as much as anyone else. I've also learned two new words today: cush and cuzzy and Jenny said as far as she can figure out that's what the girls are calling their vaginas. I know vagina is the real word for it. Mom taught me that when I was probably eight after hearing my sister call it a bird's nest, which I thought was funny even if Mom didn't. Any of them beat what I've heard some call it. I don't think I can ever call my cat a pussy again, at least not where anyone can hear me. I like cuzzy best.

Our first home basketball game was tonight. Jenny and I sat on the first row behind the cheerleaders and yelled our heads off; we lost anyway. An older boy who plays on the team asked if he could walk with us on the way home. His name is Danny Burke and he's one of the new students this year. He and his family moved into the neighborhood, across the street from Jenny, just before school started and he hardly knows anyone except the other boys on the team. I've seen boys look at girls the way he looks at Jenny and I've told her he's been looking. She said I was imagining things, but I guess she knows now I wasn't. Maybe he got the idea that Jenny's already spoken for because I made a point of walking between them on the way home and even held her hand a couple of times at street crossings. He may be older than me, and a head taller, but Mr. Burke had better keep his distance.

Saturday October 4, 1941
Night

I listened to the news tonight at Jenny's. Her dad says the Germans are running through the Russians and that the war there will be over soon, maybe even before Christmas. He says that Hitler will then invade England for sure. Everyone is so worried about Jenny's brother. They get letters from him, but they have big parts cut out; they call it censoring. Jenny read one to me and we tried to guess what he was trying to say. I wonder if he knows his letters get read before the Brewsters get them. Jenny says that their letters to him probably get read as well. He mentioned a girl in one letter and enclosed a picture of her. She was standing under a street sign and the name of the street had been cut out. I guess we can't have Hitler knowing the names of streets in London or wherever Jenny's brother was at the time.

Jenny told me today that Mr. Burke has asked her to the basketball game next week. I guess I must have looked a little disappointed because she kissed me and said that she told him she already has a date. It wouldn't be much of a date with him anyway since he'll be playing.

Monday October 6, 1941
Night

Mr. Burke has a big mouth and I'd like to put my fist in it. It was all over school today that he asked Jenny to the game and she turned him down because she already has a date. Why would he tell anyone? That seems so stupid. Maybe he thought his friends would think he was a big man for being brave enough to ask her out in the first place. I don't know, but I do know there won't be any point in him asking her out again. I've never seen Jenny so mad. On the way home, I thought she would scream.

"Just who does he think he is? Just because he plays on the basketball team, does he think he can have any girl he wants for the asking? I do have a date for the game...don't I? You'll go with me won't you? Please. All I heard today from the other girls was how stupid I was for not saying yes when he asked me. You must've heard it too. Well, I'm going to the game with a date and we're going to sit close and maybe even hold hands—and if we win and if I want to give my date a kiss in front of everybody, I will and that's all there is to it."

I knew better than to do anything other than agree with her.

She had calmed down a little by the time we got to her house. There was no one home and the note on the table said that Mrs. Brewster had gone to my house for the afternoon to help Mom rake leaves. I hate raking leaves. We should have gone to help them, but Jenny said they were probably about finished and that there were some doughnuts left from Saturday that needed to be eaten. Mrs. Brewster makes the best doughnuts in Evansville so it wasn't a hard choice. We sat across from each other at the kitchen table eating donuts and drinking milk.

"Would you really do it, Jenny? I mean, kiss me in front of everybody? You know that would get us a trip to the principal's office and probably get us banned from basketball games for the year. I've never even seen high school couples kiss in front of everyone; not ever. It's just not done."

She smiled and kept eating her doughnut.

Thursday October 9, 1941
Night

She's going to get us thrown out of school. I went with Jenny tonight to the game, but we didn't sit down front. We sat in the back row where couples usually sit. It was chilly in the gym and our coats were over our laps so no one could see us holding hands through the whole game. It was very close right to the end. Mr. Burke fouled out in the middle of the fourth quarter and I saw him looking back at us several times from the bench. At the final buzzer, we were ahead by three points. Everyone jumped up and yelled and Jenny kissed me just like she said she would. I don't think anyone noticed, but I'll find out tomorrow for sure. She's a crazy girl and I love her.

Tuesday October 14, 1941
Very early

Can't sleep. It's cold in my room and I'm under a ton of quilts and blankets. I bet if Jenny were here, I wouldn't be so cold. No one saw her kiss me at the basketball game, or if they did, they didn't talk and at my school, they would have talked.

On the news over the weekend, I heard that Hitler has announced that the war against Russia is as good as finished. How can that be? Russia is huge. I wonder if this really does mean they plan to invade England next. Surely we won't just sit by and let that happen. We have to get involved before it's too late.

Friday October 24, 1941
Night

When I got home from school, Mom met me at the door and said that Aunt Doris had just given birth to a baby girl and that she and the baby were doing fine. Does she really think I'm that stupid? That was a mean thing to write, but does she think I don't know my own sister was pregnant when she left? Half the people at school knew. Well, if my parents want to play that game, I can play along. Who cares anyway? I'm glad they're okay, but I hope both of them stay in Little Rock. Mom and Dad are going to visit as soon as he can get some time off work. Even if I'm invited this time, I don't want to go. I wonder if having a baby hurts as much as everyone says. If it does, why would anyone ever have another? Mom didn't tell me what they named the baby; I guess I didn't ask either. There was no talk of the new baby at dinner tonight. They know I know. They have to.

There's going to be a Halloween party at Caroline Hughes' house. Jenny and I both got invitations. Caroline is the most popular girl in school and I was sort of surprised being invited, though it was no surprise that Jenny was. Their moms are friends. I think they're from the same place out west. Caroline's a pretty girl, though not as pretty as Jenny, and the boys all think she's Rita Hayworth with her red hair and big breasts. I told Jenny once that I thought she stuffs her bra and was told that she definitely does not. I didn't ask how she knew.

The invitation said we had to come to the party in costume. I don't think the costume I wore two years ago will work and I'm a little worried about what I'm going to wear. Jenny's mom can make her something, but I'm afraid Mom's not much of a seamstress.

Jenny's second period came today, but she said the cramps weren't so bad this time.

Tuesday October 28, 1941
Night

The costume problem has been solved—Jenny's mom to the rescue. She's making them for us and this afternoon was the final fitting. We're going to be Abbott and Costello. We've seen *One Night in the Tropics* four times and we can do "Who's on First" perfectly. I'll need a little padding to be Costello, but Jenny's mom took care of that. We're wearing suits that Jenny's brother outgrew years ago and with my hair parted on the side and combed back and Jenny's under a hat, we sort of look like them. I'm not too sure about the shoe polish they want to use on my hair to make it black, but Jenny's mom says it'll shampoo out.

Friday October 31, 1941
Very late

The Halloween party was fun and everyone knew who we were dressed up to be. We must have done the "Who's on First" routine a dozen times. We had a couple of hours after school to get dressed and we were in no hurry. Jenny's mom wasn't home. She was at the Hughes' helping Caroline's mom get ready for the party so we had the house to ourselves.

"I know," Jenny said as soon as we were inside, "I'll dress you and you can dress me."

That wasn't an offer I could turn down. We went upstairs to her room and found our costumes laid out on her bed.

"You first. You have to dress me first," Jenny announced with a grin as she pulled her coat off, threw it in the floor and then stood motionless in front of me.

My fingers were shaking as I began unbuttoning her white blouse. When I finished I pulled it off and put it in the hamper. The weather's been cool the past few days, so she had a white T-shirt underneath. I was too much of a coward to ask if she wanted it off too. One button and a zipper later, her grey skirt fell to the floor and she stepped out of it. My buttons were undone a minute later and soon we were standing facing each other practically naked.

"There's one more thing that has to go."

She turned around and I fumbled with the bra catch under her T-shirt until it was undone. She turned back toward me and somehow took her bra off, leaving the shirt on. How did she do that? I just stood there looking at her like an idiot. She looked like a real woman. Standing up like that, her breasts looked much bigger than I remember. Maybe they've grown or maybe it was because she was standing up.

"We have plenty of time, Jenny. We don't have to get dressed just yet do we?"

"No, but it's freezing in this house."

I guess we had the same idea at the same time because we both looked at the bed. We were under the blankets by the time the thought finished crossing our minds. Wrapped around each other, we soon warmed up enough to kiss and what a kiss it was. I rolled over on my back, took her face in my hands and gave her my very best Hollywood kiss. When I moved down and kissed her neck, she seemed to melt. I learned that trick from the movies as well, but the movies never show you what comes next. She reached around me and pulled our bodies together and I felt a warmth come over me like I've only ever felt with her. I slid my hands down her back and felt her shiver.

The sound of the front door slamming made my heart stop.

"Jenny, are you home?" her mom yelled.

"In the closet; get your clothes," she whispered to me.

"I'm upstairs getting dressed, Mom. I'll be down in a minute," she yelled back.

I grabbed my clothes, squeezed into the closet and closed the door.

"Don't hurry. I just came back for some powdered sugar. We ran out. See you at the party. It starts in an hour. Don't be late. I want you to get there a little early in case we need help."

"Okay Mom. I'll leave as soon as I get dressed."

"All right, but you have to wait for Costello. I want the two of you arriving at the same time. Mrs. Hughes wants to get some pictures."

I started breathing again when I heard the front door slam. Jenny waited a full minute before opening the closet door just to make sure her mom wasn't coming back.

Maybe the look on my face was funny because she stood there half naked, laughing while I tried to untangle myself from the hanging clothes. I could barely stand I was shaking so hard. She took me in her arms and kissed me until I calmed down a little.

"We have to get dressed," I stammered.

"We have five minutes," she whispered in my ear.

We made the most of those five minutes, wrapped in each other's arms under her blankets, and we weren't late for the party.

When the party was over, we helped clean up and it was after midnight when we got back to Jenny's house. I couldn't very well sleep with shoe polish on my hair and Mrs. Brewster said it would be all right if Jenny helped me wash it out as long as we cleaned up the bathroom afterward. I never realized how much I like having my hair washed. It was a new experience for me, like a lot of things have been with Jenny.

Saturday November 1, 1941
Morning

I'm glad today's Saturday and I'm glad Jenny loves me. It was hard to get to sleep last night even though I didn't get home until late. No one was up waiting for me. I think I must have dreamed about Jenny last night because when I woke up this morning, I thought for a second I was still in bed with her. I guess I understand what Jenny said once about not wanting it to end. I didn't want the feeling of her body next to mine to end and I imagined all sorts of things that didn't actually happen.

I have to get out of bed and get a shower. I'm sure Mom has something for me to do this morning.

Saturday November 15, 1941
Night

Mom was in one of her talkative moods when I went downstairs. It was sort of funny. I knew what she wanted to talk about, but she didn't know how to bring up the subject so I helped her a little. She asked about what we've been studying in school recently, particularly in Health class and I knew what she was leading up to, or trying to anyway, so I just volunteered everything I knew about sex. Some things I know for certain and some I've just heard. We kept the conversation simple, like the stuff in our school books.

From my earliest memories, I've relied on Mom to be a mother and a father. Dad works and makes enough money for us to have plenty to eat and a good place to live, but he's always been more or less a stranger. What I know about life, I've learned from Mom and if I can figure out how to ask a question, she'll always answer it even if she has to answer for Dad. I have no uncles on my mom's side and only one on my dad's. I met him once when I was little. There were never any men around when I was younger and I don't think it mattered. Mom sometimes says I would make the perfect husband or wife. She talks to me, I think much more than she ever talked to my sister. Today she mostly wanted to make sure I knew how my body worked and that I was prepared for changes to come and she wanted to make sure I knew where babies come from. I must have had that pretty much right because she didn't have anything to add until I finished—and it was something I hadn't thought about.

"That's half right. You've learned how your body works, but it's your brain that controls it. I've always known you were the smart one and that your sister would let someone else think for her. That's what happened. Your father and I have high hopes for you."

That was as close as Mom could come to telling me my sister got pregnant. It's been a sort of understood thing between us I guess, but it's never been said outright.

The Ironworks Thanksgiving dance was tonight and it was great. Jenny and I had everyone watching us when we danced together and this year a lot more kids our age danced. Jenny was beautiful of course. Her dress wasn't new, although Mrs. Brewster made it look new. The dance wasn't at all like last year. I think we danced with everyone there at least once and Jenny had the boys lined up to ask her. They were well behaved except for one boy I don't know. He's older, definitely in high school and he kept letting his hand go too far down Jenny's back. I saw her move it a couple of times. Jenny's dad only got one dance with her. Dance has become a popular thing to learn how to do at school. Mrs. Winston even has classes during gym a couple of days a week. Jenny and I had a table of our own and when no one was looking, we held hands under it. I felt so special being with the prettiest girl there.

Tuesday November 18, 1941
Afternoon

Thanksgiving is this Thursday and it looks like we're going to Little Rock. When Mom told me this morning, she didn't sound too excited about it and I guess she could tell I wasn't too thrilled about going either. I almost asked if I could stay with Jenny, but I think Mom wants me to go. Jenny's relatives from Lincoln will be visiting anyway so it would be sort of crowded and more work for Mrs. Brewster. Is it too early for snow? We wouldn't go if we had a lot of snow. Maybe my sister has grown up a little since the baby was born. I wonder if she's been breastfeeding; probably not with those tiny breasts of hers. I'm going to miss Jenny. Someday we'll spend all our holidays together.

Sunday November 23, 1941
Night

It's good to be home again. I wish it wasn't so late; I'd call Jenny and tell her all about the trip. Everyone stuck with the story that the new baby was my Aunt Doris's. Her two boys are very young and fell for it completely. My sister even behaved as if the baby wasn't hers. It was disgusting. I had to share a room with her and I wish I hadn't.

I got the idea right after we arrived that something was wrong and I found out what it was that first night in the bedroom I shared with my sister. If even half of what she told me is true, my aunt should throw her and my uncle out of the house. How could he do that? He has a wife and two young children and besides that, my sister's his niece. I couldn't believe some of the things she told me when I asked if Aunt Doris knew. I remember exactly what she said.

"Doris doesn't have time for him, and men have needs, so he comes to my room a couple of times a week." That shook me up, but I didn't let her know it.

"And I guess you give him what he needs, huh? That's just sick. He's your uncle for Christ's sake. You just had a baby a month ago and you're already doing it again—and with him."

"We've been doing it since right after I got here. So what; we're not blood relatives. He's married to Mom's sister and she cares more about the kids and the new baby than him anyway."

"Yeah, and you could get pregnant again and how would that look?"

"Not a chance. He won't let that happen."

She then reached into her nightstand and threw a little round white box toward me. "Sultan, Thin Transparent", the label read and in fine print it said, "Sold for prevention of disease only".

"What's this?"

"Open it and you might learn something."

I opened the box and inside was a thin circular thing that looked like the rubber whatchamacallit that goes on the garden hose to keep it from leaking when it's connected to the spigot on the back porch, except it didn't have a hole in the middle. I looked back at the box and then at my sister.

"What could this possibly have to do with the prevention of disease?"

"What it prevents, is babies. Give it here."

She put the thing on the end of her finger and began unrolling it. I got the idea and didn't want any details so I turned over and pretended to go to sleep. I did learn something, although I hate that I learned it from my sister. I already knew what rubbers are from talk at school, but I'd never seen one.

She's doing it—and with my uncle. It still makes me sick. Surely my aunt knows what's going on, but she'll never tell Mom and I can't either.

Monday November 24, 1941
Night

"Prophylactics, that's what they're called," Jenny explained on the way to school when I told her all about my Thanksgiving trip, leaving out nothing. "The boys call them rubbers and I guess they can prevent spreading disease, but that's not the only thing they're used for. I found one once in my brother's sock drawer. I wasn't spying or going through his things. I was putting away his laundry. I'm just glad Mom didn't find it first. She would've had a stroke. When I showed my brother what I found and told him where I found it, I thought he would die. I didn't know at the time what it was, although I knew it was something he shouldn't have and I made him tell me what it was in exchange for me keeping my mouth shut. I didn't give it back to him either. I kept it."

"Do you still have it?"

"Maybe," she said with a smile and kept walking.

On the way home I told her the rest of the story. I didn't really want to, but Jenny and I tell each other everything.

"I saw them do it."

"What? They did it right there in front of you? You're lying."

"Well, okay, maybe I didn't see them. It was dark, but I know what they were doing. It was late Friday night and I guess they thought I was asleep. Maybe I was, because I don't remember him coming into the room. All the moaning and heavy breathing was enough to wake me up though."

"They did it in the same room where you were sleeping? That's just disgusting."

She was right. It was disgusting and there was nothing I could do at the time but pretend to be asleep.

Monday December 8, 1941
Night

A horrible day. A horrible, horrible day. We're at war. It's all over the radio. I've heard President Roosevelt's speech four times already. Yesterday thousands of our sailors were killed at Pearl Harbor in a sneak attack by the Japanese. Why would the Japanese want to bomb us? Principal Lankford called the whole school together in the gym and played the radio over the speakers used at basketball games. When the speech was over, he led us in a prayer and then dismissed school early so we could go home. Our teachers were crying. Jenny was crying. We've declared war on Japan. How far away is Japan? Will they bomb us? That was all I could think of as I walked with Jenny to her house. Her mom met us at the door; she'd been crying. She hugged us and tears streamed down her face. Jenny's brother's still in England and I know that's a long way from Japan, but it won't matter. He could be shipped out anytime to fight the Japanese. I had to get home to be with Mom. She was all alone.

When I walked in the door, I could hear her praying. She was on her knees in the kitchen and I listened as she cried out to God to watch over our country and our soldiers. I knelt next to her, but she had no idea I was anywhere around. When Mom prays, she's in another world and this one doesn't interfere with that one. She talks to God as her Heavenly Father and I'm always amazed when I hear her. It's as if she knows Him like she knows any of us. I want to remember every prayer I've ever heard her pray. If anyone knows God, Mom does and I believe He hears her. When she finished, she opened her eyes and saw me next to her. She grabbed me and hugged me and without a tear in her eyes she spoke calmly.

"You will always remember today child, for as long as you live. This world is an evil place, but our Father in Heaven will watch over us, so don't be afraid in the days to come. We're safe and He will protect us as long as we trust in Him."

She then stood up and began ordering me around as if it were any other day. We had dinner to make. Something about doing things takes your mind off of even the worst news. When Dad got home, we said the blessing and ate dinner as if it were any other Monday and that made me feel safe for some reason. Everything was all right in Evansville. After dinner, Dad showed me on the map where Germany, Japan, Italy and England are. I sort of knew, but he knew how far each of them is from the United States. He also talked to me about his work. He's never done that before. He said we've been preparing for this war for a long time and that we will win it. I listened with both ears. My dad knows a lot and he talked well past my bedtime. I hope I get to know him better. When Mom interrupted and reminded him that I have school tomorrow, he kissed me and sent me up to bed.

Germany and Italy are allies with Japan. I remember that from school last year. They signed some sort of agreement. Does this mean we're at war with Germany and Italy too? President Roosevelt didn't say that, but everyone thinks that war with Japan means war with them. I hope Jenny's brother is safe.

Friday December 12, 1941
Night

Germany and Italy declared war on the United States yesterday and we've declared war on them. So it's the United States and England against Germany, Italy, and Japan. That's three against two, but we're much bigger than all of them put together and Russia still hasn't given up. There's been war news on the radio after every program and some programs have been postponed until who knows when. *Elsie Beebe* on CBS hasn't been on all week Mom said. That'll have to change or Hitler will have every housewife in America after his head. I listen sometimes in the summers, but it seems pretty boring to me.

Eric Sevareid is my favorite news reporter. I just like his voice and I like his name. Sevareid—it sounds so Viking you'd expect him to be carrying a sword instead of a microphone. I wonder what he looks like. Jenny and I have been paying more attention to the news in the past few days than we ever have. It was always just something that came on before a radio program we wanted to hear, but now it seems a little more important than *Amos 'n' Andy*. Dad says that the Ironworks will soon have barracks for soldiers who will be guarding the whole place. The construction of those LST's, which I learned stands for Landing Ship, Tank, not Large Slow Targets, will begin right away he said, and he also said we can expect thousands of new people to be moving to Evansville to help build them. Where are they all going to live?

Two British battleships have been sunk by the Japanese.

Thursday December 18, 1941
Early morning

I had a terrible dream. We were being bombed by the Germans and the Japanese. Jenny's house was hit and almost destroyed. I was looking for her in the ruins and couldn't find her. It was horrible. I wonder how many other kids my age have had the same dream lately. I'm going to kiss her on the way to school today and tell her how much I love her and I don't care who sees me. We haven't had much time alone in the last few weeks and it's driving me nuts. Christmas is only a week away and I haven't gotten her anything yet. I have a little money saved up, but I haven't felt much in the Christmas spirit. We still don't know how many of our sailors were killed at Pearl Harbor. They know. I think they're just not telling us. Eric says there are more than two thousand. Surely there can't be that many. The last ten days have been like a bad dream, worse than the one I had last night. At dinner, Mom says the blessing as usual, but now she asks God to protect our soldiers too. I pray along with her silently and I ask Him to especially watch over Jenny's brother. War or no war, I have to get Jenny a Christmas present this weekend. Tomorrow is our last day of school until the New Year. Our class is too old for a Christmas party but we're having one anyway. Mom made two dozen cupcakes with red and green frosting for me to take. We need a Christmas party to take our minds off what's been happening.

Jenny wears the ring I got her last Christmas every day and I'm writing with the pen she gave me. What can I get her this year?

Sunday December 21, 1941
Night

I found the perfect Christmas present for Jenny yesterday. It's another charm for her bracelet; two interlocking hearts and I had my initials engraved on one and hers on the other. She wears that bracelet every day so it'll be a good present. That didn't leave much for Mom and Dad, but I managed to buy a pair of handkerchiefs with Dad's initials for him and a lipstick for Mom. I hope I wasn't supposed to get my sister anything. Maybe I'll find something for the baby.

It has snowed all day. Why can't it do that while we're in school?

If someone asked me what I know about love, I would have to tell them, not much. It's true, I don't know much about love and maybe I'm not supposed to, but I think those who write about love don't know much about it either. If they did, they would know it can't be described in words, at least not in words they know how to write or that I know how to understand. I've read a lot of love poems and stories, not the trashy ones, and Jenny's are better anyway. Love isn't just shared feelings when those feelings are good; it's shared feelings of uncertainty too and they're feelings you can't run away from, and you can't experience those feelings simply because you want to. I think you have to grow into them and that's what Jenny and I are doing. Maybe I'm feeling a little deep tonight, but I think you lose some of yourself when you're in love. You trade feelings of yourself for the feelings of the one you love and that's a little scary. If I could write like Jenny, I would write her a love poem tonight. Mine always sound like they were written by an eight-year-old as a homework assignment.

Friday December 26, 1941
Night

There might be a war on, but Christmas still came. Dad and I put up the tree on Christmas Eve right after lunch. Most people do that a couple of weeks or so before Christmas, but it's been a tradition in our family for as long as I can remember. Mom says it's because the trees are free on Christmas Eve and that my dad's just cheap. She always says that with a smile though. I don't care because we keep it up for at least two weeks after Christmas, long after everyone else has taken theirs down. The Brewsters put theirs up right after Thanksgiving. Jenny came over and helped me decorate ours and Mom let us cut one of the pecan pies she made last weekend. She makes pecan pies to kill for, but she only makes them at Christmas.

While we were decorating the tree, Jenny and I decided to meet at the park at midnight to exchange gifts like we did last year. Maybe that'll become a tradition for us. It was just as cold as I remember it being last Christmas. Both of us brought quilts from our beds this time and we sat on our bench under them. I think Jenny liked the charm I got her. She smiled and then kissed me and it was one of those kisses you see in the movies where everyone in the audience holds their breath until it's over.

"It's two hearts; does this mean we're going steady?"

I hadn't thought about that when I bought the charm, but I had an answer ready for her.

"Well I should hope so. After all, we *have* seen each other practically naked."

"That may be true, but it doesn't matter, you still have to ask me."

"Miss Virginia Brewster, will you do me the honor of going steady with me?"

"Well I don't know; does that mean I can't do this with anyone but you?"

She kissed me again and slid her hand under my coat and pajama top. Her fingers were cold on my back but I didn't mind.

"It definitely means you can't do that with anyone but me," I answered after another long kiss.

"Then I'll have to think about it."

I shined the flashlight toward her face to make sure she was smiling.

"The answer is yes. I would love to go steady with you, but only if you promise to say you like the gift I got for you."

The wide flat box she fished out of her coat pocket was wrapped elegantly of course, which made my wrapping look like the butcher had done it. I unwrapped it and didn't immediately know what I was looking at. It was a card of some sort.

"It's a subscription to *The Writer* magazine. If you're going to be a writer, you should learn how from people who already do it. It's not nearly as romantic as your gift. I'm sorry."

"It's perfect, Jenny. I had no idea you actually believed I could be a writer someday."

"Well I do and you'd better be a good one. You might have to support us. Do you think you could write trashy love story books if you had to? I know they sell. Mrs. Bender bought six of them in Muir's Drugs last week. Her face turned red when she saw I was watching."

"If you'll be my inspiration," I said with a grin, "I can write stories that would make the Gear Town girls blush."

"And just what, may I ask, do you know about Gear Town?"

"Just what I've heard at school. They say you can buy a white or colored woman there for an hour or all night—some of them are teenagers—and she'll do whatever you want."

"And what would you want her to do? The girl who just agreed to go steady with you wants to know."

"For the answer to that question, you'll have to read the book I'll write someday."

"You have a dirty mind."

We walked back home through the snow and just outside her house we stopped and I kissed her good night.

It was a great Christmas.

Tuesday December 30, 1941
Morning

Because of the war, most of the usual New Year's celebrations have been cancelled. I guess I can understand, but Mom and Mrs. Brewster aren't going to let the Germans, Japanese, and Italians ruin our celebration. They've put together a party for our neighborhood and it'll be held in four different homes at the same time. Each one will have a different dessert and at midnight, we're going to gather in the street and wish each other a happy New Year. I bet Mr. Brewster has a few fireworks for us. He always seems to come up with a box of them even if they are illegal in the city. I helped Mom make more pecan pies and this time we made them in little single serving pie crusts. Making the crusts was my job. I must have made a hundred after Mom showed me how. Jenny's mom's making something with cranberries and walnuts. The idea is to make things that people can carry with them and eat so no one will have dishes to wash on New Year's Day.

Chapter Three

1942
Thursday January 1, 1942
Afternoon

Happy New Year. This will be a good year. The war will be over and things will get back to normal. The neighborhood party was fabulous. That was such a good idea. All the food was eaten and I didn't get even one of the little pecan pies. They were for guests Mom said. The cranberry and walnut bread Mrs. Brewster made was great though and I got two slices. New Year's is one of those times I can kiss Jenny without looking over my shoulder to see who's watching. Everyone does it at midnight and no one pays any attention to us. They also don't pay too much attention to who gets glasses of champagne and we had several; one at each house I think. Our kiss at midnight was absolutely ginchy, even better than the fireworks. I may not know what love is, but right now I don't care.

Some good news came yesterday and it was perfect timing. Jenny's family heard from her brother. He's fine, although that was about all they were able to get out of his letter. It had been so cut up Jenny said, it was almost impossible to read. I guess the censors aren't taking any chances now that we really are at war, but he's okay and that's all that matters. We're off school tomorrow since New Year's came on a Thursday, and Jenny and I are going to spend the whole day together.

Tuesday January 6, 1942
Night

Girls talk. Girls talk a lot. Sarah Martin just thinks she has to know everything. She spotted the new charm on Jenny's bracelet right away and had to have a look at it. She turned it over and saw the initials and then the questions began. Who was Jenny's mystery boyfriend? That was the question all day yesterday. Finally Jenny had enough.

"No one you would ever guess, Sarah Martin and I won't tell you either," Jenny said loud enough for everyone around to hear.

Jenny told the truth. Sarah would never guess in a million years. No one would ever imagine a girl as pretty as Jenny could be anything more than a friend to anyone like me. Besides, I don't tell anyone my middle name so they don't know my middle initial. I wouldn't even tell Jenny for a long time. My middle name came from my father's family and they sure had some strange names back then. Maybe Harper was a perfectly common name a hundred years ago, but I hate it and I never use it. In first grade I made up a middle name for myself—Jesse. It was the name of my dog but no one ever knew. I loved that dog. Anyway, I'm sure Sarah will have other rumors to start tomorrow.

Monday January 16, 1942
Afternoon

I know when Jenny's periods come. She tells me, but I've wondered why she doesn't miss school with cramps anymore, so I asked her on the way home from school today. Her period started yesterday and she didn't dress out for gym today. She never misses volleyball when it's boys versus girls. It's so stupid. All the boys know when a girl doesn't dress out for gym she's on her period and some of them think they just have to say something about it. And I don't like that either. "On her period;" what does that mean? The girl isn't "on" anything. Jenny just says she's grounded when it starts and I say she's served her time when it's over. I've heard lots of other names for it and some of them are pretty bad. Anyway, Jenny's face turned bright red when I asked her about not being bothered by cramps anymore. A few steps later, she turned toward me and smiled.

"Everyone pees in the shower don't they?"

I knew what that meant.

"Yeah, everyone pees in the shower. I peed in the shower this morning."

"Really, well so did I and then my cramps went away."

We had a good laugh about peeing in the shower.

It's kinda stupid I guess.

Saturday January 24, 1942
Night

After our morning routine of stripping the beds and doing the wash, I asked Mom if I could go to the movies with Jenny. That started a conversation and she went on for half an hour about what a good girl Jenny was and how glad she was that the two of us were so close. At the end of the conversation, she went to her purse, found two quarters and gave them to me.

"You and Jenny have a good time at the movies and get home in time for dinner. Your father will be working late again and I don't want to eat by myself."

I kissed her and thanked her for the money. I really do have a good mother. When I called Jenny, she said that if I would come and help her finish her chores, she could go with me. There was a little more involved than chores. Mrs. Brewster was moving furniture again. She does that every few months.

The movie was *Dr. Jekyll and Mr. Hyde*. I like scary movies because Jenny sits really close to me. The armrests between seats fold up so it's a lot like sitting on a sofa with her. There weren't any kids at the theater, which is another reason I like scary movies. All the adults come for the evening show, so Jenny and I almost had the place to ourselves. Maybe the manager thinks since there usually aren't many people in the audience for a scary movie matinee, he can turn the heat down. Whatever the reason, it's always freezing in the place during the winter, but we went prepared this time with a nice wool throw from the Brewsters' sofa. We snuggled under it in the darkened theater and held each other close and kissed whenever we wanted. With Jenny that close, it was easy to forget the movie, except for the screaming. I want to be with her forever.

Thursday January 29, 1942
Night

Eric said tonight that Hitler's having a lot more trouble with the Russians than he expected. The Germans haven't taken Moscow and have been driven back from some of their advanced positions. The Russians are fighting and Hitler is firing any general who retreats. German planes bombed London and the southern ports last week. There was some damage but not too much and no mention was made of the number of civilian casualties. I've had to learn this new word: casualties. At first I thought it meant killed, but it means a lot of things—dead, wounded, captured, or just missing. None of them are good; then again it's not as bad as I thought. The radio reporters should remind us what that word means occasionally. I wonder if I wrote a letter to Eric if he would read it.

Friday February 6, 1942
Night

This boy in my class is bothering me. He keeps asking me questions about Jenny. Everyone knows we're friends and live near each other, but he wants to know stuff I don't want to tell him, and he's just a Daisy for asking. I've heard stories about him and if any of them are true, I'm staying away. His name is James and he's another one of the new students this year. He didn't know anyone in school so Jenny introduced him to everyone, just to be nice, and now he's in love with her or something, but he'll hardly speak to her. Maybe he thinks I'll be his Pandarus—Jenny's mom told us about that story—but he's very wrong. I'm going to tell Jenny what he's doing. He always seems to be around at recess and after school and at first I didn't think anything about it. Then he started asking me all kinds of questions about Jenny, like which house she lives in and where her father works, stuff that's none of his business. I think there's something wrong with him.

Saturday February 14, 1942
Late

Today is Valentine's Day and it was a perfect day for Jenny and me. The sky was clear and even though it was cold, it didn't seem so bad. We've had a special date planned for today; sort of our Valentine's Day gift to each other. We got dressed up and went to the Lowe's Victory Theater. We've both been there with our parents on special occasions, but this was the first time Jenny and I have gone together. It's a much nicer place than our neighborhood theater, the Rosedale. Mostly adults go to Lowe's and we wanted to act like adults. *The Bride Came C.O.D.* was playing. I just love James Cagney and Bette Davis. We had a real dinner at the theater before the movie. We felt so grown up I was tempted to order a bottle of wine. We didn't have the money to pay for it even if our waiter hadn't noticed how young we are. Everything was going great until I happened to mention James. I don't know why I did that. It was stupid. Jenny got a really serious look on her face.

"There's something I haven't told you. You were right: there's something wrong with him. He called me last Sunday and at first we just talked about normal stuff. Then he began telling me how he walks past my house late at night sometimes. That was a little creepy, but when he told me he had a pair of binoculars, I started to worry and told him I had to go and eat dinner. Monday night he called back right after I got out of the shower and told me he didn't think my yellow panties and green T-shirt matched very well. He watched me getting dressed after my shower. He saw me naked. What if he tells everyone at school? He asked me to go to the movies with him and I'm afraid if I don't go, he'll tell the whole school about seeing me. He didn't say that, but I know that's what he was hinting. What if he's seen us through the window together on my couch? What if he saw us last Saturday night when you came over?"

Jenny reached over the table for my hand and I took it in mine and squeezed. She looked like she could cry at any minute. That Peeping Tom wasn't going to ruin our date. I had a plan put together in a minute. If he was spying on her upstairs, I knew where he had to be watching from.

"You just let me worry about Mr. James, Jenny. I have a feeling he won't be bothering either of us much longer."

She smiled and I read her lips as she said, "I love you." The meal was great. We had the Valentine's Day special which was a small steak cut in the shape of a heart, a baked potato, and a salad. The place was packed and they had to delay starting the movie until everyone finished. Jenny and I were lucky to find seats together and we had to sit down front. That didn't matter to us. We had a wonderful evening and enjoyed our time together pretending to be adults.

Tuesday February 17, 1942
Very late

I can't believe it. Jenny called me about nine and said that James had just called her saying he would be watching her tonight. That guy is just sick. Did he think Jenny was going to put on a show for him? I told her to go upstairs and turn the light on in her bedroom, like she was getting ready for her shower and then leave the rest to me, that I would call her back.

My fingers were shaking as I dialed the number for the police. I'd never called the police before in my life, but this had to stop. I tried my best to sound older when the call was answered and I didn't give my name. The policeman was very nice and listened as I explained what was happening. I told him who the Peeping Tom was and exactly where they could find him and then slipped out of the house and walked around the block toward Jenny's along the back streets. I had to go all the way around the block instead of just walking five doors down, but I had to see if the police went where I told them. The local station is only three blocks away and I know all the officers who work there; not well, but I do know them when I see them. I see two of them in church every Sunday with their families. When I turned the corner on the street behind Jenny's house, I could see flashlights going in all directions, like someone running with them. I stayed out of sight in the bushes of Mrs. Walker's yard and watched. In a few minutes, a patrol car came by and stopped up the street. Two policemen loaded someone into the back and drove off. They caught him.

I raced back home and called Jenny. She answered the phone on the first ring. She'd seen the whole thing from the bathroom window.

"Once again you're my hero," she whispered. "I love you so much."

I'm pretty proud of myself right now.

Thursday February 19, 1942
Night

James wasn't in school yesterday or today and I have a feeling he won't be back. Jenny walked a little closer to me today and we held hands in my coat pocket on the way to and from school. When we got to her house, we searched through *The Press* to see if there was any mention of an arrest. There wasn't, but that doesn't matter; we know what happened. Mrs. Brewster declared it was a dance sort of afternoon and we danced until we dropped. She's teaching us some Latin steps now and they're hard to do. She wants us to learn the Cha-Cha, Rumba, and Tango and bought several new records. It's sometimes embarrassing dancing that close to Jenny with her mom right there. She got a little carried away when we finally did it right.

"The Tango is making love with your clothes on while standing up."

"Mother!" Jenny said with an awfully surprised look on her face.

When Mrs. Brewster realized what she'd said, her face turned all red and the three of us cracked up laughing. It was a fun afternoon.

Saturday February 28, 1942

Night

The Japanese attacked Australia last week. I didn't know it, but the Australian Prime Minister declared war on Japan an hour after the bombing of Pearl Harbor and it was made official the next day. Do the Australians have a navy? I guess they do. They must have. They're stuck out in the middle of the Pacific Ocean. Anyway, they're on our side. I also didn't know until last week in history class that the very first American killed in World War I was from Evansville. So far there hasn't been anyone from Evansville killed in this war that we know of. The government hasn't released many names, even of those killed at Pearl Harbor. The families of those sailors who were there must be worried sick. I'm glad Jenny's brother's still in England. He's safer there than anywhere else the Germans and Japanese are attacking. The Brewsters get regular letters from him and he's finally figured out how to write so the censors don't cut out so much.

I heard at school this week that James' family has moved. Jenny and I celebrated today by going to the matinee at The American downtown. It was a long walk but Jenny found plenty of window shopping to do along the way. We thought that since it was downtown, there might not be so many young kids there and we were right. It was an afternoon of Westerns. We were together and our hands were all over each other under our coats, so we didn't care.

Wednesday March 4, 1942
Very late

The war news is bad, really bad. The Japanese are sinking our ships right and left. I've listened to Eric so much I feel like I know him on a first name basis. He does his best not to make things sound so terrible, but I can tell he knows a lot more than he's telling us. The only good news he says is that we'll soon be building ships and airplanes faster than anyone else. What good will that do if the Japanese and Germans just destroy them? We're not even fighting the Germans yet, just sending airplanes to England. I'm so glad Jenny's brother's not in the Air Corps or the Navy.

Tonight after I went to bed, I heard Mom and Dad talking downstairs. They'd already gone to bed, but then they were up again and it sounded like they were sitting at the kitchen table like they do when they have something important to discuss. I shouldn't have, but I sat at the top of the stairs and listened. They never yell at each other; sometimes they do get a little loud and this was one of those times. I couldn't understand everything, although I heard my sister's name mentioned several times and that can't be good. Maybe Mom will tell me what's going on tomorrow.

Saturday March 7, 1942
Late afternoon

Mom has been down in the dumps all week, especially after Wednesday night, and today after we finished stripping the beds and had the wash loaded and going, I just came out and asked her what was wrong. It was like she'd been waiting for me to say something.

"Let's sit for a while and I'll tell you some things you should never have to hear, then again, I have to talk to someone and I can't bear to tell anyone else. I won't ask you to promise not to tell Jenny; she's like one of the family, but please keep it between the two of you and let me do the explaining to everyone else. You're too young to understand everything I'm about to tell you, although I know you're smart and maybe not as young as I think you are sometimes."

Tears began forming in her eyes and soon they were streaming down her face. I can't remember ever seeing my mother cry like that. She's a problem solver and always has been.

"Your Aunt Doris is getting a divorce. She and the children are coming here to live until she gets her feet back on the ground."

"What about…?"

"Your sister's staying in Little Rock and that's all I'll tell you about her."

She sounded pretty firm on that. I can only guess what my sister's up to.

"This is going to put a strain on us, but your father is a good man and he'll see that none of us go hungry. Doris and the baby will have your sister's old room and I'm afraid you'll have to share your room with the boys. Your father's going to put in bunk beds for them next week. I know this is going to be hard for you and I promise it'll only be temporary, until they can find a place of their own and Doris can find a job. That shouldn't be much trouble the way things are looking right now. She can probably get a job at the Ironworks doing bookkeeping or something like that. Your father and I are driving to Little Rock next weekend to get them. He managed to get Friday off so we're leaving Thursday night and should be back by Sunday afternoon. We'll have to help Doris pack and rent a trailer we can pull behind the car for her things. You'll have to stay here because we won't have room for everyone on the way back. I'm so sorry all of this has happened, but she's my sister, my only sister, and we have to do something. We'll manage; we always have."

It hurt me to see Mom so upset, so I pretended not to mind having to share my room and told her it will be great having them live with us for a while. She hugged me and kissed me.

"I depend on you too much. I always have. When you were four or five and my grandmother was still alive, she would scold me for the way I depended on you. I can hear her now, "You let that child be a child," she would say, but I could count on you, even when you were little, and you've never let me down. I'm sure you and Jenny will find something to do while we're gone and I think I have an extra couple of dollars just begging to be spent on whatever the two of you want. There's plenty here to eat and if you don't want to stay here alone at night, you can always go down to the Brewsters'. I've already told Mrs. Brewster that we're going to be gone this weekend and she says you're welcome at their house and I think you're old enough to make that decision for yourself."

The whole weekend with Jenny. Even if I have to share my room with two kids for a year, it'll be worth it. I'm going to go call her right now.

Thursday March 12, 1942
Night

Mom and Dad left right after dinner and now I have the whole house to myself. I can stay up to midnight if I want. Of course I won't, school tomorrow, but I could. I convinced Mom to leave the dinner dishes so they could get started earlier, so I have them to do and there's some homework due tomorrow and I think there's a test in math. I might not get to bed till midnight after all. I turned on the radio earlier and I shouldn't have. The news is bad. Eric said that a Japanese submarine shelled Santa Barbara, California three weeks ago. There wasn't much damage, but if they're shelling California, they must be planning an invasion. This happened three weeks ago and I don't remember hearing anything about it. How could they censor that news?

Saturday March 14, 1942
Very late

Jenny just left. I hope she doesn't get in trouble for staying so late. Today she and I lived together. That's what we've had planned since I told her my parents were going to Little Rock and of course I told her why. Friday after school Mrs. Brewster made me promise I would come back later and have dinner with them so I did, even though Mom had plenty for me to eat in the icebox. She wanted me to come back for breakfast this morning, but Jenny told her we wanted to make breakfast at my house. Her mom thought that was a great idea, as long as we didn't burn the place down. Jenny showed up this morning early, before I got up. Maybe I'm not so dependable after all because I forgot to lock the door last night. I thought I was dreaming when she crawled into bed with me, but I woke up when she put her arms around me. For a second I didn't know where I was.

"You sure are a trusting soul; the front door was unlocked. Just what would your mother say?"

"What would your mother say if she knew you broke into a house this morning and crawled into bed with the victim?"

"I hope you're not hungry just yet. I was hoping to get here before you got up and surprise you and you've made it easy by leaving the door unlocked."

"Well, maybe I left it unlocked for you."

"You did not; did you?"

"No, but I would have if I'd thought of it. Now, don't move. I'm going to go brush my teeth so I can kiss you."

I brushed my teeth and hair in record time and got back to my room.

It was cold in my room and I got back under the covers and gave her a kiss like I hadn't been able to give her in a long time. I noticed her clothes—all of them—were in a pile by the bed.

"Now this is the way we should start the day every day when we have a place of our own."

She rolled over on top of me, grinned and kissed me.

"Or maybe like this."

We had all morning, or all day if we wanted, and we took our time for once. Neither of us had much to go on, so we sort of figured things out as we went. We knew a lot more about what not to do than we knew about what to do.

It wasn't cold under the covers, but she shivered more than once that morning. That's the only word I can think of to describe it and then I swear she purred. I didn't know girls could purr, but that's what it sounded like. The second time she did that, I had to say something.

"Are you all right Jenny?"

It was a few seconds before she answered.

"You have no idea how all right I am," she purred. And then she said something to herself I probably wasn't supposed to hear, something like, "so much better than peeing in the shower."

I made that up about the purring and it sounds like something from a trashy romance novel. I've only ever read part of one my sister had, but I think I understand now why they use the word so much. But she did say "You have no idea how all right I am" and maybe she did purr it after all.

Jenny wrapped her legs around me and squeezed as she gave me a final kiss I was sure I deserved. The smile on her face didn't go away all day.

"Breakfast?" she asked as she rolled off me and onto her feet on the floor.

I would have complained if she hadn't looked so beautiful at that exact moment. She was just, I don't know, sort of angelic or something.

She opened my chest of drawers and pulled out a T-shirt and put it on. It was one of the oversized shirts I sometime sleep in during the summer and much too big for her. She didn't bother with putting on anything else before she ran down the stairs. In a few seconds I heard the heat come on. She'd turned up the thermostat on her way. I have to remember to turn it back before Mom and Dad get home.

I got dressed and went down to see what she had in mind for breakfast. The picture of her standing at the stove wearing my T-shirt and nothing else is one I'll have with me forever; that and the one of her with flour on her arms up past her elbows.

"Do you know what you're doing?"

"Of course I do. We're having fresh biscuits for breakfast. I've watched Mom make them since I was a little girl. Where is something I can make the dough in?"

I got Mom's wooden bread pan for her. It was a wedding present from her grandmother.

Breakfast was great. The biscuits turned out perfect, as good as any Mom ever made. When we finished, I helped clean up the kitchen and put everything away.

"We need a shower, my love."

I must have looked a little shocked. No one had ever called me that.

"Well, you are my love now. You've made love to me and that makes you my love. I feel…well I don't know how to say what I feel. I feel…like a woman I guess, like a real woman and I'll love you forever and make love to you until you can't breathe, but first a shower, or maybe I'll make love to you in the shower. I don't know… I'm just so incredibly happy right now. Did I tell you I love you? I do love you and I'll always remember this morning. Do I sound like a complete idiot?"

I hugged her and kissed her. How lucky I am.

She got the shower going, threw the T-shirt in the floor and stepped in. Steam was rising and filling the bathroom by the time I got undressed. I've seen her wet plenty of times at the pool, but not wet and naked. We took turns soaping each other and making sure every little crevice was clean. She washed my hair and I washed hers. I loved having her wash my hair, but I had no idea how much I'd like the feel of her wet slippery body touching mine. We could've stayed in the shower for a lot longer if the water hadn't started turning cool—thanks Dad for turning down the thermostat on the water heater too.

We got out shivering, dried each other quickly and got back to my room and under the covers again. I wrapped my legs around hers and rolled over on top and she rolled right back over on top of me. So that was the way it was going to be now.

"I'm never letting you go," she whispered, out of breath and shaking half an hour later.

"Home run?"

"Grand slam."

She slept and I watched her sleep until I couldn't keep my eyes open any longer.

When I woke up, she was still asleep. I slid from underneath her, got dressed and went downstairs to make lunch. For some reason, I was starving. When I looked at the clock, I knew why. It was almost three. Mom had left part of a ham in the icebox and I made sandwiches for the two of us. I was peeling potatoes for French fries when Jenny came down the stairs wearing the same T-shirt she had on before.

"So you not only make love to me, you also make lunch? Are you married? Engaged? Dating anyone special?"

"Well there is someone I'm just crazy about but she's a little nuts."

"And you wouldn't have it any other way."

She helped me finish making lunch and we ate everything. I guess she was hungry too. After we finished cleaning up the mess, we sat on the sofa and listened to the radio for a while.

"What do you want to do this afternoon?"

That must have been the right question to ask because she leaned over and kissed me. When I reached for her, she grabbed my hand and put it down by my side.

"I want to take you upstairs; it's my turn, and this time you're going to keep your hands to yourself. My starter button's broken."

"Your starter button?"

"Yeah, you know, like on a car. You push the button to start the motor. Well, my motor needs to cool down for a while."

I managed not to laugh. Starter button huh?

Jenny made me crazy in ways I hadn't even thought of and at some point I must have stopped breathing.

"Are you all right?"

"Like you said this morning, 'You have no idea how all right I am'."

"I think maybe I do," she said with a huge smile on her face. "Better than peeing in the shower?"

"Definitely better than peeing in the shower."

We could have stayed in bed all afternoon, but there were things that had to get done. We got dressed, then stripped all the beds and put the sheets and blankets in the wash. Even though Mom said I didn't have to do that, it was Saturday and we always wash bed clothes on Saturday and if we did it, she wouldn't have it to do when she got home.

While the wash was going Jenny and I talked about the changes that'll be coming after Aunt Doris and the children move in. I brushed out her hair and she brushed mine. I like that. We decided that, now that we were officially lovers, nothing as minor as a few extra houseguests would bother us. We would just spend more time at her house.

We could've gone to a movie after the wash was done, but staying home seemed to be the right thing to do. It was nice just sitting on the sofa with her and talking. At one point, she turned and looked right into my eyes.

"I won't ever forget today as long as I live. You're the perfect lover and I've never been happier than I am right now."

I leaned over to kiss her just as a knock came on the door. Jenny said her mom would probably come by sometime in the afternoon just to see how things were going. We did a quick inspection of each other and decided we were presentable and I went to the door. Mrs. Brewster came in carrying a covered pan. She was impressed when Jenny told her we'd done the laundry and made ourselves breakfast and lunch.

"I made something after lunch I thought the two of you might like. It's a new recipe I found in one of those magazines I get at the grocery store. I haven't tried it yet so the two of you will be my guinea pigs." She took the waxed paper off the pan and set it on the coffee table.

"They're called Pepper Cookies, but they don't have pepper in them. It's a German recipe. I know we're officially at war with them, but that doesn't mean we can't use their recipes. Try one."

I could smell the Ginger in them before biting into one. They were delicious and I didn't feel a bit guilty about eating German cookies. I told her we could rename them; call them ginger nut cookies or something. I got us glasses of milk and we ate most of the pan. Mrs. Brewster wanted to know all about the new houseguests that were coming.

She and Mom had no doubt talked about it a lot because she knew everything I knew.

"Well, like I told your mother; if things get too crowded around here, you're always welcome at our house."

"Thank you Mrs. Brewster," I answered. "Don't be surprised if I take you up on that offer from time to time."

When she left, Jenny gave me a hug and kissed me.

"Someday when we have a place of our own, we'll invite Mom over just like today and we'll have cookies and milk and solve all the world's problems sitting in our living room."

"We can do that, but first we have to get the bedclothes off the line."

We had lunch so late, neither of us were very hungry until it was too late to make anything complicated so we just had another couple of ham sandwiches.

"Tomorrow we'll make dinner for everyone so your mom won't have to cook when she gets home. What should we make? I know how to cook almost anything. I saw a pork roast in the icebox. We can make it. I'll think of something tonight to go with it, when I'm not thinking about you."

Jenny stayed until almost ten. I hated to see her go. It had been such a perfect day. When I kissed her goodbye, there were tears in her eyes.

"I don't know when we'll ever get to do this again, but it doesn't matter. Someday we'll do it every day."

"Do what every day?"

"You know what I mean—and yes, we'll do that every day too. Will you come by and walk me to church tomorrow?"

"I'll be there at ten-thirty sharp. I love you Jenny B."

"And I love you Emell."

"Emell?"

"Yes M.L.—My Love."

When I closed the door behind her, the house seemed awfully big and quiet. I took the sheets and blankets and made the beds. It's been a good day and I'll sleep well tonight.

Monday March 16, 1942
Night

I walked Jenny to church yesterday and on the way home afterward she gave me the note she wrote during the service, which she wouldn't let me read at the time. "HBZMBKNRDLXDXDRZMCEDDKXNTQANCXBKN RDSNLHMD"

I guess I understand why she didn't want me reading it during church. Blushing like I would have wouldn't have been understood at Central United Methodist. She always has the most romantic things to say. I wish I could learn to write like that.

Jenny invited me for lunch at her house and she didn't have to ask twice. I was tired of ham sandwiches. In the afternoon she came over to my house and we started dinner. I didn't really know what Aunt Doris likes to eat, but she's Mom's sister and I figured she probably likes the same things Mom does. The kids were the real problem. I liked corn when I was their age and could eat it every meal, but Jenny said she never liked it. We did agree that every kid likes Kraft Dinner and we had a couple of boxes, so that was settled. Dad would eat some too. He likes it and it only takes a few minutes to make. The pork roast Mom left in the icebox would be perfect for the main course. She said I could bake it if I wanted to, but I wasn't sure I could and it would be an expensive mistake if I messed up. Jenny knew exactly how to prepare it and soon it was in the oven. We had potatoes and canned corn and Jenny brought some apples. It was a toss-up whether we would bake them or make a pie. She said pork roast should be served with baked apples, but I wanted a pie. When she reminded me how much easier it was to bake apples, I gave in. That left us with no dessert, but Jenny had the answer to that. She called her mom and asked if she would bake a plain cake. We had canned cherries we could make a frosting with. There was no bread in the house though and none of the stores were open.

"You know, those biscuits you made Saturday morning were really good."

"And I'll teach you how to make them right now," she answered with a smile and a kiss.

My conniving didn't work and I had to make the biscuits. It was easy, though I managed to get flour all over myself and Jenny. Some of it was intentional, like the handprints on her blouse.

Mrs. Brewster brought the cake over in about an hour and helped us make the frosting. It looked good and I was getting hungry. Everything was finished by six and just as if we'd planned it, Dad drove up a few minutes later. Everyone piled out of the car and into the house. The two boys ran wild. When Mom walked into the dining room and saw the table set with everything we'd made, I thought she would cry. She hugged and kissed Jenny and me.

"Is there nothing the two of you can't do? I don't know why I worried about leaving you here."

Then she looked up.

"Yes, Grandmother I know; I depend on this child too much."

Mom insisted that Jenny and Mrs. Brewster join us for dinner. When everyone was rounded up, we sat at the table and Mom said the blessing. I might not remember what the preacher said in church yesterday, but I'll always remember my mother's blessing. It covered everything from thanking God for the food and those who prepared it to a special prayer for our soldiers and country.

We had formal introductions while we ate. Everyone was hungry. I remembered that the oldest boy's name is Michael, but he likes to be called Mike, the youngest is Harold who likes to be called Harry, and the baby's name is Millie. I didn't ask if that was short for Mildred. She looks just like my sister. I introduced Jenny to everyone as my girlfriend. It felt good to say that out loud. It didn't mean anything much to our guests, but it meant a lot to me. Mom knows what it means. I know she knows. She has to.

After dinner, Jenny and I cleared the table and I made a plate dinner for Mr. Brewster. Mom and Aunt Doris insisted on washing the dishes and I didn't object too much. Walking Jenny home, I tried to tell her how much I appreciated everything she did this weekend, and I didn't just mean certain things.

"It's a nice night out. Do you think anyone will be sitting on our bench in the park?"

I smiled and told her that if there was anyone in our spot, we would evict them.

It was a clear cool night and just perfect for sitting close and holding hands.

"You told them I was your girlfriend and you have no idea how bad I wanted to hug you right then. My mom knows I love you. I know she knows. She has to and she talks to your mom every day."

"Yeah, Mom knows too, but she would never say anything unless maybe she thought I might get hurt, and she knows you would never do that to me."

"So we just leave it alone for now and let them think they know, or know they know, without saying anything?"

"I guess so, but someday I'm going to tell my mom."

"And I'm going to tell mine."

I held her close and kissed her. I think I love her more every day.

Wednesday March 25, 1942
Night

Dad finally got the bunk beds put together last night and the boys slept in my room for the first time. They've had to sleep on pallets in their mother's room and I guess they liked the change because they were quiet as church mice. They're not bad kids, just kids. Yesterday Harry told me he thought my girlfriend was pretty. He's three and Mike's five. Millie seems to be perfectly content and I think Mom likes having a baby in the house. Dad takes everything as just another job that needs doing and he does it without complaining. So far things are working themselves out with Aunt Doris helping Mom do a lot of the things I used to. No one's mentioned my sister or my uncle. What if they got married? Would my sister then be my aunt or would my uncle be my brother-in-law? I'm not going to think about that again.

Jenny and I danced this afternoon at her house. That's probably as close as we're going to get for a while, but it was nice anyway. When Mr. Brewster got home, he was all excited about the new Republic plant at the airport. They're going to be making airplanes and he applied for a job with them last week. They let him know today that he got it. Things are happening so fast in Evansville, it's hard to keep up. There was big news in the *Sunday Courier and Press* last Sunday about Gear Town too. The Army and Navy big shots want the city to shut it down. Who do they think the biggest customers of the girls there are, and shouldn't they be worried about more important things, like the war?

Eric said tonight that some German spies have been caught in New York. With all the war work being done in Evansville, I wonder if Germany will send spies here. If Hitler wants to find out everything we do in E'ville, all he has to do is send his spies to Gear Town.

Monday April 6, 1942
Night

Yesterday was Easter Sunday and we all got together at the Brewster's for a cookout after church. I must be growing up a little because last week Mom gave me some money and said I could go into town and buy something nice to wear for Easter. Jenny's mom did the same thing, so Thursday we left school a little early and went shopping. We had notes, but I don't think Principal Lankford believed they came from our mothers. We tried on clothes all afternoon before we approved of what the other had chosen. Jenny looked like a movie star yesterday and her father took about a hundred pictures of us at the cookout. I want to see the one of us in a dance pose we staged for him.

Thursday April 16, 1942
Night

Every week the newspaper's full of stories about new industries in Evansville. Chrysler was the first, back in January, and now the Ironworks has real orders for LST's. They're calling the new place the Evansville Shipyard and Dad says it'll be bigger than anything I can imagine. There are advertisements everywhere looking for workers. Aunt Doris has a new job at the shipyard and they want her to work all the hours she can. She's going to be a welder. A lot of women tried out for the job, but she got it. She'll be making good money too, even at part-time, as soon as she's trained and certified. That'll take about two weeks. Some places are even taking colored men and women. Mostly they live down near the river and Dad has driven us through that area, but we kept our doors locked and didn't stop for anything. The paper has stories all the time about trouble with the coloreds and it looks like a lot more of them will be moving in soon. Dad says they won't ever live anywhere around our neighborhood, that the Indiana Klan will see to it. We've read about them in school, but I didn't know they're still around.

Mike and Harry have been pretty good roommates so far. Last night we had a terrible thunderstorm and I woke up to find Harry asleep in bed with me. He was curled into a little ball at the foot of the bed, like he didn't want to bother me. When I got up, I helped him back into his bed and I'm sure he won't remember any of it.

Monday April 20, 1942
Night

Eric announced on the news tonight that today is Hitler's birthday. He talked on and on about the celebrations all over Germany. Maybe it'll be his last. Last night the big news was about the first bombing of Tokyo Saturday. The Japs thought they were safe being so far away, Eric said. I guess we showed them.

Yesterday it was Jenny's idea for us to take the bus up to Oak Hill Cemetery where the Queen of the Gypsies is buried. It's quite a ways from home and too far to walk. We learned in school that Evansville used to be the home of the gypsies—if they had a home. Her grave is well marked and a lot of people come to see it. The story goes around at Halloween that if you stand at the foot of the grave at midnight with your back to the headstone and throw a silver coin over your shoulder, your wish will come true. I've never tried it and I figure it's just a way of getting younger kids up there so the older ones can scare the life out of them. Jenny and I walk around there on Sunday afternoons sometimes because it's usually deserted and we can talk, hold hands, and kiss whenever we want. What she wanted to talk about yesterday sort of surprised me.

"Have you ever thought about going over to Gear Town just to see what goes on? I mean, aren't you a little bit curious?"

"That's way down by the river, on the east side and miles from here. The coloreds don't like white people walking through their neighborhoods, and besides, didn't you read in the paper about the military wanting the place shut down?"

"But it's Sunday and we could be back before dark. They won't shut it down before then. Don't tell me you haven't wanted to go down there and just look around. It'll be fun."

She can talk me into anything. We took the bus to First Street and we got a few looks when we got off. When we started up the street, I knew we were somewhere we shouldn't be. People were looking at us from porches and storefronts, but no one said anything. There were no other white people anywhere. We turned the corner and started up Second Street and I noticed a colored girl following us. She looked to be about our age. When we stopped, she stopped and I finally turned around and spoke to her.

"Hi, do you live here?"

"I live two streets over, but I come here sometimes. The question is—what are you doing here?"

"We're just out walking," Jenny said. "It's such a nice day."

"You here to make money? 'cause if you are, I can make things real easy for you."

"What do you mean?"

"Fuckin's ten dollars and suckin's five. You can make fifty dollars this afternoon and tonight. I can show you around for five dollars, make sure you only get white men if that's what you want. They's plenty of white soldiers from Camp Breckinridge hanging around on High Street. I can set you up in a real nice place. Hell, I know girls that would pay you and you wouldn't have to do nothing, just let them lick you a little and play with your titties."

"Let's go Jenny," I finally spoke up. "We're supposed to be home by now."

"Your skinny friend can probably find work too."

Then she turned to me.

"Hell, I bet you'd get on your white knees for a fiver, wouldn't you? It's easy money. That's how I started and now I can make fifty easy on a good weekend and I don't have to worry about gettin' knocked up with some white man's baby. If they want in my pussy though it's gonna cost 'em fifteen on account of I'm young and not wore out—and I put the rubber on; got 'em right here. My sister's got a white baby now and we don't need no more."

"What's it like, doing it with a stranger? Jenny asked before I could get us turned around.

"Ain't nothing to it. Suckin's over in five minutes if you know what you're doing and most white boys don't squirt more than a thimble full, and if they wanna fuck, that don't take much longer. It's easy money I tell you."

"Could we watch once?"

"Cost you five dollars…each."

"We don't have five dollars."

"That don't matter. You can make it back in no time after you watch me. I'll trust you and get you a couple of nice white boys to show you on. You can make a whole lot more than that if you want, especially if you got a cherry to pop and I bet you do. White boys pay extra for that and most wouldn't know the difference anyhow. You carrying around a gold mine between your legs, girl."

"We really need to be going Jenny."

We walked on up Second Street with the colored girl talking the whole time. I just wanted to get back home. She turned around when we got to High Street.

"Y'all come back when you want to make a little money. I'll be here. Just ask for Mandy."

We didn't go down High Street and headed straight for home instead.

"She seemed nice, don't you think?"

"Nice? Jenny, she's a whore and what was all that about watching?"

"Okay, but she seemed like a nice whore and what would it hurt to watch just once? It's not like we'd be doing anything."

Sometimes, I just don't know about her.

Saturday April 25, 1942
Night

There was a big party tonight for Aunt Doris. She's now a certified welder. A reporter from *The Sunday Courier and Press* is going to write a story about her. He took pictures at work last week and today he came out to our house and took more. I hope the news makes it all the way to Little Rock if that's where her worthless ex-husband's still living. A couple of weeks ago I saw a picture of Aunt Doris in *The Invader* dressed in her welding clothes. She's such a pretty woman and I bet she could find another man if she wanted. There're plenty to choose from in this town and they all have jobs.

Jenny and I talked a lot this week about our visit to Gear Town. That colored girl was no older than us and white men are paying her to do things I can't even imagine.

I've heard rumors about that place for as long as I can remember, but I never knew whether to believe them or not, and Jenny seemed a little too interested in what we saw and learned.

"Do you ever think about what it would be like, being a whore?" she asked this afternoon. "Can you imagine doing it with a complete stranger?"

"No I can't. It sure seems like you've thought about it though."

"Oh, Emell, you take me too seriously sometimes. I could never really do anything with anyone but you, but I could watch, I think."

"I think you're crazy."

"And I think it's been too long since we were alone together and I'm getting tired of peeing in the shower."

She was right about that. It's been six weeks since we spent that wonderful Saturday together and we've hardly been able to kiss since then. It's just torture.

Thursday April 30, 1942
Night

If Jenny and I don't get some time alone together soon, I think I'm going to shrivel up and die. The way she teases me sometimes doesn't help either. Like today, when we got to her house after school and she went upstairs to change. She yelled something to me and I went to the foot of the stairs to find her standing at the top of the stairs naked. She blew me a kiss and darted back into her room. Her mom was in the kitchen and it was a good thing she didn't happen to walk by. In a few minutes, she came back downstairs fully dressed as if nothing had happened. Maybe she just wanted to remind me of what I'm missing. She's always doing things like that and it drives me crackers.

Mom said at breakfast that she, Aunt Doris, and Dad are going out to dinner tomorrow night. She asked if I could watch the kids and I couldn't say no. With everything that's been going on, they deserve a night away from all of us. Besides, Aunt Doris has taken practically all my chores since she's been here. Maybe Jenny can come over. I don't expect much privacy unless maybe we can put the kids to bed early.

Friday May 1, 1942
Late

It was a great evening, better than I expected for sure. Jenny came over and we made dinner for the two of us and the boys. Mom, Dad, and Aunt Doris left about six with orders that Harry and Mike were to get baths before bed. We read them a story after their baths and they were asleep by eight. I knew we had at least another couple of hours before everyone got home and all we had left to do was feed Millie. Her formula, that's made right here in E'ville, was already mixed up and in the icebox. After I got it warmed and tested it, I sat down to feed her.

"Can I feed her?" Jenny asked.

I put the baby in her arms and gave her the bottle. Millie didn't seem to care who held the bottle.

"Remember when I said that I'd like to know what it feels like to nurse a baby? Do you think Millie would mind?"

"We can find out."

Jenny unbuttoned her blouse—with a little help from me. Millie knew exactly what to do when Jenny put her up to her breast and she found her nipple without any help.

The expression on Jenny's face was priceless when Millie latched on like a shark. She'd finished most of her bottle already and seemed to be more than happy with her new pacifier. I swear that baby smiled the whole time.

"It's an amazing feeling. She bites a little sometimes, but not enough to hurt." One of those bites must have been pretty hard though because she sort of jumped and then switched nipples.

In fifteen minutes, Millie was fast asleep and Jenny's nipple slipped free of her mouth. I managed to take her upstairs and put her in the crib without waking her. When I got back, Jenny was inspecting her nipples.

"See those tiny bite marks. Aren't they cute?"

"I can make some bigger ones if you like those so much."

Finally, everyone was asleep and we had precious little time before everyone got home. I locked the front door, which Mom had told me to do and I had forgotten.

"Thank you for letting Millie do that. Now I know what it feels like. Maybe I could be a mother some day after all."

"Don't thank me. Millie seemed to be happy and you didn't look too miserable yourself. Now is it my turn?"

The sound of a door key going into a keyhole is unmistakable.

"The kitchen."

We got into the kitchen and turned the light on just as the door squeaked open.

"We're home," Mom announced.

"We're in the kitchen," I answered.

Buttons were never buttoned faster in the history of the world.

"Jenny and I were just thinking about a snack. Is there any of that peach pie left?"

"Yes, there's plenty in the icebox. Get all you want," Mom answered as she came into the kitchen.

I fixed Jenny and me a bowl of the cobbler and Mom sat down at the table with us while we ate it.

"Jenny dear, are you all right? Your face is awfully flushed. Do you have a temperature? You know there's a terrible cold going 'round."

"I'm fine. I guess it's just a little warm in here for me."

"That's my fault. I turned the heat up when we left. It's been a little chilly these last few days and I didn't want the baby to get cold. This time of year you can never tell what the weather's going to be like."

Neither of us were hungry, but we ate the pie. When we finished we washed the bowls and put them away.

"Well, I guess I'd better be going. It's getting late and I don't want Mom to worry," Jenny said as she started toward the door."

"Can I walk Jenny home, Mom?"

"Sure, but come straight back, okay? It's too late to be out."

We laughed all the way to her house. I teased her with "Jenny dear are you all right? Your face is awfully flushed."

There were no porch lights on anywhere around Jenny's house so I gave her a kiss on her doorstep. That had to do for tonight.

Saturday May 2, 1942
Night

"My nipples are sore," was the first thing Jenny said to me this afternoon when I got to her house. "When I looked at them this morning in the mirror, they're both red and have little bite marks all around them."

She then grinned wide, "I would hate to have to explain to Mom where they came from."

It was furniture moving time at Jenny's again. This time we rearranged the living room, twice. I wonder if Mr.

Brewster thinks he's in the wrong house sometimes. It was nice out today, so after we finished moving furniture Jenny and I walked down to the park. A few parents with their children were there, but mostly we had the place to ourselves.

"Do you think we'll get married someday?" Jenny said as we watched one kid push another into the water at the edge of the lake.

"Absolutely, and we'll both live happily ever after."

"I'm serious. With the war going on, girls are getting married even before graduating high school if their boyfriends join up and who knows how long this war will last or how it'll end. We may be drafting women if it goes too long. The Germans or Japanese could be running the country by the time we're old enough to get married. I listen to the news same as you and right now, we're losing the war."

"I'm sorry Jenny. We really will get married someday and we will live happily ever after. I know we will. My grandmother got married when she was thirteen and my father was born when she was just sixteen so maybe we're not too young to think about it. I'm just a dumb kid sometimes."

Jenny seemed ten years older than me today. She thinks seriously about a lot of things I don't think about at all. I have to grow up.

Sunday May 10, 1942
Night

Today's Mother's Day and I know Mom got a call from my sister this afternoon. I could tell because she started crying when she hung up the phone and wouldn't tell me who it was. She'll tell me later if she wants to. The rest of the day was fun. This week Jenny and I helped Harry and

Mike make Mother's Day cards for Aunt Doris. They were cute little hand prints they drew out and colored and I helped them write their names on them. Dad got Mom and Aunt Doris a dozen roses each and we took them out to lunch after church. Today's sermon was on the love Jesus had for his mother and after he finished, the preacher had all the mothers stand up and everyone applauded. Jenny and I sat next to our mothers and next to each other like we do every Sunday, but today we were extra proud of them. I think Mom and Mrs. Brewster are the prettiest mothers in our congregation. I guess I never thought of Mom as pretty, although she really is a pretty woman. She didn't get all fat and old after my sister and I were born like most of the other mothers her age and she still cares a lot about how she looks. I made breakfast this morning for everyone. I couldn't very well just make breakfast for Mom. Aunt Doris helped and everything was delicious. We weren't late for Sunday School either. We had to go this Sunday; it was Dad's turn to teach my class and he always gets really nervous about it. I don't know why. He's a good speaker and spends a lot of time preparing. He began with Proverbs 31, verses 10-31, which I've heard all my life, but it's kinda different when it's your father speaking to a group of soon-to-be teenagers. Verse 28 is the one I had to memorize in first grade for Mother's Day and I still remember it, "Her children arise and call her blessed; her husband also, and he praises her".

Jenny and I are so lucky to have the mothers we do, and someday I'll tell Harry and Mike how lucky they are to have Aunt Doris for a mom. She's been put through a lot, but she's every bit as strong as Mom. I hope someday I'll be as smart and strong as they are.

Friday May 15, 1942
Night

Today was the last day of sixth grade for me and a big day. The graduation from grammar school to junior high is an achievement and recognition of the completion of a basic education, or that's what Mom says. Neither of my parents graduated high school and they have high hopes for me—which I'm constantly reminded of. Parents were invited to the ceremony, but it was mostly mothers in the crowd and a few grandparents. I wish I had grandparents. Mother's parents were killed by the influenza in 1918 when Mom was only seven. She and Aunt Doris were raised by their grandparents and an aunt. Daddy's father was killed in the Great War and he says his mother worked herself to death trying to keep him fed after the two of them moved southeast, leaving Dad's younger brother with relatives because she was afraid he would starve on the trip. We're so lucky to be living in a country that, even during a war, people don't die by the thousands from disease or starve to death.

The girls were all dressed in white and the boys in black as we waited for our names to be called after Principal Lankford gave a graduation speech and presented special awards. Jenny and I got an award for athletics for helping start the dance club and for our first place win in Chicago last school year. That trophy is the best looking one in the trophy case on the wall just outside the principal's office. I look at it every day and remember the nose to nose finish of our "Blue Danube" Viennese waltz.

There was a reception after graduation and our teachers were all there. You'd think we were leaving for the other side of the country instead of just moving a few blocks to Reitz. Next year we get to choose classes beyond the required ones for the first time and we got all kinds of suggestions from our teachers who know our abilities better than we do. My and Jenny's fathers didn't get to come to the ceremony, so after it was all over the two of us decided we would stay dressed in our graduation clothes until they got home and we reenacted the whole thing for them. It was a lot of fun. Mom and Mrs. Brewster played along. I was surprised how much of Principal Lankford's speech Mom remembered, but she got it pretty much right.

I'm looking forward to being able to spend every free minute with Jenny this summer. She'll need a new swimsuit and maybe I will too; at least I'm taller than I was last summer.

Monday May 18, 1942
Night

The weather has warmed up finally. I love the spring and fall. Mom had me planting flowers this past weekend, like every spring, and I've learned not to argue with her regardless of what she chooses. This morning Aunt Doris took the kids and headed out for who knows where. I think she did it just to give Mom a break. After she made my breakfast, Mom sat down at the table while I ate and I could tell she wanted to talk.

"You listen to the news every night closer than I do, so you know how bad things are. We've surrendered all of the Philippine Islands and it's just a matter of time before the Japanese invade Australia. Your father's always optimistic, but sometimes I think he doesn't believe what he says and he won't tell me what he really thinks. I know it's not fair for me to burden you with my worries, but you're a lot older than your years and I can't talk to Mrs. Brewster about the war. She has a son who could be in the thick of it at any time and she worries enough as it is without having to listen to me. When the Germans get finished with the Russians they'll invade England for certain and they can't hold out for long against the whole German army."

"Mom, I had no idea you kept up with the war this close. You should've been a reporter."

"I may be a woman and some might think I ought to be more concerned with cooking, cleaning, and children than with world events, but I see what's happening and there's no use trying to keep it from you. You hear it on the radio every night and see it in the theater and you can bet the news is a lot worse than they're telling us. I just get so worried sometimes that I have to talk to somebody and now with a new baby on the way..."

She froze.

"A new baby? Mom, back up—what are you saying?"

She was quiet for a long time and when she looked up at me there were tears in her eyes.

"It's true. Not even your father knows yet. I don't know how I'm going to tell him and I didn't mean to tell you. It's just so stupid. I'm so stupid. I'm forty-two years old. What am I going to do with a new baby?"

"We could sell it to the gypsies."

She laughed and it was good to see her laugh. She hasn't done much of that lately. Then I thought of something pretty deep.

"Maybe it's God's way of reminding us that life goes on even during a war."

"I knew talking to you would be the right thing to do. I lied when I said I didn't intend to tell you, and you're right about life going on. I just wish God had reminded me of something else three months ago."

Then it was my turn to laugh when her face turned beet red.

"How am I ever going to tell your father? We sort of agreed we wouldn't be having any more children."

"Dad is Dad, you know that. He'll take it like he takes everything else that comes up unexpectedly, as just another predicament this family gets into and he'll be happy whether he shows it or not. I think it's about time the two of you had an evening out without the rest of us. Aunt Doris and I can handle things next Saturday night so the two of you can go into town, have a nice dinner and maybe see a movie. Order a bottle of wine. Dad will be fine with the news."

We talked for over an hour this morning and she talked to me like I was an adult. So I'm going to have a new baby sister or brother. Well, I'm happy about that and I hope it's a brother. Mom made me promise I wouldn't tell Jenny until she told Dad and I'll keep that promise even though I'm dying to tell her. Her first doctor appointment is next week and she wants us to go with her. She could ask me to babysit so Aunt Doris could go, but I get the idea she wants Jenny and me. I can't imagine what Mom will look like a few months from now.

I guess I never realized before just how much the war affects her.

Wednesday May 27, 1942
Night

Eric said tonight that England and Russia have signed a new treaty promising cooperation until Germany's defeated. I'll have to talk to Mom about this, now that I know she keeps up with the war news. I didn't hear any mention of Japan or Italy, like they were going to leave them to us. Eric said the treaty was mostly to guarantee neither side made a separate peace with Germany. I don't think there's much chance of that, so I don't see what the big deal is, but Eric seemed to think it's important. All I know is that if we have to fight the Japs by ourselves, a lot more of our boys will be drafted into the Navy. I'm glad Jenny's brother's in the Army. According to his letters, not much is happening in England right now. They still have air raids even though most of the German air force is busy with the Russians.

Last Saturday night Mom and Dad went out to dinner. She was nervous when she came up to my room to tell me they were leaving.

"Wish me luck."

"You look gorgeous Mom and I think Dad knows what a lucky man he is. Things will be fine."

Sunday morning when I got up I went downstairs to find Aunt Doris making breakfast.

"Your mom and dad aren't up yet."

I could tell by the smile on her face that she knew, and that she knew Mom was supposed to tell Dad last night. That's an awful lot to figure out from just the smile on someone's face, but Aunt Doris is so easy to read. I also guessed that since Mom and Dad weren't up yet, things had gone pretty well.

It was almost nine when Dad came into the kitchen and asked where the tray was. I knew what tray he was talking about and found it for him. He put together breakfast for Mom and took it in to her without saying a word about why he was doing it.

"Your mother was never any good at keeping secrets," Aunt Doris whispered to me. "So I'm sure she's told you already, nevertheless we have to look surprised when they tell us."

Mom and Dad came out of their bedroom in half an hour, sat down at the kitchen table and asked Aunt Doris and me to join them.

"We have some good news and the two of you can pretend you don't already know," Dad smiled as he began. "Just to make it official, there will be a new baby in the house soon and I'm sure the new mother will get all the help she needs from my favorite soon-to-be teenager and sister-in-law."

Aunt Doris hugged Mom and I hugged Dad, then we switched. When everyone was well hugged, Dad reminded us that church would be starting in half an hour. I couldn't wait to tell Jenny. We were a little late but our seats next to the Brewster's were waiting for us. My note to Jenny was done before we left home.

"LNLVHKKADDZSHMFENQSVNENQSGDMDWSRH WLNMSGR"

When she finished reading it, she gave me a puzzled look until I nodded. She smiled and hugged me.

After church I asked if I could walk home with Jenny. She wanted to know all about how everyone was taking the news. Then she said something I hadn't thought of.

"Your mother will have a baby only a year younger than her granddaughter."

That's kinda strange even for our family.

Sunday June 7, 1942
Night

Jenny and I went with Mom to see the doctor last week. She's knocked up all right. I'm sure she wouldn't like me saying it that way, but I like how it sounds for some reason; not that I'd ever say it out loud where anyone could hear.

Jenny and I had our birthday party at her house today after church. Finally we're real teenagers, although Jenny's looked like one since she was eleven and I still don't. Mrs. Brewster made a chocolate cake this year, Jenny's favorite. We had our first date in a long time last night as our gift to each other. We saw *To Be or Not to Be* with Carole Lombard and Jack Benny. I didn't want to see it when it first came out because Carole Lombard was killed in January, two months before it was first in theaters, and I really liked her. She was from Fort Wayne and so pretty. We saw her in *Mr. and Mrs. Smith* last year and decided that we really should see her very last movie. It was sad knowing she was dead, but it was a great movie. Most everyone's seen it already so the Woodlawn wasn't crowded at all, even though it was a Saturday night. We sat in the back row and couldn't keep our hands off each other. There weren't any "home runs" but there were a couple of triples for both teams. We held hands on the way home and I got a kiss on her doorstep. It was a good birthday, although I can't wait until I'm sixteen and can drive. We're already planning places we want to go.

We also got an extra special birthday present neither of us was expecting. Tonight on the radio, Eric said we've just won a major battle in the Pacific. We kept the Japs from taking a place called Midway Atoll and sank a lot of their ships. Last month there was good news about a battle in the Coral Sea where we didn't exactly win, but we stopped the Japs before they could get to Australia. Maybe the war against Japan is turning around and we can help the British fight Hitler.

Mrs. Brewster has joined the "Wives and Mothers Club" of Evansville. It's for the wives and mothers of servicemen from the Evansville area and she says they're putting a sign at city hall with the names of all our servicemen on it. There are over a hundred now. Jenny says her mom and the other women support each other and share information they get from the letters their loved ones send. Some of that information doesn't make it to the newspapers through official channels for months. It must be hardest for those who haven't heard from their husbands and sons for a long time. Eric says the Japs have thousands of our boys in captivity. I'm going to say a prayer for them before going to sleep tonight.

I wonder if Jenny's thinking about me right now.

Tuesday June 16, 1942
Night

There was trouble in Gear Town this past weekend. Three soldiers from Camp Breckinridge and one colored girl were arrested. Probably the colored girl was a prostitute. The Army's going to crack down on that place if the city doesn't do something. There's trouble almost every weekend. "Fuckin's ten and suckin's five," I remember. Jenny wanted to go back there for her birthday, to watch, but I wouldn't go with her. Sometimes she gets the craziest ideas. What if we'd been there when those people got arrested?

Mom's doing great. Aunt Doris and I are doing all the normal housework when Mom will let us. She thinks we're silly for treating her like an invalid or something. Today she, Jenny, and I went shopping for maternity clothes. Mom gave away all of hers years ago. We felt a little out of place, but she wanted us to go. The saleslady was trying to be funny when she asked who the clothes were for. Mom didn't think it was so funny.

Monday June 22, 1942
Night

Dad got his pork chops, gravy and biscuits yesterday for Father's Day. We wanted to take him out for breakfast, although he always says our breakfasts on Father's Day are much better than any we could buy. He's such an easy father to please. He was supposed to work yesterday but his boss made someone who didn't have children trade days with him.

There was a phone call from my sister yesterday afternoon while I was at Jenny's. If I had been home and answered the phone, I would've told her Mom wasn't home. It really depressed Mom and this morning at breakfast after Aunt Doris and the children were finished eating, she told me about the call and wanted to talk. She waited until there was no one in the kitchen but the two of us and asked me to sit with her for a while.

"Your sister's back in town and living on Second Street somewhere. She wants to come over next Sunday for lunch. What could I tell her? She's still my daughter. I talked to your father about it last night and he agreed to let her come, but I wanted to tell you. No...that's not right. I want to ask if it will be okay with you. You live here too and your opinion matters—you being a grown up teenager and all."

The smile on her face didn't quite hide her concern. Second Street; that's Gear Town and the only reason a white girl would live there is to make money. Mom knew that and I knew she knew that, but neither of us said anything.

"Sure, she can come Sunday—as long as she doesn't stay long and doesn't bring anyone with her. You didn't tell her about the baby did you?"

"No, there's no reason she should know and she'll only be here for lunch after church. I told Doris she was coming and she and the children are going to the park. I don't blame her for not wanting to be around."

My sister's a whore in Gear Town. Isn't that just wonderful? I would write "just fucking wonderful" if I talked like that.

Sunday June 28, 1942
Night

Lunch could have been worse. My sister showed up just as we got home from church and thankfully she was alone.

She has a car or at least she was driving one and she was dressed very nice. Mom's blessing at the table turned into a lesson on the importance of families, from the Old Testament to the new, from Adam and Eve to Jacob to Jesus' family. She knew them all by name and spoke as if she were talking about her own relatives. Special petitions were sent up for my sister although no names were mentioned. I don't think my sister got the Whore of Babylon reference, but I did, "the woman was arrayed in purple and scarlet color, and decked with gold and precious stones and pearls." That's straight from Revelations, chapter 17, verse 4. For some reason I remember that verse. It certainly wasn't one of the morning devotional readings at school and our Sunday School teachers stay away from such things. I guess they think we won't understand what it's really about.

After that prayer sermon, we had a nice lunch as a family. In her prayers, Mom shows just how deeply she feels things and how knowledgeable she is, particularly on the Bible, even if she never went to high school. She's talking to God when she prays, and for me it's like listening to my favorite teacher. At the table there were no discussions of my sister's current living arrangements or employment. Conversations were kept cordial and there was no mention of the coming new baby. After lunch everyone sat on the front porch like we used to do when I was very young. Several neighbors came by and stopped for a few minutes. The talk was about normal things and hardly anything was said about the war. There's not much good news now on that front and everyone just chooses not to talk about it. I walked my sister to her car when she was ready to leave after saying goodbye to everyone. Mom invited her back for our July Fourth cookout.

"Are you all right?" I asked. "I mean, are you living in a good place? Do you have enough money? What about Uncle…"

"That bastard? I have no idea where he is and I don't care. Aunt Doris is lucky to be rid of him. You think I was the only girlfriend he had while he was still married? There were three that I know of. I'm living with one of them right now. She came back to E'ville with me. As for money, I have plenty. I bought this car and paid cash for it. It took me a while to figure out I'd been giving away what men would pay good money for."

"Aren't you ever afraid that some man will hurt you? You could get some kind of disease."

"I keep a thirty-eight under my pillow and my nightstand drawer full of rubbers. I don't fuck niggers or white men with big dicks. I let the colored girls have them. On a good night I can make fifty dollars easy and I only work when I want. Don't worry about your big sister; I'm doing fine. What about your little girlfriend, Jenny? The two of you still all over each other? I have a white girl about her age who pays me ten dollars almost every week for a little fun. A colored girl named Mandy sets up special things like that for me."

"Stop it. I don't want to hear any more and I don't care how much money you make or what you do to get it. I just wanted to know if you're safe."

"I'm fine. If you're ever in the neighborhood, look me up, kid. I'll show you around. Oh, and ask for Maybelline. I don't give anyone my real name anymore."

With that, she drove off. I hope she's okay. I wonder if she was talking about the same Mandy Jenny and I met—probably. Maybelline? Where did she come up with that?

Tuesday July 7, 1942
Night

So hot today I can hardly breathe. Jenny and I went to the pool and took Mike and Harry with us. They were a handful, but Aunt Doris deserves a break occasionally. She's working part-time permanent at the Ironworks now and I know she feels bad about having Mom babysit all the time. Mom looks pregnant now and the hot weather seems to affect her more than the rest of us.

With Harry and Mike in the room with me, I can't very well sleep naked on top of the covers like I sometimes did before in the hottest part of the summer. Jenny says she sleeps on a pallet on their screened-in back porch. If I were brave enough, I'd sneak out of the house some night and surprise her.

Our July Fourth cookout was this past Saturday, but my sister didn't show up. I guess it was a busy time for her. That's a terrible thing to think, although it's true. There've always been girls who would sell it and men who would buy it, I know. I just never imagined my sister being one of the sellers, a buyer maybe, not a seller. That was a terrible thing to think too, but I can't help it. In spite of everything, I miss her, especially since seeing her again.

Thursday July 16, 1942
Very early

Jenny and I went roller skating last night. The rink is air conditioned and the place was packed with about a million people from little kids to grandparents looking for a cool place to spend the evening. We didn't stay very long. It was too crowded to skate and with all the people, it wasn't much cooler inside than out. On the way home I told her about my back porch plan.

"That would be perfect. Daddy will be working the graveyard shift for six weeks beginning tonight. He'll leave at ten fifteen without waking Mom and she won't get up until seven tomorrow morning to make breakfast for them. A bomb wouldn't wake Mom up from a sound sleep. You could come over every night. I'll leave the screen door unlatched for you."

"I'll have to make sure my two roommates are asleep and that I don't go to sleep myself."

"I don't think you will, not tonight," she said with one of those smiles I love to see.

Getting out of the house was easy. The boys were asleep by the time I went to my room and they looked like they were out for the night. Mom and Dad went to bed at their usual nine o'clock and I counted down the minutes until ten past ten. With every fan in the house running on high speed, I could have fallen down the stairs and no one would've heard me. Aunt Doris is riding to work with Dad now, so she and Millie were already sound asleep when I stuck my head out my bedroom door to have a look around. Everything was dark and quiet.

I walked on the street behind our house to Jenny's. Around the corner of the house I could that see the Brewster's car wasn't in the driveway, so I knew her dad had already left for work. There were no lights on anywhere and when Jenny's flashlight blinked twice, I had no trouble seeing it. She was waiting for me at the screen door. In the moonlight I could see she was wearing just a white T-shirt that was too big for her. I didn't say anything when she let me in. I just kissed her and held her close for a long time. It had been a while. Our eyes were already adjusted to the pale light and I could see the pallet she'd made with both pillows from her bed, but the floor was just as hard as I imagined it would be. The neighborhood was quiet except for an occasional dog barking and there were no cars on the street. Holding her close and kissing her made the chance of getting caught seem so small it was barely worth imagining.

If there was a cool breeze anywhere, it didn't reach Jenny's back porch. We didn't care and soon we were a sweaty pair wrapped in each other's arms and legs. I could taste the salty sweat wherever I kissed her and I kissed her everywhere. She was beautiful in the moonlight—like the leading man always says in the movies. We arranged the pillows under her so she wouldn't have to feel the hard floor my knees were being punished by, not that I noticed at the time, but I have bruises now. Unexpected lights over my shoulder caused me to fall flat over her once. It was just a passing car that didn't slow down as it went along the street behind her house.

"This is crazy," I whispered as I leaned back up off her.

"I know; isn't it great? I love you Emell and I've missed you so much."

She hadn't called me that in a while. I wanted to feel her body touch mine everywhere at the same time. She pulled my face to hers and kissed me as she wrapped her legs around me and squeezed me tight. We were wet with sweat and our bodies slid over each other like we'd been drenched in oil.

"This is what I've thought about," she whispered as I tried to melt into her. She pulled me up over her and pushed me back with her hips and legs again and again until I felt the little twinges I knew too well.

"Bases are loaded Jenny."

She didn't say anything. She didn't have to. We held our breath at the same time and I'm pretty sure we felt the same identical shivers at the same time. It was like nothing I can describe; fireworks maybe, or thunder that shakes the ground and rattles the windows. We lay still for a long time not wanting the moment to end and then I realized it was raining. A fine mist of water came through the screen as if it had been ordered to cool us down. There was no storm, no wind, just gentle rain and I lay there thinking how perfect everything was at that moment.

More headlights; this time I thought they were coming from the street in front of Jenny's house and bouncing off something, but it was the kitchen lights. Her mom was up. What time was it? Had I fallen asleep? The sun wasn't up, but I could see the sky was lighter in the east and it was still raining. I had to go and go soon. Jenny woke up and for a moment she had the same look on her face I probably had. Then she smiled and kissed me.

"Come back tonight?"

"I'll be lucky to be alive."

My clothes were soaking wet. We both looked like we'd just stepped out of the shower. There were no sounds from inside the house and I was careful not to slam the screen door after getting a last kiss.

I ran through the rain back home. The lights were on as I knew they would be. I couldn't go through the back door; Mom would be in the kitchen and if the front door had been locked, I don't know what I would've done. The living room lights weren't on, but they would be soon. The front door opened with a squeak I never remembered being that loud. Inside, the fans were still going full blast. I closed the door behind me and made it up the stairs in three steps. The light was on in Aunt Doris' room. She came to the doorway with Millie in her arms just as I was about to make the turn into my room. We looked at each other without saying a word. I got undressed and slipped under the sheets. The boys were still asleep. My heart pounded in my chest as rainwater dripped from my hair. I was dead and I knew it.

I've been lying here expecting Mom, or worse, Dad to come in and demand to know where I've been. The car just started. Dad and Aunt Doris are leaving for work. I have to do something with my wet clothes, and then face Mom.

Sunday July 19, 1942
Night

Aunt Doris didn't tell Mom and Dad about Wednesday night. This afternoon they went to the USO to volunteer for something. They're always doing that. After they left, Aunt Doris invited me to sit with her at the kitchen table. It wasn't too hard to figure out what she wanted to talk about.

"Do you really know how much your mother means to me? Although she's just a little more than a year older than me, she's always been ten years wiser and everything a big sister's supposed to be. I only went against her wishes once—when I got married, and I should have listened to her then. Our parents, your grandparents, died when we were very young. I barely remember them and your mother had to grow up fast. I'm afraid I didn't grow up quite as fast and she became my mother out of necessity. I was probably ten or eleven before I realized she was only a year older than me. She married a wonderful man and they have let me and my children move in with you when I had nowhere else to go."

I was at the point of crying by that time.

"When she called me and said your sister was pregnant and needed a place to stay, I saw it as a chance to pay her back for some of the things she's done for me. I don't regret saying yes, even though my marriage fell apart soon after your sister arrived. It would have sooner or later anyway. You're her hope for the future and I want you to know just how much she loves you and how proud of you she is. In her eyes you can do no wrong.

I don't have to ask where you were Wednesday night. I didn't say anything to your parents, but don't ever expect me to lie to them either. Your mother thinks the world of Jenny, and she's convinced herself that your infatuation with her is completely innocent and just a phase the two of you are going through. It's none of my business, but maybe I see things she doesn't."

She finally smiled a little.

"…and nobody sneaks into the house at the crack of dawn during a rainstorm after playing cards with a friend all night."

I didn't say anything after she finished. I just hugged her and told her how much I love her. She knows about Jenny and me and so does Mom, but some things are better left unsaid.

Saturday July 25, 1942
Late

Jenny and I went to a Reitz baseball game this afternoon. A lot of the boys playing went to Centennial and after the game (Reitz won) several came over to talk. Mostly they flirted with Jenny. I wish I could get used to that and I can't really blame them. She was far and away the prettiest girl there. Sitting next to her and not being able to touch her definitely does something to me. On our walk back home, I asked if it would be all right if I came over later, much later.

"The screen door will be unlocked and there's no forecast of rain. Daddy's still working the graveyard shift and Mom will sleep all night."

She smiled that smile that makes me want to rip her clothes off.

"I don't think she'll be expecting you for breakfast though."

I left the house at eleven fifteen and returned at two. Everything was dark and quiet this time. It was hard for me to leave Jenny and the sight of her sweaty on those pillows will be with me a while. I think we could've made love till dawn. I made her promise that someday we will. Maybe we still don't know what we're doing, although we're getting better at it according to Jenny.

Tuesday August 4, 1942
Night

Daddy's asleep in bed with Mom and tomorrow morning he'll get up, eat breakfast, and go to work just like he did today, and tomorrow night we'll have dinner, listen to the news and maybe *Blondie* and then he'll smile and tell me not to stay up too late before he and Mom go to bed.

None of that is going to happen ever again.

Monday August 24, 1942
Night

Tomorrow it will be three weeks, and then it will be a month, then two, and then a year.

I was on my way downstairs from feeding Millie and happened to look out the window to see Aunt Doris pull into the driveway. It was the middle of the day and Daddy wasn't with her. I knew something was wrong, but I walked on into the kitchen and sat down with Mom and began helping her peel potatoes. I'm so glad I was home. Aunt Doris didn't say anything and I could tell she'd been crying. She just looked at Mom, shook her head and tears filled her eyes. Not a word was spoken between them. Mom knew and I knew. The cry I heard as she fell to her knees came from her soul, not her lips. It was the sound of a heart breaking. The two sisters prayed and I'll never forget how Mom pleaded with God for His help in keeping our family together and safe. Toward the end, she thanked Him for my father and asked Him to hold his soul in the palms of His great hands. She then hugged Aunt Doris and me and the three of us emptied our hearts of every tear. I never saw my mother cry for my father again. Aunt Doris stayed with the children while Mother and I went to St. Mary's hospital where Dad had been taken after the accident. She knew exactly where the burial policy and life insurance papers were and brought them with us. She was calm as she spoke to me of the funeral plans she and Dad had agreed on years ago.

"Promise me you won't ever leave me Mom," I tried to say without crying.

"Listen to me and remember what I say," she answered in a very firm voice. "Your father did not leave us. He's a good man and would never do that. He was taken from us through no fault of his own—and don't believe anyone who says it was 'God's will'. God doesn't cause accidents and neither does he 'allow' them to happen. Life is uncertain and that's His plan. It's what makes us human. It's what makes us love life and each other like we do."

Maybe it was then that I realized just how wise my mother is.

At the hospital, we were allowed to spend a few minutes with Daddy before the funeral home director showed up. Mom talked to him in a calm voice as if he were listening to her every word and answering her every question. I managed to tell him I loved him before Mr. Graves (yes, that's his real name) came into the hospital room. Mom gave him the burial policy and he assured her he would take care of everything. Mr. Graves is well known and liked in our neighborhood and seems almost like a member of the family we're glad not to see very often. His funeral home even sponsored a baseball team before the war and Dad always said something funny about their uniforms with "Graves Funeral Home" emblazoned on the back of the jerseys. Undertaking was a job that had to be done and Mr. Graves was the perfect man for it, he always said. I've never heard anyone say a cross word about him. When we turned to leave, Mom kissed Dad and wished him a good night's sleep, just like she probably had the night before. I learned a lot about life, love, and death that day.

On the drive home, Mom asked me if I knew how to get in touch with my sister. I didn't want her going near Gear Town and told her not to worry, that I would find her. It was late when we got home, but Aunt Doris was still up and the kitchen table was already covered in food brought over by our neighbors. I asked Mom if it would be all right if I called Jenny.

"Jenny and her mom came over earlier," Aunt Doris answered, "and Mrs. Brewster said that if you wanted, you could come over when you got home regardless of what time it was."

Mom nodded and I was out the door running for Jenny. I needed her to tell me things would be all right. All the lights were out when I got there, but I knew Jenny would be sleeping on the back porch. The screen door was unlocked.

I lay down next to her and hugged her tight. She turned over and kissed me, brushed away my tears, and then we both cried.

"Promise you won't ever leave me Jenny."

"For the rest of my life; body and soul, remember? A promise is a promise."

We talked until I was so sleepy I couldn't hold my eyes open. We talked about little things and she promised we would see Abbott and Costello someday. We missed them at the Coliseum on the fourteenth. They came for a War Savings Bond drive and we had plans to go. I wanted to stay with Jenny, but I knew I should be home when Mom woke up. With a final cry together and a kiss, I left and made my way back. I slept well for some reason. It was late morning when I went downstairs to find Mom and

Aunt Doris explaining to the boys what had happened. Mike understood and began to cry; Harry probably didn't, but cried anyway because his brother was crying. I had to get out of the kitchen or I would've come apart all over again.

Mrs. Brewster must have seen me walking back and forth in front of their house because she came to the door and invited me in. She hugged me and asked if I'd eaten breakfast yet. When I told her no, she asked me to go out on the back porch and wake Jenny up so the two of us could eat together.

Jenny was wrapped up in sheets and pillows and still sound asleep when I eased the door to the kitchen closed behind me. I sat on the porch next to her and brushed the hair out of her face. She looked like an angel. I leaned over and kissed her until she began to wake up. She had a smile on her face when she wrapped her arms around me and pulled me down to her face and kissed me the way I needed to be kissed at that moment.

"Mom's looking out the kitchen window," she whispered.

I froze.

"It's okay. She knows."

Jenny wrapped a sheet around herself and went upstairs to get dressed while I sat at the table watching Mrs. Brewster make our breakfast.

"If there's anything my family can do, I want you to tell me and I mean it. Your mother's my best friend in this world and there's nothing I wouldn't do for her, but you know as well as I do she won't ask for help. These next few months will be especially hard for her with a baby on the way and I'm counting on you to tell me how she's really doing. Jenny and I and Mr. Brewster are here for your family. I don't want to butt in but I will if I have to."

She walked over to where I was sitting and hugged me. I'd thought about something already. Aunt Doris will be working full-time now to help pay the bills and the boys and the baby will be mine and Mom's responsibility. We can handle that just fine for now, but when school starts in a few weeks, it'll be too much for her, especially in her condition. My quitting school would be out of the question for Mom; there's no point in even bringing it up.

"School will be starting soon and Mom will have the boys and Millie to care for. She would never ask you, but if you could do something to help with them, at least until the baby's born…"

"And I won't take no for an answer. Harry and Mike can stay here every day until Doris gets home from work. It's been a long time since I've had boys around the house and I would be glad to watch them."

"Boys are different, that's for sure, but they're good kids."

"They still pee standing up?"

Jenny wanted to know what we were laughing about when she came down the stairs but Mrs. Brewster wouldn't tell her.

The funeral was last Friday. Jenny and I went to Gear Town Wednesday after lunch. We figured business would be slow at that time of day. When we got to Second Street, I couldn't find anyone who would tell me where "Maybelline" lived. Maybe they thought I was sent by the police or something. I had better luck when I asked how to find Mandy. Then they probably figured we were customers. It wasn't hard finding the Larson Hotel on High Street and there Mandy was, standing out front dressed like…well, dressed like a whore. Made up the way she was, she looked much older and at first she didn't recognize us. Jenny and I both had a little trouble talking to her with her nipples clearly visible through the thin white taffeta blouse she was wearing. Advertisement, I thought to myself.

"Yeah, I remember you and I know that white girl Maybelline. I'll take you to her, but I won't tell you how to find her yourself. You see, I get a dollar for every paying customer I bring with me, but I don't get nothin' for telling you how to find her. You two paying her full price? 'Cause if you are, I can do anything she can do for less money. How about a two for one deal? I guarantee satisfaction, just like Sears and Roebuck."

She talked a lot as we followed her back to the residential end of Second Street to a little white house that looked like any of the other little white houses. Colored men and women yelled things to Mandy from their porches and from benches in front of stores as we walked by. I couldn't understand most of what they said, but I did hear one man ask Mandy if we were paying her or if she was paying us. Jenny heard him too.

"You think she would pay us?" she whispered.

My best cold stare told her what I thought about that idea.

When Mandy knocked on the door, a white woman maybe as old as Mom answered. She didn't look like a whore.

"I told you Mandy, I don't work on Wednesdays so I'm not paying you anything for bringing this jailbait here. You know what we've been told about fucking underage kids; now get the Hell out of here."

"We came to see Maybelline," I managed to say during all the yelling.

"Well, you'll have to wait. She's with a regular and old Basil don't get in no hurry. When he can get it up at all, he pays double, but he only pays if you can make him finish. The colored girls won't take him, but Maybelline always gets his money."

"I took that bet once," Mandy interrupted, "but I ain't doin' it again; sucked on that old man's dick for an hour for free."

"If you think Maybelline's gonna give you two dollars for finding these customers, you can hang around—

outside, but you might be missing a fine paying customer at the Larson. You could suck two dicks and make two dollars this afternoon."

"I don't suck no dick for a dollar."

"Not even your daddy's?"

Mandy stormed off shouting things I didn't understand and didn't want to.

"My name's Annemarie. You can come in and wait if you want. Maybelline shouldn't be much longer. I just didn't want Mandy hanging around."

Her voice and personality changed into that of an educated white woman as soon as Mandy left. She wasn't crude and I noticed the house was clean and well kept. We sat on the sofa and Annemarie brought us Coca-Cola to drink.

"You don't look like customers, but I've been fooled before. Maybelline has quite a few local white boys—and girls who venture into Gear Town to spend time with her through the week, before the soldiers show up on the weekends. I know most of them and I don't remember seeing you here before."

I decided to just tell the truth. I don't know why, and I saw no reason to tell her I knew something about who she was—a former girlfriend of my former uncle.

"She's my sister. Our father was killed in an accident at the shipyards yesterday and I've come to tell her."

She came over to the sofa, sat down next to me and took my hand in hers. It would have been a touching moment if not for the groans coming from my sister and her customer in the next room.

"I'm so sorry. Give me a minute to get rid of our guest and Maybelline will be right out."

In a few minutes, an older man zipping his pants walked out of the bedroom and through the front door without taking any notice of us. A few minutes later my sister and Annemarie came out. I ran for her and hugged her. The tears came and I couldn't stop them.

"What's wrong? Why've you come? Are Mom and Dad all right? Aunt Doris?"

"Daddy."

I guess she could tell what I was trying to say, when I could talk at all.

The two of us stood there holding each other and crying. It was the first time we had hugged in a very long time. In a little while, she walked with me back to the sofa and sat down on the floor in front of me. We talked for an hour and I told her everything I knew about the accident, which wasn't very much.

"Let me get my keys and pack a few things. I'm going back with you."

She walked back into her bedroom just as a knock came on the door. The voice I heard was that of a woman, a well-spoken woman.

"Is Maybelline free?

"No Victoria, I'm sorry she isn't. There's been a death in her family, her father, and she'll be away for a few days."

"Is she here? I would like to express my condolences."

"Yes, please come in."

My sister came out of her bedroom just as the well dressed woman came in. She went to my sister, hugged her and kissed her. It was a kiss like none I've ever seen. It was passionate and sincere and beautiful. Jenny and I were sort of frozen and I guess a little amazed. The two women were alone in the world for a minute. They tenderly touched each other's faces with the tips of their fingers and the woman wiped away my sister's tears and kissed her again; this one being just as passionate as the first. Jenny reached for my hand and squeezed it. She felt it too.

"I'm so sorry for your loss, Maybelline, and if there is anything I can do, and I mean anything, please tell me. You're the light and love of my life and I'll always be there for you."

The two of them then left through the front door, arm in arm. The woman took no notice of Jenny and me sitting there. In a few minutes I heard a car start and my sister came back in the house and went to her bedroom. No one said anything, but Annemarie looked nervous as a whore in church, like we'd seen something we shouldn't have. I've heard that expression since I was in fifth grade but I never thought about what it meant until that moment.

"Okay, I'm ready," my sister said as she closed the bedroom door behind her. "Let's go. I'll be back on Saturday, Annemarie. Keep the doors locked and don't let anyone in you don't know."

We got into her car and she began talking before we'd gone a block.

"The two of you will forget that woman and what you saw. Forget what she looks like and forget her name."

"She loves you," I said before thinking.

"She loves what I do for her, that's all. She'll go home to her husband and children and forget about me until she wants me again."

"You're wrong. She loves you and you love her. I saw it."

"She's a woman for Christ's sake and she's twenty years older than me."

"So, what does that have to do with it?"

She didn't answer me and things were quiet for a long time. At a red light, she turned around to Jenny.

"Thank you Jenny for coming along. It's not safe to walk alone in Gear Town and it's getting worse."

"It's what you do for the one you love," she answered.

Jenny then leaned over the front seat and kissed me; not a melt your brain kind of kiss, but not a kiss like your mother gives you either. My sister didn't say a word, but out of the corner of my eye, I saw the smile on her face. She already knew, but now she really knows and I don't care. Virginia Brewster loves me and I love her. Write it in stone, put it on a billboard, let Eric tell the world on the radio tonight, let President Roosevelt put it in his next speech to congress. Virginia Brewster loves me.

When we got home, Mom ran to the car and practically dragged my sister out. The two of them hugged and Mom turned her face toward Heaven and thanked God in a prayer right there on our front lawn. I hope the whole neighborhood heard her.

The kitchen table was piled high with more food and the icebox was full. It's a nice tradition. At a time like this no one wants to cook. We were all hungry and sat down to eat.

"When's the baby due?"

There was no hiding the fact that Mom was very pregnant.

"Mid to late October the doctor says, but I think it'll come sooner."

The funeral was at our church, Central United Methodist, and I didn't know until then how well liked my father was. There were people there I'd never met who worked with him, and several were in military uniforms. I was introduced to Captain Redgrave and his wife by someone else I didn't know. I was told later that he's the supervisor of shipbuilding at the shipyard. After Pastor Knott finished with the eulogy we sang "I'll Fly Away," Daddy's favorite hymn. At the end of the song a distinguished looking man stood up at the back of the church.

"Pastor Knott, I wonder if I might be allowed to say a few words this afternoon."

Whispers traveled through the congregation. Jenny knew who Mayor Dress was; I didn't. The mayor spoke for a few minutes. I didn't know it but Daddy was the first wartime civilian casualty of Evansville and the mayor spoke as if he knew him personally, mentioning his civic volunteer work and his devotion to the community. At the end of his speech, another man from the mayor's office presented Mom with a plaque of recognition for my father's years of service to Evansville and the war effort. When he sat down, a naval officer stepped forward and presented Mom with a War Department plaque and a sealed envelope with the presidential seal on it.

Mom told me that Daddy had said he wanted to be buried at Oak Hill. She said that he joked about being buried near the Queen of the Gypsies. At the funeral I remembered walking through the cemetery so many times before with Jenny as Daddy's coffin was lowered into the ground. She was by my side the whole day. I don't know how I would have gotten through it without her.

Saturday August 29, 1942
Very late

This afternoon there was a family meeting at the kitchen table, where all our important meetings are held. Mom wanted Aunt Doris and me to know exactly what kind of financial shape we were in. I was pleased at being invited and did my best to act like an adult. Mom spoke to me first.

"Your father left exact instructions as to what I should do in case something like this happened and I intend to follow his wishes as best I can. His burial policy covered the funeral except for twelve dollars and Mr. Graves covered that himself. There's a life insurance policy and your father wanted it to be used to pay off the house. I intend to do that Monday. We will have a place to live and we should all thank your father for that. There will be about five thousand left over from that, and until this morning, I thought we would have to live on that for a long time. But, do you remember at the funeral when that naval officer gave me the plaque and an envelope? I didn't open it until this morning."

She laid the opened envelope on the table. It was a letter signed by President Roosevelt. I started reading every word out loud, but when I got to the last paragraph, I couldn't go on. Aunt Doris took the letter and continued reading. Daddy had signed up for a separate payroll deduction and hadn't told anyone. It was for a ten thousand dollar War Department workers life insurance policy and if death occurred on the job, the government would match that value. A check for twenty thousand dollars made out to Mom was enclosed. I just stared at it.

"By Monday afternoon, this house will be paid for and we will have over twenty thousand dollars in the bank."

She reached for my hand and I reached for Aunt Doris'. Mom raised her face toward Heaven and talked to my father and God as if they were in the room; maybe they were. When the final "amen" came, her face was radiant. She was Mom again.

After the meeting, Mom told me that part of the money would be put in a savings account, not to be touched until it was used to pay my college tuition. College? I haven't even thought about going to college. Anyway, with the life insurance money and with Aunt Doris now working full time, we'll make it just fine even if we'll soon have four children in the house to feed.

Tuesday September 8, 1942
Night

School starts next week and I'm a little nervous about it—seventh grade. Reitz is a big school and there'll be lots of people I don't know there. Jenny and I walked to the school Sunday afternoon so we'd know how long it'll take us every morning. It's farther than Centennial, but if we walk, we don't have to ride the bus and we can sleep half an hour longer every morning. We decided walking was better. Mom let me go shopping with Jenny Saturday. I already have my new school clothes so I was Jenny's official fashion critic. What did I know about fashion? I just know what she looks good in and she looked good in everything she tried on. I did say that one blouse she picked out was a little too sheer for school. She bought it anyway and said she would wear it for me.

When we got back to her house, Aunt Doris was there with the boys. Mrs. Brewster has offered several times to watch them when school begins and I guess she kept offering until Aunt Doris accepted. I found out later that night that she agreed to it only after Mrs. Brewster agreed to accept some payment for her trouble. Aunt Doris told me that Mrs. Brewster would put the money toward Jenny's college tuition. College for Jenny too? That would be perfect. On Sunday, while we walked to Reitz, we talked about what college we want to go to and what we want to study. I know it's really early to be thinking about such things. Then again Jenny and I like to plan things together. Indiana University in Bloomington is huge, but there's a branch in Jeffersonville, which isn't far away at all and it's a lot smaller. Oh well, we have lots of time to think about it.

Mom had a doctor's appointment yesterday and Jenny and I went with her again. He told us everything was fine and Mom seems to be handling things well. I want to be that strong someday. The final mortgage paperwork arrived Saturday and we had a mortgage burning party Saturday night. The house is ours for better or worse.

Monday September 14, 1942
Night

Our first day at Reitz was crazy. Jenny and I were lost most of the time and we didn't see many familiar faces. We chose the same classes, but we're in different homerooms. The high school is separated from the junior high by a long hallway and we're supposed to stay on our side. Classes are packed. I counted thirty-two of us in history today. We don't have assigned seats in any of our classes, so Jenny and I were able to sit together, even if we did have to sit in the back of the room. I have science, math, history, English, art, and gym. Jenny and I decided to take art as our elective this year. She's going to try out for the volleyball team and I know she'll make it. We're both going to join the dance club too. It meets for the first time this Thursday right after school. We got homework assignments in every class. Homework on the first day; that's just cruel.

I saw a high school girl I recognized after school today. I don't know her name, but I remember seeing her picture in the paper months ago. She was at one of the new business openings and they always put pictures of the event in the paper. I remember her because she was much younger and prettier than the women usually involved with such things. I have to ask someone who she is. She was surrounded by boys so it shouldn't be too hard to find out. I tried not to stare as Jenny and I walked past the group.

When we got back to Jenny's after school, Mrs. Brewster and the boys were just starting to make dinner. Mike was having a great time mashing potatoes and Harry was trying his best to shell peas. Jenny and I sat down to help.

"Just because they're boys doesn't mean they can't learn to cook," Mrs. Brewster announced. "The best chefs in the world are men and who knows, maybe Mike and Harry will have their own restaurant someday and we'll have to pay a lot of money to eat there."

"You can eat for free Mrs. B.," Mike answered, "but you have to help wash dishes."

"They don't like washing dishes, I discovered this morning," Mrs. Brewster said with a grin.

When Jenny asked if she could walk home with me, Mrs. Brewster said yes, but there was a favor she wanted from her.

"We're having German potato cakes for dinner, but don't tell your father that's what they're called or he won't eat a bite."

"I know who that girl is you were staring at today after school," Jenny said as we walked toward my house.

"I wasn't staring."

"Yes you were; your tongue was hanging out."

"It was not. Don't you think she's pretty though?"

"She's beautiful. She also happens to be the daughter of Charles Bosse. Her name is Evelyn."

Even I knew the name Bosse. Half the buildings in Evansville and the baseball field have that name on them. They own Globe World Furniture that's been in Evansville forever. We studied about it in history at Centennial and there've been lots of stories in the paper about the beautiful furniture they're making.

"So she's pretty and rich; just what I'm looking for."

That got me a punch in the ribs.

Mom was changing Millie and seemed to be glad to let Jenny and me take over. Only about a month to go now and Mom looks pretty tired most of the time. I didn't smell anything cooking in the kitchen either. Meals have been pretty simple lately. She made my breakfast this morning, but I insisted on doing it myself from now on, until the baby's born, and I can make enough for her, Aunt Doris, and the boys just as easy. I want to contribute something to keeping things running and I can cook a good breakfast. My biscuits are every bit on par with Mom's.

When Aunt Doris arrived home from work, the boys came in with their arms loaded.

"Mrs. Brewster has decided to cook dinner for us until the baby's born and you know how it is trying to argue with that woman. Besides, she said the boys helped make it and they should get to eat it."

"Your mother's an angel, Jenny. Please tell her how much we appreciate this."

"Well, I guess dinner is ready at my house too," Jenny said, "so I'd better be getting home."

I walked with her to the door and had a look around. There was no one on the sidewalk, so I gave her a quick kiss and a promise to do better soon.

I set the table while Mom and Aunt Doris unpacked our dinner. We ate like wolves. During dinner, Mom asked the boys what the pancake looking things were that tasted so good.

"They're not German potato cakes," Harry answered.

After helping with the dishes, I turned on the radio. Eric says it's hard to figure out who's winning in Russia. Last month the Germans attacked Stalingrad and it looks like they'll capture it, but they've been pushed back from Moscow. The British are winning in North Africa, that's for sure, and we're taking back some of the islands the Japanese occupied at the beginning of the war. No one seems to think the war will be over anytime soon though. Jenny's brother has been busy in England, but he can't tell us what he's been busy doing. He just says they'll be ready if Hitler decides to cross the Channel and I know that's not going to happen as long as the Russians fight. I guess if you have to be a soldier somewhere, right now England is the safest place to be. Eric says the Russians are trying to get us and the British to invade Europe. If that happens, it will surely start in England and Jenny's brother will be in the middle of it.

Sunday September 20, 1942
Night

It was a big day for Evansville today. The Republic Aviation plant rolled out their first fighter airplane. Jenny's dad wouldn't have it any other way but for us to all go and see. He's so proud of Republic and I bet he'll be a manager there someday. I think the whole town turned out, but since Mr. Brewster works there, he was able to get a pass that got us close to the stage that had been set up for the event. The US Army Air Forces Band was there along with a dozen officers. I don't really know their ranks as well as the Navy's, nevertheless they looked pretty important. When Mayor Dress introduced Governor Schricker, I knew who he was. The speeches were long, but the band was great and after everyone was finished, they unveiled the airplane. It's amazing we can build something like that right here. It looked ferocious and ready to bomb Hitler or the Japs. Mr. Brewster gave us a private viewing after the official ceremonies. It was a lot bigger up close. There were four gun barrels coming out of the front of each wing. My thumb would fit in the hole where the bullet comes out.

It was long day for Mom and her poor ankles were swollen double their normal size when we got home. I helped her into bed after we ate sandwiches for dinner. Tuesday is her birthday and Jenny and I are making a cake for her tomorrow after school. She hasn't mentioned anything about her birthday coming up and I bet she thinks

I won't remember, but Aunt Doris and I have had a little party planned for a month.

Tuesday September 22, 1942
Night

No one said anything this morning about today being Mom's birthday. I made breakfast as usual and she came in and ate with Aunt Doris and me. It was a normal day, and then Jenny and I nearly ran to her house after school. Her mom had all the ingredients set out for us and we had the cake done in less than an hour. Mike and Harry did the frosting and decorations. We didn't have forty-three candles though. Mrs. Brewster said Mom would be happy not to see that many on her cake anyway. We had enough to put one candle for each member of our families on it, though. When Aunt Doris came from work to pick up the boys, everything was done. We all, including Mr. Brewster, paraded into our house singing "Happy Birthday." Mom cried of course, but they were happy tears. Aunt Doris had a beautiful bouquet of flowers for her. After we explained the number of candles on the cake, Mr. Brewster lit them and Mom made a wish and blew them out.

Jenny and I cleaned up the kitchen after the party and I walked her home. It wasn't too late so we stopped by the park and sat on our bench for a while. No one was around so we caught up on the kisses we've missed. I wonder if she's thinking about me right now.

Wednesday September 30, 1942
Night

Jenny's first volleyball game was today after school. She didn't have any trouble making the team and she played really well. We won, but she didn't seem very happy as we walked home. When I first asked her what was wrong, she didn't want to talk, so I had to drag it out of her.

"Am I ever going to be your real girlfriend?"

"Jenny, you are my real girlfriend."

"No I'm not. Everyone thinks we're only friends."

"You are my girlfriend, Jenny. I love you. You know that."

"Then kiss me. Kiss me right here for everyone to see—if I really am your girlfriend."

"Jenny, people don't do that, not in public."

"You're right, they don't and why don't they? What's wrong with everyone knowing someone in the world loves you. You don't have to rip their clothes off and make love to them on the sidewalk. Just a little kiss; what harm could…"

I didn't let her finish. On the corner of Hartmetz and Sonntag, two of the busiest streets in our part of the city, I took Jenny in my arms and kissed her as passionately as I know how in full view of anyone who happened to be there at the time. If the whole world had been watching, it wouldn't have mattered. It was like group ballroom dancing in front of a crowd. You don't really know if anyone's watching you in particular, but you don't want to fall on your butt just in case. I didn't fall on my butt and women passing by didn't faint and no one called the police. No one noticed us at all—however Jenny wasn't able to speak for a few minutes as we walked on down Sonntag.

"Out of the park grand slam," she leaned over and whispered. "If I ever start talking crazy like that again, just kiss me in front of hundreds of people and I'll be fine. I guess I just need to know sometimes that this is all real, that we're not just kids pretending to be in love."

"Body and soul, Jenny B."

I don't know if anyone we know saw us this afternoon. There were lots of people around and probably some of them were students from Reitz. I guess I'll find out tomorrow.

Thursday October 8, 1942
Night

Wasn't it Peter who denied Christ three times? And didn't Christ forgive him? I wonder if Jenny would forgive me if I denied kissing her last week; probably not. I haven't heard any rumors at school, but there are so many kids I don't know, maybe one of them saw us and just didn't know who we were. Things are still a mess at school with students showing up in the wrong classroom or not showing up at all. Our history teacher, Mr. Jacobs, is my favorite so far. This is our first full year of world history and he talks about the war a lot. We get a daily update on how things are going in Europe and at sea. He has maps that are much better than the ones we have at home and he shows us where the places are that we hear about on the radio. His son's in England, so he and Jenny have something in common. She brought in some of her brother's letters this week and Mr. Jacobs was able to fill in some of the censored information.

I don't like the way our science teacher, Mr. Mattox, looks at Jenny. He's too young to be a teacher and he told us the first day of class he wasn't married. Why did he do that? Is he looking for a girlfriend in the seventh grade? That's just sick. The way he stands over her at her desk, I know he's trying to get a look down her blouse. I make sure it's buttoned all the way up before we go into his class. I might've been the only one who thought Jenny was the prettiest girl in fifth grade, but a lot of us think she's the prettiest girl in seventh.

Last night, Mom asked me if I would mind sleeping in her room until the baby comes. She thinks it could be any day now. Mrs. Brewster is just a phone call away during the day and the two of them have a plan for how Mom will get to St. Mary's. The local police station is only three blocks from here and they've arranged for a police car to take her. Officer Mabry and his wife are truly nice people and they sit right behind us in church every Sunday. After Dad died, Mrs. Mabry volunteered her husband to make sure Mom gets to the hospital in plenty of time. He's delivered several babies himself, so if things get out of hand he can make sure my little brother or sister arrives safely. I still hope it's a boy. Mom and I have picked a dozen names for boys and girls. I like David if it's a boy and Sherry if it's a girl. William David was Mom's father's name.

Saturday October 10, 1942
Night

Mom didn't sleep well last night and today I stayed close to home. Aunt Doris is working a double, but Jenny's dad was home all day in case we needed a ride to the hospital. There have been a few labor pains, but Mom says they aren't the real ones. It's been thirteen years since she had a labor pain and I hope she hasn't forgotten what they're supposed to feel like. Maybe it's not the kind of thing a woman forgets.

Jenny spent the day with us, beginning with helping me make breakfast, and we took care of Millie for Mom. Aunt Doris took the boys to the Brewster's when she left for work. Millie's a very happy baby and no trouble at all. She has her first birthday coming up on the twenty-forth. Wouldn't it be funny if the new baby was born on her birthday? Maybe funny's not the right word for it.

Mom took a nap right after lunch and Jenny and I fed Millie, then we took turns rocking her until she went to sleep. Jenny's "pacifiers" finally did the trick; Millie has a good memory. I knew Mom would sleep for hours, so Jenny and I had the afternoon to ourselves as long as we stayed in the house. It's Saturday so Jenny wasn't wearing a bra and that drove me crazy all morning, even before Millie had her turn. When she got up from the rocking chair, with her blouse unbuttoned and Millie still attached, there was something special about that image. I can't explain it. It was something like a painter would see. Maybe I'll study art in college so I can paint that picture someday. All I know is that I won't ever forget that split second.

Jenny took Millie upstairs to her bassinet and I followed along behind her. As soon as she put her down, I reached from behind and put my arms around her waist. I'd wanted to do that all day; then she turned around and kissed me. What happened later is probably not a story I'll tell Millie when she grows up.

A knock on the front door and the sound of it opening a bit put a temporary hold on anything more I had in mind. I walked down the stairs just in time to see Mrs. Brewster come through the door.

"Come in Mrs. Brewster. Jenny and I are just putting Millie to bed and Mom's taking a nap."

"I'm so sorry if I woke anyone. I just wanted to make sure everything's all right and I brought some sandwiches you can have now or for dinner."

"Hi Mom," Jenny said as she came down the stairs, and I checked to see that her blouse was buttoned. "Millie's been fed and she's sound asleep. I'll be such a good mother someday."

Jenny and I put the food in the icebox and I thanked Mrs. Brewster for bringing it.

"Just call if you need me. Mr. Brewster's having a good time with the boys this afternoon. It's been a long time since he had anyone to do boy things with. You should see the little boats they made. I think they're going to the park later to see if they'll float and I'll be home if you need me."

I thanked her again for the food when she left and locked the front door when I was sure she was far enough away not to hear.

Jenny turned on the radio, but kept the volume low and we danced a slow waltz together. When the music stopped, I walked her to the sofa and sat down, turned sideways and leaned against the arm. I pulled her to me so that she had her back to me and I could wrap my legs around hers. I like that feeling; her lying on top of me, and my hands free to explore. Her face was close enough to mine I could kiss her and reach everything else—until she squirmed and grabbed my hands.

"You're going to make me pee on your sofa and how will you explain that to your mother?"

"I'll just say, 'Mom, Jenny peed on the sofa' and she'll say…"

"You wouldn't dare."

It was getting late by the time we tore ourselves away from each other and I walked Jenny back to her house. We walked fast because I didn't want to leave Mom alone for more than a few minutes, although there was still time for a good night kiss and a check to make sure all her buttons were buttoned.

"I love you Jenny B. and if Mom feels like it, I'll see you tomorrow in church."

"I love you too, Emell, even if you are a little mysterious at times. Are you going to think about me tonight?"

"I think about you every night."

"And every morning in the shower, I bet. Go home and watch after your mother and Millie. Mom says the boys are staying here tonight."

Everything was quiet when I got home so I crept into Mom's room to sleep on my pallet next to her bed. She was awake and wanted to get up. I helped her stand and found her robe. She wanted to stay up until Aunt Doris got home. I was tired but I couldn't sleep with Mom awake. So Jenny thinks I'm a little mysterious, huh? I think she's the one who's mysterious. I learn things about her every day I didn't know.

Wednesday October 14, 1942
Afternoon

I don't have time to write much. I have to get back to the hospital to Mom and my new baby brother. He was born last night just before eleven. Both he and Mom are fine and I just came home to get a shower. I'm going back as soon as that's done. Jenny should be here any minute and she's going with me. We have a little more than an hour before the next bus so there's no rush. Maybe a shower with Jenny?

Friday October 16, 1942
Night

It has been a crazy three days…and I did get that shower with Jenny.

Tuesday afternoon when I got home from school Mom was in bed and didn't look so good, so I called Jenny and asked if she would come over. I checked on Millie and she was wet and hungry as usual. Jenny changed and fed her while I cleaned up the kitchen. Mom had left it after lunch and that wasn't like her at all. I was about to start washing the dishes when she came out of her bedroom.

"I guess I left the kitchen in a mess after lunch. At least let me wash the dishes."
I told her I would do it, but she insisted. Jenny came in the kitchen with Millie and the two of us sat at the table talking to Mom. When I saw her hands grip the side of the sink hard and her head droop, I knew something was wrong.

"Mom, are you okay?"

"Just help me back to bed. I don't think I can..."

She turned around and I saw her gown was wet and there was a puddle of something on the floor between her legs.

"Her water's broken," Jenny screamed. "We have to get her to the hospital right now."

"There's no emergency, Jenny," Mom answered in dead calm. "Call your mother and then the two of you can help me get cleaned up and dressed. My bag is next to the bed. Be sure to bring it when we leave."

Jenny called her mom and the great plan was put into operation.

We helped Mom back to bed and got her out of the wet gown. I ran for a couple of wet washcloths and Jenny and I gave her a quick bath. I can't remember ever seeing my mother naked before. When we finished, she sat on the side of the bed and I noticed her breasts dripping.

"Bring my bra and a handful of tissues. I remember this when you were born," she said, looking at me and smiling. "Your poor father needed a doctor more than I did by the time we got to the hospital."

Tears welled up in her eyes; not one escaped. I could hear the siren by the time we got her dressed.

Officer Mabry was cool as a cucumber, like he'd taken a dozen pregnant women to the hospital that day. When we got Mom safely in the back seat of the police car, she reached for Jenny and hugged her.

"Thank you Jenny for everything. I don't know what my family would do without yours."

I don't know if anyone was watching, but I gave Jenny a quick kiss before getting into the police car with Mom. She stayed behind and took Millie to her house. Of course we forgot Mom's bag, but Jenny brought it to the hospital and she was there when the baby was born. It was a long night, even though they let us stay with Mom until they took her to the delivery room. We learned a lot that night. I guess moms really do forget labor pains or they would never have more than one baby. Jenny and I held her hands when the pains came and it was hard not to cry. We sat in the waiting room with a man whose wife was also in delivery. He works at the shipyards and remembered when my father was killed. He didn't know Dad, but he talked as if he did, to make us feel better I guess. Everyone stared at the clock to make it run faster. At exactly six minutes to eleven a nurse came out and told us Mom and baby were fine. I asked if it was a boy or a girl and she wouldn't tell me. She just smiled and said we could come and see for ourselves. Normally only mothers and fathers are allowed inside the nursery, but she let us in. There was only one baby there and the nurse picked up the bundle and put it in my arms. It was a beautiful baby and I forgot all about whether it was a boy or girl. The nurse left Jenny and me alone with the baby and I handed the bundle to her.

"I thought it was a pink blanket for a girl and a blue one for a boy," she whispered. "It's white."

I looked around and the blankets in all the empty bassinets were white too. Maybe there's a wartime shortage of pink and blue blankets, I thought at the time. We could have looked on the basinet's nameplate to find out if the baby was a boy or a girl, but we didn't think of that.

"It's definitely a girl," I said. "Just look at her face. A boy wouldn't look that pretty, and look how she smiles. Boys don't smile like that."

"There's one sure way to find out," Jenny said with a grin as she undid the pin on one side of the diaper.

Everything was kinda swollen between the baby's legs, but there was no doubt about it, I had a new brother.

"Someday I'll tell him I was the first girl to see him naked," Jenny said with a grin.

After I held him a while, the nurse came in and put him back in his bassinet. She said we could see Mom in an hour. That was a very long hour and she was still groggy when we went in. She gradually came to her senses and I got to tell her she had a new son.

"A boy... Your father would be so proud. Does he look like a David?"

"He looks like a Sherry," I answered, "but Jenny and I had a look. He's a David for sure."

The nurse brought little David in and I asked her about the white blanket and she told me all the dyes used for unnecessary coloring have been restricted. I don't think there are too many pink uniforms out there; blue sure, but not pink. Mom had a long look at David and then asked us to take his diaper off. She pulled her hospital gown off over her head and reached for him.

"This is the way a baby should meet his mother," she said with a smile. "It's how I first met you and your sister."

The nurse put David on her stomach between her breasts and he just lay there. It was a perfect picture.

"Let's see if he's hungry," Mom said after a few minutes. "He's been through a lot."

She leaned up slightly and Jenny put a pillow under her shoulders. When Mom squeezed her nipple, a drop of milk came out and maybe David smelled it or something because he opened his mouth and moved around. Mom helped him and he latched on like he'd been doing it for months. It was a very satisfied smile that came to Mom's face at that moment.

"I had forgotten what it's like, having a baby nurse, but I remember it all now."

Jenny opened her mouth to say something, but I poked her in the ribs just in time.

We slept in the room with Mom and David the rest of the night. No one came to chase us out and Wednesday morning, they brought breakfast for all of us. I told Mom I would make a much better breakfast for her as soon as we got home. Aunt Doris came by on her way to work and brought a beautiful bouquet of flowers.

"There's something else that has to be done before we take David home," Mom said after Aunt Doris left. "I'll arrange for the doctor to circumcise him sometime tomorrow."

The nurse came and got David, and Jenny and I followed her back to the nursery.

"I don't want them to circumcise him," I told Jenny when we were alone in the nursery with David.

"Why not?"

"Do you even know what it is?"

"No, not really, I just know it's something they do to boy babies."

"Did you get a good look at David? Notice anything different about him?"

"No, he just looks like a boy."

I unpinned David's diaper and folded it down.

"Look closely. You see this skin? They're going to cut it off." I felt like an expert knowing something she didn't.

"Cut it off? Why? It looks fine to me; a little different maybe, but fine."

"I don't know for sure why they do it, but I know that's what they do. I've read about it in one of those baby books Mom bought."

Jenny and I talked about it for a long time before going back to Mom's room. We spent most of the day with her and caught the bus home in the afternoon.

Thursday morning I rode with Officer Mabry back to the hospital to bring Mom home with baby David—uncircumcised, but I got a warning from her that we would get it done later if there were any problems. I didn't ask what the problems could be and she didn't tell me.

Mrs. Brewster was at our house with the boys and Millie when we got home. She'd made lunch and brought it over. We were all hungry. When school was out, Jenny came straight to our house and I told her David came home with all his parts. I really don't see what the problem could be. He certainly pees just fine, and often.

Neither of Aunt Doris' boys is circumcised; I noticed that during the first bath I helped them with, and they seem to be okay down there. In fact they delight in showing me they can pull the skin back over their little wangers and wash there. Jenny taught me that word and I like it—or wang—better than some names I've heard. David will be fine. If there's a problem, Aunt Doris can help. Surely she knows all there is to know about baby boys.

Tuesday October 27, 1942
Night

Happy two week birthday to David, although we're already calling him Dave. Mom's doing very well and seems to have recovered completely. She's breastfeeding Dave and Millie now and it's a beautiful picture to see both feeding at the same time. That was Mom's idea and I guess Aunt Doris understood her wanting to breastfeed her granddaughter. Millie will be too old pretty soon anyway. Women are a lot tougher than men I've decided, but it has to be a little strange breastfeeding your son and granddaughter at the same time. We even made it to church Sunday and everyone wanted a look at the new baby. So far, he hasn't been any trouble. Mom and I completely forgot about a bassinet though and he had to sleep with her for the first few nights. Mrs. Brewster came to the rescue as always. She'd kept Jenny's and when she found out we needed one, she brought it down. It's nice knowing the bassinet that once held Jenny now holds Dave. It's hard to believe Jenny was ever that small. Dave's eating well and Mom has more than enough milk for him and Millie. For the first couple of nights, I stayed in Mom's room with her and the baby, but after that, she told me I could move back into my room. Even with Dave crying occasionally, I think her room was quieter than sharing a room with the boys. It's getting harder to get them to sleep now and Mike wanders all over the house in the middle of the night. I don't know if he's sleepwalking or what. I keep checking to make sure he's in his bed.

October 31, 1942
Night

Today we went to the christening of the ship Daddy was working on when the accident happened and Jenny and I got a real surprise. It was her, Victoria, sitting next to the wife of Captain Redgrave. I remembered who he was. He was at Dad's funeral and his picture's in the paper almost every week. So this is why my sister wanted me to forget what she looks like and why Annemarie was so nervous. Neither Jenny nor I got a good look at her before, but it was her for sure. We decided she must be someone important. She's a very pretty woman and she was dressed to the nines in the latest style. I have to find out more about her.

There were Halloween parties in the neighborhood, but Jenny and I stayed at my house and handed out candy to the trick-or-treaters this year. That was fun. Maybe I've grown up a little.

Saturday November 7, 1942
Night

Things have settled down at home after all the excitement baby Dave caused. Both he and Mom are doing well. Baby Dave, I like the way that sounds.

School is school. We get daily updates on the war from Mr. Jacobs and he tells us about all the new business E'ville is getting from the War Department. The Russians are still hanging on in Stalingrad even though the Germans are throwing everything they have into the battle. Mr. Mattox is still trying to get a peek down Jenny's blouse, but I don't think she believes me when I tell her. There's something about that man I don't trust. Maybe it's because he's so young. Teachers should be old, like my teachers were at Centennial. Even the young ones there were old. In art class Jenny and I have discovered we have no great talent for drawing, but that's only part of the class. We're also going to study the famous artists of the world and their paintings. We have to write a report this semester on an American artist and I already know who I want to write about and told Mr. Weimer. I've had a print of a Mary Cassatt painting on my wall for as long as I can remember. My father bought it for me when I was a baby, Mom said. It's called "Child in a Straw Hat" and Mr. Weimer knew it when I told him. Someday I'd like to see it in real life.

Victoria Meckler; that's her name and anyone important in this state knows it. The George Meckler Company has been around as long as anyone can remember and they're a huge government contractor for steel products. She wasn't hard to find. I just looked through the newspapers in our school library until I found the one with her picture and name in it from the christening. Mrs.

Landers, our librarian knew right away who she was when I asked.

"Victoria Apperton was her name before she married Charles Meckler. I remember her well. She and I went to school together here at Reitz. She was the most beautiful girl in her class and Charles was head over heels in love with her when he was a senior. They got married right after he graduated. That wedding was the biggest this town has ever seen. She was still in school and I remember she was quite pregnant at graduation. They had two children. Both are married now and living here in Evansville. She's still a beautiful woman; the most beautiful grandmother in Evansville most would say."

So my sister's girlfriend's not only beautiful, she's also rich.

Saturday November 14, 1942
Night

This afternoon there was a meeting about the Thanksgiving dance coming up a week from today. It will be at the USO this year. The Ironworks management has decided to open it to all servicemen in uniform. I guess that's why they moved it. City schools will be out Friday to help with decorations as usual and it's going to take a lot more time than before. I've never been inside, but they say the USO is huge. We have a lot to celebrate. British and American forces have invaded French North Africa and Eric says the French loyal to the Germans have been chased out without much of a fight. Jenny and her family are worried sick because the American soldiers involved in the operation were those stationed in Great Britain. They're waiting on pins and needles to hear from Jenny's brother. I just know he's okay.

My paper on Mary Cassatt is finally finished. I never knew about all the other famous paintings she did. In the library at school I found a book that had a photo of one in it that really caught my attention and I had to show it to Jenny. It's called "Maternité" and I love it, even more than the one of the girl in the straw hat. The young mother nursing her baby looks just like Jenny. Maybe her breasts aren't quite that big, but I bet if the woman in the painting wasn't nursing, they would be the same size. Mom's breasts are huge, although their normal size is small, like those of all the other women in my family.

Aunt Doris has volunteered to babysit if I can get Mom to go to the dance. She says that Mom needs to get out without baby Dave for a while and I think that's a good idea too. He's doing fine and doesn't need Mom to watch him every minute. Maybe I'll get Jenny to help convince her to go. It'll be her first time out since Dad died. I know it'll be hard for her, but she can't stay cooped up in this house forever. Dad wouldn't want that and she doesn't have to dance with anyone.

Monday November 16, 1942
Night

Yesterday Aunt Doris told me why she volunteered to watch the kids. She wants Mom to go to the dance, but she's also met someone at work and wants to invite him over after she gets everyone to bed. I think that's great. She's a beautiful woman who could easily pass for someone ten years younger. They haven't gone out together yet and she's not quite ready to introduce him to everyone, however she told me a little about him and said she's told Mom a little as well. I guess this is a chance for the two of them to be alone, or as alone as they can be with four kids in the house. He's from North Carolina and is divorced with no children. His name is Bob Crandall and he's a little younger than Aunt Doris, although according to her, not enough that it matters. I can't wait to meet this mysterious stranger who has Aunt Doris grinning like a teenager when she talks about him. I think she likes him a lot.

With a little convincing from Aunt Doris, Jenny, and me, Mom has agreed to go to the dance. She and Mrs. Brewster are going shopping tomorrow and that has Mom in a good mood. It's been a long time since she bought herself a new dress and she deserves one. She can't fit back into any of her others yet anyway. She told me it only took a few months for her to lose the extra weight after my sister was born, but a year after I was born. I can help with that maybe, starting this Saturday night. Dancing is good exercise and she can dance with Jenny and me if she doesn't want to dance with anyone else. She could dance with Mr. Brewster, and Jenny said she would talk her dad into asking her. I'm going to talk Mom into accepting.

Saturday November 21, 1942
Very late

Some very good things and some very bad things happened tonight at the dance. Mom was absolutely beautiful in her new dress, as I knew she would be. Mrs. Brewster talked her into buying a red one that made her look thirty-four instead of forty-three. She almost didn't wear it, saying it made her look like she was on the prowl for a new husband, but it's not that kind of red. After a little persuasion and making her look at herself in a full-length mirror, she walked out the door of our house looking like a million bucks. She knew she looked good and it was great to see her smile again.

We rode with the Brewsters in their Plymouth to the USO. Mrs. Brewster was stunning as she always is when she dresses up and Jenny wore a dress I'd never seen before. It was a beautiful yellow, which she knows is my favorite color, and she looked fabulous in it. I found out later it was her mom's and Jenny convinced her to shorten it, which turned it into the perfect dance dress. It was strapless and had a little white jacket that matched. She looked like a princess. I wish I'd taken Mom up on her offer to let me buy some new clothes for the dance, but I thought it was an expense we could do without.

We left an hour early so we could get a table and I was able to claim one for Jenny and me, and Mom and the Brewsters found one for themselves. We could've sat with them, but Jenny wanted us to have a table of our own like last year. We held hands under it when the lights went down and everyone started dancing. She's such a romantic. Little things like holding her hand mean so much when we're not able to be alone together. It's saying, "I love you and I miss being close to you" without using words. And then sometimes she just teases me, like tonight on the way to the dance. I was in the front seat and she leaned forward so her dad couldn't see her in the rear view mirror and pulled down the top of her dress just enough. She wasn't wearing a bra. Do they even make bras for strapless dresses? She laughed when I whispered later that I would make sure she kept her jacket on all night.

Mrs. Winston was at the dance with several students from Centennial and she came over to our table and sat with us for a while. When the band played a Viennese waltz, she looked at us and smiled. I would have asked Jenny to dance if she hadn't asked me first. It felt so good to hold her close again and we remembered every step of our old routine as if it we'd practiced the day before. With everything that's been going on, we haven't danced much lately. Everyone cleared a path for us, and for that song, we were back at Centennial practicing for the competition in Chicago. I guess that's what they mean by a magic moment. After that, we had all the dance partners we wanted. We were enjoying ourselves more than we had since last year until a very smartly dressed young man walked over to our table and asked Jenny to dance. It was Mr. Mattox and I guess we were both sort of surprised seeing him there and all dressed up; I sure was. It was a slow waltz, but Jenny kept her distance and I watched for any roaming hands. It's too bad he wasn't a terrible dancer. He was good, very good and after the music stopped, he brought Jenny back and sat down with us. We couldn't think of anything to talk about with him so we just sat there until the next song started. He asked Jenny to dance again and she put him off by asking him to get her a glass of punch.

"What's he up to, Jenny?"

"I don't know, but he's a really good dancer don't you think?"

"I think he has a lot more in mind than dancing. You're not his date."

"You worry too much. He's just being nice."

When he came back to our table with Jenny's punch, a tango was playing and he asked Jenny to dance. I couldn't believe she accepted and I accepted the first offer I got so I could be on the floor with them. He was all over her this time and I think her dad must have noticed because when we got back to our table, he was sitting there. She introduced Mr. Mattox as if she'd just met him herself and I noticed she never mentioned he was our teacher. Mr. Brewster gave him the once over—twice, and I think he got the message because he went back to wherever he came from. I didn't see him again the rest of the night.

Mom hadn't danced a single dance with anyone so I went over and asked her. It was a Rumba and I knew she knew the steps because I've seen her sort of do it with Dad who sort of knew it. She was pretty unsure of herself, but I led her and she followed, just like she always danced with

Dad and she remembered right away. When I walked with her back to her table, Mr. Brewster didn't let her sit down and led her right back out onto the floor. It was a West Coast swing and Mr. Brewster taught her the steps in no time. It was so nice to see her having a good time. I was a little worried with all the military men at the dance, but they were well behaved as far as I could see. Maybe it was because there were so many officers there.

Tonight was my first time to see women in uniform. They're called the Women's Auxiliary Ferrying Squadron or WAFS in the Air Corps and the Women's Army Auxiliary Corps or WAACs in the regular Army. Jenny noticed them too and said that the WAACs at the dance were the very first women to complete training at Fort Des Moines. How did she know that? To begin with, the WAACs only danced with each other, but our local soldiers were pretty determined and convinced some to dance with them. Photographers took hundreds of pictures of the couples in uniform. When another Viennese waltz came around, Jenny and I were out on the floor immediately. We didn't get to finish the dance together because two very pretty women in uniform cut in and we couldn't very well say no. The woman I danced with was best friends with the woman dancing with Jenny. They were both good, very good. I was perfectly happy leading or following my partner and after the music stopped, they followed us back to our table and we talked through the next few songs. We didn't dance with anyone else the rest of the evening. When the Brewsters and Mom came over to our table to remind us how late it was getting, we introduced our dance partners to them. Mary Ellen and Barbara were from Southern California and offered to take Jenny and me home after the dance. I don't know why Mom and Jenny's parents said yes, but they did; probably because they were in uniform.

The last dance was a slow waltz. I danced with Jenny and Mary Ellen and Barbara danced together. The lights were low and most of the couples on the floor were younger and pretty drunk. I pretended not to notice when Mary Ellen and Barbara kissed at the end of the song and maybe they pretended not to notice Jenny and me kissing. It didn't matter; no one was noticing anything by that time. They dropped us off at Jenny's house just after midnight and walked us to her door and thanked us for the dances we had together. Jenny and I turned to go inside and before Jenny could open the door, we were both spun around and kissed. It wasn't one of those kinds of kisses, although it was a real kiss. Out of the corner of my eye, I saw Mary Ellen holding Jenny's face in her hands just like Barbara was holding mine. We were both sort of caught by surprise I guess. Still, it was a very nice kiss and maybe I was a little flattered that a grown woman would want to kiss me. After we got inside, Jenny and I started breathing again.

Tuesday December 1, 1942
Night

Ever since the dance, Mr. Mattox has been especially nice to Jenny in class. Everyone's calling her teacher's pet and I don't like it one bit. I also don't like that he always seems to find us after school and make small talk, like he's carrying a torch for her or something. And maybe she thinks I don't see her when she unbuttons a button or two on her blouse in his class, but I do, and then she buttons them back just before class is over. She's giving him the look. She told me on the way home today that he called her twice on the phone over the weekend and that all her parents know is that it was some boy who called. Why would she even tell me?

"We didn't talk about anything, just school and stuff."

"It doesn't matter, he's our teacher and he shouldn't be calling you like you're his girlfriend."

"I'm not his girlfriend. You're jealous and you have no cause to be. He's just lonely and doesn't know anyone in E'ville. I think he's nice and only wants someone to talk to."

"I think he's just horny."

I wish I could have taken that back because Jenny didn't speak to me the rest of the way home. It was a terrible word to use, but I hear it all the time at school; I know what it means and I think that's what he is. If he's going to charm his way up Jenny's skirt, he'll have to go through me.

Sunday December 13, 1942
Very late

I think Jenny's been sneaking out of the house to see Mr. Mattox, or Jerry as she's started calling him. The phone book gives his name as Gerald and from his address I know he lives in one of those new apartment buildings near our church. I'm going to find out which one.

Yesterday afternoon, I called Jenny and asked her if she wanted to come over and help me babysit so Mom and Aunt Doris could do some Christmas shopping. She said she couldn't because she was going shopping with her Mom and Dad. I'm not normally a suspicious person, but something just didn't ring true. After Mom and Aunt Doris left, I called Jenny's house. Her mom said Jenny had gone shopping with some friends from school; that she was going to meet them downtown. I covered her story by saying I had forgotten and that I'd planned to go too but had to babysit. Last night when I called back and talked to

Jenny, she didn't mention anything about not going shopping with her parents and even told me about some of the things they'd bought.

Today in church, I noticed Jenny turning around and looking back several times before the service started. The last time she looked, she turned back around with a smile on her face. I turned to have a look for myself and there sat Mr. Mattox three pews back. The look I gave him would've killed him if we hadn't been in church. She was out with him yesterday afternoon, I just know it. After church, we stood around and talked with everyone like we normally do and Mr. Mattox walked up and joined in like he was an old family friend, and that's the way Jenny introduced him. When her parents came over, she introduced him as someone she met at the dance. I don't think Mr. Brewster remembered him. It was awfully dark in the USO that night.

Jenny and I usually walk home from church if it's nice weather. It gives us a chance to talk. She invited Mr. Mattox to walk with us today. When we got to her house, I said goodbye and kept walking. I turned around just in time to see them go into her house. What's going on? Am I being pushed aside for him? Jenny didn't call tonight. She has no idea what she's getting into and anytime I bring it up, she refuses to talk about it.

There was some good news this past week though. The Brewsters have finally received a letter from Jenny's brother. He's alive and well and Jenny and I figured out the code he used to tell us where he is. He wrote that he wished he could be home to take the family to New York on November twenty-sixth; that he would take everyone to the movies. Mrs. Brewster had no idea what that meant but Jenny and I figured it out. We looked up the new movies opening in New York on that date in *The New York Times* at school. We laughed out loud and got a stare from Mrs. Landers when we saw *Casablanca*.

Monday December 21, 1942
Night

We're out of school until after the first of the year and Jenny and I went Christmas shopping today. She agreed to go with me only if I wouldn't bring up anything about Mr. Mattox. I have no choice but to go along with her rules now if I want to spend any time with her. I can't believe she's being such a pushover for that wolf. That's what I've started thinking of him as, a wolf in sheep's clothing. There's only one thing he wants her for and I have no one I can tell. I keep having these awful thoughts, like my sister told me once, that someday Jenny would find a real man and kick me to the curb. How far have things gone between them? Jenny's not stupid, but this wolf has her thinking all screwed up. There's not one person I can talk to who would understand.

We split up for a little while so we could shop for each other. I already knew what I wanted to get her and it had a special meaning for me. We met back at Muir's Drugs and shared a hot fudge sundae. It might be our last for a while. There are rumors that sugar will be rationed beginning next year sometime. Not one word was mentioned about Mr. Mattox. I wonder if he's buying her a Christmas present. It was getting dark when we started for home, but we decided to stop off at the park anyway. We hadn't really been alone for a month and I wanted to hold her and kiss her. I guess I thought I could tell if she still loved me by how she kissed me. Although it had started snowing earlier in the day, it wasn't too cold out. We sat on our bench in the fading sunlight and I looked straight into her eyes with our noses almost touching.

"I love you Jenny and I've missed being with you so much I hurt inside."

I slid my hand inside her coat and under her blouse.

"Your hand is freezing; let's see how you like it."

I was glad to have her touching me even if her hand was freezing too.

When we kissed, she seemed like Jenny to me and for a little while I forgot all about Mr. Mattox. Maybe I've been making a mountain out of a molehill. On our walk back to her house from the park, we agreed to meet Christmas Eve at the same place to exchange gifts and I got a kiss on her dark front porch before she went inside. Maybe everything's okay after all.

Friday December 25, 1942
Night

Christmas morning at our house was crazy. The boys were up before daylight and I think I got about two hours sleep after helping Mom and Aunt Doris put up the Christmas tree. It was almost midnight when Aunt Doris and I got the boys to sleep and there was no way to sneak out. I just told Aunt Doris where I was going as I put on my coat and grabbed a flashlight.

"It's a tradition, I guess. Jenny and I meet at the park at midnight on Christmas Eve to exchange gifts. I don't know why; we just do."

"I know why," she said with a smile. "Just don't stay too long. We have lots of presents to wrap before morning and I have a surprise for you tomorrow. Bob's coming to Christmas dinner. I think it's about time everyone met him."

"I think that's great Aunt Doris and I promise not to do anything to scare him off. I'll be back in an hour and help with the wrapping."

It was still snowing when I left and just past Jenny's house I saw her up ahead of me. We walked together holding hands in her coat pocket until we came to our bench. She thought to bring a quilt, I hadn't, and we curled up together under it and kissed. It was a soft tender kiss with our lips barely touching; the kind of kiss that always makes me wish we were somewhere in bed together. I took her gift out of my pocket and this year I was not ashamed of the wrapping. I had the saleswoman at the store do it. It was a tiny silver necklace with a pendant in the shape of two small red cherries and green leaves intertwined. If you didn't look closely, you would think they were holly berries and leaves, which would be perfect for Christmas, but they were cherries.

"So you took my cherry and now you're giving me back two," she whispered as she kissed me again. "Is that the idea?"

"Yes, one of them is mine. Merry Christmas Jenny."

"So I have the ring, the steady charm for my bracelet, and now a necklace. Everywhere I look, I see something that reminds me of you."

"That's the idea. I don't ever want you to forget how much I love you."

"Oh, Emell, you worry too much. I'll always love you."

I didn't like the way she said that. It was like she was talking to her best friend instead of her best friend and lover, but I tried hard to put that thought out of my mind. After all, she had kissed me like a lover, not like a friend.

"I hope you like your present. I never know what to get you. Getting you that magazine subscription last year was about the stupidest present in history. I could've done a lot better."

"No it wasn't. That subscription to *The Writer* told me you believe in me and that I might really be a writer someday. It was the best present ever and I read every issue from cover to cover. I've learned a lot from it and I have you to thank."

"Then maybe you won't think my gift this year is so bad."

I unwrapped her present and smelled the scent of new leather. It was a leather bound book: *Far from the Madding Crowd*, by Thomas Hardy.

"I've read parts in the school library and I know you'll like it. It's a wonderful and tragic love story set in England."

I knew very well who Thomas Hardy was from my magazine and I knew the story. It's a tragic love story, she was right, still there's a happy ending I reminded her. Perhaps that's what she means to say to me in choosing that particular book, or maybe I'm reading too much into things. I do that all the time. It was a very special edition of the book in any case and probably cost a lot. I thanked her with a kiss and a promise.

"I'll be your Gabriel even if I have to wait as long as he did."

We trudged through the snow back to her house and had a final good night kiss on her porch. I really want to believe things are all right again. I have a plan. I'll beat this bastard at his own game without him ever knowing I'm competing. He's just another horny teenager, only older.

Christmas dinner at our house was perfect. Aunt Doris and Mom did most of the work while I watched after the kids. The babies are easy but those boys can be a terror. Just before dinner, I put them in the tub and gave Millie and Dave their baths. A couple of weeks ago when Mom was bathing Dave, she called me to come watch her.

"Okay, this is what we have to do. Since you wouldn't let me have your brother circumcised, you'll have to do this whenever you give him a bath. The skin they would have removed is called the foreskin," she explained as she gently took Dave's little wanger in her fingers. "You have to push it back until the head of his penis pops out, like this, and then you wash it with just soap, no washcloth. When you're finished, rinse it and make sure it goes back inside the foreskin."

I didn't bother telling her I'd already seen Aunt Doris's boys doing that during their baths. I guess she doesn't know they aren't circumcised and it wasn't something I wanted to talk about.

Penis—I know that's the right word and I really didn't expect Mom to call it a wanger. That would have been pretty funny. Unfortunately for Mom, baby Dave's wanger had a mind of its own and after she rinsed it, there was no putting it back where it came from and the more she tried, the bigger it got. I could tell Mom was a bit embarrassed.

"Never mind, it'll go down by itself in a few minutes, but always check on him to make sure it goes back inside. Mrs. Brewster says that sometimes they don't, which can cause a problem. If that happens, just put a little Vaseline on the end and it will slip right back…once it goes down."

I finished giving the babies their baths and didn't have any trouble with Dave's little wanger although when I pushed the foreskin back he peed straight up and I barely got out of the way. The end slipped back into its little cocoon, after I finished washing it, without any help from me.

We got a nice surprise when my sister came through the door with an armload of presents. We never really know when to expect her. She looked great and seemed happier than I ever remember seeing her. After dinner, I found out why. She's moving from Gear Town and into the home of Victoria and her husband as their housekeeper. That will be about perfect as long as her husband doesn't ask too many questions, or maybe asks the right ones. Bob showed up exactly on time and was the perfect gentleman all evening. I think we're going to like him just fine. Aunt Doris was like a teenager in love head over heels. She didn't even seem to mind that my sister was there, although they didn't really speak to each other. Even the boys were well behaved. They never ask about their real father anymore and that's okay with the rest of us. I just love the way people are during Christmastime. They are so much nicer to each other than during the rest of the year.

Chapter Four

1943
Friday January 1, 1943
Morning

This year there were New Year's celebrations all across the country. The president says the war has turned in our favor against the Japs and that the Russians are beating the Krauts at Stalingrad. The mood in our town is a lot better than it was this time last year; that's for sure. According to the newspaper Evansville has become the place to go if you're looking for work and just about anything else.

Aunt Doris wanted to go to a party last night with Bob so I volunteered to stay home and help Mom watch the boys. She can manage both babies just fine, but I thought it would be too much for her to have the boys by herself as well. I'd hoped Jenny would come over, but she said her parents wanted her to go to a party with them being hosted by her father's boss. So it was a pretty quiet New Year's at our house until midnight when all the fireworks started. I went outside in my pajamas and coat to watch for a few minutes, and then went back to bed. Aunt Doris wasn't home when I got up this morning and Mom was still asleep with the two babies in her room. I was cutting out the biscuits when I heard the front door open. Aunt Doris and Bob were standing in the doorway kissing. His hands were firmly grabbing her behind as she tried to push him away, but she didn't try too hard; pretty romantic I thought. She closed the door slowly and crept toward the stairs. I wasn't about to let that moment pass.

"And just where have you been missy? Do you have any idea what time it is?"

She took off her coat trying not to laugh, then hugged me and threw her open purse onto the kitchen table. She was beaming.

"I have had the most wonderful night. Bob is wonderful. Life is wonderful. We had a little too much to drink and his boss insisted we stay at his house. I hope you and your mother weren't worried."

"No, we weren't worried," I said with a huge grin as I picked up her bra and a hotel key from the kitchen table where they'd spilled out, "but really Aunt Doris, if you're going to make up a story, you should leave the key at the hotel next time and put your bra back on before coming inside."

She was much too excited to let anything I said bother her.

"You just have no idea how wonderful I feel this morning. It's like being in love for the very first time. Last night I wasn't anyone's mother; I was a woman for the first time in, I don't know how long, and he was a man, a real man. I know I shouldn't be talking like this, but I'm so incredibly happy."

So, Aunt Doris got a little loving last night; good for her.

Saturday January 2, 1943
Afternoon

Jenny didn't go to a party Thursday night with her parents. I went over to her house this afternoon and Mrs. Brewster said, without my asking, that she and Mr. Brewster had slept through the fireworks altogether. I didn't ask where she thought Jenny was. Maybe she told her mom she was with me. I could guess where she was or at least whom she was with. Last night I decided that confronting Jenny would be the wrong thing to do. From now on, Mr. Mattox will be the farthest thing from my mind. He won't exist and I'll make sure Jenny doesn't have a moment to think about him. I love her and she won't choose him over me. Somehow we'll be together tonight and every night I can arrange it. Mr. Mattox can't do that. If he's touched her, I'll know it and I'll kill him. I swear to God, I'll kill him.

I'm going to call Jenny right now and ask if I can come over tonight after everyone's asleep. I know my way to her bedroom even in the dark and they never lock their front door. This can work, and it's not the first time I've thought about it, but I never wanted to risk it until now. So what if I get caught; I'll make up something.

Monday January 4, 1943
Night

I got up my nerve and called Jenny Saturday night and asked her about coming over. I could tell someone was listening to her conversation.

"That'll be fine. I think probably ten will be enough. I'm looking forward to it. There shouldn't be any problem."

"I'm going to make love to you until your toes curl up and cramp."

"That sounds nice and I've been thinking about doing the very same thing, so you might have some competition."

"Do you love me Jenny B.?"

"Well, of course I do and I'll do everything I can to make things perfect."

"Do you still have that light blue T-shirt with the red design around the sleeves that I like so much? I know it's way too small now, but I think about how you look in it all the time."

"As a matter of fact, I do," she answered, "and I'm sure I can find it for you."

"Okay, I won't torture you on the phone any longer. I'll see you tonight at ten."

"That's a good time and I'll make sure everything is ready."

"So you won't be wearing anything but the T-shirt?"

"You'll have to find that out for yourself."

I had no idea what story she would make up in case her parents asked what that conversation was about, but I knew she would be expecting me.

Everyone, even the boys, was asleep before ten. Aunt Doris was out with Bob and I knew she wouldn't be home before midnight, or even Sunday morning if she got lucky again. She's been a different person since New Year's Eve and I like the new Aunt Doris a lot. It was easy for me to slip out of the house a few minutes after the clock struck ten, and the front door of Jenny's house was unlocked. I slowly tested the steps to see if they squeaked and made my way to her bedroom. The door was open and with the moonlight through her window I could just make out the lump on her bed. She heard me come in and close the door and pushed back the covers for me. She was warm and only had on that T-shirt, and we wrapped ourselves together like we'd been apart for a year. I'd missed her and Mr. Mattox hasn't touched her; I could tell from our first kiss.

Jenny noticed I was nervous as a cat, but I couldn't help it. Her mom and dad were just downstairs and could come up anytime.

"They're both dead asleep and won't be coming up here unless the house is on fire. I have something special planned for you tonight."

The smile on her face that came next didn't make me forget where I was or what would happen if I were caught in Jenny's bed, but that risk wasn't nearly as important as it had been just a minute earlier. She leaned over, turned on her bedside lamp and sat back on her knees, pulling the cover off me. I had no idea what she had in mind when her kisses moved from my lips down my neck and farther, though I was about to find out. "You're going to remember tonight, Emell and don't pretend you haven't thought about this. Your toes are about to curl up and cramp. It's time you knew what you've been doing to me."

I probably moaned a little. I don't remember. Of course I'd thought about what she did. It wasn't as if I could simply come out and ask her though. Soon she made me forget where I was and that her parents were downstairs. I may never pee in the shower again. When I finally stopped trembling inside and relaxed a little, I pulled her face up to mine and gave her a kiss I hoped would say what I couldn't put into words.

"That's why we'll be together forever," she whispered through a smile when our lips parted, "and one of the reasons you love me. You can't predict what I'll do next and that drives you crazy."

"And I suppose you know me inside and out now."

When I laughed a little, she punched me with her finger.

"That's not what I meant. You have a dirty mind."

She then turned her head.

"What color are my eyes?"

"A beautiful blue."

I leaned up from the bed, pulling her up with me, wrapped my arms around her and rolled over on top. During the next hour I don't know how many times she had to put a pillow over her face and scream into it. Then it was my turn to get a kiss because she couldn't speak. When she leaned over and turned the light out, what she did manage to say was perfect, like she'd been rehearsing.

"It's like being pushed off a cliff and suddenly realizing you can fly, or being a flower that blooms every minute with each being a more intense color than the one before. I'm talking crazy because I'm madly in love with the world's greatest lover. I have to be the luckiest girl in the world."

I waited until she was asleep and slipped out of bed and got dressed. That was the hardest thing for me to do. All I wanted was to curl up with her for the rest of the night. It was freezing cold on the way home. I didn't care. I crept up the stairs and into my bed and thought about everything that had happened that night. Blooming huh? I like that word for it. Maybe tonight was planned to show me there's nothing going on with Mr. Mattox. I shouldn't be thinking about him right now, not after the most wonderful two hours of my life. She got one thing wrong though; I'm the one who has the world's greatest lover.

Sunday January 10, 1943
Late

Fat-head Mattox was in church again today. He does have a fat head or maybe it's because he's so skinny his head just looks fat. I ignored him as he walked us home afterward, but when he asked Jenny if she was enjoying her Christmas present, I thought I would die. He bought her a Christmas present? I just kept walking and didn't listen for what she said back to him. When we got to her house, I told her goodbye and kept walking. I didn't say anything to Fat-head and I didn't turn around to see if she invited him in. How could she still be with him after last Saturday night? She doesn't unbutton her blouse for him at school the way she used to; I have noticed that. She didn't call tonight and I didn't call her. Tomorrow I'll pretend none of this happened. If she wants to talk, she will. I won't bring it up. My plan to just ignore him isn't working out too well.

Monday January 11, 1943
Night

When I stopped at Jenny's this morning, her mom told me she wasn't feeling well and wouldn't be going to school today. I knew what that meant and her mom knew I knew what that meant. Mrs. Brewster's a good mother, like mine, and she told me I could go upstairs and check on my best friend. She was on her way out to do grocery shopping with my mom like every Monday morning.

Jenny wasn't doing well at all. She was wrapped up in her bed quilts and didn't say anything when I walked in and spoke to her, but I kept talking. The electrical cord going from her bed to the wall told me the cramps were really bad this month.

"Are you okay, Jenny? I'm here and I'll be here all day if you want me to be."

"I want you to hold me when the cramps come and make them go away. I hate being a girl. It hurts so much."

"I'm glad you're a girl."

"It hurts so bad I couldn't even pee in the shower this morning."

I heard the front door slam shut. School could wait. I got under the covers with her and put my arms around her.

"But…my mom."

"She's gone grocery shopping with my mom and they won't be back for hours," I whispered in her ear. "We have the morning together. School can wait."

When the cramps came, I rubbed her stomach until they went away. It was as if some monster was inside her when her muscles tightened and cramped on their own.

"They'll go away in a little while, when my period starts, but they really hurt right now. I'm never having a baby if it's anything like this. You're so lucky not to have this torture every month."

The next cramp caused her to double over in pain and begin to cry. I can't listen to her cry. I put my arms around her and held her tight, trying to do anything to make it go away. She took my hand and pushed it farther down her stomach.

"Everyone does it."

I smiled and kissed her.

"Yes, but not everyone has someone to do it for them like you do. I love you Jenny B. and I won't ever let anything or anyone hurt you."

"He doesn't mean anything to me."

There were tears in her eyes and I didn't know if they were because of the cramps or what she said. She lay there next to me in my arms for a long time and didn't have another cramp. It wasn't just because of what I was doing; her period had started in a big way. Without saying anything, I slid from underneath her and went to the bathroom for a washcloth. While the water was warming up, she came in.

"I think it's going to take more than that. What we need is a shower."

She bent over and turned on the water to the shower and I saw a trickle of blood making its way down her leg. I guess I'd always wanted to see that for some reason. It didn't bother me and it didn't seem to bother her. It's just the way things are.

It'd been a long time since we'd had a shower together—since Mom was in the hospital with Dave—and the hot water and soap and being that close to her was even better than I remembered. She had to help me out of the shower my knees were shaking so bad. It's really hard doing that standing up—well, when someone's helping anyway. We dried each other and then changed the sheets on the bed before getting dressed. Jenny's mom had left the radio on downstairs and one of mine and Jenny's favorite songs came on as I was leaving her house; Gene Kelly and Judy Garland singing *For Me and My Gal*. It's funny that Judy sings most of it and it's like she's singing about her girlfriend. When Jenny called this afternoon she told me that I left only minutes before our moms showed up. I got to school just before lunch and when asked where I had been, I said I was with a sick friend, which was the truth. No one asked for any proof. Fat-head didn't have Jenny's blouse to look down today, but I noticed him looking at another girl the same way. I don't even know what the word is to call him, but I know who would.

Friday January 15, 1943
Afternoon

Lecher, that's the word. Mrs. Landers knew it when I described what I was looking for and when I looked it up, it was perfect: "A man given to excessive sexual indulgence; a lascivious or licentious man." I had to look up lascivious and licentious too and Mrs. Landers let her curiosity get the best of her.

"It's a very serious word. I hope you don't know anyone it fits."

"I wish I didn't, but I do and he's here at Reitz."

Mrs. Landers and I are pretty close and have been ever since she saw me reading my copy of *The Writer* at the beginning of the school year. I can talk to her.

"Mrs. Landers, what happens if a teacher gets too friendly with a student?"

"Well, all teachers are cautioned against such things, but it has happened, even here at Reitz and it almost always results in the teacher being dismissed at the end of the semester. In some cases, especially if the student is very young, there can be charges filed. It's a serious matter that has to be dealt with early before the student is emotionally harmed."

Emotionally harmed? That sounds really bad. I've thought about it all day and I think I should talk with Mrs. Landers again. She'll know what to do. Keeping this from Jenny is wrong, but I can't tell her. She doesn't see Mr. Mattox as someone who could hurt her or maybe she's carried away with all the attention an older man's giving her. I can't let it go on until he does something, and I know he will. Jenny's a beautiful girl and there can only be one thing he wants her for. I'm not just worried about the emotional harm he could cause her.

Eric said tonight that the British have started drafting women nineteen years old and older. I get the feeling things are a lot worse than even he knows. Kraut submarines are still sinking ships faster than we can build them. We only hear good news from the Pacific and now I'm wondering if it's true.

Monday January 18, 1943
Night

I have to write this down now. Eric said on the news tonight that the government has banned all sliced bread beginning tomorrow. It would be funny if it weren't true. What are we coming to?

Saturday January 23, 1943
Night

I did it. Tuesday at noon I told Mrs. Landers everything with the condition she would never tell anyone who told her. She didn't hint for a minute she didn't believe me. I don't know what I would've done if she'd doubted any of what I said. We had a long talk and she promised to look into things herself. She started that afternoon. She just happened to be outside where I told her Mr. Mattox usually caught up with Jenny and me after school. The lecher was right on schedule and she saw him casually pass a note to Jenny and walk away. I've seen him do that several times, but what happened next was not in Mr. Fat-head's plans. He didn't see Mrs. Landers walk right up to Jenny and take the note out of her hand. She didn't say a word and Jenny was too surprised to say anything. She was quiet all the way home. I didn't say anything, afraid of giving away my part in what had happened. If he called her later, I'm sure she told him everything, but he didn't act any different all week. There was another note on Thursday, but Mrs. Landers didn't get it. If Jenny keeps the notes, I can guess where she hides them. She has a heavy wood and metal jewelry box that came from her grandmother that locks. It's very old and looks like one of those strongboxes for holding money you see in western movies. The key's above the door on a nail inside her closet, but even if the notes are there and even if I could get them, she'd know who the thief was. I can't do that. All I can do is hope Mrs. Landers does something.

This afternoon Jenny and I went to the movies. We didn't get to see *Casablanca* over the Christmas holidays and we'd both wanted to. I guess most people have seen it already because the Rosedale was practically empty. Usually they show Westerns or something else for the younger kids on Saturday afternoons. There were no kids in the theater at all. Jenny and I got a seat near the back and covered up with our coats. It was freezing in there as usual. As soon as the lights went down and before the movie started we were wrapped in each other's arms. Jenny's first kiss was like no kiss she'd ever given me in a theater and her hands were all over me during the newsreel. We should've been paying attention. My eyes were closed and I recognized the voice of Ed Murrow from the radio, but I can't remember a thing he said.

"I've never let him touch me."

I didn't answer.

Someday we'll have to see *Casablanca*. Everyone says it's a great movie.

Sunday January 24, 1943
Night

"Thanks for Friday night." That's what the bastard said to Jenny today after church. He thinks I didn't hear him whisper that to her as he walked us home, but I did. She was with him Friday night and then me Saturday afternoon. I could kill him.

Friday January 29, 1943
Night

I skipped homeroom this morning and went to the library. Mrs. Landers had to be told what happened this past weekend. I thought about it all week and decided to talk to her again. She invited me into her office and told me she'd been watching Mr. Mattox and that as soon as she had enough evidence, she would go to the principal.

"What did the note say you took from Jenny?"

"I couldn't read it. They have some sort of code, but I kept it for evidence."

She took the note out of a drawer in her desk and handed it to me.

"KNNJENQVZQCSNRDDHMFXNTZFZHMEQHCZXM
HFGSZSLHCMHFGSLX
ZOZQSLDMSHKKADVZHSHMF"

"That bastard," I said under my breath as soon as I saw the writing. He'd used our code and I translated the message quickly. How could she have given him our code? It's ours.

"Can you read it?"

"No, no I can't. Thank you Mrs. Landers for everything you're trying to do for Jenny."

I stumbled over my words a little more and left her office as soon as I could. I have plans for that wolf and I don't want Mrs. Landers to go to the principal just yet. She would have if I'd translated that note for her. I don't want him fired. I want him arrested. So they're meeting at his apartment every Friday night at midnight. Tonight's Friday night and in a couple of hours it'll be midnight. Everyone's asleep and Aunt Doris is out with Bob. Fat-head might not have touched her yet, but if she keeps meeting him at his apartment, he'll have her out of her clothes soon enough and he knows it. I see through him. I know his little scheme. Either he just wants to fuck her or the sick bastard is in love with her and the only way he can have her is if she gets pregnant and has to marry him. Either way, he wants to fuck her. I knew that, but I hadn't thought what else he might want until now. If she gets pregnant before school's out for the summer, they can get married before school starts in the fall and the principal would probably turn a blind eye. Jenny's parents would be heartbroken of course, but if Mr. Mattox agrees to marry her, they would go along with it. They would almost have to, or send her away, and I don't think Mrs. Brewster could do that.

Saturday January 30, 1943
Early morning

I sneaked out at quarter past eleven last night and waited on one of the benches outside our church with my back to the sidewalk. It's a pretty far walk and I wanted to get there before Jenny. I had my coat and its hood on so she couldn't see who I was if she happened to look in my direction. I knew she'd have to walk past the church on the way to his apartment. At ten minutes before midnight, I heard footsteps. When she passed me without slowing down, I turned around. Her coat and long brown hair were unmistakable. I sat there and cried for a while and then walked back home, slipped into bed and cried some more. How many Friday nights has she been doing this?

Wednesday February 3, 1943
Night

I've known Officer Mabry and his wife for as long as I can remember, but I was trembling when I walked into the police station this afternoon and asked to speak with him alone. He was surprised to see me and even more surprised when I told him I was there on official business. I started out being very careful of what I said after he shut the door to his office. There was a little small talk about Mom, Aunt Doris, and little Dave before I got up my nerve and told him why I was there.

"I know you're not a priest or a lawyer or anything like that, but I need to talk to you about something important, and I can't if you have to tell anyone else."

"I only have to report what you tell me if a crime has been committed, otherwise it stays in this room."

"Well, I don't know if it's a crime or not, but it should be, and even if it is a crime, I can't say for certain it's been committed."

"Then there's nothing to report. Why don't you tell me what's bothering you and if I can help, you know I will. Your father was one of the finest men I've ever known, so if there's anything wrong, I want to know about it."

"It's not about my family, but someone I know. Let me just ask. Is it a crime when an older man has a young girl in his apartment at midnight without her parents' knowledge?"

"Well, just how young is this girl?"

"Suppose she's my age, thirteen."

"It's called lascivious behavior. Now I don't expect you know what that word means, but yes it's a crime."

"Oh, I know the word. I'm going to be a writer someday. Would the man be arrested?"

"Yes, he would be arrested and held until he can make bail in most cases. If there's been any sort of contact between him and the young girl, it's statutory rape and he would be held on those charges."

"What about the girl? Would she be arrested too, even if she hasn't done anything with him?"

"Whether she says the two of them have done anything or not, she wouldn't be arrested. In the eyes of the law, she hasn't done anything wrong, but he has, just because of her age. Now this is pretty serious talk. Maybe you'd better tell me everything you know."

"Would you have to tell her parents?"

"By law, her parents would have to be informed, but a lot is left up to the discretion of the arresting officer. If the girl hasn't been harmed and she says there hasn't been any contact, I personally would not inform the parents, but I would encourage her to tell them herself."

"Officer Mabry, if I called you at home at midnight this Friday and told you I knew for a fact that a young girl was in the apartment of an older man, would you come and would you come alone?"

"My phone is next to my bed and I would be there. All you have to do is call, and I never discuss work with Mrs. Mabry; this would be between us. If there's someone living here who's trying to corrupt a thirteen-year old girl, I want to know about it. We don't need people like that in our neighborhood."

I stood up to leave and Officer Mabry shook my hand. Before I left I gave him the address where he should come if I called and he gave me his home phone number. He told me I was brave to come and talk to him. I don't feel very brave. I feel like a rat.

Saturday February 6, 1943
Night

Last night I wasn't sure they'd planned to meet again, but they had. This time I followed Jenny instead of waiting for her at the church because I wanted to make very sure which apartment was his. I had it right when I wrote it down for Officer Mabry. After he let her in, I walked up to the door and wanted so much to just break it down and rescue Jenny. A million thoughts went through my head as I walked to the phone booth across from the church. I was crying when Officer Mabry answered the phone.

"Please don't hurt her. The girl's name I told you about is Jenny, Jenny Brewster and she's in his apartment now. His name is Gerald Mattox and he's our teacher at Reitz. Please don't arrest her and please, please don't tell her parents."

"Don't you worry about a thing. I know the Brewsters as well as I know your family. They're good people. Jenny will be fine and I'll make sure she gets home all right. I know who Mr. Mattox is too. I've seen him hanging around you and Jenny after church. He'll get to spend the night in jail tonight and if he's so much as touched Jenny, he's in for a lot worse. Now you go home and leave this to me. Everything's going to be all right, I promise."

I was shaking so hard when I hung up, I could hardly walk. Officer Mabry told me to go home, but I couldn't until I knew Jenny was safe. I stood beside the church out of sight and waited. He must've been expecting my call because in ten minutes the Mabry's Dodge drove slowly by the church. I made my way to the apartment building in time to see him drive up and park. When he got out I could see he was in uniform. Crouched down between parked cars, I had a good view of Fat-head's apartment. Officer Mabry walked right to it and the sound of his banging on the door could've been heard a block away. When the door opened a little, he pushed it open wide, walked inside and closed it behind him.

It seemed like an eternity before the door opened again and I was almost frozen to the pavement by that time. Mr. Mattox's hands were behind him, in handcuffs I imagine. Officer Mabry followed him. Jenny seemed okay and stayed behind Officer Mabry as the three of them walked to the car. He put Mr. Mattox in the back and then talked to Jenny for a while. I couldn't hear what was said, but I could see she was crying when she turned to get in the front seat of the car. They drove away slowly and I followed. When I got to Jenny's house there were no lights on and everything was quiet. I made it back to my house and into bed, but I stared at the ceiling the rest of the night wondering how Jenny was.

This afternoon I called her and asked if I could come over. She seemed to be glad I called and said she and her mom were just about to start one of Mrs. Brewster's experiments and that I shouldn't miss it. The afternoon was like any other Saturday afternoon and Mrs. Brewster's pineapple upside-down cake was delicious. She said she saved up her sugar rations for three weeks for that cake.

Jenny walked me home afterward and didn't mention anything about last night. She doesn't suspect that I had anything to do with it and I'll never tell her. When we got close to my house, she put her hand in my coat pocket and we held hands, just like we always do.

Sunday February 7, 1943
Afternoon

Today in church, the Mabry's sat behind us like every Sunday and after the service they talked with Mom, Jenny's parents and Aunt Doris, just like they do every Sunday. It really was as if nothing had happened, but before the service started, I didn't see Jenny looking back for Mr. Mattox. She and I walked home, her hand in my pocket. Everything's going to be all right.

     Last night Eric said the battle of Stalingrad is over. The Russians have won and the Krauts are retreating. It's the first time the Germans have been pushed back. Maybe this war will be over soon.

Friday February 12, 1943
Night

A substitute teacher took Mr. Mattox's classes this week. We were told he had a family emergency. The substitute is Dr. Haley and she's about a hundred years old, but she knows a lot. She's a retired professor from the University of Kentucky. I've never had a doctor for a teacher before and I like saying her name, Dr. Haley. It sounds so important. Mrs. Landers came to homeroom Monday morning and asked to speak to me. When we got to her office she told me Mr. Mattox had been arrested. I pretended not to know anything. She said Officer Mabry had told the principal earlier that morning and that he had told her, and only her, since she's also the assistant principal. She told me that she was going to turn her evidence against Mr. Mattox over to the principal right after our conversation and that she was sure Mr. Mattox wouldn't be back. She then opened a drawer and placed the note she took from Jenny on her desk.

"This is the only hard evidence I have and I don't know what it says. It will be my word against his."

I smiled at her and took the note.

"I might be able to help with that, Mrs. Landers."

After explaining the code to her, she translated the note.

"This is more than enough. I can assure you that lecher won't be back in our school."

I looked in the newspapers this week to see if there was any mention of Mr. Mattox's arrest but there was nothing and I'm glad. If the news gets out, some of the students might connect Jenny to it. Everyone saw the attention he gave her in class. So far, there haven't been any rumors.

Sunday is Valentine's Day and in spite of the cold, Mr. Brewster says he's going to barbecue. Jenny says he sometimes does it when it's snowing outside. I've got her a card already. *The Writer* sponsored a contest last fall for the best Valentine greeting. I entered about a dozen times, but I didn't win. The winners got cash prizes and their greetings put on cards for sale. I saw one that was just perfect and bought it. It's not one of those silly ones like everyone buys. Outside, there's a photograph of the night sky and inside it says: "Before you were in my life the stars shined, but I never saw them twinkle."

Sunday February 14, 1943
Night

A perfect day; there was no snow and no wind. After church, Mr. Brewster fired up the barbeque grill and cooked steaks for everyone. I'm sure President Roosevelt wouldn't have approved, even though we didn't use any rationed rubber or sugar. Jenny liked the card I got her and when we went outside to bring in the barbecue utensils, I got a kiss; a very nice kiss for it being in broad daylight and in her backyard. We didn't realize we'd been caught until later when Harry whispered in my ear that he'd seen us, but that he would keep it a secret. I whispered back that I would appreciate that very much. Both Aunt Doris' boys are such good kids. I think Bob should marry her and be a daddy for them.

Jenny didn't give me her present until my family left. I helped clean up everything and when we finished, Jenny asked if I'd like to go for a walk. We sat shivering on our bench at the park. There was a tear in each eye when she handed me the narrow bright red box. When I opened it, I looked around quickly and gave her a kiss. It was a steel bookmark with two interlinked hearts on top, made here in Evansville. I noticed that one heart was missing half of one of its humps but I didn't say anything.

"The salesman at Muirs offered to find me another one since this one has one heart that's damaged, but I knew when I saw it that it was the one I wanted. One heart is slightly damaged, but they're still connected, and I knew you would understand. I love you more than you'll ever know."

It wouldn't have mattered who was watching at that moment. I hugged her and kissed her with everything I had. Jenny Brewster loves me and life is finally good again.

Wednesday February 17, 1943
Night

When I got home this afternoon, Mom was walking through the house praying. Walking through the house praying; that's something no one else understands, but I've seen Mom do it lots of times and it's something I won't ever forget. She's not in this world when she talks to God like a best friend and neighbor who knows everything about her and the things that trouble her. I know she misses Dad and she talked to him as if he were there with her. Her beautiful voice was strong, loud and clear and it made me hope that someday I might be more like her. Her words weren't meant for anyone else but God and I feel fortunate to have heard some of them. She cried out to our Heavenly Father in a powerful voice, praying for strength and the wisdom to care for and guide those who depend on her. I felt like I was in the presence of someone who knows Him as well as she knows me. When she came back through to the living room, she noticed me, hugged me and prayed to God for His blessings on me. It was as if we were in the presence of the Holy Spirit and when the "Amen" came from Mom's lips, I was on my knees thanking God for giving me a mother like her. Things will be all right in our house, whatever happens to the rest of the world.

Saturday February 27, 1943
Afternoon

My sister showed up unexpectedly at school yesterday in a new car just as we were getting out and Jenny and I got a ride home with her. She looked good and said that her job at the Meckler's was working out well. She stopped the car at the corner instead of taking us all the way home.

"Do you think it would be all right if I brought Victoria around to see Mom? She asks about her all the time, but I'm not sure what Mom might think."

"I think Mom would see her as a wonderful lady who has been very kind to her daughter. Our mom loves anyone who loves her children."

"Yes, but you know there's more to it than that."

"Not to Mom there isn't. Let me talk to her first, but you should tell Victoria to keep next Sunday open."

Eric says the Krauts have started drafting women. He says this is an admission by the German government that they're losing the war, but I don't think the British are winning either. The only ones winning are the Russians and even if they are our allies, I don't trust them.

Sunday March 7, 1943
Night

When I told Mom on Monday that my sister would like to visit today and bring a friend along, she was as happy as I've seen her in a long time and insisted they meet us at church. There was something special about sitting next to my sister and Jenny at church today. She brought Victoria, and between us, Jenny's parents, Aunt Doris, Bob and the children, we took up the whole pew. It was one of those perfect pictures we never take but nevertheless keep in our memories.

After church, Mom invited the Brewsters to our house for lunch and wouldn't take no for an answer. Mom, Aunt Doris, Jenny and I worked all day yesterday preparing things and I'm glad she invited them too. I think Mom got the idea from me that Victoria's pretty important to her oldest daughter and Aunt Doris didn't think up an excuse to be gone today. The afternoon was perfect and Victoria stole the show. She was elegant and beautiful, but still insisted on helping us with all the food. She and her family are at the top of the social heap in E'ville, but you'd never have known it by the way she behaved. I guess I didn't realize that she, Mom, Aunt Doris, and Mrs. Brewster are all about the same age, and the women talked as if they'd known each other twenty years. They knew some of the same people and I noticed that Victoria didn't drop any of the really important names in our town even though I'm sure she knows all of them. Poor Mr. Brewster and Bob were left out, but they finally escaped and took the boys to the park later in the afternoon. Victoria made a point of saying several times how fond she is of my sister and how close the two of them have become, but it wasn't like she was talking about her as some kind of servant or anything. Aunt Doris was civil to both of them and I will always admire her for being able to be in the same room with my sister.

At the table, I sat next to Jenny and my sister sat next to Victoria. We held hands as we always do as Mom said the blessing. She mentioned Victoria in her prayer and thanked God for bringing her and my sister together. I almost laughed when she thanked God for the end of the ban on sliced bread that takes effect tomorrow. That's my mom.

Friday March 12, 1943
Afternoon

Mom wanted to talk this week, all week. She wanted to know everything I know about Victoria.

"Well I think Victoria is the best thing that's happened to your sister in years. Did you see how the two of them get along? I think she'll be a good friend and help your sister turn her life around."

"Mom, you do know they're more than just friends, don't you?"

"All I know is what I see and what I see is a very different daughter."

I let it go at that. Mom's such a realist. She sees the world as it is, not what other people tell her it is and that's just one of the reasons I love her so much. She's my anchor, firmly set in the real world while praying to God in Heaven. That's who I want to be.

Monday March 15, 1943
Night

It's not really news anymore but another new plant opened in Evansville last week and yesterday there was a big spread in the newspaper about it. There must be a dozen new plants already. We're making everything from ammunition to airplane engines right here. The newspaper said there are more new people showing up in town now every week than a year ago and that they're all looking for work and a place to live. There are no empty houses anywhere around here I know of. New students showing up at school almost every day has become normal. We don't bother learning their names until they've been around a few weeks.

I've started reading everything I can find written by Ernie Pyle. I've seen his articles in the newspaper before, but I never realized until recently that he's from Dana, up in northern Indiana about thirty miles north of Terre Haute. Mom says we have some distant relatives who live there. From now on I get my news from Eric, Ernie, and Jenny's mom and her Wives and Mothers Club. They find out stuff from letters they get even though they're censored. When Jenny's mom invited her to one of their meetings a few months ago, she dragged me along to keep her company. I thought I would be completely out of place, but soon found out I could be useful. All the women brought letters with them and talked about what they said, but there was no organization to the conversation. I picked up bits and pieces and when one woman, Mrs. Yarbrough, said she still had no idea where her sailor son was, I had the envelope she passed around in my hand and spoke up without thinking.

"He's in Australia."

Everyone stopped talking and looked at me.

"How can you possibly know that?" one woman I didn't recognize asked.

"It's all here. All you have to do is put together the little pieces of information each of you have. Different censors cut out different things and mail comes through different routes to get here. Mrs. Yarbrough said her son's letter is dated February twenty-sixth, but the postmark on the envelope is dated February twenty-fifth. How could the letter be postmarked the day before it was written?"

Mr. Jacobs' history class was paying off.

"That puts him on the other side of the International Date Line and the only place a US sailor could have mailed that letter from, unless he's a prisoner of war, is somewhere close to Australia."

It was like I'd performed a magic trick or something and soon all the women were digging out their old letters and giving them to me, wanting to know where their son or husband was. So I became a sort of unofficial member of the club. I've taken dozens of letters home from the meetings and Jenny and I piece together the information in each of them. It's like a giant jigsaw puzzle you don't have the box for and it makes Jenny and me feel like we're doing something for the war effort. Some of the ladies have already lost sons and husbands and from their letters we can sometimes guess where they were killed. That's the sad part about doing this, but it does seem to give them some consolation. We have funerals for servicemen killed in action whether their bodies have been returned or not. Most are being buried near where they died or at sea. For those who've lost loved ones, I think a funeral's important and it's important for the community to show up.

Saturday March 27, 1943
Night

Jenny and I went to the first baseball game of the season today. It was an early morning game so we got started right after breakfast at my house. We don't have the Bees anymore because of the war, but we do have the Blues of the Home Talent League and I've heard the city is trying to get major league teams to play some of their games here this season.

It was cold and windy in the bleachers, however Jenny and I were prepared with heavy quilts from home. We played a team from Indianapolis and got beaten badly. There was a good turnout for the game though, and it was something to take everyone's mind off work and funerals for a little while. We sat right behind our dugout and I think every one of our players flirted with Jenny sometime during the game. I told her that's why we lost; they were paying too much attention to her. I finally told one guy that Jenny was only thirteen, and he asked if she had an older sister. I've had to accept the fact I'm in love with a beautiful girl and that I'm not the only one who notices how pretty she is. Giving her a big kiss to let everyone know she's taken was what I really wanted to do and someday I'll do that.

It was a long walk home and it took even longer because Jenny had to do some window shopping. When we got to Peggy Hale's on Main Street there was a beautiful short little spring dress in the window she just had to try on. It was beige with a tiny floral pattern of pink and blue and was gathered tight at the waist. It's nice to see a little more color coming back in clothes. The neckline was cut low, too low and it looked really good on her. While she was modeling it for me, a well dressed older man and a young woman, who couldn't possibly have been his wife, came into the shop. He sat down while the woman looked through the dresses on a rack behind him. The man didn't try to hide the fact he was staring at Jenny and I didn't try to hide the fact I was watching him. When he left the shop and came back in a few minutes with an expensive looking camera, I got suspicious.

"Excuse me," he said to Jenny while ignoring me, "my name is Walter Evans and I'm the fashion editor of *The Press*. I was wondering if you would allow me to take a few pictures of you in that dress for our next Saturday's spring fashion edition."

At that point, I butted in.

"Could we see some identification please?"

The saleslady who'd been helping us disappared for a moment and returned with an older woman I guessed was the manager.

"Mr. Evans is very well known in this shop," the lady said to Jenny, "and when he brings models in to try on the latest fashions, he has the run of the place. If he wants to photograph you in that dress, I'm prepared to pay you a few dollars for your time."

"We want the dress," I interrupted before Jenny could open her mouth.

"I couldn't very well do that."

"Sure you could," Mr. Evans said with a smile.

"All right Walter, you have me over a barrel, but I want this girl's picture wearing my dress on the front page of the fashion section this Saturday."

"Done. Now dear," he said to Jenny, "if you would allow Miss Payne to assist you in getting ready, we can begin right away."

The pretty woman that came in with Mr. Evans led Jenny back to the dressing room. In a few minutes she came out and collected shoes, hose, hats, purses, bras, slips, panties, and other things I didn't even recognize...and a bottle of Houbigant Chantilly perfume. I had no idea what the perfume would have to do with taking Jenny's picture, but she sure smelled nice wearing it. And where did the hose come from?

"Just a few accessories we need," she said as she disappeared back into the dressing room.

"This is costing me a fortune," I heard the manager say to Mr. Evans, "and those pairs of hose are the last in the city."

"I can assure you, the result will be well worth it. In fact, if you're not one hundred percent happy with the spread on Saturday, I'll pay for everything myself."

When Jenny came out of the dressing room almost an hour later, she was transformed into a model any designer would kill for. The heels she wore made her look even taller than she already is and I knew the moment I saw her that the shop manager wouldn't be asking for her money back.

Mr. Evans took about a million pictures of Jenny in the store and then after some dressing room adjustments by Miss Payne, they moved outside. It was cold and windy but the sky was a bright blue, just perfect Mr. Evans said. After every few photos, Jenny had to come inside to warm up.

The photography session outside collected a crowd of onlookers. I sat inside mostly and didn't particularly notice the well-dressed lady and a boy a little younger than me when they came in. It's not really unusual to see boys in Peggy Hale's in the spring. They sell swimsuits this time of the year for boys and girls and they get them in before anyone else. When he came over and sat next to me, I guess he noticed me watching Jenny through the store window.

"She's beautiful, but the hat's all wrong."

"Really," I said with a smile, "and which one would you choose?"

He left and the next time I saw him, he was outside handing Jenny a different hat. She put it on and the photographing continued. When he came back inside and sat down, we started talking.

"It seems Mr. Evans likes your choice and so do I."

"You have a very attractive girlfriend."

"Who says she's my girlfriend?"

"If she's not, she should be."

"You think you know a lot. Who are you?"

"Roy Frowick, but nobody calls me Roy. Everyone in my family calls me by my middle name, Halston."

Friday April 2, 1943
Night

We walked out of Peggy Hale's with an armload of clothes last Saturday and Jenny had to put them all back on to show her mom when we got to her house. She couldn't believe they were free and that Jenny's picture would be in the paper wearing them. Jenny also managed to keep the bottle of perfume. I didn't ask if anyone knew she took it. We didn't tell anyone at school this week what had happened, but Sunday afternoon I got all the details from Jenny about her first modeling job.

"I never knew there was so much to getting dressed. If Miss Payne hadn't helped, I wouldn't have known how to put on half of it. I've never worn hose before and had no idea how a garter belt and garters work, but she knew everything. She had me try on five pairs of panties and she never found a color she liked. The garter belt was next, but she liked the first one she put on me. Hose were as big a problem as the panties and I don't know how many pairs I tried on before she found the right shade. The bra she chose was one of those new "bullet" bras in light pink. I wonder if they're made in E'ville. We make every other kind of bullet here. The slip was easy; she just chose the sheerest one Peggy Hale had in beige. The dress itself was perfect the first time she put it on me. She then put on my makeup and lipstick, but did nothing with my hair. The idea was for me to be someone who wasn't made up, although I was thoroughly made up. She spent some time choosing a hat, but after we started doing the shots, that boy in the shop brought out one she and Mr. Evans liked even better. He talked a lot and for a boy, he sure seemed to know everything about women's clothes. Maybe he'll be a famous designer someday. A lot of women's fashion designers are men, you know. Anyway, before we went outside, we went back to the dressing room and Miss Payne took off the bra, saying that I didn't need it."

That got me to thinking and Wednesday afternoon when we got home from school there was a note on Jenny's dining room table saying that her mom had gone to the Willard library for some special Wives and Mothers Club meeting and wouldn't be back until six.

"I want to watch you get dressed like you did for the pictures Mr. Evans made."

"I thought you might," she said with a smile and then she kissed me. "You seemed awfully interested when I was talking about it Monday and I decided then I wanted to get dressed for you sometime. But you have to help me undress afterward."

Watching her get dressed was almost better than watching her get undressed.

Saturday April 3, 1943
Night

There was one half-page picture of Jenny on the front page of the fashion section of the paper and six smaller pictures on the next page. Jenny and I were standing in her front yard this afternoon waiting when the paper was delivered. The half-page picture is my favorite. It was taken outside and has Jenny holding her hat with one hand and her dress down with the other just when a gust of wind came up. Her dress blew up enough to see one of her garters in the photo if you look closely. She's facing into the wind and everyone will think it's the bra pushing through her slip and dress, but I know different. Oh, and the dress looks good too. Her pictures would pass for those of any professional eighteen year old model in the best fashion magazines. The only thing I don't like is that Jenny's name wasn't mentioned anywhere. Maybe that's a rule or something. Her mom took one look at the pictures and tears came to her eyes. Her father hit the ceiling and grounded her for a month.

Wednesday April 14, 1943
Night

There's a new celebrity at Reitz and her name is Miss Virginia Brewster. All the girls are jealous and all the boys are horny. I was expecting both. Since she's been grounded, the only time we get to talk is at school and walking to and from. She says her mom is pleading her case with her dad though, and that she might get some time off for good behavior. I'm not allowed to go over to her house and she can't come to mine. We haven't been apart this much since they moved into the neighborhood and I miss her so badly. I guess Mr. Brewster figures he's punishing me too because I didn't talk Jenny out of the fashion shoot. At least I can still walk with her to school and back and her mom says we can sit together at church. Maybe we'll just write long love letters to each other before peeing in the shower.

Two seniors have already asked her to the Junior-Senior Prom but she can't go because she'll still be grounded, and she's only a seventh grader anyway and you have to be in the eighth before you can be asked. I guess the boys who asked her thought she was old enough. That's one less thing for me to worry about for now, but there's always next year and she'll be asked again by some handsome boy. I don't like thinking about it.

There's some very good news in our house. Bob has asked Aunt Doris to marry him and she's accepted. She told me yesterday even before she told Mom and I said it was about time he made an honest woman of her. The wedding will be June twelfth and I was glad to hear that it'll be a church wedding. She says they don't want a big to-do over it, but I know Mom will ignore that. She loves weddings.

Sunday April 18, 1943
Late afternoon

Today on the way home from church—we still get to walk home from church together—Jenny wanted to talk.

"You knew how much I wanted that dress and I knew how much you wanted me to have it."

"It's a beautiful dress and you look great in it. It'll be perfect for Easter next Sunday." I smiled and continued, "I have to say it was one of the best deals I've ever made."

"There was a little more to it than you know."

"You didn't sign anything; the dress is yours fair and square."

"It's nothing like that. You remember Miss Payne and how helpful she was, right?"

"Sure, she seems like a very nice lady."

"Well, she is, but she was more than just nice that day."

"What do you mean, 'more than just nice'?"

The expression on her face told me the answer to that question.

"It's not what you think… Well, it probably is what you think, but it's not what else you think. In the dressing room, there was a bench and she sat on it as she kept changing my panties, trying to find a pair that couldn't be seen through my slip and dress outside in the sunlight. To change panties, I had to take the dress and slip off as well as the garter belt and hose. It was a lot of trouble and she had to do it because I didn't know how everything worked. She finally decided I should go without panties and just wear the garter belt and hose."

"You mean in all the pictures Mr. Evan took, you weren't wearing panties?"

"Why do you think I was trying so hard to hold my dress down in the wind? Anyway, after getting me into the fifth pair of hose—out of nowhere she leaned forward and...she kissed me."

"No, Jenny. That's enough and please don't ever tell me what happened next."

"Nothing else happened. I don't know why she did it. It just happened. I didn't plan it and I don't think she did either. How could she? She apologized and said she didn't know what had come over her and I believe her and I really wanted that dress and she'd been so nice helping me and all. She didn't try anything else and I didn't kiss her back, I promise."

"There are some things you shouldn't tell me Jenny. I'll never be able to look at you in that dress again and you'll be struck dead if you wear it Easter Sunday. Every time I see your picture in it, all I'll think about is her."

"But it didn't mean anything. It just happened and it won't happen again."

"Earthquakes just happen, not things like this."

We were at her house by that time and I just kept walking; she didn't have to tell me all that stuff. Isn't it enough that every boy in school is horny for her; now I have to worry about grown women too.

Monday April 19, 1943
Early morning

I didn't sleep much last night and I have to get up in a few minutes. Is this the way it's going to be forever? If it's not some horny teacher or senior, it's a complete stranger—and a woman. I've been thinking about how I would have reacted in that situation and I don't have a good answer—not that it would ever happen to me anyway. Maybe I'd do the same thing, just let it go, but I don't think I could ever tell Jenny. Anyway, she didn't do anything. That's right. Jenny didn't do anything…and she did tell me about it and it won't happen again. If she doesn't mention it today, I won't, but I don't want to see her in that dress again ever. If I hadn't bargained for it, none of this would have happened. What a SNAFU. I learned that word from a magazine I read in the Willard library last year and I know what it really means.

Saturday May 8, 1943
Night

Nothing else has been said about what happened and I'm never going to bring it up again. I don't think it'll be one of those things we laugh about years from now.

Jenny's not grounded anymore and this afternoon we went to the movies. It was the first time we've been out in over a month and I had no idea how famous she'd become in our corner of E'ville. I must have heard "Hey sugar, are you rationed?" a hundred times today from complete strangers; from men old enough to be her father to a boy who couldn't have been more than ten; some knew her name. They completely ignored me except for one boy who looked eighteen who wanted to know if I was Jenny's cousin. We had no privacy in the theater either. Boys sat all around us and talked so loud I couldn't hear Jenny or the movie. After the movie, there were six offers of a ride home. When I saw a group of boys following us, I got a little worried, but we eventually lost them. Jenny said her father was still mad and that the dozens of phone calls for her weren't helping any either. I hope all this fame goes away soon. It's driving me bananas.

Tomorrow's Mother's Day and I'm hoping my sister comes. I helped the boys make a card for Aunt Doris. It's really cute with things they cut out of magazines pasted on it. Blackman's Florist gave me a good deal on a bouquet for Mom and I'm going to make breakfast for everyone.

Saturday May 15, 1943
Night

Yesterday was the last day of school; we all survived our first year at Reitz. I'm so glad school's out. Maybe things can get back to normal now, and we have a wedding to plan. Mom's already sent out invitations, without Aunt Doris knowing, and I bet half the town shows up. Wedding dresses aren't rationed, not yet anyway, and Mom and Aunt Doris went shopping for one today. I knew it would take all day so I invited Jenny over to help me watch the kids. We didn't get much time alone, but at least we were together. What we need is a vacation, but no one's getting vacations, what with the war and all. Anything made of rubber is rationed and that definitely includes car tires so there are no unnecessary trips anywhere.

I just had a funny thought. I wonder if the rubber shortage is hurting business in Gear Town. I'm so glad my sister doesn't live there anymore. She showed up for Mother's Day and that was nice. She looks good and seems to be very happy. Victoria didn't come with her. I guess her children were visiting.

Monday May 17, 1943
Night

This girl, Caitlan Propst, who's a fourth grader at Centennial, and her mother Mary Ruth live two houses down from Jenny. She says her unusual name comes from a combination of her parent's names, Kate and Lanny. Mr. Propst is some high ranking naval officer and Jenny's mom says they haven't heard from him in a while. Mrs. Propst and Mrs. Brewster are good friends and Caitlan sometimes comes over to Jenny's on Saturday or Sunday afternoons when I'm there. Anyway, Caitlan and her mom came over to my house Saturday afternoon after finding out where we were from Jenny's dad. I could tell Mrs. Propst had in mind to ask Jenny to watch Caitlan because she showed up with sandwiches and what looked like a change of clothes. When she saw that Jenny and I already had four little ones to watch, she didn't ask, so I just volunteered for both us in a roundabout way.

"You know, Mrs. Propst, we could really use some help watching this bunch today. Do you think you could spare Caitlan for a little while? She would be a lot of help to us and it might be good training for her. She'll be babysitting on her own pretty soon and I'm sure Mom and Aunt Doris would want her to watch Dave and Millie if Jenny and I aren't around."

"How about it Caitlan?" her mother asked. "Would you like to stay and help? It would be good experience and you could indeed have a babysitting job yourself in a couple of years and you need to learn all you can now while you have these two as teachers."

Of course Caitlan was all for that and Mrs. Propst, who knew very well what Jenny was doing, thanked us before she left. She didn't say where she was going, only that she would be back before dark.

Jenny and I had already fed Dave and Millie, so I knew the next thing they would need would be changing. Dave is easy but Millie's older now and what she leaves in her diapers is enough to scare anyone so I changed her first. I told Caitlan she could change Dave.

"But I've never changed a diaper before on a real baby, just dolls."

"It's easy. I'll show you and you can do it next time."

After I got Millie changed and on a pallet in the floor I sent Caitlan for a warm washcloth while I tried to do something with the present Dave left in his diaper. I decided a bath was easier than trying to clean him up so I sent her back to fill the sink with water. We still bathe Dave in the sink and he loves it. Mom and I have started taking Millie into the tub with us for her bath. When Caitlan had the sink full of warm water, I picked Dave up, and holding him out away from me, headed for the kitchen. That was a mistake. I don't know if maybe there was a draft in the house or what, but his little wanger was starting to grow by the time I got to the kitchen with him. I've learned that if it does that while I'm changing him, it usually means he's about to pee and I didn't want him to pee in his bathwater, although he usually does anyway. I thought about yelling for Jenny, but she was outside with the boys and I didn't want her to leave them. Caitlan got an eyeful when I sat Dave down on the edge of the sink. His wanger pushed out of its skin all the way, but he didn't pee. It was just sticking out there, and for some reason I thought I had to say something.

"It seems to want to be washed first," I said with a laugh, "so that's the way it'll be."

"Boys are sure different down there aren't they?"

"Is Dave the first baby boy you've had a look at?"

"No, no, of course not. I mean yes, he is," she said in a whisper.

Caitlan got a quick lesson in the difference between boys and girls "down there" and Dave loved every minute of it. As soon as we put him in the warm water, his wanger went back into hiding.

"But you were going to wash it first."

"We'll save it to last and I'll show you something I've learned about boy babies."

When baby Dave was clean as a whistle, I lifted him out of the water and sat him back on the edge of the sink.

"Watch this."

I took a deep breath and blew it on his wanger. It was much easier than trying to force it out with my fingers. When it was out again, I took a little soap on my fingers and rubbed it in and then took the sink sprayer and sprayed it. Dave didn't mind at all; nice and clean again. Another good thing I learned about baths is that babies will go right to sleep afterward and Dave was asleep by the time we got his diaper on. Millie was already asleep. Caitlan went outside with Jenny and the boys while I cleaned up the sink.

Jenny came in and began making a pitcher of Kool-Aid for all of them, which gave us a few minutes alone. While she stood at the sink filling the pitcher with water, I reached around her and slipped my hands up her blouse. It was Saturday, so no bra. She pretended not to notice what I was doing until it got to be too much. When she turned around, I gave her a kiss I'd been saving all day. It was one of those whole-body kisses that make us both crazy.

"I'm going to drag you upstairs if you don't stop."

"Promise?"

That was as far as things got. We didn't dare leave those three in the back yard for very long. Those wild Indian boys would have had Caitlan tied to a tree. Jenny took the Kool-Aid out with some cookies and I used the lull for a chance to sit down on the sofa and close my eyes for a few minutes. I must have dozed off because when I opened my eyes again, Caitlan was sitting on the sofa just looking at me.

"Do you think Jenny's pretty?" she said out of the blue. "I think she's really pretty. Is she your girlfriend?"

It took a moment for me to wake up all the way and give her an answer.

"Yes, I think Jenny is very pretty and she is a girl and she is my friend."

"I saw you kiss her in the kitchen when she came in to make Kool-Aid. I wasn't spying; I just looked through the window in the door and saw you. I won't tell anyone. You're not mad at me are you?"

"Of course I'm not mad at you. Jenny's been my girlfriend since I was not much older than you, but it's a secret only a few people know and now you're one of them. Can you keep a secret?"

"I can keep a secret forever. I promise never to tell, but you'll tell everyone someday won't you?"

"Yes, someday, when we're older but for now, it's a secret."

Mom and Aunt Doris got home about mid-afternoon and Jenny and I annoyed Aunt Doris until she went upstairs and put the new wedding dress on. It's nice, but it doesn't look much like a wedding dress to me. It's not even white.

Thursday May 20, 1943
Night

We went to the pool today for the first time this year. It just opened on Monday and the water wasn't very warm. Jenny has a new swimsuit her mother bought for her. She doesn't like it much because, even though it's padded, when it gets wet all the boys stare until she can get her robe on. One boy needed punching when he came up to Jenny and me and announced he sleeps with her picture from the newspaper every night. I told him to enjoy it because that was as close as he would ever get. He gave me the finger and walked off.

We got our first "War Ration" book of stamps last week. I had no idea they were going to ration so many things, but Mom's been preparing. We have enough dried beans and Ketchup to last us into the next century. Mom and Mrs. Brewster bought the last freezer in all of Evansville and it's filled with meat and butter. Everyone seems to think that, even with rationing, we'll have plenty, but they want to make sure. The problem is, after Aunt Doris moves out, there'll be no one in the house with a job critical to the war effort which means we won't get much gas for our car. Mom's already filled the car up and filled two five gallon metal cans. That'll have to last us a long time.

Sunday May 30, 1943
Night

Today was Memorial Day, or Decoration Day as a lot of people still call it, and the parade through town was bigger than ever. Mr. Evans, the photographer, convinced Jenny it was her civic duty to appear on a float...wearing a new swimsuit from Peggy Hale's of course. I don't really see what that could have to do with Memorial Day, but at least she wasn't the only pretty, half naked girl in the parade.

Her father knew about the float and didn't ground her this time. Maybe he thought it was for a good cause or something. Naturally she was beautiful and just as naturally, she was the center of attention at the end of the parade. I brought a robe for her and she put it on as soon as the float stopped. She walked home wearing it, with me by her side fighting off the boys.

"She's someone's girlfriend," I yelled at the last two boys escorting us home—I recognized them from Reitz—" and if you don't want me to report that a couple of horny high school boys followed us home, you'd better get lost."

"What are you; her bodyguard or something?"

"Yeah, I am and I can tell you it's a body worth guarding, now scram."

I don't know why I said that last part, but I'm glad I did. When we got to Jenny's house, there was no one home and as soon as we got inside, she pushed me back against the door and kissed me like I'd saved her life.

She then whispered in my ear, "So who's going to save me from my bodyguard?"

Jenny and I have a birthday coming up and what I would like more than anything is to get out of E'ville with her and go somewhere—anywhere.

Saturday June 5, 1943
Night

This year we decided to celebrate our birthdays on Jenny's birthday. It was Saturday after all and a perfect day. It was warm and Jenny wore her shortest shorts. She really could be a model someday. She could be another Jane Greer or Anne Gwynne, the swimsuit models. Jenny looks like a million bucks in a swimsuit. Mr. Evans has already told her he wants to take some more photographs this summer. Who knows, she might really make it as a model.

Aunt Doris's wedding is only a week away and I've been helping Mom get ready. In spite of that, I found a little time to shop for Jenny's present. I didn't have much money to spend, as usual, but I met an Army Air Corps soldier at Muir's while I was shopping for her present and he was wearing a pair of sunglasses like I've never seen before. I asked him where he got them and he said they were only available on base, and that he could get me a pair for five dollars. A few days later we met again at Muir's when he came to pick up the ring he was having engraved for his girlfriend and he had the sunglasses. They're gold plated metal with dark green lenses and have their own leather case. I spent every cent to my name, but Jenny'll look great in them.

Jenny's mom insisted on a cake and we didn't argue very hard, although cakes are rare with the sugar rationing we've had to live with. I wonder why sugar's rationed. Rubber, I understand, but sugar; what is the military doing with sugar, making sugar bombs to sweeten up the Krauts? The cake was coconut this year and Mrs. Brewster found twenty-eight candles to put on it; fourteen for each of us. I guess everyone was hungry for cake because we all had seconds. We even had ice cream. Mrs. Brewster used syrup instead of sugar in the recipe and it was really good. You can't get ice cream in town anymore. Mike and Harry turned the churn until they couldn't and then Mr. Brewster took over when his barbecuing duties were finished.

After lunch, Jenny and I helped Mrs. Brewster clean up and then we went for a walk to our favorite park bench. We should carve our initials on it or something. Since the weather was so nice, there were lots of families out, so our birthday gift exchange had to be pretty proper and not at all what we wanted.

"So, who goes first?" I asked.

She reached with both hands toward me and grinned.

"I would win, you know, so I get to choose and I want you to open mine first."

As usual, her gift to me was beautifully wrapped and I tried not to destroy the work she put into it. Inside the wrapping paper was a box, a pale blue box. I didn't know what the horseshoe shaped object was at first, although I knew it was silver and that it looked expensive.

"It's a key ring and I want your car keys on it someday, but for now this key will have to do."

She took the cardboard thing out the key ring was attached to and under it was a silver key, but it wasn't really a key. The engraving on one side read: "The key to my heart; don't lose it." I got the shock of my life when I turned the key over and read: "Tiffany and Co. Makers Sterling Silver 925-1000".

"Jenny, I can't accept this. It's much too expensive. Even I know what Tiffany's is. I love you more than anything in this world, but this is too much."

"Would you take it if I told you all I paid for was the engraving?"

I guess I must have looked as if I didn't believe her.

"Mr. Evans does some photography for Tiffany's and they sent him enough of these for all his models."

"All his models; how many does he have?"

"He has six but only Lisa and I live here. The others live in Indianapolis and Chicago."

"Lisa? Is that Miss Payne?"

"Yes and don't worry, she hasn't done anything since that one time. Mr. Evans would like some outdoors pictures of us next week. He wants my hair a little darker and Miss Payne said she would help with that. She said it would wash right out. I hope you can come."

"Wild horses couldn't keep me away and I'll be watching Mr. Evans and Miss Payne. I thought he was just the photographer for *The Press*. Are you getting paid for any of this?"

"Not exactly. I get to keep the clothes and if the pictures sell, I get paid, but Mr. Evans says that right now, just getting my photographs out there is the most important thing."

"Do your parents know about this?"

"Daddy would kill me, but I thought that if someone does buy the photographs, I could tell him then and he would see it as me contributing something to the family. I know...I don't believe that either, but I can't tell him now and I can't miss this opportunity either."

"Just promise me you'll wear panties this time and not let Miss Payne help you dress."

"I promise. Now do I get to open my present?"

Jenny liked the sunglasses and she looked like a movie star wearing them. I love the key ring. I've never had anything from Tiffany's before, but someday, I'm going to New York and I'm going to buy Jenny something there in person.

Saturday June 12, 1943
Very late

Aunt Doris was a beautiful bride and the wedding went off without a hitch. Since she had insisted on a simple wedding, Mom and I couldn't talk her into having bridesmaids, but she did agree to have Mom as her Maid of Honor, or as Jenny corrected me, Matron of Honor, and Caitlan as her flower girl. She's a little old to be a flower girl, but she wanted to do it. Bob chose Mr. Brewster as his Best Man and they both looked very handsome. The church was full with all the people we'd invited, and as a wedding present, Jenny arranged for Mr. Evans to do the photography for free. The reception was held at the USO club and no one paid too much attention to who was drinking the champagne. Jenny and I had our own bottle. There wasn't a live band, but the music was perfect for dancing and I think everyone got a dance with the new bride, including me.

"Do you know what I would really like?" Aunt Doris asked as we were dancing our second dance, and I could tell she was a little drunk, "I would like to see you and Jenny do that waltz thing. You know which one I'm talking about; the one where you spin around a lot. Do you think the two of you could teach Bob and me how to do that?"

"When the crowd thins out a little and everyone left is a little drunk, I promise we'll do it."

"You know, the two of you have something very special that most people would kill for. I don't pretend to understand it, I'm old; but I'm your mother's sister and, like her, I see the world for what it is, not what someone tells me it is. Do you love her so much you can't sleep at night? Do you wake up in the mornings hoping she's next to you? Do you want to dance naked with her in front of a thousand people?"

I kissed her.

"Aunt Doris, you understand it all…and you're not old. Now, you're a new bride and I expect you to behave like one on your honeymoon."

"It's not going to be much of a honeymoon. Bob and I had to sell our souls for three days off, but that's the best anyone will get until this war's over. We're going to Chicago and stay in the finest hotel in town and I'm not going to let him out of bed except to pee."

"The Drake?"

"How did you know?"

When the "Blue Danube" started, I walked over to Jenny and offered her my hand and she took it without a moment's thought. Our routine came back as if we'd practiced this morning. Everyone stepped back and gave us the floor. We were a little tipsy so we missed a few steps, although no one knew. The change-up from me leading to her leading was perfect and our fleckerls were pretty good too. I held her close, the way the dance is intended and we moved as one over the entire dance floor. We danced naked in front of a thousand people, except we weren't naked and there weren't a thousand people. The ending was supposed to have us just touching noses, but when we got there, we touched noses and then kissed. It wasn't a romantic kind of kiss, just a kiss, but it was in front of everybody and the building didn't collapse and no one fainted.

Tuesday June 15, 1943
Night

Aunt Doris and Bob should be back from their honeymoon tomorrow. It's been extra work watching the boys without her, but Mom and I managed. She says Bob has found a house not too far from ours. The lady living there lives alone and wants to move to Indianapolis to be near her children. If word gets out that a house is for sale, they won't have a chance. Luckily, Bob knows the lady and she told him he would be first in line. Aunt Doris and Bob make a lot of money, although I know she wants to quit and be home with her boys. Jenny and I have already volunteered to babysit when they need a night out.

Jenny had a photo shoot today—that's what they call it—with Mr. Evans and Miss Payne and I went along as the bodyguard. He gave Jenny this really short pleated skirt to wear and a white blouse and he wanted her hair straight. She caused a traffic jam just walking to the park from her house. Thank goodness her mom didn't see her leave in those clothes; she would have had a stroke. This time I made sure Jenny was wearing panties in case there was any wind. Mr. Evans took about a hundred pictures of Jenny and Miss Payne, and I'm sure he'll be able to sell them to someone. When we got to the park, Jenny put on the sunglasses I bought her. Mr. Evans noticed right away and wanted to have a look at them. I gave him the story about how I was able to get them.

"I know the company, Ray-Ban, and if they know what's good for them, they'll pay me dearly for pictures of a pretty girl wearing their sunglasses. They're going to sell millions of these after the war and I don't see why Jenny can't be one of their models."

I like that idea. At least Jenny won't have to take most of her clothes off to sell sunglasses. Her father might even go along with it.

Jenny insisted that Mr. Evans take a photograph of her on our bench and she's going to get me a copy when it's printed. She was posed on her back with a white hat over her face. You can't see her face at all, but the picture will show off those beautiful legs. I know Mr. Evans got a good look up her skirt when deciding how to take the photo. He was pretty discreet about it though—and she was wearing something underneath.

Sunday June 20, 1943
Night

We spent the weekend helping Aunt Doris and Bob move. They bought the house and it's only a few streets over from us. We're practically neighbors. I really like Bob and he seems to adore Aunt Doris and the boys. They've been calling him Daddy and I can tell he likes that. I'm going to miss having those two boys, Millie, and Aunt Doris around the house. Tonight it's just Mom, Dave and me, although Mom and I will be watching the boys and Millie during the day as long as Aunt Doris works. She says she's applied for a spot at a nursery school for Mike and Harry for when school starts back and I won't be able to help Mom with them. I do have my room back, but it wasn't so bad sharing it with the boys. It's quiet at night now and that'll take some getting used to, although I do get to sleep naked again. I bet Jenny could sneak in and spend the night and no one would ever know. Mom never comes up here during the night and she has Dave's bassinet in her bedroom. That would work; I have to tell her.

There was some really horrible news tonight from Eric. I've read stories about the Jews being killed in Europe, but I guess I never realized just how bad it is. There's now real proof, Eric says, that the Krauts are trying to kill all of them. Why would they do that, just because they're Jews? It doesn't make any sense. Eric also says we have our Tenth Fleet helping the British hunt for submarines and that we've destroyed several already. The Krauts have given up in the Atlantic. That should be good news for Jenny's brother. They hear from him regularly now. He's back on British soil safe and sound after his stay in Casablanca. His letters are easier to read now too. It seems the censors aren't as careful as they were. The war in North Africa's over. The Germans and Italians have surrendered to the British.

Friday June 25, 1943
Very Early morning

Jenny just left. She showed up last night about ten. I was waiting for her and made sure the front door was unlocked before I went to bed. We had a special night together. I just hope she got back to her room before her mom and dad got up. The plan was to do this tomorrow night because her parents wouldn't be getting up so early, but she wanted to come over last night and I couldn't say no. It's not quite five yet and still pretty dark outside. Everything's so quiet. She's only been gone a few minutes. The bed is still warm beside me and I can smell her scent on the pillow—Chantilly. I'll always remember that scent as hers. Last night we held each other like we had all the time in the world and it felt special. I pretended to be asleep when she slipped into bed next to me, but I'd already watched her undress in the dim light. She's gained a little weight back and that's good. She was getting too skinny. When things happen, Jenny stops eating and that worries me. She can gain or lose ten pounds in a week depending on her mood. I stay scrawny whether I eat or not.

She was quiet for a long time lying next to me with her arm across my stomach and her leg across mine. There was no hurry. Her head was wedged between my neck and shoulder and I could feel every breath she took. When her hands started exploring, I decided it was time for me to stop pretending to be asleep.

"If you're a burglar, take whatever you want, just don't stop doing what you're doing."

She rolled over on top of me and it was good to feel some meat on her bones again.

Soon we were holding each other tight and struggling to breathe without being too loud. There were lots of home runs before we curled up for the night and I don't know how she managed to wake up early enough to get home. It was nice having time to take things slowly, tenderly, the way it should be. Maybe I'll sleep a little longer this morning and dream about last night. She's all I'll ever want if I live to be a hundred.

Wednesday June 30, 1943
Night

It's been the best day ever. When Aunt Doris and Bob came to pick up the boys after work today, they had a smile on their faces that told everyone they were hiding something and all she would say was that she had some very good news for me. Mom was just finishing making dinner and insisted they stay and eat with us. Aunt Doris made me wait all through dinner before saying what the good news was about. She turned to me and I thought her face would break with the smile she had.

"I've never won anything in my life, ever. Today during our lunch break, Bob and I were eating our sandwiches when Mr. Bankston, our supervisor came over and sat down with us. I could tell something was up by the way he was grinning from ear to ear, and he hardly ever smiles.

He handed me an envelope and said loud enough for everyone at the table to hear, 'Congratulations Mr. and Mrs. Crandall. The two of you are the winners of the all-expenses paid Fourth of July Florida vacation sponsored by the Evansville Chamber of Commerce. The prize was just delivered to me to give to you, although I don't think you'll be needing the two rooms that come with it.'

I enter all those stupid drawings, but I've never won anything until now. That's the good news. The bad news is that Bob and I took off for our honeymoon only two weeks ago and there is no way we can go. The good news for you is that the prize is transferrable and I want you to have it. I called your mom earlier from work and she says you can go. Everyone should go to Florida when they're young enough to enjoy it and I can't think of anyone who deserves it more. It's a trip for two, by the way and you'd be crazy not to invite Jenny."

I grabbed Aunt Doris and Bob—Uncle Bob now, and hugged them both so hard they couldn't breathe.

"What I said, Doris," Mom interrupted, "was that it would be all right with me *only* if Jenny can go too. They can take care of each other and I won't worry so much if they're together. I haven't spoken to Mrs. Brewster yet, but I will tomorrow and find out what she thinks. There'll be no trip for you unless Jenny can go and I don't want you telling her about any of this until I talk to her mother either. I don't want her worrying her parents to death trying to get them to say it's all right if they really don't think it would be a good idea for her to go."

She said that in her "I'm your mother" voice so I knew it was law and there was no point in discussing it. Jenny's parents just have to say yes and I could tell that Mom wants them to, but I also know she won't put any pressure on them about it.

Thursday July 1, 1943
Night

Mom spoke with Mrs. Brewster today and she didn't say no and agreed to discuss it with Mr. Brewster tomorrow morning at breakfast. The bus tickets are for Saturday morning and I don't know whether to pack or not. I wish we had more time. The tickets are for Panama City Beach and I looked it up on a map to see where it is. It's just barely in Florida, but that's okay; it's still Florida and there'll be a beach and the ocean. I haven't breathed a word about anything to Jenny. Keeping secrets is not something I'm very good at so I've just tried to avoid her as much as possible. She can read me like a book and I would crack if she started asking questions.

Friday July 2, 1943
Late

We leave for Florida tomorrow morning at six. I can't believe it. That's only seven hours from now and I still haven't finished packing. According to Jenny there wasn't too much discussion at her house about her going. She said her parents trust the two of us together more than either of us alone. I've heard the same thing from Mom about a million times. Mrs. Brewster told Jenny the news early this morning and she was at my house in time to eat breakfast with Mom and me.

"Jenny, I think of you as my own daughter," Mom began. "Your parents and I are trusting the two of you to behave and that covers a lot of ground. We also expect you to be safe. Your rooms are supposed to be right next to each other and when you get there, if the place doesn't look safe, I want you to find somewhere else to stay. Mrs. Brewster and I are giving each of you fifty dollars and you can spend some of it on a better hotel if you need to. You have to promise me you'll do that."

Then she hugged both of us and grinned.

"If you don't come home broke, I'll be very disappointed. Have a good time, but behave and be safe."

We got the same talk from Jenny's mom later.

The reservations at the Aquaterra hotel are for Saturday night through Wednesday night. That gives us four whole days before we leave on Thursday morning. Mom made sandwiches for us before she went to bed and they're in the icebox. She doesn't want us eating strange bus station food on the way down. Jenny and I did some quick shopping this afternoon. Mostly we bought shorts and T-shirts because Mom said they would be terribly expensive in Florida. Anything else we need, we can buy there. I have to finish packing and try to get some sleep. Jenny's dad is taking us to the bus depot, but I know Mom will have some last minute instructions for me and she'll insist I eat breakfast before leaving. I want to pack this diary as well. Maybe I'll get to write some while we're gone.

Thursday July 8, 1943
Very late

I took this diary with me but not once did I think about writing in it. There was too much to do and see. Five whole nights of sleeping with Jenny would have been worth the trip even if we hadn't gone to Florida.

Neither Jenny nor I had ever ridden on a Greyhound before and we enjoyed the trip even with all the stops in every little town along the way. We arrived in Panama City Saturday night very late and had no idea where our hotel was. I had an address and when I asked the man at the depot, he told me we were within walking distance.

"Just past The Hangout and you'll know that place when you see it. Kids are there all hours of the day and night. Just follow the loud music. You can't miss it."

He was right about that. It was well after midnight and the parking lot was packed. No one knew or cared about the war and I decided I wouldn't care either; no radio news and no newspapers for as long as we stayed. The hotel was busy and we had to wait to talk to the night manager. He didn't look old enough to be the manager, but that's what the nameplate on his shirt said. After having a look at our vouchers for the rooms, he handed us two keys for each room, in case we lost one I guess. He then gave us directions how to find them.

"No loud music in the rooms. That's about the only thing we'll throw you out for. Don't tear up the place and don't steal the towels. They aren't worth stealing. There's no room service so don't bother calling me unless the place is on fire. There's a phone but it's only for local calls or collect calls. The beach is across the street about fifty yards from here. Feel free to pee in the ocean but please don't pee in our pool. Enjoy your stay at the Aquaterra."

He probably gave that speech about a hundred times a day, but he still smiled when he mentioned about peeing in the ocean.

We found our rooms without much trouble and, even though it was very late, we called home collect to let our moms know we'd arrived safely. The rooms were clean, but there wasn't even a radio. I guess if you wanted music, you had to bring your own. Jenny was out of her clothes as soon as the door shut on the room we decided was the nicest.

"I want to go pee in the ocean. There's plenty of moonlight and I want to see what the ocean looks like at night."

"You're crazy. It's late and we've been on the road since seven this morning. We'll see the ocean tomorrow."

She had my clothes off before I could argue anymore. We dug our swimsuits out of our suitcases, put them on and headed across the street with a couple of the hotel's towels. It was very busy even at that hour and lots of cars slowed down and boys whistled at Jenny. Then they sped away as if we were going to chase them down and beat them up or something. After going up a little rise across the road, we could look down and see the ocean. The moon wasn't full but there was enough light to see the waves rippling and coming toward the shore. It was the first time either of us had ever seen the ocean. We walked down to the shoreline and out into the water up to our knees. It was warm and the motion of the waves was like someone rocking us in a giant bathtub. Sand squished between my toes and I didn't think about what might be swimming around me. There was no one around as far as I could see so I took Jenny in my arms, wrapped my legs around hers and kissed her.

"Are you going to do it?" I asked.

"I will if you will?"

I felt her pee going down my leg before I could get started, then I caught up. There's something truly American about peeing on things that are ours. Mom told me a story once about when she and Dad moved into our house; on their first night there she caught him peeing off the back porch. She never told me if she did it too.

We walked on out until the water was above our waists and then swam back to shore. The towels weren't big enough to lay on so we just sat on them. I wasn't tired anymore. We sat there motionless and stared out at the ocean. Groups of teenagers came by occasionally and said hello. Everyone was friendly and I'm pretty sure drunk as well. One girl wrapped in a towel came up behind us and when she said hello, it startled us for a moment. She unwrapped the towel and sat down on it next to us. I don't know if Jenny noticed first or if it was me, but the girl wasn't wearing a top. There wasn't much light, but she definitely wasn't wearing a top.

"I think you forgot something," Jenny said with a little laugh.

"Oh, I couldn't find the top to my swimsuit so I just wrapped a towel around myself. I didn't think there would be anyone down here at this hour and if there were, they would probably be drunk and not notice. I'm Marcella, Marcella Feinstein, but everyone calls me Marcie. I'm down here with my sister and some girlfriends from New York. We were on our way to Miami but this is as far as we got. There are six of us in the room and only two beds. I'd rather sleep on the beach than try to sleep with that bunch, especially with the boys they've dragged in."

Jenny introduced us and we sat and talked with Marcie for an hour. She was nice and not at all drunk, but it's hard to carry on a conversation with a girl who isn't wearing a top. It was so dark I couldn't see much but I looked, trying hard not to stare. I knew what Jenny was going to do, so when she invited Marcie to stay in the room we weren't using, it wasn't a surprise. She wrapped the towel back around her and we walked to her room so she could collect her things. I could see through the curtains that the lights were on and when Marcie opened the door, we got an eyeful; a naked girl on top of a boy. They had a sheet over part of them, but it wasn't hard to imagine what was going on.

"See what I mean?" Marcie said. "Every night those two go at it like there's no tomorrow. I guess the rest of the girls aren't home yet."

The couple on the bed ignored us as Marcie went looking for her things. Jenny got her wish to be able to watch that night. The girl rode that boy like she was on a bucking horse and kept going until she screamed at the top of her lungs and fell forward on him. He flipped the two of them over and then it was his turn. He kept going until his body stiffened for an instant and then relaxed. It was all over in a few minutes and then the girl pulled the sheet up over them and they lay there motionless until we left. It was quite a show, but Jenny and I are better.

On the way to our room, Jenny asked about the boy and girl.

"That's my older sister and I don't know who the boy is, except his name is Nicky or something like that. She met him our first night here and she says they're madly in love. On the way down here, we all promised we wouldn't go home virgins, and so far I'm the only one left, although I'm pretty sure my sister wasn't one when we got here. We leave Monday morning going back home so I don't have much time."

Sunday July 11, 1943
Night

It'll take me several nights to write down everything that happened on our trip, but I don't want to leave anything out and there's some unbelievable war news. According to Eric, we've just invaded Sicily. That's the first step in taking Italy and taking Italy is the first step in ending the war. This whole thing will be over by the end of the year. Mom saved *The Sunday Courier and Press* from July 4 for me. It has the names and photos of almost a thousand men and women from Evansville now serving in the military. I had no idea there were that many.

Marcie moved into the room next to ours that night, or I guess it was about two o'clock Sunday morning. Jenny and I got a quick shower to wash the sand off and crawled into bed. The room had an air conditioner, which we didn't know how to work, and sometime during the night, I woke up freezing and turned it off. It was so nice to curl up with her and not have to worry about sneaking out before sunup. Neither of us heard the knock on the door Sunday morning and we were awakened by a young colored woman standing at the open door asking if we wanted maid service.

"Just a couple of towels," I managed to stammer.

She came in and collected the dirty towels from the bathroom floor and left clean ones. Before she left, she asked if we knew the girl next door.

"Maybe you should check on her," she said. "I left towels but she never moved."

Jenny and I pulled on shorts and T-shirts and went next door. I used my extra key to open it. Marcie was on her back on the bed, naked and for an instant I thought she was dead. We went over to the bed and sat down next to her, expecting the worst.

"She's breathing," Jenny whispered and then I noticed her chest moving up and down.

"Marcie, Marcie; are you all right?" I said loud enough I thought to wake her up.

I touched her face and she opened her eyes.

"Oh. Hi…is it morning already?"

"It's almost eleven," Jenny said, "and we were worried about you. The maid thought you were dead or something."

"No, I'm sorry. I'm just a really sound sleeper. I once slept through a car crashing into the side of our house. The police came and everything and I slept right through it. I only heard about it the next day from Mom. Let me get a shower and we'll go looking for something to eat."

She didn't seem to care at all that she was naked, and in the daylight I could see much better what I'd tried to see the night before. She looked older than Jenny and me, maybe a junior, I thought, and definitely pretty. Her hair was short, but not too short and done by someone who knew what they were doing, sort of a Vivien Leigh or Olivia de Havilland look. I know Feinstein is a Jewish name and she looked Jewish, not that I really know what a Jew looks like except for the Cohens here in E'ville, and she was much prettier than any of the girls in that family. Her breasts were larger than Jenny's. I noticed that the night before and Jenny said she saw me staring. She left the bathroom door open and I watched her as she showered. I saw Jenny steal a few glances as well. When she finished her shower and dried off, she began looking through her suitcase for something. She turned around and caught me looking straight at her.

"I'm sorry, I didn't mean to stare."

"It's okay. You've already seen me as naked as I can get. There's not much left to see, but I'm not going out with hairy legs. I have a razor here somewhere."

I'd never seen a woman shave her legs before and I guess Jenny hadn't either because we both watched her like we were watching brain surgery. She had a jar of some sort of cream and spread it over her legs all the way up. She was really hairy down there, or a lot more than Jenny and me anyway. Marcie knew what she was doing and had her legs done in a few minutes and then put one leg up on the side of the tub and shaved some between her legs, I imagined so that nothing would show with her swimsuit on.

When she finished, she took a washcloth and removed the rest of the cream. Her legs looked so smooth and the hair between her legs was perfectly trimmed.

"I want to try that someday," Jenny said loud enough for Marcie to hear her.

"You've never shaved your legs? Well, there's no time like the present. Here, you can use my razor and cream."

"I couldn't. I'll cut myself to shreds."

"No you won't. I'll show you. It's the least I can do for letting me stay here. Last night was the best sleep I've had in a week. Come over here and I'll teach you. Legs are easy; it's the other part that's hard. Sometimes I just shave it all off. It's easier."

Jenny walked over to the bathroom and Marcie took out a handful of the cream and spread it on her legs. In no time, she was finished.

"You have to feel this. It's so smooth."

She didn't have to ask twice and when I ran my hand over her legs, they were smooth as silk, like a baby's bottom.

"I don't know what your swimsuit covers, but you might want to shave a little farther up so the boys don't have anything to stare at."

"I'm buying a new swimsuit today, and I'm not sure what I want or what it'll cover."

"Let me have a look and I can tell you if you'll have a problem."

I couldn't believe it when Jenny pulled off her shorts, just like that, in front of a girl we'd only met the night before. In our hurry, neither of us had put on underwear that morning so everything was there for Marcie to see. I guess if you look like Jenny you don't mind being naked in front of strangers.

"You'll have a problem with some suits."

Then she ran her fingers along the top of Jenny's thigh, through the hair that had started growing at her panty line.

"This definitely has to go."

Marcie took out another handful of the cream and spread it along a line where she imagined a swimsuit would go.

"Sometimes you shave all of it?"

"Yep, just for the fun of it. I like the way it feels, at least until it starts growing back."

"Then shave it all."

This took a lot longer and Marcie took her time, but I could tell Jenny didn't mind and I liked watching; definitely another first for me.

"Done," Marcie announced after wiping the extra cream off. "Now you look like an eight year old with eighteen year old boobies."

Jenny ran her hands between her legs and smiled.

"It's perfect. Thank you so much Marcie."

"What about you? I have more razor blades and cream."

"Oh no," I answered. "It took me years to grow what little I have and I'm keeping it."

Marcie got dressed with a swimsuit under her shorts and T-shirt and we went next door so Jenny and I could put on something we could go out in. Marcie followed us into our room and sat on the bed while we changed. I was a little hesitant about changing in front of her, but the thought came to me that, after she left Monday, we'd never see her again, so why should I care if she saw me naked. Marcie didn't pay much attention to me anyway with Jenny to look at. The three of us started off walking down the beach looking for a place to have breakfast. Marcie knew where to go.

Thursday July 15, 1943
Night

Sunday afternoon we went shopping with Marcie leading the way. Jenny wanted a new swimsuit and there were lots of places that sold them. They had the latest two-piece suits like Marcie lost the top of and that's what Jenny wanted. There weren't too many color choices though. The saleslady said it was because of the dye rationing still in effect and I told her about baby Dave coming home from the hospital in a white blanket for the same reason. There were plenty of white and black suits, but Marcie said the white ones go transparent when they get wet and that the black ones fade out really fast. Jenny compromised by buying a black and white striped suit that had enough padding in the top that the saleslady said it would be all right to swim in. Next we bought beach towels and suntan oil that was advertised as being guaranteed to keep us from burning. We had T-shirts we could put on if the sun was too hot. I also bought a cheap camera and film. Naturally I forgot to bring mine from home. Finally we were ready to hit the beach and so were about a million other people. Marcie found a place to spread our towels and Jenny and I took a swim in the ocean. It was a lot different from our neighborhood pool in E'ville and the sun didn't seem so hot. When we got out of the water, I saw a problem with Jenny's suit and told her to get back in the water until I could get a towel. The lady was right, you couldn't see through the top, but the bottom clung to her skin like it had been painted on and every nook and cranny was visible.

"Yeah I forgot to tell you about that," Marcie said when I brought Jenny back to our spot. "Swimsuits have a lot more to stick too when there's no hair down there, but in this sun the suit will dry out fast and everything will be fine."

Marcie had the suntan oil ready for us. She rubbed it on Jenny while I rubbed it on her; then Jenny rubbed it on me. I liked putting it on Marcie and the feel of Jenny putting it on me was a lot nicer than the feel after it was on. I felt greasy as a fried catfish. We pretended to like lying on the beach for a little while, but it was pretty boring so when Marcie suggested we go for a walk, we agreed. The whistles from boys as we went by were meant for Jenny and maybe Marcie, but neither of them paid much attention. It seemed like we walked for miles.

"Fuck boys," Marcie said as she put her arms around Jenny's shoulders and smiled at me. "Let's go find something to drink. I don't intend to spend my last night in Florida sober. I'd rather go home a virgin than give my cherry to one of these goys. Do you know what a goy is Jenny? Well, I'm not going to tell you, but it's not someone I want to give my cherry to—unless he's really cute. Now, there's a liquor store just across the street from the hotel I was in and my sister bought a bottle of rum there right after we got here. The old man running the place is some kind of lecher and she had to let him feel her boobies to get it, but I'm prepared to make that supreme sacrifice for the two of you. If he tries to kiss me though, I may have to kill him and I expect the two of you to help me bury the body."

"Aye Aye Captain," I replied with a salute.

It was still early in the afternoon when we got to the liquor store and there weren't any customers around when Marcie went in. She was back out in a few minutes with a brown paper bag.

"That old bastard pinched my nipples so hard I thought I would scream, but I got us a bottle of rum."

"I know what would make them feel better," Jenny said with a smile.

"Now, to the grocery store for some Coca-Cola and ice and I'll make the two of you the best drink ever invented; guaranteed to make your dick hard or your pussy wet."

Marcie was a character but I liked her. When we got back to the hotel, she made all of us a drink and we sat down on the bed.

"To Florida, may we all have trouble remembering what we did here and may we always be glad we came," Marcie toasted.

The taste was sweet, like Coca-Cola with some of the fizz taken out. I couldn't taste any liquor, but after my second glass, I could feel the effects. It was a warm, kind of calm feeling and I liked it.

Tuesday July 20, 1943
Night

I'd never been drunk in my life, but after that second glass of rum and Coca-Cola, I was well on my way and so were Jenny and Marcie.

"You're not a virgin;" Marcie slurred to Jenny, "I can tell, and you're both younger than me. I bet I'm the only sixteen year old virgin in all of Panama City Beach and it looks like I'll be going back to New York that way too; hungover with sore nipples. That old man didn't have to pinch. I said he could feel them; he didn't have to pinch. That was just rude and I should report him to the Better Business Bureau or something. Anyway, I'm not a real virgin. There are two men I can have anytime I want, although I prefer Lefty here."

She raised her middle finger and we all laughed. I think Marcie made her drinks a lot stronger than ours.

"You don't have to go home a virgin."

I don't know why I said that; maybe it was the alcohol or maybe it was because I sitting on a bed with two very pretty girls or maybe it was because Marcie kept rubbing her nipples.

"I think your girlfriend might have something to say about that and I don't want to piss her off."

Marcie and I had a long drunken conversation about Jenny with her sitting right there on the bed with us. She wanted to know everything and I was drunk enough to tell her. Jenny thought it was hilarious and just sat there and listened. I got up to go to the bathroom and when I came back, they were kissing. I'd never seen Jenny kiss anyone before, certainly not a girl and for some reason I wasn't jealous. After all, I'd sort of started it. When they parted, Marcie had a grin on her face like she had been caught with her hand in the cookie jar.

"Your girlfriend and I talked it over while you were gone."

Then the expression on her face changed.

"My God, I just kissed a girl didn't I?"

"Yes, and I just kissed a Jew," Jenny laughed, "and neither of us got struck by lightning." As soon as she said that, as if on cue, the Fourth of July fireworks started on the beach.

Marcie didn't go back to New York the next day a virgin. She was gone when I woke up and Jenny was still asleep. She left a note on hotel stationery and I kept it after letting Jenny read it.

> Sorry I had to leave so early. I have to find my sister and get to the bus depot by seven. My head feels terrible, but the rest of me feels great. Thanks so much for everything and I mean everything. If you're ever in New York, look me up. My father's name is Karl J. Feinstein and that's how it's listed in the phone book.

Love you both,
Marcie

Jenny and I talked a lot about Marcie that day. We both liked her and neither of us is upset about what happened. We did things with her we'd only ever done with each other, but we weren't in love with her—and she was a girl after all, and it was Florida.

Wednesday July 21, 1943
Night

After Marcie left, Jenny and I missed her terribly. She was a lot of fun and already knew her way around the place. We spent the day Monday wandering up and down the beach and playing in the ocean, just relaxing in the sun like any other tourists. In the late afternoon, we went to The Hangout to see what that place was all about. It was huge, like a giant amusement park right there on the beach and everyone just wore their swimsuits. We rode the roller coaster about a dozen times. It wasn't very busy, so after the first couple of rides, the man running it let us ride for free after flirting with Jenny for a while. There were lots of parents with young children wandering around. After the roller coaster, we sat and ate hamburgers and drank root beer. We'd missed breakfast and were both pretty hungry. They had everything at The Hangout, food, rides, shops and everyone was so nice to us. The place started filling up by sundown and I was glad we'd gotten there early or we wouldn't have had a place to sit near the dance floor. There wasn't a live band but they had the latest records on the jukebox. It was a Wurlitzer and the sound was a million times better than an ordinary record player. The more people showed up, the louder the music got. Maybe we lose our shyness on vacation, knowing we probably won't ever see the people around us again, because the dance floor was full of teenagers who had no idea what they were doing and not all of them were drinking. There was plenty to drink, not officially of course, but bottles were passed around and liquor got poured into whatever soft drink you had if you weren't careful, whether you asked for it or not. Jenny and I passed on the free liquor until a bottle of rum came around. We both liked rum and Coca-Cola we discovered the night before and poured some into our cups. Rum and root beer's not bad either.

Sunday July 25, 1943
Night

It's been horrible not getting to sleep with Jenny since we got home, so last night she sneaked out after everyone went to bed and came to my house. We've figured out how to make wonderful things happen really easy. I guess we learned a lot about each other in Florida—and from Marcie too. Neither of us would deny we liked having her around and somehow it was okay.

Jenny slipped into my bed about eleven and we had a perfect night together—until I heard the phone ringing downstairs. I jumped out of bed to answer it before Mom could. Jenny was still in my bed and it was almost daylight. Standing naked at the bottom of the stairs, I prayed Mom hadn't heard the ringing. When I answered, Mrs. Brewster asked in a very nice voice if I knew where Jenny was, that she wasn't in her bed.

"Yes, Mrs. Brewster, she's here," I whispered. "She and I are making breakfast for Mom this morning. She's still asleep. It's a surprise Jenny and I cooked up last night. I guess she forgot to tell you and didn't want to wake you this morning when she left. I'm so sorry if you were worried. Jenny's in the bathroom right now, but I can go and get her if you want."

Lying to Jenny's mom was almost as bad as lying to mine and I surprised myself with how easy the words came.

"No, that's okay. I wasn't really worried, but she should've told me. Her father has to work today and after he left a little while ago, I just couldn't find her. Tell her to be home in time for church."

"Okay, Mrs. Brewster, I will. Bye."

There was no sound from Mom's bedroom and by the time I got upstairs, Jenny was dressed.

"Quick. We have to make breakfast. I'll explain later."

I pulled on my clothes and we went downstairs and began making breakfast, making as much noise as we wanted after we got the biscuits in the oven. Mom was soon awake and came into the kitchen to find us both sitting at the table peeling potatoes. Mom likes grated fried potatoes for breakfast but she hates making them and only does it on special occasions.

"What's all this? Have I died during the night and gone to Heaven?"

"It's Amelia Earhart's birthday, or yesterday was and I thought we should celebrate."

"I completely forgot about it and you're right, yesterday was the twenty-fourth. I must be getting old."

Jenny didn't have any idea what we were talking about, but Mom's been a big fan of Amelia Earhart since she was a young girl and every year since her disappearance, she reminds us of her birthday. Mom taught my sister and me everything there is to know about America's greatest woman aviator and I can remember how heartbroken she was when she disappeared. She was sort of Mom's hero I guess. I remembered the date yesterday and forgot to say anything about it to her. It was perfect.

"Oh what a tangled web we weave when first we practice to deceive" and I had woven one big enough to catch a bomber. Mom used that line on my sister and me, mostly my sister, when we were small and it came back to me just now.

We finished making breakfast while Mom saw to Millie and baby Dave. Millie stays with us now most of the time. Mom says it's just easier than having two of everything at our house and Aunt Doris's. We don't usually say a blessing over breakfast, but this was a special day. In her prayer Mom thanked God for Jenny and me and asked that he watch over the soul of Amelia Earhart. I silently asked Him to forgive me for lying to my mother and Mrs. Brewster.

Monday August 2, 1943
Night

There haven't been any more late night visits from Jenny since our last narrow escape. I think our luck has been stretched as thin as it can be. She didn't get into trouble for being AWOL and her mom didn't say anything to her father about it. She has to know Jenny spent the night with me and probably Mom does too. Maybe they think that if we were going to sleep together we would certainly have done it in Florida.

I never finished that Florida story and I want to before I forget anything—and there's major war news. Eric said tonight that Mussolini's been arrested by order of the king. I didn't know Italy had a king. Why didn't he arrest Mussolini a long time ago? Ernie had a story in the paper about a battle going on in a place called Kursk in Russia that may decide the war. He says that if the Russians win, there'll be nothing to stop them from invading Germany. If the British invade from the other direction, the Krauts will have to give up.

At The Hangout Monday night a lot of boys came over and asked Jenny to dance and she danced with some of them, then she started asking if they knew how to dance before she would accept. Most were scared away by that. One beautiful really tall girl came over and asked her to dance and she asked the same question.

"Baby, I can do anything from Shag to Jitterbug and I'll even let you lead," she said with a smile and a southern accent. "My name's Luanne and you just turned down my new boyfriend. I like that; he can't dance worth a damn and I bet him five bucks you would dance with me. I'll split it with you and let you pick the dance."

"Well, Baby," Jenny replied with a grin, "you're on. Let's show these damn Yankee tourists how it's done."

The next song was the Andrews Sisters' "Boogie Woogie Bugle Boy" and it was perfect for a fast swing or Shag. When Jenny stood up, she took my hand.

"You're coming with me. If she's as good as she thinks she is, she can dance with both of us."

We took off our shoes and followed Luanne onto the floor. Apparently she was well known at The Hangout because the other dancers backed off and gave us some room. We blew them all away. Luanne was good and she switched between Jenny and me like a pro while still letting us lead. At the end of the dance, everyone on the floor and those standing around applauded. We took a bow and walked back to our table. Luanne sat down with us and had a smile on her face that said she was up to something.

"How would you two like to make some money? This place is really slow on Tuesday nights so they've started having a dance contest to bring people in. I came last week but I didn't have a good dance partner and didn't do very well. They have two categories: swing and everything else and they pay fifty dollars to the winners of each. We can compete in both. A girl couple won everything last week. They were good, but they can't compete again for two weeks. Do you know how to Waltz, Quick Step, and Cha-Cha? If you do, we have it covered."

I was quick to tell her we placed first in Chicago two years ago in our division and sixth overall, and my bragging pretty well committed us to the contest as far as she was concerned.

"Meet me here tomorrow morning at seven. There's no one around at that time and as you can see, there's no way to lock the place up. We'll have the floor to ourselves all morning. The jukebox plays twenty-four hours a day seven days a week so we'll even have music. Please say you'll do it."

"And we split the money, right?" I asked.

"Absolutely, and I'll buy the liquor if we win."

Jenny and I left The Hangout early. If we had to be back at seven, we needed to get some sleep. Mostly I wanted to make sure we had time for lots of other things before going to sleep. That night, after we were peacefully wrapped in each other's arms, Jenny whispered something that has had me thinking ever since.

"What if Marcie had been a boy?"

Wednesday August 4, 1943
Night

Today when I got home, I heard Mom praying before I opened the front door. It's been a year and I know she misses him even more than I do. She was on her knees in the kitchen and I stood at the door and listened and prayed and cried. Over the past year I've realized just how little I know about my father. Mom talks about him all the time now and I've learned more from her about him than I ever learned from him. He never talked much about his family and Mom said that he always felt he was marrying above his class when he married her, although her family was not well-to-do by any means. Mom said he had a relative who had been in prison and that when they first got married, he would go to Kansas every summer to visit him. Mom said she never asked what he was in prison for, but she told me once that the only prison she knew of in Kansas was Fort Leavenworth and that it was a military prison.

Wednesday August 11, 1943
Very late

Tuesday morning we were at The Hangout at seven. Luanne was already there and warmed up. She and Jenny began with an East Coast Swing and they were great together. If the contest winner is based on looks, I thought to myself, they would win hands down. Jenny and Luanne both had their hair tied back in a ponytail. Luanne's was longer and when Jenny would whip her or lead her in a spin, it would wrap around her face. Luanne was taller than Jenny and led most of the time, then when Jenny thought of a new move, she would take over. Each of them had led and followed enough that to someone who didn't know, the switch wouldn't be noticed.

When a waltz started playing, it was my turn. Luanne was strong, muscular and didn't have the smooth grace needed to waltz. Although she knew all the steps, something wasn't right. We were dancing, but not with each other. I could tell she'd been taught by someone she really didn't want to be that close to. The next song was a Tango and she started out just as rigid as she'd been during the waltz. This wasn't working and then I remembered something Jenny's mom had said once and whispered in her ear.

"The Tango is making love while standing up with your clothes on. I want you to make love to me like it was your last day on Earth."

We were both wearing shorts; hers were very short, and when I pulled her close and slipped my leg between hers until our thighs touched, I felt a little shudder come from her. We were so close, our hip bones touched. I led and didn't let her make a move without me. At the end of the dance, we separated and I saw how flushed her face was. Mine probably was too.

"That was so unbelievably wizard," Jenny yelled over the music. "The two of you'll win if they don't throw you out and arrest you on obscenity charges."

"I've never danced with anyone like that before," Luanne said when we sat down for a break. "I don't know if I can keep it up for an entire song."

"Don't worry," I said with a smile, "I can."

We rehearsed the rest of the day, only stopping long enough for lunch. Jenny and I didn't bring any clothes that even resembled dance clothes so we went shopping. The competition didn't start until nine so we had plenty of time. We discovered that Panama City was not the place to shop for dance clothes, but we found outfits that would work. It was exciting getting ready. It was the first time we'd competed since Chicago and all the same feelings came back. Jenny was beautiful in her pink skirt and white blouse and I couldn't resist kissing her before we left for The Hangout. I slipped my hand up her skirt as we stood at the door.

"Just checking to make sure you're wearing something underneath," I said with a smile. "We don't want to spend the night in jail."

"It's awfully itchy down there. We have to find a razor tomorrow."

When we got to The Hangout, the place was packed. Luanne saw us and gave us our numbers to wear during the competition.

"Okay, we don't dance with anyone until the competition. Everyone's trying to see what the others are going to do and I don't want to give away anything; also, no booze until afterward. When the competition begins, there'll be a group dance and the judges will wander through tagging people to be dropped. The three of us will have to dance together and we have to be good enough to get through that first. Then comes the individual dances and we won't know what the dance will be until the music starts, so we have to stick together until we know if it's a swing or something else."

"Okay Coach," Jenny said with a grin. "We have the game plan and we're gonna kill 'em."

The three of us dancing together was awkward for the group dance because there were so many people on the floor, but we didn't get tagged. Thank goodness the music was swing so we didn't have to keep switching partners.

The judges chose five finalists and we got a good look at the competition. There was one girl couple and one that was dressed like pros. The rest looked average. The pro couple looked as old as our parents and we figured they'd been dancing together for a long time. They were also the first couple up for the individual competition. We were scheduled third, right where I wanted to be. When the older couple finished their two dances, I had a sinking feeling we were outclassed by a mile. They were pros, no doubt about it, just out to make a few easy bucks.

"They were pretty good," Luanne said when the music stopped after their second dance.

"Good? They were perfect," I answered. "If we have any hope of winning this thing ladies, we have to pull out all the stops. Technically, we don't have a chance; they're a lot better than us, but that's not how competitions are won. The judges are all young men and we have to put a bulge in their britches if we expect to win. It's as simple as that."

Luanne blushed, but Jenny knew exactly what I was talking about. The second couple was the girls. They were terrible but they were pretty and that counts. It was then our turn. The three of us walked out onto the floor and waited for the music. I recognized it in two notes.

"It's 'Bugle Call,' go."

"Got it," Jenny yelled back over the music.

I ran off the floor and took a seat. Jenny and I knew the song very well, but I didn't know if Luanne did. It was fast—really fast—and Jenny knew precisely what to do. Their dresses didn't come down for the whole dance and the judges didn't take their eyes off their legs. They used the entire dance floor and could have used more. Jenny made up stuff and Luanne followed like they'd rehearsed for weeks. It's not supposed to count, but they got a huge round of applause when the dance ended. There was no break between dances, only the amount of time it took to change records and I was worried Luanne might be worn out. I ran out onto the floor and hugged them both and Jenny hurried back to take my seat.

"Tango," I whispered to Luanne when I heard the first few notes, "making love standing up."

I pulled her so close to me every step I made was hers. My thigh never left hers except for a moment during the paseos. Our cortes were perfect and our promenade positions were strong. Luanne was breathing heavy and I thought it was because she was getting tired, but during one of the back cortes, her thighs squeezed me especially hard and I added an unexpected second's hesitation as her body shook for an instant. You're not supposed to, but I turned and looked at her face for a half-second. Her eyes were closed and I knew little explosions were going off inside her. A few steps later she was fine and we ended the dance with a classic Tango pose we'd rehearsed. I hugged her and led her off the floor to the sound of even more applause than she and Jenny got.

"Okay ladies, if that doesn't do it, we're sunk," I shouted above the noise.

"If that didn't give the judges a cheap thrill," Jenny yelled back, "then nothing will. You two were fantastic and should be arrested for what you did out there."

"I guess you can make love standing up with your clothes on after all," Luanne said with a smile in my direction. She liked me and I knew it.

Sunday August 15, 1943
Night

Jenny and I spent the day at the pool yesterday and went to a ballgame last night. On the way home, she brought up something that I guess has been bothering her.

"You liked that girl Luanne, didn't you?"

"Yeah, I liked her; didn't you?"

"Yes, but I mean, you really liked her. You wanted to make love with her, I can tell, and if we'd stayed another day, you would have, wouldn't you?"

"Maybe, but only if you wanted to."

"Well, I wouldn't have and you know why? It's because you liked her and she liked you."

"But we made love with Marcie."

"That was different. There was nothing going on with her. She was just there and we were just there and we had fun together. That was all there was to it. I saw what you made Luanne do on the dance floor."

"I didn't make her do anything, she just did it."

It was a long walk home from the ballpark.

I don't know if I want to finish the Panama City vacation story or not. Jenny's mad at me about something that didn't happen.

We won the dance competition in both categories and afterward, one of the judges told me the decision was unanimous. The other three couples were okay, but nothing special, so the contest came down to the pros and us and we won. We split up the money and insisted Luanne get more since she'd won in both categories, then she invited us back to her hotel for a drink. It was already well past midnight and we were all tired, but we decided some sort of celebration was in order.

"And now we're gonna drink all the liquor we can hold," Luanne yelled over the music as we walked up the sidewalk.

"I know a place we can buy it," Jenny answered and smiled, "but you'll have to go in. Just tell the old fart at the counter you'll do anything he wants and he'll sell it to you."

"Really? And what do I have to do?"

"Not a thing. Just stand there and look beautiful."

"Jenny…," I interrupted.

"No, really; all she has to do is stand there and look pretty. That's all Marcie had to do."

"I know the place," Luanne said with a grin that said she knew more than we thought. "Old Ernie is well known around here—guess he'll want a feel."

Our favorite lecher was working and when Luanne went in, I sort of felt bad letting her go by herself, but Jenny thought different.

"She's a big girl. She can take care of herself."

In a few minutes Luanne came out with a paper bag and a very upset expression on her face.

"That son of a bitch pinched my nipples. He didn't have to do that. I've a good mind to call the cops."

"Really?" Jenny said. "Why he was a perfect gentleman when a friend of ours was in there. She said she just smiled and asked him nicely and he sold her what we wanted."

"Your friend lied. Ernie won't sell anything at all to underage boys and he always gets a feel from the girls."

When we got to Luanne's hotel, it wasn't just any hotel. She had a bungalow at the Long Beach Resort and it was huge. There were two real bedrooms and a kitchenette. We sat around drinking something Luanne made and talking about the competition until almost two when Jenny announced we should be getting back to our hotel.

"Why don't you just stay here? It's late and I have plenty of room. My parents are gone for the evening. We've been here three weeks and they finally left for Clearwater the day before yesterday to see some cousin. They won't be back until late tomorrow."

"I think we should take Luanne up on her offer," I answered. "I don't want to walk all the way back to our place. I'm really tired and a little drunk."

"Perfect. I'll show you to your bedroom. I can have a cot delivered if you want."

"That's okay," Jenny quickly replied. "We've been sleeping together since we were in fifth grade. We're not just friends."

"Oh, I see. Well, make yourselves at home."

Jenny hardly said a word to me that night and we left early the next morning.

Tuesday August 24, 1943
Night

To finish up the story, Jenny and I spent our last day in Panama City on the beach, not really doing anything. We had fifty dollars extra between us and we hadn't even spent all of the fifty we each had been given before we left. I suggested we have one really nice dinner somewhere and that seemed to be the right thing to say.

"And we're going to buy some new clothes to wear to dinner. I'm going to buy something I'll probably never wear again."

"And a razor," I added.

"Definitely a razor."

We took a taxi and told the driver we wanted to shop at the best clothing store in the area. He knew where to take us. It was a twenty-minute ride into the city and he dropped us of at a busy intersection saying there were several nice clothing stores in the area. We didn't have to walk far before Jenny spotted something in a window she liked. The mannequin was dressed in a very short light blue pleated skirt and wore a bright floral print low neck blouse with puffy short sleeves. The mannequin was in a dance pose with another, who was supposed to be the man I guess, wearing grey pleated pants and a light blue padded shoulder sports jacket.

"That's what I want," Jenny said after studying the mannequin for several minutes.

I didn't argue. If she found something she liked at the first store we came to, so much the better. We went in and the saleslady got the skirt and blouse in her size and gave them to her to try on.

"Don't you just love seeing colors again. Someone must think the war's about over. We just got this collection in today and I'm sure we'll sell out when word gets around."

It was good to see clothes in something other than grey, white, or black, but Jenny wanted more. "I don't suppose you have hose to go with this do you?"

"Hose are still only available on the black market and I'm afraid they're rather expensive."

"How expensive?"

"Twenty dollars a pair when you can find them."

"Suppose I have an extra twenty dollars and wanted a pair right now; do you think you could help me?"

"Let me see what I can do. Will you be needing a garter belt and perhaps a bra and panties?"

"A garter belt, yes, a bra yes—your most revealing please, panties no. I don't intend to wear any."

The lady smiled and disappeared. In a few minutes she came back with everything Jenny had asked for. When she walked out of the dressing room, I think even the saleslady was a little impressed. Jenny looked beautiful, like she was on her way to a Hollywood party. There was a minor problem with shoes though. I didn't know it, but there is an official government ban on heels higher than one inch. It sounds as crazy as the ban on sliced bread, nonetheless the saleslady assured us it's true. She said everything made of leather was in short supply. Jenny tried on a dozen pairs and I noticed the saleslady looking up her dress every time she helped her.

"You're going to buy something new too," Jenny said to me, "so find something outrageous you like that you'll probably never wear again."

We spent the afternoon in that one store trying on clothes, although Jenny had already decided she was going to buy the outfit in the window. It was almost sunset when we walked out wearing our new clothes with our shorts and T-shirts in bags. The wind from the ocean caught Jenny's skirt right away, but she kept on walking.

"Jenny, you really should have bought panties while you were in there. In this wind, it's just a matter of time before…"

"Before what? Before I get you to look? Maybe that's the idea."

We had dinner in what everyone said was the nicest place in Panama City and took a taxi back to our hotel after stopping off at a drugstore for a razor and cream. When we were just inside the door, she pushed me back against it and kissed me.

"Do you love me Emell?"

I like it when she calls me that.

"Of course I love you Jenny B."

"Then make love to me right now."

I reached up to unbutton her skirt.

"No, I want to leave it on and everything else too so that when we get home, I can look at these clothes and remember exactly what I was doing the last time I wore them."

We barely made it to the bus depot the next morning and we never got to use that razor she bought.

Monday September 6, 1943
Night

Labor Day's my least favorite holiday. It's the end of summer and it's not during the school year. We only have one more week of freedom before going back to the grind.

That last night in Panama City Beach was probably the last time Jenny and I will get to spend the entire night together for a long time, but it was a night to remember. She's never been that? What's the right word? Horny's so crude, although that's what she was. It was like she thought we'd never get to be together again and I don't think we slept at all. Maybe it was the clothes.

We had the usual cookout today at the Brewster's and everyone showed up, even my sister. I think Mom was a little disappointed that she didn't bring Victoria. When Jenny and I went inside to get the watermelon, she kissed me behind the icebox door.

"I have a surprise for you. I finally used that razor we bought in Florida and I didn't cut myself either. The hair growing back out drove me crazy and I didn't know when you would be able to do it so I did it myself this morning in the shower. I like it and I'm going to keep it that way…if it's all right with you, that is."

"I love it, and I love you. You're nuts; did anyone ever tell you that?"

"Only you. Everyone else thinks I'm quite sane."

I helped Jenny and her mom clean up after the cookout. Then she and I took a walk and sat on our favorite bench. It was dark by the time we got there.

"I wish I could curl up with you naked on a big bed in the fanciest hotel in Paris. I would make love to you until you begged me to stop."

"Like our last night in Florida? I thought you were going to kill me."

"Well, I was jealous. I saw how Luanne looked at you and I wanted to show you I was a much better lover than she could ever be."

I took her face in my hands and gave her my best movie star kiss.

"Well, I never…" came a woman's voice from behind us.

"And you probably never will," Jenny yelled back.

The woman kept walking. I hope she didn't recognize us.

Monday September 13, 1943
Night

The first day of school is always crazy, but at least now I know my way around. I remember when Jenny and I were in fifth grade we thought eighth graders were so mature, almost adults. I don't feel so mature, except maybe when I'm with Jenny. On the way home, she didn't say much and I could tell something was bothering her.

"I have to go to the doctor tomorrow at noon and I'm scared. It hurts when I pee. What if he wants to look down there? What if he says something to Mom about me not having any hair?"

"Do you want me to go with you?"

"I already asked and Mom says no. I don't know why; she wouldn't discuss it. We talk about everything, but when I asked her what was wrong with me, she just said the doctor would talk to me about it. I don't want to talk to some strange man about how it hurts to pee and I sure don't want to talk to him about why I shave down there. What kind of mess have I gotten myself into?"

She was almost at the point of crying by the time we got to her house. I had no idea what was wrong, although I knew who would and told Jenny I'd call her later with some answers. When I got home, Mom was out so I called my sister and asked about Jenny's problem. She was very nice about it and told me Jenny had an infection that was pretty common and that the medicine the doctor would give her would take care of it right away. She also told me I could get it if I wasn't careful and that I was probably the cause of it in the first place. I'd already guessed that. Before we hung up, I asked if the doctor would say anything if Jenny looked a little different from other girls down there.

"Like how different?"

"Like if she doesn't have any hair. She shaved it all off and if you tell anyone, I'll kill you."

After she stopped laughing, she told me the doctor wouldn't care at all about that kind of thing and that he wouldn't tell her mom anything except about her health. I called Jenny right after I hung up and told her what my sister said. I was going to tell her that the doctor might tell her mom that she has a serious disease that made her hair fall out, but I decided against it.

Tuesday September 14, 1943
Night

Jenny was in a much better mood on the way home today. She went to the doctor and it was just as my sister had said.

"The doctor had me undress and looked me over but there was a young nurse in the room with me the whole time. I'm so glad it wasn't some old fat woman. She said I could have Mom with me if I wanted but I told her no. The doctor felt my breasts first. I don't know what that could have to do with it hurting when I pee, but I didn't ask. Then I had to lie down on this table thing and put my feet in these metal braces with my knees in the air. The nurse covered me with a sheet, which was pretty funny since they'd both already seen me as naked as I could ever get. He poked around inside me for a while. I couldn't see with what and then he left. The nurse said I could get dressed and that she would talk to me after speaking to the doctor. She wasn't gone long and when she came back, we talked for a while. She said it looked like I had a bladder infection and that it was easily treated. Then she asked if I had a boyfriend. I must have hesitated because she said that if I did have a boyfriend, I should tell him to keep his hands in his pockets until this infection clears up. She also asked if I had any problems with my periods and if I had any questions about other girl stuff. She then invited Mom in and told her I would be fine. I cringed when Mom asked how I got this infection, but the nurse told her it happens to most girls at some time and that there wasn't any specific cause. That seemed to satisfy her and after getting a prescription, we left."

There was big news on the radio tonight. Eric says Mussolini's been rescued by the Germans and that he's raising a new army in the northern part of Italy. There weren't many details. Did the Krauts just walk in and take him? The southern part of the country is on our side now it seems, although no one thinks we need them.

Sunday September 19, 1943
Morning

I'm lying in bed and it's a beautiful morning in Evansville, Indiana. We're making bullets by the millions and Jenny's infection is almost gone. In a little while I'm going to sit next to the prettiest girl in eighth grade, maybe even in the whole city and I'm going to write her a love poem that will make her blush so much the preacher will think she has a fever. I want to tell the whole world I love Miss Virginia Brewster. It really is a beautiful morning.

Night

It's just cool enough for a light jacket and in church this morning, Jenny and I took ours off and spread them over our laps so we could hold hands underneath. I never get tired of holding her hand. It's such a simple thing, but we can be close to each other even in a crowd if we can hold hands. After church, we walked home together and talked.

"Do you think your mom would hate me if she knew about us? My mom knows, she has to, even if she's never said anything. I just don't want your mom to hate me."

"My mom could never hate you Jenny, and she knows too. She only wants what's best for me, like your mom. Someday they'll tell us they know; when they're ready."

Wednesday September 22, 1943
Night

Mom's birthday started off with a minor disaster. Millie's sick and has been running a temperature since yesterday. I had planned to get up early and surprise her with breakfast, but when I went downstairs she was sitting in the living room rocking Millie. She looked like she hadn't slept all night and Millie was crying. I took the baby and told Mom to go back to bed. Jenny called when I didn't show up at her house to walk to school with her and I told her what was going on and that I wouldn't be going to school.

Mrs. Brewster was knocking on our door a few minutes later. She took one look at Millie and felt her forehead and said that we were taking her to the doctor. I didn't argue. Millie was burning up. I went in and told Mom what we were doing. I don't think she heard me. She was sound asleep. Dave was just waking up so I grabbed him and took him out to the living room and changed him. I left Mom a note telling her I had Dave and that Mrs. Brewster and I were taking Millie to Dr. Berger's office downtown.

I held both babies while Mrs. Brewster drove our car. Early morning traffic was horrible and the babies were wet again and crying by the time we got to Dr. Berger's. We didn't have an appointment, but we were early and the nurse managed to get us in before the doctor started seeing regular patients. He'd been practicing in our town since Mom was a little girl and was the first white doctor in Evansville to take colored babies and she sort of liked that.

Dr. Berger was Millie and Dave's regular doctor and I'd come with Mom several times but he didn't remember me. He said that his patient load had doubled in the last year with all the new people moving to E'ville and having babies. He was pretty sure, even without looking, that Millie had strep throat, that half the babies he'd seen in the last week had it. I held Millie and the doctor had a look down her throat and confirmed his guess. He wrote out a double prescription saying that Dave would probably have it in a few days and then we left. Mom was still asleep when we got home and Mrs. Brewster helped me with the babies while I made lunch. We missed breakfast altogether. Both babies take a bottle and breastfeed so I mixed up formula and Mrs. Brewster fed them and gave Millie her medicine.

It was after noon before Mom woke up. When Mrs. Brewster and I told her about our morning adventure, she couldn't believe she'd slept through everything. Then we surprised her by singing "Happy Birthday" at lunch. She didn't think anyone would remember, but I will always remember her birthday—and Amelia Earhart's.

Thursday September 30, 1943
Night

Maybe we're finished with strep throat at our house. Dave got it just like the doctor said. We started giving him the medicine early so he's just about recovered. Millie's fine and once again a happy baby.

Aunt Doris says the boys are doing well at St. Vincent's Day Nursery, but I wish she would quit her job and stay home with them. That's probably not going to happen because she just got a new job at the shipyard and a nice raise. She's working in the purchasing department now and gets to dress nice every day. Mom and I can take care of Millie permanently and she's perfectly at home with us. It's strange how my sister has never acknowledged Millie as her daughter and still barely pays any attention to her. She just treats her as Aunt Doris's and doesn't even want to hold her when she visits, which isn't very often. Maybe she's put that part of her life out of her mind. How could anyone do that? Especially a mother?

Reitz is overflowing with students this year, even worse than last year and classes are a lot harder. Jenny and I are going to the first football game of the season this weekend. We watched them practice for a while this afternoon after school and some of the players look big enough to be on our high school team. When one of the boys whistled at Jenny, the coach made him do push-ups. That's when we decided to go. With all of them wearing helmets, I couldn't tell who it was, but I'm sure we'll hear about it tomorrow.

Friday October 1, 1943
Night

Those boys looked big enough to be on our high school team because they were our high school team and Sarah Martin knew which boy it was that had whistled at Jenny. Of course she did; she knows every bit of gossip in school and I think she starts a lot of it herself. She told Jenny, with me standing right there, that Tony Bingham wants to ask her out. He's in tenth grade and I remember him from Centennial. He was okay then and I haven't heard anything bad about him at Reitz. If Sarah knew any rumors she didn't repeat them, and she would have, so I guess he has a pretty good reputation.

Jenny and I have talked about her dating someone else and even though she's always told me she never would, I know that's impossible. Boys are going to ask her out and Tony wouldn't be so bad; at least he's good-looking. He's probably going to call her this weekend and I won't go crazy if he does.

Tuesday October 5, 1943
Night

On the way home from school today Jenny told me that Tony called last night and asked her to go with him to the movies next Saturday night. That was a respectable amount of time. No girl would go out with a boy who called only a day or two in advance.

"I think you should go. Tony was a nice boy at Centennial and it seems like he still is. I don't think he'll be grabbing for anything on the first date, unless you grab first of course."

"He'd better not. I'm not even going to kiss him and I sure won't be grabbing anything. It doesn't matter; my parents have already told me they're not going to let me date until I'm sixteen."

I was hoping for that but I didn't let on. Jenny didn't try to hide that she was sort of flattered that Tony had asked her out.

"You have to ask your parents anyway if you can go."

"I'll ask, although I know what the answer will be."

Jenny called tonight and told me she'd asked her parents at dinner about going to the movies with Tony. She didn't get the answer she was expecting.

"They said I'm too young to go out alone with a boy even if I do know him well, but that it would be okay if Tony and I doubled with someone, namely you. I couldn't believe they would even let me do that. Would you go? I know you can get a date and I would feel a lot better if you were there anyway. I think the reason they said I could go is because they met that way; on a double date. Will you think about it?"

"And just who am I supposed to go with?"

"Kelly Smithers likes you; Sarah told me so."

"Sarah doesn't know everything, but if I happen to run into Kelly at school, maybe it'll come up."

"You might get a phone call."

"I might? Why, do you know something?"

"Maybe. I just think it would be fun to double date."

"I don't know if Mom would even let me go. She's told me I can't date until I'm sixteen either."

"It wouldn't be like a real date for either of us. Promise me you'll ask."

Mom gave me the same answer Mrs. Brewster gave Jenny. I think they've been talking again. I could go with Kelly as long as Jenny and a date were the other couple.

I don't know if it was curiosity or what, but when Kelly called, I said yes, so it looks like we'll be sort of double dating with Jenny and Tony this Saturday night.

Eric said on the news that we've taken Naples. I know where that is.

Saturday October 9, 1943
Very late

We had a choice: Alfred Hitchcock's *Shadow of a Doubt* or *My Friend Flicka*. They're showing at the Grand Theater on Sycamore, which seemed to be about the same distance for all of us to walk. Tony has his license but he's not allowed to drive at night. Kelly won't be sixteen until next month, so we just agreed to all meet at the theater at seven. We're having a cold snap so Jenny and I dug out our winter coats this afternoon.

"I'm wearing a bra," Jenny announced as we walked toward downtown.

"That's too bad for old Tony. He'll just have to work a little harder if he wants a feel."

"That wasn't very nice. He's not getting a feel."

Kelly and Tony were there waiting for us when we arrived. We were early but they were earlier. I was the first one into the theater and I chose seats in the middle. I wasn't interested in any back row adventures. Jenny and I sat together between Kelly and Tony; just as I'd planned all week. Kelly was all right and I did my best to make small talk until the movie started, although I was more interested in trying to hear what Tony and Jenny were talking about. It was freezing in the theater so Jenny and I spread our coats over our laps as we always do. Kelly and Tony spread theirs over ours and themselves. I like Alfred Hitchcock movies and I hadn't seen this one; it's been out for a while though. A half hour into the movie, I felt Kelly's hand under the coats looking for mine. I didn't think a little hand holding would hurt so I let mine be found. I'd been holding Jenny's since before the movie started. It wasn't so bad, and that's as far as things went with Kelly and me. My other hand was up Jenny's skirt by the end of the movie and I kept thinking of the story I would write someday. If old Tony only knew. If Kelly only knew. I could write that story and sell it to a trashy men's magazine. Do they ask the age of their authors?

After the movie we walked to Muir's and sat in a booth; me next to Jenny and Kelly next to Tony. We drank Coca-Cola and talked mostly about school until after ten. I reminded Jenny that we had to be home by eleven. Since we lived in opposite directions from downtown, we said our goodbyes in front of the drugstore. There was a little hand holding but no kissing, not even an attempt and I think Jenny was a little disappointed, so I gave her one as soon as we were out of sight of our dates.

"He didn't even try to kiss me. He could have tried. I wouldn't have let him, but he could have tried. He only held my hand for a few minutes and he didn't even ask me for another date. I think I'm done with Mr. Bingham. From now on, I only date seniors."

That got her an elbow in the ribs.

Thursday October 14, 1943
Night

Mom didn't ask much about last Saturday night and Jenny hasn't talked about it at all. Maybe it really was nothing, although I know it won't be the last time. Next year Tony will be a junior and he can ask eighth graders to the Junior-Senior Prom. If he doesn't ask Jenny, someone else will. Kelly and I speak when we see each other at Reitz, which isn't often, mostly after school before Jenny and I start home. There's been no talk of a second date, although Sarah said that Kelly had a good time on our first one—like she would know. She needs a boyfriend to pinch those perky nipples of hers she's so proud of. She never wears a bra and I don't know how she gets away with it.

Some girls are already being asked to the Thanksgiving dance. I wonder if Mr. Bingham knows how to dance. Someone will ask Jenny for sure. *The Press* has already had a story about the event and I bet it'll be even bigger this year than last. I hope Mom decides to go again. She had a good time before and she needs a night out away from the babies. I would volunteer to babysit if she'd go.

Eric and Ernie say the Russians are continuing to push the Krauts back to Germany. What will happen then? Some say that's when the fighting will really begin, that Hitler will never surrender an inch of Germany as long as a single soldier is left to fight. The new government in southern Italy has declared war on Germany. I don't think that means anything much, but it's something else for Hitler to worry about. The war will be over by New Year's for sure.

Monday October 18, 1943
Very early

Jenny didn't tell me who the boy was who asked her out for Saturday night, only that he called Friday night and that she told him she already had a date. That date was with me, but I doubt she told him that. We went back to the Grand to see *My Friend Flicka*. We got there a little early and walked around the block to kill time. We stopped in front of the Vendome hotel, which is just up from the theater.

"I wonder how much it costs to stay a night."

By the time Jenny had those words out of her mouth, I was inside the huge doors. She followed me, not knowing what I had in mind. The man at the desk was about a hundred years old and I walked up as if he should have been expecting me.

"Excuse me sir, but could you tell me if our parents, John and Jane Smith have checked in yet."

I could have been a little more original in the names I thought up, but I hadn't planned any of this.

"I'm sorry, there doesn't seem to be a reservation under that name."

"What are we going to do? My sister and I are supposed to meet them here. We just flew in from Charlotte and they were flying in from Dallas. We're staying the night here to visit my grandparents tomorrow and then going home to Atlanta."

"Perhaps their flight was delayed. There's been some bad weather southwest of here this afternoon."

"That's probably what happened. I'm sure they wouldn't want us wandering the streets of Evansville until they land. Is there a room we could have just until they arrive? I would kill for a shower."

"Well, it is rather slow tonight. I could let you have a room until your parents arrive and call you then, but if they don't arrive tonight, you'll be responsible for paying for the room tomorrow morning."

"Oh, that would be perfect and we have enough money to pay if they don't get in tonight. You've been very kind and we'll make sure our parents hear of it."

Jenny was completely dumbfounded at my acting abilities. We followed the bellhop to our room and I tipped him a dollar. When the door closed behind him, she hugged me and gave me a kiss I'd been waiting for and thoroughly deserved.

"You are simply amazing. I'll never believe another word you say."

"Well, you don't know how much I've wanted to be alone with you. We have five whole hours before we have to be home."

We took off our coats and had a look around. The room was fantastic with elegant furnishings and a bathroom larger than my whole room at home.

"Do you realize we've never had a real bath together?" We'd only ever had showers. "That tub looks big enough for six and I'd love to try it out; and look, there are all sorts of bath salts and things I don't even recognize. We have to do this." She had that look in her eyes that makes me agree to anything. I would rather have started our five hours together doing other things, but Jenny knows an opportunity when she sees one and I liked the idea of a real bath together.

"All right my queen, your wish is my command. I only have one request. Before your royal bath is run, I want to make use of these."

The bathroom was also furnished with a razor and shaving cream.

"That's a great idea. It's awfully scratchy down there. I'm afraid I don't do such a good job in the shower at home. I have to sneak my razor into the bathroom and sneak it out afterward and I'm always afraid I'll cut myself if I hurry."

I took the razor and cream and grabbed a towel. I had never shaved anyone, but I was pretty sure I could do it. Undressing Jenny took a while; after all, I don't get that chance very often, and of course she had to undress me too. She lay down on the towel I spread on the bed and I sat between her legs with her knees in the air; a very undignified pose, but I wanted a good view of what I was about to do. At Jenny's suggestion, I got a washcloth soaked with water as hot as I could stand and placed it on the stubble first. Maybe that's supposed to soften the hair or something. The cream mixed with the moisture left by the washcloth and became slippery as oil. It was easy and in a few minutes, she was smooth as silk again, even in the hard to get to places. I wiped off the extra cream with another washcloth and inspected my work—perfect. This gave me a chance to do something I'd never done, have a really good look at her down there. I had wanted to, but that would be a strange request I guess. It was fascinating seeing things up close I'd only felt before. I've had a look at myself with a mirror lots of times. I wonder if Jenny's done that. Her little starter button, as she calls it, was right there and I got a good look at it while moving things out of the way for the razor. After I finished, I had something else in mind. I went back to the bathroom and got the bottle labeled "body oil" and poured half of it on her and rubbed it into her skin from her toes to her nose. It didn't have a bad taste either. She poured the rest of the bottle on me, and oiled up like that, it was like we could get even closer than just being naked.

Later, the bath and hair washing in that huge tub was the perfect ending to a perfect evening. We got dressed afterward, sneaked out the hotel's back entrance, and walked home arm in arm.

Sunday October 24, 1943
Night

Jenny and I talked all week about our stay at the Vendome and she said we would certainly go to Hell for stealing. I told her that someday we would go back as paying customers and leave a really nice tip. Her note in church this morning made it hard for me to pay attention.
"LZCDDUDQXSGHMFMHBDZMCRLNNSGZFZHMSG HRLNQMHMFITRSENQXNT"

No boys called her last week asking for a date or if they did, she didn't tell me. We babysat for Aunt Doris last night and I think Mike and Harry both have a crush on Jenny or maybe they've just discovered that boys and girls are different. When it was time for their baths, Jenny turned down the offer from Harry to let her bathe him saying that he was too old now to need any help. He looked pretty disappointed and when he came back downstairs wearing his pajamas, his little wanger was pushing his pajama bottoms straight out in front of him like a blind man's cane. Neither Jenny nor I said anything, even when Mike came downstairs wearing his pajamas and having the same bulge in them.

"They're just boys," I tried to explain to Jenny in the kitchen when we went looking for a cookie for them.

"I bet if I grabbed their little wangers and squeezed real hard..."

"You should try that on your next date."

That got me a "go to Hell" stare I probably deserved.

Aunt Doris and Bob were home soon after we got the boys to bed so Jenny and I had almost no time alone.

Friday October 29, 1943
Very late

The last volleyball game of the season was this afternoon. Jenny got to play a lot but we still lost. A photographer made team pictures before the game and I want to buy a yearbook this year. All our girls looked good in their blue and grey uniforms. Since Halloween comes on Sunday this year, the children are trick-or-treating tomorrow night. There was a party tonight at Sarah Martin's house for Reitz students in our class who graduated Centennial and Jenny and I went. It was good to see a lot of them. We may all go to the same school now, but there are so many students there, we rarely see some except in the hall between classes. It wasn't a costume party and I didn't really dress up, but Jenny wore one of her photo shoot outfits and had the eye of every boy there, and some of the girls too. She looked like a million bucks and the girls all asked her about the photographs Mr. Evans has taken of her and if she really was going to be a model someday. These were not at all like the stuck-up girls at Reitz who mostly come from well-to-do families and barely speak to us. I've known most of these girls since first grade. The boys looked a lot, but I think they're afraid of Jenny. Sarah told me that she'd heard that Jenny was secretly dating a senior and didn't want her parents to know. I tried to put her off that line of questioning, but she was determined.

"You're her best friend; just tell me if she's seeing anyone special and we'll let it go at that."

"Yes," I replied. "Yes she is. The two of them are madly in love and that's all I'll say."

"Is she coming to the Thanksgiving dance with him?"

"I don't think so and that really is all I'll say."

I've decided I won't be going to the dance. Jenny can choose whom she wants to go with, but I'm staying home. I've thought about it a lot and I really do want Mom to go and I don't mind watching the kids.

Sarah had dozens of records at the party and her mom made cookies. I have no idea where she found the sugar, but if she's anything like Sarah, she found a way. We waited to see if anyone would dance, but it was just like fifth grade. All the boys stayed together in a group and the girls did the same thing.

"Watch this," Jenny said with an evil smile on her face.

She walked over to Sarah, took her hand and practically dragged her out into the middle of the floor. Jenny had no idea what song would be coming up next. It was a brand new one by Ella Mae Morse called "Shoo Shoo Baby." I've heard it on the radio, but I didn't know it was in record stores already. It's a sort of slow swing that Jenny figured out right away and she taught Sarah the basic steps as they danced, although it looked like she knew some of them already. Jenny didn't let Sarah go at the end of the song and when Harry James's "Two O'clock Jump" came up next, Jenny took charge and had poor Sarah spinning so fast everyone knew by the end of the dance she was wearing green panties to match her dress. When Jenny came back and sat down, she had a smile that wouldn't stop.

"That's nothing," I whispered to her. "Watch this."

I got up, walked slowly around the room and came back to Jenny and asked for her hand. She shook her head and turned away. I got the cue immediately and walked to the other end of the room and sat down. As soon as I got seated, Jenny came over and asked for my hand. I shook my head and turned away. It was the old Viennese waltz routine and we had everyone watching us. They had no idea what was going on. It was Benny Goodman and Peggy Lee with "Why Don't You Do Right" and it was perfect for what we were doing and the words just fit the mood. There wasn't nearly enough room for a Viennese waltz, but it was just right for a slow waltz. When the music slowed, we looked at each other, stood up and walked to the middle of the floor. I took Jenny in my arms and made love to her while everyone watched. They might've thought we were dancing, but in our minds we were all alone with our legs wrapped around each other. We couldn't have danced any closer—not with clothes on, and when the music stopped there were a lot of mouths hanging open. I didn't care. We left just before midnight and laughed about it all the way home. That should be enough to keep Sarah gossiping for a month.

Wednesday November 3, 1943
Night

I told Jenny on the way home from school today that I wouldn't be going to the Thanksgiving dance, that I wanted Mom to go with Aunt Doris and Bob and that I would be babysitting the kids.

"Then I'm not going either."

"Yes you are Jenny. You haven't said anything but I know you've been asked by a dozen boys by now. You're a beautiful young woman and I don't own you. I want you to go. You should date and do things a normal teenager does. I love you, but I also want you to be happy and I don't know if I can ever make you happy the way someone else could."

She exploded.

"I have heard this bullshit from you since fifth grade and I'm sick of it! I don't know if you're intentionally trying to get rid of me or if you just haven't been paying attention these last three years. I'm tired of hearing this 'poor pitiful me' crap you pull every year or so. If I want to go to the fucking dance, I'll go to the fucking dance and if I want to stay home from the fucking dance, I'll stay home from the fucking dance. I won't do either because you want me to; because you know what… I haven't been naked with you every fucking minute I could be because you wanted me to. I didn't fall in love with you because you wanted me to. I'm not going to spend the rest of my life with you because you want me to. Can't you get that through your fucking head?"

"If it were a fucking dance, I'd probably go."

My attempt at humor didn't slow her down.

"You make me crazy; do you know that? I was normal before I met you. Just don't keep telling me what I should do, because I'm already doing what I want to do and I believe it's what I should be doing. If I have to make love to you every day to convince you I love you, then I will. I'll find a way, but I can't listen to you tell me what a 'normal' teenager should be doing. Do you really not believe I love you as much as I say I do? Nothing has ever come between us, has it? We've never had a serious fight, have we? If I go to that dance with some boy, do you really think I'll let him do anything afterward? Do you really think I'd spread my legs for anyone but you? Do you honestly think I can be talked into anything I don't want to do? I'm happy with you. I'm horny just talking to you and I can't think of anything I'd rather do than take you up to my room right now and rip your clothes off. Can you say the same thing about me? Do you want to make love to me more than take the next breath? There are some things I don't know and maybe never will and there are things I know for absolute certain and the only one that matters is that I love you."

I love that woman. I even love her when she yells at me.

Thursday November 11, 1943
Night

Today is Armistice Day and that holiday never meant too much to me until now. It was always just nice to get a day off school, but now maybe I know why they made it a holiday. I would sure be in favor of a holiday marking the end of this war. I didn't know until this week that the armistice was signed the eleventh hour of the eleventh day of the eleventh month in 1918. It would be perfect if the Krauts surrendered at noon on December 12, the twelfth hour of the twelfth day of the twelfth month. Maybe that's what I'll pray for.

We had a nice surprise early this morning. My sister showed up with Victoria right after breakfast. I thought something might be wrong, but it was just a visit. Mother and Victoria get along so well when she visits. It's like they're long lost relatives or something and they can talk for hours catching up. Under different circumstances, they would probably have been best friends for years by now. My sister followed me around while I saw to Millie and Dave. I'm glad she did; I wanted to know how she was getting along.

"I have a really nice room and Victoria pays me much too much for the work I do. Mostly I just see to it that everything gets done by someone else, like maybe the gardener and the maid. Victoria buys me everything I need so I've saved almost all the money she's paid me. You're definitely going to college by the way. Mom told me she has a savings account for that, and whatever else it takes I'll cover. I want to come to your graduation and sit in the front row. The big news in my life right now is that I have a boyfriend. His name is Stanley, but everyone calls him Stan and he has a good job at Sunbeam. We've gone out every Saturday night for the past month and I think I might be in love."

"What about Victoria?"

"Victoria's the best thing that ever happened to me and I'll always love her. If she told me tomorrow that she didn't want me seeing Stan anymore, I'd break it off with him without a second thought, but she hasn't done that. She loves her husband and has never given me any reason to think she doesn't, but she loves me too. He doesn't see me as a threat and I don't see him that way either. Maybe Victoria thinks the same way about Stan and me. I haven't quite figured out how to explain Victoria to him. He's such a sweet man, I know he'll understand. Anyway, things are not at that point yet. What about you? Jenny still keeping you around until she can do better?"

"I think that sometimes, I really do, but it's been three years now so maybe I should grow up and believe her when she says she loves me."

"Well, I'm the last person you should take advice from, but I'd believe her if I were you. She's grown into a beautiful girl and if she had plans to dump you, she would've done it a long time ago."

It was a good visit and when they left, Mom hugged Victoria just like she did my sister and made them both promise to visit more often. After they left, I heard Mom praying. She was on her knees in the kitchen and God was in our house, listening.

Monday November 15, 1943
Early morning

I have to get up in a few minutes. I can already hear Mom downstairs starting breakfast. She knows I don't mind doing it, but she likes doing it herself. Jenny went to the movies with Tony Bingham Saturday night and I'm sure her parents don't know that it wasn't a double date with me and someone—I didn't ask. I thought she was done with him, but then sometimes I think she likes him, at least more than the other boys who've already asked her to the Thanksgiving dance. She got home by eleven and after making sure her parents knew she was home, she went out the back door and came to my house. She stayed until almost daylight and neither of us slept. Tony asked her to the dance weeks ago and she told him Saturday night that she would go. Of all the boys she could have said yes to, he's my choice and I told her so. He's a nice guy and I know he doesn't know how to dance. That's a mean thing to think, but he'll make sure she doesn't dance with anyone I wouldn't approve of. I don't have to tell Jenny everything do I?

Monday November 22, 1943
Night

The Thanksgiving dance was Saturday and I watched the four brats, but it wasn't so bad. Mom, Aunt Doris, and Bob had a good time and I heard that Mom even danced a few times, and not just with Bob. I guess I've never thought about Mom maybe remarrying someday. She's a good-looking woman and there are plenty of eligible bachelors her age around, although not too many who would meet our standards.

Tony got special permission from his parents to drive Jenny to the dance and when he suggested they leave the place a little early, Jenny agreed. He didn't know that she would insist they come here. All the kids were in bed and I had my pajamas on when the knock on the door came. It was a little awkward at first, but Tony was so glad to be out with Jenny, he got over it quickly. He had to be home by eleven so at about fifteen till, he left with Jenny telling him it was okay for her to stay at my house until our parents got home. She walked him out to his car and of course I was watching. She probably figured I would be. It was a very simple kiss, one that I approved of.

As soon as she was back inside, she grabbed me and kissed me and slipped her hand inside the back of my pajamas. I wanted to ask if being out with Tony had made her horny, but I thought better of that and kept my mouth shut; not completely shut. It was easy to fold down the top of her strapless dress, but that's about as far as we got. Mom, Aunt Doris, and Bob drove up just as things were getting started. I pulled my coat over my pajamas and walked Jenny home in time to see her parents pull into their driveway. It wasn't a bad night after all. Not bad at all.

Saturday November 27, 1943
Night

Thanksgiving Day Mom and I went to Aunt Doris.' She'd insisted and had gone to a lot of trouble so we couldn't very well turn her down. I missed being with the Brewsters, and Jenny said it wasn't the same without us. She came over after we got home and the two of us went skating. The place is always open on Thanksgiving so parents will have someplace to send their kids while they entertain guests. I'm getting better and when the all-couples skate was announced, Jenny and I didn't hesitate for a minute before going out onto the floor. It's very different from dancing. I'm not nearly as sure of myself and let Jenny lead most of the time. After the skate, we sat down and it was a surprise when Sarah walked up to Jenny and offered her hand. Jenny smiled at me and accepted. The two of them were beautiful together and Sarah's an excellent skater. There weren't any rumors at school after her Halloween party and maybe now I understand why. I think Sarah has a crush on Jenny but doesn't want to admit it to herself. On the floor Sarah took charge and held Jenny close. I should probably be jealous. At the end of the song, Sarah's face was close enough to Jenny's to kiss her and it was plain to see she wanted to. She now knows Jenny and I are more than friends, but that's something even Sarah wouldn't tell anyone about.

After the skate, they came back to our table and we talked for a long while. Sarah's a very different person away from other people, even likeable, and she sat as close as possible to Jenny. She would never do anything like that at school or around her other friends. When Jenny and I were getting ready to leave, Sarah suggested that the three of us do something together sometime, like go to a movie or something and I wasn't upset when Jenny answered for both of us and said we would love to. On the way home I kidded Jenny about her new girlfriend.

"You're just jealous she didn't skate with you."

Really, I wasn't. For all her faults, Sarah's one of us, one of the Centennial gang and we stick together even if we don't like each other sometimes.

Sunday December 5, 1943
Night

Jenny and I went to the movies last night with Sarah. We saw *Phantom of the Opera* with Nelson Eddy. I like him and I think Susanna Foster is just beautiful, although I never know what color her hair's going to be. It was a stunning red in this movie and I think I like that color best on her. Jenny sat between Sarah and me and I held Jenny's right hand. While we were walking home she said Sarah held her left hand through the whole movie. Sarah was dressed to the nines and I know she was wearing make-up.

Our parents don't really wait up for us anymore when we're out together so everyone had gone to bed by the time we got to Jenny's. It wasn't hard for her to talk me into going up to her bedroom for a few minutes and as cold as it was in the house, it didn't take us long to get warm under her bed covers. Soon we were as close as two people can possibly be.

"Jenny, can I come in?"

I rolled over behind Jenny and tried to disappear.

"Sure Mom; what's wrong?"

Thank goodness she didn't turn the lights on before she came over and sat down on the bed. The light from the bathroom down the hall wasn't bright enough for her to see me—I hope.

"Nothing's wrong, not with us, but I heard on the news about some trouble downtown tonight with three white soldiers from Camp Breckinridge getting into a fight with a group of colored teenagers and just wanted to make sure you were home."

"We didn't see anything. It must have happened while we were in the theater."

Jenny sat up in bed, kissed her mother and told her good night. I started breathing again when the door closed.

Friday December 17, 1943
Night

Hurray, we're out of school until after the New Year and I'm expecting Eric to announce the end of the war any night. Maybe the Krauts will give up before we have to invade across the Channel. The Russians aren't letting up, that's for sure and all the news from the Pacific is good.

Last weekend Mom and Mrs. Brewster decided Jenny and I should stay close to home. There's been more trouble with the coloreds in Gear Town. If some high-ranking military officers don't do something soon, it's going to get worse. On the weekends, soldiers from the camp flood into the city and a lot of them wind up in Gear

Town after they've made it through the bars. I've heard it's easier to buy a girl there than at the Trocadero in Henderson. That's the other place the soldiers go. They can find a white girl at that bar, but she'll cost them a lot more and the chances of getting killed are about the same. We get *The Gleaner* at school and there's always a story about the Trocadero in it. Jenny wants to go sometime, but I told her I wouldn't be caught dead in that place, and besides it's too far away.

Saturday at noon Sarah called Jenny and asked if we were going to the movies or anything. Instead of just telling her no, Jenny invited her over for the afternoon. We didn't have anything planned so it was okay with me.

"Are you going to kiss her and give meaning to her dull life?" I asked with a smile. "She'll let you and I bet she faints. I dare you."

"No, I'm not going to kiss her, but you can if you want. I dare you."

"I will if you will."

"All right sweetheart, I'll take that dare. You have to go first and you have to kiss her on the lips."

"Okay, but if I do, you can't chicken out—and it can't be just a peck on the cheek either. Your kiss has to be on the lips too and it has to last at least as long as mine. She'll absolutely die."

It was mean of us to plan such a thing, but I guess we were bored. We were sure Sarah had never been kissed before, because if she had, she would've told everyone already.

Jenny's mom going Christmas shopping with my mom that afternoon made the plan that much easier to carry out. Mr. Brewster's working most Saturdays now so we had the house to ourselves. I would much rather have been there alone with Jenny and that could have happened if she hadn't invited Sarah in the first place, so it was really her fault.

We both chickened out. Sarah came over dressed for a date with her blonde hair perfectly curled and we played records, but there was no kissing and not much dancing.

Saturday December 25, 1943
Night

It was snowing hard and bitterly cold last night when I left for our bench in the park. I took a quilt from my bed and told Jenny when I talked to her on the phone earlier to bring one too. Our bench was covered in snow and I had to brush it off before I could sit down. There was ice underneath and my butt was frozen by the time she arrived.

"Promise me that someday we can exchange gifts sitting by a warm fire in our own home," Jenny said as she sat down next to me and I wrapped us both in the quilts.

"I hope we come here on Christmas Eve when we're old and grey. There's something special about being here on this night with you. Everything's so quiet and when it's snowing, it's like a Christmas story come to life. There's nowhere I'd rather be tonight than right here with you."

"Okay so I'm not as romantic as you, but I am here."

"You're romantic enough," I whispered just before I kissed her. "You're my Christmas candy that lasts all year long no matter how much I lick you."

"Can I remember that line and say it back to you someday?"

Sometimes she's the romantic and sometimes I try to be. Her Christmas present to me was perfectly wrapped as usual and so was mine. I got Mom to do it for me. She wanted to know what I got Jenny so I opened the box.

"But Jenny's not Catholic," she said when I showed her.

Jenny unwrapped the small case and took out the silver St. Christopher medal and necklace. A lot of girls are wearing them and even some of the boys.

"It's beautiful and I've wanted one of these since the girls on the volleyball team started wearing them this year. Almost everyone has one but me. You notice things like that don't you? Help me put it on."

My fingers were freezing but I managed to undo the clasp and put the silver chain around her neck. She turned around and kissed me and I slid my freezing hand under her coat and blouse. She shivered a little and I don't know if it was from the cold or not. Her kiss was nice, although it wasn't the kiss I wanted, so I tilted her head back just a little and gave her my best Christmas kiss. Her fingers were cold and I had to pee—I always forget to pee before leaving home to meet her on Christmas Eve—but I didn't want her to stop. Just a few seconds of her making goosebumps run all over my body and I had to back away.

"You're gonna make me pee and I'll freeze to this bench. They won't find me until New Year's and I can just imagine the story in the paper."

"Well, open your present. It's not as nice as yours, although it's something you haven't had in a long time."

I slid my hand down her stomach.

"I can think of something else I haven't had in a long time and it doesn't come in a box."

"But this is sweet and you'd do anything for it."

"I know."

"You're terrible. Now move your hand and open your present."

I unwrapped the perfectly wrapped box and I swear there was music from Heaven. It was an assortment of the most delicious looking chocolates I've ever seen. It's been almost impossible to get good chocolate for years and when you can find it, the price is more than a pair of hose and it tastes old. I looked at the box lid and saw it was made in England.

"I got my brother to buy it for me almost two months ago. The box just arrived last week and it was all I could do to stay out of it. I didn't even tell Mom what it was."

"Jenny, this is the best Christmas present ever."

I took out a piece and put it in her mouth and she took one and put it in mine. The expression on her face was one I've only ever seen when…and I probably had the same expression on mine. Half the chocolates were gone by the time we started for home.

"By the way," Jenny said as we walked, "my brother had a message for you in with the chocolates. I told him about you helping a lot of the wives and mothers figure out where their loved ones are right now and he gave me this message for you. 'I hope your Uncles Harold and William Hastings get their differences settled by the middle of October. It would be a shame for them to miss the family Fourth of July celebration next year. I'm sure they'll have lots of fireworks. The men really appreciate all the presents we've been receiving from Evansville lately. They will all be put to good use in the coming year'."

"Do you have any idea what he's talking about?"

"No, but I know who would. We're going to the city library tomorrow. Mrs. Landers works there during the holidays and summers. She can help us."

Monday December 27, 1943
Night

Jenny and I went to the library today and Mrs. Landers was working. She seemed glad to see us and the place was practically deserted. I told her I had a puzzle for her.

"What do the words Harold, William, Hastings, and October have in common?"

"That's easy and you should know the answer yourself," she replied, "although you may not have gotten to the Battle of Hastings in Mr. Reeves' history class yet."

I didn't know what she was talking about.

"The Battle of Hastings led by the French king, William, was in October 1066 and it represented the final major battle of the Norman invasion. The English king, Harold II was killed. It's a date you should remember."

I thanked her and pulled Jenny aside.

"We're going to invade at Normandy sometime around the Fourth of July next year. The presents from Evansville are the LSTs, airplanes and bullets we're building here. You can't tell anyone about this Jenny. They'd put us in jail as spies."

I know where Normandy is. Eric's talks about it a lot. It's one of the places on the French coast where the Krauts are building up their defenses, but everyone seems to think that the invasion, if it comes at all, will be at Calais and I know where that is too. Maybe the Germans will give up before that happens. They can't win. Just here in E'ville, we're making enough stuff to fight the whole war. Jenny's dad told her the government was really worried about spies coming to see what we're doing, but I think we should invite them and give them the grand tour. It would shorten the war.

Chapter Five

1944

Sunday January 2, 1944
Night

The New Year's celebration this year was enormous. It's like everyone believes the war will be over soon. The best fireworks were on the river and Jenny and I showed up early. There was a huge crowd so I didn't expect to see anyone I knew, but right there next to us was Sarah and her family. We watched the fireworks for a couple of hours, well after midnight, and when we were ready to start for home, Jenny invited Sarah to her house for this afternoon.

She showed up early in the afternoon today and she was dressed like she was expecting her date to arrive any minute to take her out someplace nice for an evening of dancing. She came with a stack of records and some were new ones we didn't have, so Jenny set up the record player and put one on. The first song was perfect, *Put Your Arms around Me Honey* by Dick Kuhn's Orchestra. It was a swing and soon the three of us were dancing with each other. Mostly it was me dancing with Jenny for that song. Jenny and I danced with Sarah alone for the next few swings; then Jenny put on a slow waltz and waited for me to ask Sarah to dance. Her waltz was perfect even with the limited amount of space we had and I held her like she was my best girlfriend. At the end of the dance I thanked her for dancing with me and kissed her. It wasn't one of those pee yourself kinds of kisses, but it was on the lips and it did last a couple of seconds. Sarah didn't back away; in fact she smiled, held on to me and waited for Jenny to put on the next record. Jenny knew what she was doing. She sneaked in one of her mom's Tangos, a long one. Sarah was completely lost.

"It's a Tango…and Jenny's mom says it's like making love standing up with your clothes on," I said with a smile. Sarah smiled back; it was a nervous sort of smile.

I gave her a quick lesson and showed her the basic steps. She soon picked them up, but when I slid my leg between hers and pulled her so close I could feel every muscle in her body tighten, I was afraid she would back away. She didn't and after the first few steps, she relaxed and let me lead her through the rest of the song. During the promenades, with our faces turned sideways, I brought her so close our cheeks touched and I could feel how warm her face was. At the end of the song, she thanked me for teaching her—and then she kissed me. It wasn't a passionate kiss by any means but it wasn't a kiss like your mother would give you either. It felt good. Jenny applauded and took my place while I searched through the records for just the right one. I started with a Cha-Cha, which Sarah didn't know either. Jenny taught her the steps and then I played the record again. Cha-Chas are danced with the couple far apart and I thought it would be a good warm-up. I then put on the same Tango Jenny had played. Their faces were less than an inch apart through the whole dance and when it was over, Sarah took Jenny in her arms and kissed her and what a kiss it was. I think it surprised Jenny for a second when she realized it wasn't going to be one of those quick kisses like Sarah and I had exchanged, but then she wrapped her arms around Sarah and the girl just melted. It was something to see. It was like Sarah had been waiting for that kiss a long time. Her face was fire engine red when they separated and I noticed she held onto Jenny's hand.

"I'm sorry, I shouldn't have done that. I've never done anything like that in my life," she stammered. "You have to believe me."

Jenny and I looked at each other and burst out laughing. Sarah just stood there; then finally smiled a little.

"I kissed a girl… I've never kissed anyone before today."

"Yes you did," Jenny said with a smile, "you kissed a girl and you weren't turned into a pillar of salt."

Sarah kissed both of us a lot that afternoon—saying it was practice of course and we practiced enough to be experts. I think Jenny and I were like new toys for her and I wanted so much to accidentally touch those perfect bumps in her blouse that seem to always be asking for someone's attention, but I didn't get up the nerve. Her father arrived about eight to pick her up and when she heard his car in the driveway, she gave me a kiss first. I wasn't going to let her get away without getting at least a feel of something so I slid my hands around behind her and got a good double handful. She squirmed but she didn't try to back away. Things would have gone a lot further if she hadn't had to go. She then kissed Jenny. It was just an ordinary kiss, but Sarah's hands went low, like she'd learned something from me, and Jenny said later there was a little squeeze.

Friday January 7, 1944
Night

It was hard going back to school this week after being off so long. I haven't written much about school this year. It's not so different from last year, although our classes are larger and harder. Jenny and I have most of our classes together and we both like science and history best. Miss Jimmerson is our science teacher and Mr. Reeves is history. Neither of them is married and Sarah says they're dating. I think that's nice even though Sarah says there's some rule against it. That doesn't seem very fair. English is divided this year between composition and American literature. We start literature Monday and I'm looking forward to it. The grammar part of composition was so dull, but Mrs. Hammond got us through it and maybe she's right, that good grammar is a sign of a good education. Our first reading assignment will be *The Scarlet Letter* and I've already started reading it. This isn't like other books we've been made to read, not at all. Jenny and I are reading it together and tonight we read to each other. I haven't been read to since Daddy used to read me bedtime stories. He would never read the stories exactly the way they were written. My favorite was *Goldilocks* because he had a different ending every time. Sometimes I would make him read it for a week straight. I'd forgotten that. It's sad that I'm already forgetting things about him.

Tuesday January 11, 1944
Night

There was so much freezing rain and snow over the weekend, the roads are iced over and school was cancelled yesterday and today. Jenny's dad has been stuck at the shipyard since Saturday and soldiers have been called out from Camp Breckinridge to help workers get to their defense jobs. They're clearing the main roads today so probably tomorrow we'll go back to school. Jenny and I finished *The Scarlet Letter* last night. Neither of us cheated by reading ahead, although we guessed Dimmesdale had to die sometime in the story. I didn't like the idea of Hester being buried next to him and I really didn't like the letter "A" being put on their gravestone. This was the first book I've read where everyone didn't live happily ever after. We can hope that Pearl, their illegitimate daughter, had a good life at least.

Mr. Evans called Jenny yesterday and said he wanted to get some pictures of her and the snow in the park before it melts. Sarah called me bored out of her mind so I asked if she would like to come along. The three of us met Mr. Evans and Miss Payne at Peggy Hale's. The store wasn't open, but Mr. Evans had the key and we had the run of the place, helping Miss Payne and Jenny pick out clothes to model. I thought Jenny would be modeling coats and hats and winter clothes. It turned out that wasn't at all what they had in mind. The newest swimsuits had just arrived and they wanted pictures of Jenny in a swimsuit in the snow. I thought it was crazy, but Miss Payne said the pictures would sell for sure.

"We need a couple of extras for the snowball fight," she said, looking at us with a smile. "How about it?"

"I dare you," Sarah said before I had a chance to.

Sarah and I tried on swimsuits, in separate dressing rooms, until Miss Payne was happy with how we looked. Jenny of course looked like a New York model in all the suits she tried on.

"But how are we going to get to the park? All the roads are closed," Sarah asked. "We'll freeze out there if we don't have some place to warm up between pictures."

I hadn't thought of that and the park was too far away to come back to the store after every shoot.

"Mr. Evans has that taken care of," Miss Payne answered, "and I think you'll be plenty warm. Put your clothes on over your swimsuits for now."

In a few minutes, a huge military truck with snow chains pulled up in front of the store and another smaller truck followed. I had no idea what was going on when six soldiers in uniform got out.

"Our ride is here," Miss Payne announced, "and I understand there was a lottery at Camp Breckinridge last night to see who would get to escort us today, so be nice to them."

We grabbed armloads of swimsuits, hats, boots, and coats and followed Mr. Evans to the back of the biggest truck. The rear was covered and it had a huge heater in the middle and seats along the sides. It was a warm comfortable ride to the park. When we arrived, Mr. Evans came inside.

"Okay, we're going to shoot the snowball fight first. I'm going to get set up and then I'll call you. Come out in your swimsuits, boots and hats and let's start the shooting with the three of you walking toward the lake. Jenny, you'll start the fight and let's just see what happens. The whole thing will only take a few minutes and then you can come back and warm up. I want to see lots of smiles."

"And perky nipples," I added after he closed the flap on the truck.

"I don't know about this," Sarah said as Jenny and I began undressing down to our swimsuits.

"Come on; it'll be fun," Jenny replied, "and who knows, we might even get paid."

Sarah undressed and as soon as she did, those fabulous nipples of hers rose to the occasion and pushed out of her swimsuit like lighthouse beacons in a storm.

Jenny had one look at her and smiled.

"Those might just steal the show."

When Mr. Evans yelled, we piled out of the back of the truck to whistles and cat-calls from the soldiers who had escorted us on this, no doubt, vitally-important-for-the-war-effort mission. The cold air hit us like a sledgehammer. I could hardly breathe and goosebumps covered every square inch of skin on my body.

"Now walk toward the lake like it was a nice spring day," Mr. Evans yelled.

He wanted photos of our butts; Jenny's for sure and I heard his camera click about a hundred times as we walked slowly toward the lake. When we were within a few yards of the frozen bank, Jenny peeled away and scooped up a handful of snow and made a snowball. She was playing it out like a professional and teased us with throwing it. Sarah and I did the same thing and soon it was an all-out battle, which ended with the three of us rolling in the freezing snow. It was over in about two minutes and we ran back for the truck, giving the soldiers a close-up eyeful. One asked Sarah if she needed any help getting changed. Mr. Evans had nothing but good things to say about our supporting roles.

Miss Payne said that Sarah and I could get dressed, that we were finished for the day. She then picked out the next swimsuit for Jenny and handed it to her. Sarah pretended not to notice Jenny as she changed, but she was taking it all in. After a few minutes' warming, Jenny walked out to the next shoot with Miss Payne as if she were walking out into the summer sun. Our swimsuits were wet from the melting snow we'd collected on them and I decided to take mine off before getting dressed. Sarah would just have to look or not. I didn't care. I undressed as if I were in my own private dressing room, hoping of course Sarah would do the same. Maybe she thought that since she'd just seen Jenny naked and now me, it didn't matter if I saw her because she peeled off her swimsuit with me looking straight at her. Finally I had a look—and that flaming red hair down there—what a surprise. I tried not to stare, but I didn't intentionally turn away either. I didn't know that sort of hair came in red.

We got dressed in our coats and by that time Jenny was back inside for another swimsuit change. She was shivering as she opened my coat up, wrapped it around her and hugged me.

"I'm freezing. Warm me up quick."

Sarah came over, opened up her coat and we both hugged Jenny between us until she stopped shivering.

"Help me get out of this and into the next one. My fingers are frozen."

Sarah and I rolled the swimsuit off her down to her ankles and she stepped out of it. We helped her dress for the next five swimsuit photos. When Jenny went out for the last shoot, Sarah and I stayed in the truck and sat on the floor near the heater.

"Maybe I shouldn't ask but I'm going to anyway," Sarah began. "Why doesn't Jenny have any hair, you know…down there?"

"She shaves it. It's something models do because they have to change clothes a lot and don't want to take the time to make sure nothing spoils the shot. Mr. Evans would get into a lot of trouble if he took pictures of an underage girl's pubic hair." She didn't need to know the real reason.

"God, I hope I didn't have anything showing."

"You didn't; I looked."

"I'm going to shave it all off someday. I hate it."

"Red hair is one in a million," I guessed, "and I think it's stunning. Don't you dare shave it off."

"Well, don't you dare tell anyone either. You're the only one who's ever seen it. I always get gym as the last class of the day so I don't have to shower afterward."

"Your terrible secret is safe with me," I said with a huge smile, "and trust me; someday your red surprise is going to make a lucky boy, or maybe a girl, very happy."

I don't know why I said that.

When Jenny came back in after the final shoot, the truck pulled out and headed back toward downtown. By the time we stopped again, Jenny was dressed and warm and we got to keep all the things we'd worn that day. Of course I told Jenny about getting to see Sarah naked, complete with a description of her red hair down there.

Sunday January 16, 1944
Night

We're all grounded for life. The photos came out yesterday in *The Press* fashion section. Jenny's dad hit the ceiling, although there's not much he can do because he signed a contract letting Mr. Evans take pictures of Jenny. Sarah's parents and my mom however haven't signed anything. Sarah's father says he's going to sue the newspaper and Mr. Evans for taking indecent pictures of his daughter. Mom just said she was very disappointed in me. I would rather she'd beat me with a belt than say that.

I think the photos are great and, like we expected, Mr. Evans did make sure almost every shot had pointy nipples in it; Sarah's were the pointy-est of them all. I don't understand what the big fuss is all about. We weren't naked or anything. I think it's because one of the photos showed the soldiers staring. Sarah's father informed Jenny's mom that his daughter would no longer be allowed to visit Jenny or me and that we were not welcome at his house either. We can't even talk on the phone. Jenny's dad sat between Jenny and me today in church. This afternoon Mrs. Brewster came over and she and Mom talked a long time in the kitchen. After she left Mom told me Mr. Brewster was plenty mad and that I shouldn't hang out with Jenny or walk to school with her for a while.

Thursday January 27, 1944
Night

This is torture. Jenny has to leave for school fifteen minutes earlier than before so I won't be walking with her and she can't walk home with me. That only lasted one day. She just waits for me a couple of blocks from home. Unless her father hires a private detective to follow us, we'll at least be able to walk to and from school together and now Sarah's joining us for the last few blocks. She's been asked out twice since the photo shoot and can't go with either boy. One of them is a senior, Rudy Meckler, the son of probably the richest man in town.

"Well, I don't care," she said this morning. "No one ever asked me out before and I would rather be asked out and not be able to go than not be asked out at all."

"That's okay, seniors ask us out for only one thing," Jenny added. "They think we're too young and stupid to tell them no when they reach up our skirts for a feel."

"I might let Rudy have a feel. I think he's adorable."

"If he ever got a look at that fiery red cuzzy of yours, you'd have him for life," Jenny said with a smile.

"You told her," Sarah said as she turned to me, but she wasn't angry. "I knew you would."

"Relax, I haven't told anyone else and I won't. Your horrible secret is safe with us. Old Rudy will just have to find out for himself."

At least the three of us get to talk for a few minutes every school day. The weekends are going to be hardest.

Monday February 7, 1944
Night

Sarah told us this morning she sneaked out of the house Saturday night and Rudy picked her up in his car. He didn't even take her to a movie, just took her parking down by the river. Jenny and I really need to talk to her before she does something stupid. She said they just kissed, but girls lie almost as much as boys when it comes to things like that.

I've torn down a few of our pictures from the newspaper that were posted on bulletin boards and in bathrooms at school. All of them had something vulgar added to them. One of the pictures of us taken from behind had a stiff wang drawn pointing toward Jenny's butt and the one that really showed Sarah's nipples had both of them circled with "bite here" written underneath—and this was on the junior high side. Who knows what the high school boys have done with them.

Tony has asked Jenny out again and suggested we double date with him and Kelly like before. If we weren't grounded, we would probably go. A popular senior named Sandy Cosworth, who is good friends with Rudy has put the word out that I'm lickable. I thought it was likeable at first until Sarah told me different. I guess I don't mind being called lickable, not by someone as good-looking as Sandy. Sarah wants me to sneak out this weekend and double date with her and Rudy. She said she would get him to arrange it with Sandy. I think she just doesn't want to be alone with him again. I know he's tried something and she probably let him and now he wants more. If she gets caught sneaking out of the house, her father will kill her, but if she doesn't get caught, something even worse might happen. I can't very well call her parents and tell them to keep an eye on their daughter. If she had a brother or sister though, I think I'd tell them. There's a big Valentine's Day party coming up next weekend and Sarah's hoping Rudy will invite her. If he does, she'll sneak out to go with him.

Tuesday February 15, 1944
Night

Rudy went to the party but he didn't go with Sarah. He went with that stuck-up bitch Dorothy Fulton whose family's just as rich as his. Sarah said on the way home yesterday that he had to go with her and then she told me Rudy came by her house and picked her up after he took Dorothy home. I blew up before Jenny had a chance to.

"So you're good enough to fuck, but not good enough to be seen with. Is that it?"

I shouldn't have said that. Sarah didn't speak to me all day today and I can't call her on the phone; so damn frustrating, and I haven't had any time alone with Jenny and I miss her so bad. I got her a Valentine's card and had to give it to her on the way to school yesterday. She got me one too and it was very sweet, although nothing takes the place of her hands all over me. Jenny and I have to figure out some way to get our parents out of the house for an evening. Sarah's problems will have to wait.

Monday February 22, 1944
Night

There was no school today. It's Washington's Birthday and it would have been the perfect day to lie in bed with Jenny and listen to the rain. Mom has cooled down a little and she's speaking to me regularly again, although I still hear her pray for me every night. Jenny said a letter arrived from Mr. Evans last Thursday with a check inside for three hundred dollars. He sold our photos to a magazine in New York. Her father says she has to divide the money with me and Sarah and maybe that will help smooth things over with everyone. I wrote Jenny a really long, really dirty letter earlier tonight, which just made me hornier (if that's even a word) than I was before. Last night I pulled out my copy of the newspaper with our pictures in it and that was enough to give me a dream that sure seemed real. We were in her room and I could hear the rain on the roof just above us. Her parents were gone for the night; doesn't matter where, and we were alone, and then Sarah was there. The two of them were all over me. That was as far as I got before squeezing my pillow so hard my muscles ached this morning. It was nice, but nothing like the real thing. Sarah would be with Jenny and me, I know she would if I could think of how to bring it up to Jenny. She has no reason to be jealous. Anyway, Sarah's probably spreading her legs for old Rudy by now and wouldn't want anything like that with us. Sometimes I have the craziest dreams.

Sunday February 27, 1944
Night

Tuesday's paper had pictures from another one of those ship christenings that seem to happen almost every week, but the girl in the picture looked familiar. I asked at school and found out it was Katherine Kohl. Everyone says she's the prettiest girls in school and hers is just about the best known family in town. She's a senior and her brother Jimmy recently asked Sarah about Jenny. He's a junior. I took the paper with me to school Friday and showed Jenny the picture. She knew who Katherine was.

"She's beautiful," Jenny said. "She also happens to be the daughter of Robert L. Kohl, one of the richest men in town. Her brother's asked me out—and I'm grounded for who knows how long."

"I have an idea. You get me a date with her and you can go out with Jimmy."

"You're a dreamer, but you dream big don't you?"

Everyone knows the name Kohl. George Kohl and Sons is a metal working business that has been in Evansville forever. We studied about it in history at Centennial and there've been lots of stories in the paper about the things they're making for the war. How could old Robert have a daughter that beautiful? Maybe I was dreaming, but I'd sell my soul for a night with her. Thank goodness Jenny doesn't take me too seriously. Not being able to be with her is making me crazier by the day.

Saturday March 4, 1944
Night

Okay, I'm sneaking out tonight and I hope Jenny's front door isn't locked. I'll crawl in through the window if I have to. There's something I have to show her. I don't normally look at the men's magazine rack behind the counter at Muir's, but something caught my eye today when I went in to pick up medicine for baby Dave. He has colic and when he cries, Millie cries and no one sleeps. The copy of *Spot* caught my eye for some reason and when no one was watching I stretched over the counter and pulled it off the rack—and there on the front cover were three butts I recognized. They belonged to Sarah, Jenny, and me. Mr. Evans sold our pictures to one of those "true story" magazines, or that's what I thought it was at first. All I could think of was that if anyone in town finds out, we'll be branded for life. I ran home, got my money, and went back and bought every copy Muir's had. They had ten and it was hard to ask for them. I wasn't sure the girl working would even sell them to me. Thank goodness she didn't know me and I'm never going in there again when she's working. I spent an hour going to the other stores in town that sold magazines and bought all they had. My last stops were at Hart's Drugs and Readmore Magazines on Main Street. They each had ten copies. I bought fifty copies in all and I pray no one I know saw me. There were some strange looks but I don't care. I don't think any of the stores had sold any yet because each one had exactly ten copies. It wasn't exactly the same photo that was in the paper, but I knew it was us. I hadn't even taken time to look through the magazine before I sneaked them into the house and up to my room. I hid the stack under my bed, slipped back out of the house and came in through the front door with the medicine.

Sunday March 5, 1944
Night

The medicine worked and Mom went to bed last night as soon as the babies were asleep. She hasn't slept much in the last few nights with Dave being sick. I sneaked out of the house at ten with a copy of the magazine and went the back way to Jenny's. The lights were still on so I figured her father was going in at eleven to work third. I waited until he left and all the lights were out before trying the front door. It was unlocked, but I wasn't sure Mrs. Brewster was asleep yet. There were no sounds in the house so I crept up the stairs, putting my weight on each step slowly so as to not make them creak. There was a dim light under the door at Jenny's room, which meant her lamp was on, but the overhead light was out. She wasn't expecting me so I didn't know exactly what to do. I turned the doorknob slowly and pushed open the door just a crack. Jenny was lying on her stomach with her hands under her and soon enough I knew what I was watching. The first thing I thought was 'so that's how she does it.' It would have been rude for me to interrupt, so I just watched, feeling like the most successful Peeping Tom in history. It was a picture Mr. Evans would sell his soul for. Her face was turned toward me but her eyes were closed. I imagined what she was thinking about and hoped I was a part of it. In a few minutes, I recognized the long sigh that came from her. When she reached down for the covers and pulled them up, I thought it was time I let her know I was there. It seemed a shame to intrude, but I'd already made it that far. I waited a few more minutes.

"Jenny, are you awake?" I whispered as I walked into her room. "It's me."

"Don't say another word. Come over here—if you're real and I'm not dreaming."

I slipped into her bed and stayed there until she let me go.

"I'll love to you forever for showing up tonight. You have no idea how much I wanted you to be here, and then you were."

Maybe she was thinking about me after all.

"You have to see this, Jenny. I bought every copy in town this afternoon."

"What are you talking about?"

We looked through the magazine together. They were photos we recognized from the last shoot, but they weren't the ones in the paper and all of our faces were blurred out. They also changed our names and where the pictures were taken to fit the story. My name was Jesse and I thought that was funny. It was my dog's name when I was little. Jenny's name was Ursula and Sarah's name was Sugar. Ursula's butt and Sugar's nipples were the stars of the spread. There was a whole story about the three of us being imprisoned by Nazis on a mountaintop somewhere in Bavaria and being rescued by brave American soldiers. Sugar was particularly grateful. The stories in that magazine were there just to take up space between the pictures of mostly naked girls and some mostly naked men. This was no "true story" magazine. It wasn't like any magazine I've ever read and now I really hope no one I know saw me buy all those copies.

"This is something for us to show our grandchildren someday," Jenny said with a smile.

She always knows the right thing to say. I didn't risk staying any longer and sneaked back to my own bedroom. I wasn't missed and today in church, I was allowed to sit next to Jenny again. Maybe our penance is coming to an end.

Wednesday March 15, 1944
Night

Mom told me today after school that my grounding is over. She also said that she hoped I'd learned something from the experience. I kissed her and promised to never disappoint her again and I meant it. According to Mom, Sarah's parents and the Brewsters have also agreed to lift their wayward daughters' sentences. I called Jenny as soon as Mom finished talking to me. She'd just hung up with Sarah. The three of us are going to meet tomorrow afternoon at my house. Mom's meeting with her USO group and she's already asked me to babysit so we'll have some privacy. I can't wait to catch up on everything. Maybe Sarah's forgiven me for my comment about her doing it with Rudy. I want to know what's going on and I want to show her the magazine.

There's been a lot more trouble in Gear Town between local colored boys and white servicemen. Mom says there'll be a big conference next month between colored leaders and white military officers to try and resolve the problems. She says that Gear Town is going to be shut down or the base commander at Camp Breckinridge will make E'ville off limits. That'll hurt all the businesses in town. They can shut down Gear Town if they want, but there are enough colored and white teenagers willing to sell it somewhere else. I'm not sure anything they do will make much difference. You can buy a night with a girl at almost any hotel in town if you have the money and shutting down Gear Town isn't going to change that. I've heard there are girls at Reitz who make extra money on the weekends by "dating" servicemen, and they're all white girls.

Thursday March 16, 1944
Night

Today after school Sarah, Jenny, and I met at the exit between the junior high and high schools. We were standing talking when this boy I don't know walked up and spoke to Sarah.

"How's it going Red?"

And then a girl who looked to be a senior called her Red as she walked by with her nose in the air. She wasn't very nice and it was plain to see she was talking down to Sarah.

"Red?" I said as we started toward home.

"It's my new nickname I guess. It's what Rudy calls me and everyone else just picked it up."

Jenny and I knew where it came from and it wasn't from Katharine Hepburn's nickname in *Philadelphia Story* either.

When we got to my house, Mom had baked shortbread cookies for us. I knew what that meant. She always makes shortbread cookies when she wants to talk and I guess she figured the three of us had a lot of talking to catch up on. The babies had been fed and were asleep. Mom left for her meeting and reminded me to check on them occasionally. We sat around the kitchen table and waited for someone to recognize the elephant in the room. Jenny didn't wait very long.

"So if you get pregnant is he going to marry you?"

"I'm not getting pregnant. We've only done it once and you can't get pregnant just doing it once."

"Oh yeah; how long did you do it? Did he hurt you?"

"How long? I don't know, until he stopped, I guess; not very long. It didn't hurt at all. I barely felt him inside me. I guess he's not very big down there."

"When he stopped, did he back off quick or did he just lay there on top of you?"

I was beginning to wonder how far Jenny was going to go.

"He held me close for a long time after. It was wonderful. I felt like a real woman for the first time ever."

"When did this happen?"

"Last Saturday night, why?"

"When should your next period start?"

"I don't know, in a couple of weeks, why? I told you we only did it once."

"And I don't suppose your knight in shining armor was wearing a rubber was he? Did you see him put a rubber on?"

"No. Stop it Jenny, you're scaring me."

"You listen to me Sarah. We love you. You're one of us and whatever happens to you happens to us. You can't keep doing this. He's going to get you pregnant and then forget who you are. It happens all the time. There are other things you can do that he'll like just as much, but don't let him back inside you."

"There was something else he asked me to do before we...but I just couldn't."

"Well you won't get pregnant doing that."

We talked all afternoon and then Jenny and I walked Sarah home after Mom got back. I gave her a copy of the magazine and made her promise to hide it. I never asked Jenny how she knows so much. She just knows stuff I don't and maybe I'm glad she does.

Thursday March 30, 1944
Night

Now Sarah has the reputation at school she's often created for others with her rumors; strange how that happens. Students, both boys and girls who don't even know her, call her Red and everyone knows why. She has the most famous cuzzy at Reitz, but old Rudy isn't getting any more of it according to Sarah. I didn't ask if she's had anything in her mouth she couldn't swallow. The bad news is that her period was supposed to have started Tuesday and it didn't. Jenny's worried Sarah might be pregnant. I don't know what she'll do if she is. Maybe Rudy's family will pay her family to send her away to have the baby somewhere. I seriously doubt there'll be wedding bells. I don't know if it makes sense to pray for someone's period to start, but tonight I did anyway.

Friday March 31, 1944
Night

Sarah called this morning and said she wouldn't be going to school, that she had cramps really bad and that they had just started. I told her Jenny and I would come by on our way to school. Her house isn't at all on our way, but I knew it wouldn't matter if we were a little late to homeroom.

We got to Sarah's early this morning. Her parents both work and had already left so we let ourselves in. They live in a beautiful new house and when we yelled for Sarah, we heard her answer from her bedroom. She looked terrible and I recognized the doubled over position I'd seen Jenny in many times before.

"You didn't have to come over. I'll be fine as soon as my period starts. I've never had cramps this bad before though. Maybe I'm being punished for not keeping my knees together."

"Well, we're here to make you feel better," Jenny replied with a smile that told me what she had in mind. "We know just the thing to stop those cramps, although you have to trust us."

Sarah has a huge bed and we crawled in with her and lay down on either side. She had no idea what we were up to.

"Now just relax and let us take care of your problem," I whispered as I pulled her over onto her back and then kissed her.

Those nipples I'd dreamed of touching were right there under her thin pajama top. No one said anything as buttons down the front got unbuttoned. I thought maybe we were going too far trying to help, and then Jenny's hand disappeared under the covers. That's when I decided that too far was just far enough and my hand went under the covers to join hers. Soon our patient was all smiles and kisses—when she wasn't purring. Do I do that too when I…?

With the next cramp, Sarah moaned and dug her butt into the bed. Jenny and I might not be experts even if we do practice a lot, but there was this one final long, bases loaded, out of the park grand slam that took Sarah's breath away for what seemed like a full minute. I thought she'd fainted. She said something but I couldn't understand her.

"What?"

"I said I've never, and I mean I never have…I've tried. Some girls talk about it. I've never made it happen. It was so easy and so…I don't know…just easy and I know I sound like an idiot, but I don't care. I love both of you."

After a few minutes, Jenny and I got up to leave. Sarah's cramps were gone for good. She rolled over and was probably asleep by the time we got to her front door. We didn't miss any of our first period class and we kept a smile on our faces all day. Maybe my crazy dream about being in bed with Sarah and Jenny wasn't so crazy. After school we stopped back by Sarah's and she met us at the door with kisses that would melt an iceberg. It was a good day. It was a very good day.

The evening wasn't so good. Jenny called me late and said that she just got off the phone with Darryl Bertram. He asked her to the prom and she said yes. I don't blame her; Darryl's about the most handsome boy in the junior class and he was the first boy to ask her. He's not one of the society types and I guess I approve. I told Jenny I did anyway. I was kinda hoping that if she went, it would be with Tony.

Friday April 7, 1944
Very late

Jenny, Sarah, and I went skating tonight and afterward came back to Jenny's for a couple of hours. Mrs. Brewster was home, but she gave us the living room after we promised to keep things quiet. Mr. Brewster's still working third shift and sleeps from about two in the afternoon to ten. Mostly the three of us just wanted to talk and catch up. The really big news of the last two weeks happened Wednesday. Since Sarah has refused to sneak out of the house to meet Rudy he's been saying some pretty awful things about her and making sure that everyone, even the junior high boys, knows her new nickname is Red—and why. Sarah's been hanging around Jenny and me as much as possible to get away from their hateful gossip, but Wednesday after school, Rudy and his high society girlfriend Dorothy—with the perfectly made up face and hair— and a group of their friends made a point of yelling at Sarah and calling her Red. Maybe she had rehearsed it or maybe it just came to her, and Sarah had the perfect comeback for them.

"Did Rudy tell all of you about his new nickname? He promised me he wouldn't say anything to anyone about my beautiful red hair, but he did. I promised him I wouldn't say anything about his little pinky size dick, but I am. Sorry about that P.D. but I guess both our nicknames fit. It's just that no one will wonder why you're called P.D. and they're all dying to know why I'm called Red. I'll show them if you will. How about it P.D.? Anytime you're ready."

Sarah stuck the pinky of her left hand up in the air as she walked away. I've heard a lot more people call Sarah by her nickname in the last couple of days, and not in a bad way. It's sort of like everyone wants to know her now and only her friends call her Red. The nickname's been turned completely around. I've heard a lot of talk about Pinky Dick too and I see people with their pinkies in the air after school, but it's not because they want everyone to think they're friends with him.

Sunday's Easter and I don't think anyone has anything special planned. There will be an Easter parade this year though. Jenny's not in it so maybe we'll go and watch. I'm supposed to help her pick out a prom dress tomorrow and I'm not looking forward to that.

Thursday April 13, 1944
Night

Jenny got an interesting letter from her brother today. It was addressed to her, not the family and she wanted me to read it. The censors didn't cut out too much. He's figured out how to write without saying the wrong things. The letter was sort of depressing. He knows the invasion is coming and that he'll be right in the middle of it. He wished Jenny and me a happy birthday but said that we would remember this birthday for the rest of our lives. I told Jenny that somehow he's found out when the invasion will start. He never writes about exactly what he does in England, but I told Jenny that he definitely knows when the invasion's coming. It'll be on our birthday, less than two months from now. I told Jenny to write him back tomorrow, so that he might possibly get it before it all started. His letter ended with him saying that she probably wouldn't hear from him for a while, that he expected to be really busy with work. I know what kind of work he was talking about. Jenny knows too.

Not even Eric or Ernie has that kind of inside information and we can't tell anyone what we know. I thought the Krauts would have given up by now, but I guess it's going to take a full-scale invasion to get Hitler's attention, although some are saying he's dead already. He's lost Italy and the smaller countries around Germany are switching sides the closer the Russians get to them. There are reports almost every day of a city once held by the Germans being recaptured by the Russians. Most of them I can't find on my map. The names sound real though.

On the way to school this morning, before we met up with Sarah, Jenny had one of those "I know something you don't" looks on her face.

"Guess who called me last night asking for a date in two weeks?"

I guessed all the usual suspects and Jenny kept grinning and shaking her head.

"You'll never guess. It was Jimmy Kohl. It turns out that his family and the Meckler's hate each other. When Jimmy found out about Sarah telling off Rudy and giving him his new nickname, he asked around to see who her friends were and someone mentioned my name and he just called me out of the blue. I hope Mom'll let me go."

"Well, before you get too hot and bothered, just remember that you can't go out with him unless you get me a date with his sister."

"How am I going to do that? I barely know him and I don't know his sister at all."

"You'll find a way."

Tuesday April 18, 1944
Night

The prom was this past Saturday night and Jenny went with Darryl. I didn't ask her many questions about it and I won't ask to see the prom picture of the two of them either. She said before that it wouldn't really be a date, that he just wanted to go and someone suggested her. If it was Sarah, I'll kill her. Her dress was beautiful, but I don't want to see her in it again.

Jenny's talked to Jimmy Kohl a couple more times and I can tell she really wants to go out with him. I really want to go out with his sister too. Now I try to get a glimpse of Katherine right after school every day before I meet Jenny. Today when she walked outside through the door that joins the junior and senior high, I was waiting for her as usual. She has gym last period and today it was warm enough she didn't change out of her shorts and T-shirt afterward. It was the first time I've seen her legs, at least that much of them. Her shorts were short—and tight, and I'm pretty sure I stopped breathing for a while. I wonder if she would talk to me if I called her. She probably gets a dozen calls every night.

There's a new record out that Jenny and Sarah are crazy about. Sarah's mom bought it for her today and we danced to it till we dropped this afternoon after school. Sarah's father won't let her play music by colored groups, but her mom lets her play what she wants. It's called *G.I. Jive* by Louis Jordan and His Tympany Five. All the best swing music comes from colored groups and some whites won't dance to it. We don't care who it comes from. I've never been to a dance where colored are allowed, but I don't think it would bother me, although I wouldn't dance with one.

Jenny's parents still say she isn't allowed to date unless she doubles with someone and that it doesn't matter that the richest most handsome boy in school has asked her out. I was at Jenny's tonight when Jimmy called again and she broke the news to him. My name never came up and when she hung up, I asked why she hadn't suggested double dating.

"I'm not going to ask him to ask his sister out on a date with you. I barely know him. You're going to have to do that yourself. Here's the number; call her. You don't even have to make it sound like a date. It could just be doing me and her brother a favor or something like that."

"You don't think I'll call do you? Just how bad do you want to go out with him?"

"How bad do you want to go out with her?"

"All right, I'll do it tonight. What's the worst that could happen? Maybe she tells the whole school tomorrow? She wouldn't do that."

On my way home I wished I hadn't promised I'd call, and after dinner I thought of a dozen reasons not to. My fingers trembled a little as I dialed the number Jenny gave me.

We talked for an hour. It was amazing. She's a normal person or at least normal for someone that rich and beautiful. She knew I was Jenny's best friend and that she really likes her brother and all that stuff, and how Jenny's parents wouldn't let her date unless she doubled. I finally got around to suggesting that the two of us could be their chaperones sometime if she wouldn't mind. She laughed and I wasn't sure what that meant for an instant.

"It would be perfect payback for all the times my parents made me take him along on dates when I was Jenny's age. I would love to."

My hands were shaking by the time we hung up. I'm going out with the prettiest girl in Reitz High School. I don't care if it's not a real date. It's real enough for me. I called Jenny and gave her the news. Her parents must have wondered why she screamed.

Sunday April 23, 1944
Night

Jenny wouldn't like me saying it, but last night was one of the most wonderful nights of my life. We spent all day yesterday shopping. Actually, she spent all day shopping and dragged me along. I picked out something for myself in the first store we went in. She must have spent all the money she earned from the last photo shoot. She looked good in everything she tried on and I think all the fashion houses believe the war is over already because I've never seen so many new styles.

Jimmy and Katherine picked us up in his car at Jenny's and we saw part of *Heaven Can Wait* at Lowe's, and I have no idea what it was about. I was afraid we would be overdressed, particularly me since I was officially just one of the chaperones, but Jimmy and Katherine were dressed nice so I'm glad we went shopping. Katherine wore this elegant light blue skirt that hugged her hips and legs like paint and that pale yellow sweater blouse I could almost see through made it hard for me to carry on a conversation. Jenny sat with Jimmy in the front and I sat with Katherine in the back, trying not to get caught staring at her. I decided that Jenny and I didn't look half bad if we happened to be seen out with the two richest students at Reitz. And the way she smelled; God it was…arousing I guess would be the right word. I could have kissed her there in the back seat on the way to Lowe's. She would probably have had Jimmy put me out at the next light.

I was disappointed when we sat down because Jenny and Jimmy were between Katherine and me. That wasn't at all what I'd planned, however I couldn't very well just get up and go sit down next to Katherine. How would I have explained why I wanted to sit next to her? I sat there petrified and angry at myself for not arranging things better. Before the shorts started, I saw Katherine lean over and say something to her brother and then get up and walk toward me. She sat down next to me and smiled.

"I can sit next to my brother anytime. I hope you don't mind if I sit next to you."

From somewhere I thought of something to say.

"Well, I was going to be disappointed if I didn't get to sit next to the prettiest girl in school."

"And I was going to be disappointed if I didn't get to sit next to the best dancer in school. I was a little let down when you didn't come to the Thanksgiving dance this past year. I shouldn't tell you, but that was the only reason I went. I thought I might have a dance with you. Jimmy and I have been taking lessons since we were children and it's so hard to find someone who knows what they're doing on a dance floor. We have a floor at home that's perfect for dancing and I would love to have you and Jenny over sometime."

"If I'd known you were going to be at the dance and that you would have danced with me, I wouldn't have missed it for anything. I didn't think you even knew who I was. Anytime you want to dance, just call—anytime."

"I didn't know who you were until someone told me what a good dancer you are and pointed you out to me at the Thanksgiving dance a couple of years ago. Now I see you every afternoon after school waiting for Jenny."

Then I got up my nerve.

"I haven't just been waiting for Jenny. I've been waiting for you too."

I thought for an instant I shouldn't have said that.

We sat there and I tried to get as close to her as I could, and that's not so easy to do sitting in theater seats with the armrest folded down between them. I didn't dare try to hold hands with her, but Jenny reached for Jimmy's even before the lights went down and he moved the armrest up between them. The movie must have been boring because about half an hour into it, Katherine leaned over Jenny, said something to Jimmy and he nodded.

"Did you mean it when you said we could dance anytime?"

"Anytime you want."

"How about right now? Our parents are out of town until tomorrow night and Jimmy and I have the house to ourselves. We can turn the music up as loud as we want. What do you say?"

"If Jenny says it's okay, then it's okay with me."

Katherine leaned over to Jenny and I saw her nod. We were out of the theater at the next lull in the action.

We got back into Jimmy's car and drove to the far eastern part of town to a community I never knew existed. The houses are huge with acres of lawns and marble statues everywhere. It was like something out of the movies. It seemed like we drove for fifteen minutes after we turned into their driveway before we got to the house. All I could think was…Sarah is never going to believe this.

It's late and I have to get up for school tomorrow, but I won't forget anything before I get to finish this story.

Tuesday April 25, 1944
Night

I waited for Katherine outside after school yesterday just as I have for the past few weeks. When she came out, she walked straight to me and hugged me in front of everyone. She introduced me to all her friends and when Jenny came up, she repeated the introductions to include her. That group of six or seven young adults represents the future of Evansville and I know it. They're from the richest most powerful families in town, maybe even the state and now I know their names. They might not remember mine, but I'll remember theirs.

"I'd have his baby," Jenny said on our way home today. "Of course he'd have to marry me first. But maybe I'll let him have a feel if he tries."

"Jimmy? Maybe you'd let him? I think if he ever started anything you'd be all over him."

"You're probably right. I just hope he doesn't try anything. And don't tell me you wouldn't trade a year off your life for a night with Katherine."

"Maybe two."

We talk like that sometimes, especially when we know it'll never happen.

The Kohl's house was just as magnificent as I'd imagined. The living room was as big as our whole house I think, and it had a beautiful polished wood floor laid out in a swirling design, perfect for dancing. Katherine told Jenny and me to make ourselves at home, but it was not a place either of us could ever do that in. There was a huge cabinet style record player in the far corner of the room and Jenny and I were told to look for records we wanted to play. There were hundreds of them, all arranged alphabetically by the artist's name. Luckily Jimmy came over and helped us choose a few he thought we would like. I was afraid to touch the record player and waited for him to turn it on and get the music going. Katherine went upstairs to change into something she could dance in. I didn't recognize the music and couldn't figure out what dance would be done to it either.

"The music is from Cuba and the dance is called the Bolero. Katherine and I have just learned it and we haven't had anyone to do it with, only our dance instructors and they're both old and don't like it. They told us this dance is for the young and horny."

Katherine came downstairs dressed in a long flowing bright red skirt and a skimpy little white top that just covered her braless breasts. I was in Heaven. She went over to a little cabinet on wheels next to the record player and took out bottles of liquor and made all of us drinks with ice. We sat on the sofa, sipped our drinks and talked about dance. Katherine sat close to me, not close enough, but closer than she had to. My drink was sort of fizzy and after two of them I was in a very happy place and so was everyone else. Katherine had three by the time I finished two.

Jimmy walked over to Jenny and like a gentleman, asked her to dance. The steps looked sort of like a Rumba, except there were three steps to four beats. The first step is on the second beat, not the first and it's danced very close like the Tango. I liked it right away and wanted so much to ask Katherine to dance, or wanted her to ask me. It didn't matter who got asked.

"If we're going to dance the Bolero," Katherine announced, "I want to dance it to the music that makes any woman feel like making love with her husband and her lover—and maybe her husband's lover."

"I know what you're going to play," Jimmy answered, "and it's not even a Bolero. It just has Bolero in the name of the piece. The timing is all wrong. It's a slow waltz."

"We'll make it a Bolero."

I had no idea what we were in for. Katherine was a little drunk and it took her a few minutes to find the record she was looking for. The first flute notes had me spellbound. It was the most beautiful music I've ever heard, haunting and mysterious and a tingle inside me started as if on cue. The Tango might be making love standing up, but listening to this music—without dancing—was like making love slowly, with time stopped, on an enormous bed with crisp white sheets, somewhere near the ocean with waves crashing on cliffs so far away you can barely hear the noise.

When Katherine gave me her hand, I wanted to pull her to me right there and kiss her. She held me close and I let her lead, picking up the steps she created to fit the music and adding some I knew from Rumba and even a few from Viennese waltz. The timing of the two distinct rhythms was close enough. I felt her leg between mine, pushing them apart so she could reach even higher and soon I was on a cliff looking down. If the music had gone on for another minute, I would have jumped. Her eyes were closed and I made sure the hesitations I added were long and that my leg was between hers as far as it would go, until my upper thigh pushed into hers and I gave her an intentional squeeze a couple of times. Maybe I was a little drunk too. I could feel how warm she was and wished there were no clothes between us. When the music stopped we separated slowly. Her face was flushed and I'm sure mine was glowing.

"That's about all of Ravel's Bolero I can listen to standing up," she said with a smile, "and this is the short version. Thank you so much for the dance. Now that we're all thoroughly warmed up, how about some swing?"

I didn't want to swing. I wanted another Bolero or whatever that was. She's a great swing dancer and so's Jimmy. It was eleven chimes I counted before I noticed the time, or was it twelve? I told Katherine we had to be leaving, but then she put on "The Blue Danube" and insisted Jenny and I dance the Viennese waltz for her. The room was large enough that we did every move we knew and then I told her we really had to go.

"You have to promise to do that with me someday. It's like flying without wings."

I promised that Jenny and I would teach her and Jimmy as soon as we could and started walking toward the door. We had to get home before our parents had the police out looking for us.

When we got to Jenny's, the front porch light was on. Jimmy walked her to the door and gave her a very respectable, socially acceptable kiss. When we got to my house, the front porch light wasn't on. I guess Mom forgot it. I thanked Jimmy and Katherine again for a wonderful evening. Katherine took my hand for just an instant before I opened the car door; then I heard her door open. She got out and I turned to see her coming around the back of the car. She walked me to my door and with every step I thought I would faint. I had no idea what I was supposed to do. I opened the screen door and turned around to thank her again for everything.

"I've had the best time tonight being a chaperone with you, Katherine. Thank you so much for a fantastic evening."

For two seconds we just stood there, face to face, our lips separated by only a few inches; each of us waiting for the other to make the next move. She put her hand to my face and lightly touched my cheek. That's exactly what I wanted to do, so for another two seconds we touched each other's faces like we were made of cotton candy. She wanted to kiss me and I wanted to kiss her. The tension was unbearable until Jimmy honked the horn and she turned away.

"Call me tomorrow," she said as she walked toward the car.

I went inside and straight up to my room. I relived every moment of that night until I heard Mom downstairs making breakfast. Maybe I know what people mean when they say the night was magical.

Saturday May 6, 1944
Afternoon

I've just spent a thoroughly delightful afternoon with Jenny and her mom. She taught us how to dance the Bolero. We didn't tell her why we were so interested. I didn't know she knew the dance and when we asked her about it, she blushed a little and said that it was not a dance unmarried couples should do. I understood what she meant, then we kept nagging her until she agreed to teach us the basic steps. Jenny and I caught on pretty fast; maybe because we paid attention and we weren't drinking this time.

"I have a record that I haven't played in years. It's in my chest in the bedroom. Maybe the two of you are old enough to hear it now. They say it does something to women, but I think it has the same effect on men. Of course they would never admit it."

When she put the record on and the first soft drum beats began, I knew it was the music Katherine and I had danced to—Ravel's Bolero. I think she sort of forgot she was forty something, and then the flute took her off this planet. She danced alone and it was beautiful. I could see the man she was dancing with and if it hadn't been Jenny's mom I would say the dance was the most arousing thing I've ever witnessed. Like Katherine had done, she made the Bolero steps fit the music. She didn't care that Jenny and I were watching while she made love to the imaginary man she was holding. It was a different version and it ran almost fifteen minutes. Jenny and I sat there with our mouths open. Neither of us knew she could dance like that. It was a beautiful performance that's stuck in my mind forever.

When the music stopped, Mrs. Brewster became aware again that she had an audience and her face flushed bright red as she turned to Jenny and smiled.

"I danced that with a young man when I was your age, in front of three thousand people at a recital in Norman, Oklahoma. It's hard to imagine I still remember the choreography, but I guess some things you never forget. That was the most wonderful night of my life and if I want your father to know about it, I'll tell him."

The smile on her face said there was a lot more to the story we would never hear. I was hoping that Jenny and I would be able to go out with Jimmy and Katherine this weekend, although Jimmy said both of them were expected to attend a party given by some of their parents' friends and that their dates had already been arranged for them. I guess that's how things are done in the high society world they live in.

Thursday May 11, 1944
Night

I can't believe how fast this school year has gone by. Graduation is in two weeks and I'm going to the ceremony this year to see Katherine walk. An invitation addressed to me came last week. It was nice of her to send me a formal invitation, and that means a graduation gift in my family. I have no idea what I could get her. There's a big party afterward at her house and Jenny and I are invited. She told me last night that right after graduation she and Jimmy are leaving for California for the summer. In the fall she starts college at Vassar and classes begin as soon as they return. I'll be lucky if I get to see her at all before Christmas vacation. Poughkeepsie, New York is a long way from Evansville unless you have your own airplane, and Mr. Kohl does. I don't think he'd fly me up to see her on the weekends though. I didn't even know Poughkeepsie was a real place when she first told me that's where Vassar is. I did know that Vassar's an all-girls school though. I can't imagine what it's like being as rich as they are. Maybe it's like being poor; you get used to it.

Sunday May 14, 1944
Night

I love Mother's Day. No matter what I do for Mom on that day, whether I just get her a card or we have a daylong celebration, she loves it. All the mothers were asked today at church to stand up and we applauded. While they were standing, the younger children presented them with a rose each. Blackman's Florist donates the flowers every year. It was an especially nice service today and I saw Jenny scribbling a note after the mothers were recognized.
"RNLDCZXHVZMSSNADRSZMCHMFVHSGSGDL"
     That's one wish I bet comes true.
     Mr. Brewster didn't have to work today and he insisted we join them for a barbecue. It was a nice afternoon and we enjoyed celebrating the day. This was the first time our families have gotten together since Jenny's big date with Jimmy and Mom wanted to know what she had to say about it. I let Jenny do the talking because I didn't know for sure what she'd told her parents. Mom hadn't asked me too much about it, since I was just the chaperone, so I went along with whatever was said. She told them about our leaving the movie early and going to the Kohl's and dancing, but she left out the part about the Bolero and the drinking and the parents not being home. When my sister and Stan showed up, Jenny had to repeat the story for them. They were suitably impressed that we were spending time with the high society of E'ville. She's doing something different with her hair. It was styled up on her head in huge curls and it made her look very dignified. Stan is a handsome man and I think he's head over heels in love with her. I was a little worried about what Mom would think about him, but the two of them seemed to hit it off. He's a good listener and with Mom, that matters a lot.

Mom asked me tonight after we got home if I thought we would be seeing more of Stan, that she liked him. She also asked about Victoria. I told her what I knew, which wasn't much.

Friday May 19, 1944
Night

Today was my last day as an eighth grader. Next year I'll have some classes on the high school side and have a real reason for being over there. Sarah had a little end of the year party at her house after school today and Jenny and I demonstrated our latest Bolero attempt for her after everyone left. We taught her what we've learned so far. Jenny and I tortured her with our thighs until I thought she would scream. Sarah's leaving Sunday to visit her grandmother in Fort Smith for two weeks. She doesn't really want to go, but it's already been arranged.

It's just not fair. Jenny will have a whole year left dating Jimmy, and Katherine will be away at Vassar. We know we don't have a hope of anything serious developing. Then again it's a fun sort of game. They're so far out of our league, we're not even playing with the same ball. When we talk about what we would do alone with them, it's just talk and if anything did happen, we'd tell each other first. It would never mean anything. That's a sort of trust Jenny and I have and it's hard to explain. If I had the chance to spend a night with Katherine, I would and I'm sure Jenny would do the same with Jimmy, but it wouldn't make either of us jealous—as long as we were both there. I don't know what Jimmy or Katherine would have to say about that, however that's the way it would have to be. If we're together, it doesn't matter who else we're with at the same time. I know that's not normal, but Jenny and I promised ourselves to each other a long time ago and nothing's going to change that. We did a lot of fun things with Marcie in Florida and we like kissing Sarah, but they're both just friends. Well, maybe Marcie wasn't a friend, but she would have been if we'd gotten to know her better and maybe we did help Sarah with cramps once. Katherine and Jimmy are still just friends we're fortunate to have and if some miracle happens and we can be with them in another way someday, it'll be the same sort of thing. That's pretty deep thinking for a Friday night.

Saturday May 27, 1944
Night

Graduation was as boring as it should have been, but the party at Katherine's was like nothing I've ever experienced. It must have cost thousands. There was more food than I've seen in my life and there were two live bands. Only the highest of the high class seniors and juniors were invited and there were relatives of the Kohl's in from all over the country. I did notice there weren't any of the Meckler family in attendance. Jenny said the Kohl and Meckler families have been enemies for decades and I guess she was right. Katherine sort of let it slip too and told me it's because her family's German and the Mecklers are Jews. I didn't happen to mention that my sister is a housekeeper— and a lot more—for one of them.

There were two champagne fountains set up in the garden behind the house where the bands were playing and Jenny and I had plenty. The bands were far enough apart you could dance in the marked off areas without hearing the other too much. One band played mostly modern stuff for the younger guests and the other played the classics. Katherine and Jimmy dragged Jenny and me between the two all afternoon. At sundown, Mr. Kohl had the bands stop for a rest and he gave a little speech saying how proud he was of his only daughter and that he was sure he would only hear good reports from Vassar about her. When he said that, Katherine leaned over and whispered in my ear.

"What he means is that he hopes I won't become a lesbian like his sister, my Aunt Eileen, who graduated Vassar twenty years ago. She and her lover live in Maine somewhere and write children's books. They're quite good. I've read them, but Daddy wouldn't let them in the house when I was little."

I didn't know what to say to that and started talking about how beautiful their house was, what I'd seen of it anyway.

"Then allow me to give you the grand tour. It's a fucking museum really and we were never allowed to even go in most of the rooms when we were children."

She led me into the house through a kitchen that was larger than I imagined would be found in most restaurants. I didn't count the number of rooms we went in, although there must have been more than a dozen on the first floor alone. There were two libraries, one for her mother and one for her father because she said her parents could never agree on what books they should have. We ended up in the great room, which I had seen when we visited before. The bedrooms were on the second floor and the master bedroom was the size of our house. The next room was a guest bedroom and the one after that had a pink door.

"And this is my room. It was sort of a mess. Daddy gave Beatrice the day off and I'm afraid I just left it this morning."

It's exquisite with furniture that looked heavy enough to build a battleship out of. Her bed has a canopy on top with fringe that hangs down halfway to the floor. Katherine gave me the tour and told me the story behind each piece of furniture.

"Some of it's English and some's French. Mother hates it and wanted me to choose one or the other but I couldn't. I just picked what I liked. I'm sure she'll change it all after I leave."

She even had her own bathroom with a tub big enough for a small family to fit into. I imagined it filled with bubble bath, Katherine and me. When we got back to the door of her room, I opened it a bit, then she pushed it closed. When I turned around her face was as close to mine as it had been on my front porch.

"Did you think about kissing me when I walked you to your door three weeks ago? I've never wanted to kiss someone so much in my life, but..."

I didn't let her finish. I stood on my tiptoes, took her face in my hands and kissed her. Her lips were soft, her lipstick had the taste of cherries and her perfume had a faint hint of vanilla. I kept my mouth closed until she took over and pushed her tongue past my lips. Maybe the champagne gave me the courage to slide my hands from her waist upward or maybe I thought I would never have the chance again. Her lips separated from mine just long enough for her to take a deep breath.

The flute had stopped and the clarinet had already begun when I heard the music coming up from the garden. I didn't move my hands when she spoke up.

"I asked them to play it for us. I want to dance with you to Ravel."

"It's fifteen minutes fifty seconds long," I whispered. "The b-flat clarinet you hear begins one minute into the piece. Our music doesn't begin for another six minutes."

"Our music?"

"Yes, I asked them to play it too. I've dreamed of dancing to this music with you again, but you have to let me lead. Jenny will be leading Jimmy. We've had it all choreographed for a while, hoping we would have the chance to do it today."

"So we have another six minutes?" she said with a smile.

We kissed again and I thought my knees would give way when she moved her hands down and pulled me into her. Only a few thin layers of clothing separated us. We stood there trying to crawl inside each other's bodies until there was no more time left.

"We have one minute until our music starts and we should be going, unless you want to take me over to that wonderful bed of yours."

"That's exactly what I want to do," she said with a grin, "but right now I think we'd better get downstairs. Do I look all right?"

"Like a million bucks; just wait for my signal. When I say 'go' you'll know what to do."

I wiped some smudged lipstick from her face and she did the same for me.

This story is too long for me to write down all at one time and I don't want to leave anything out. Katherine and Jimmy are leaving Monday morning. I wish Jenny and I could go to the airport with them, but there's no one to drive us. Mom could, although I hate to ask her. Katherine said they'll try to come by Sunday afternoon for a little while. I just have to see her again before they leave.

Tuesday May 30, 1944
Night

Jenny and I went to the Memorial Day parade today. It didn't cheer us up much though. We're both a little blue because we didn't get to see Katherine and Jimmy before they left. I waited all Sunday afternoon for her to call and I called Jenny a dozen times asking if she'd heard from

Jimmy. It was after nine when Katherine finally called and I didn't try to hide my disappointment. She'd been tied up with family things and packing all day and I understood that. It was probably too much to hope for to see her again and say goodbye in person.

"I'll be back in the fall for a few days before I leave for school and I promise we'll spend some time together."

She was just being nice, but I told her I would be looking forward to it anyway.

To finish my story of what happened at the party...after we wiped lipstick from each other's faces, I gave Katherine final instructions before we left her bedroom.

"When I say 'go,' we run out to the center of the floor and do fleckerls. Let me lead. Remember, the percussion beat is the Bolero. I'll make it fit, and the wind instruments will sound like a waltz; strings go both ways so ignore them. We dance to the oboe first and then Jenny and Jimmy come on as soon as the oboe stops. They'll dance the Bolero in a big circle around us. After that, just follow Jenny and me. She really likes Jimmy in case you haven't noticed."

"I know, and there's something I should tell you about my brother."

I heard what she said, but we had to get downstairs. Katherine and I joined the crowd standing around the dance area. Hardly anyone was dancing. I couldn't see Jenny and Jimmy and they were supposed to be across the floor from us if things were going according to plan.

"I don't want Jenny to get hurt; nothing will come of her chasing my brother."

Ten seconds.

"Why, does he have a girlfriend already?"

"Go."

I grabbed Katherine's hand and pushed our way through the crowd.

"No, a boyfriend."

There was no time to think about what she said. We ran out onto the floor to the center and began our fleckerls to the waltz music. Mrs. Brewster had taught Jenny and me well. I could recognize every instrument and we had memorized when each would come in. Ten seconds…go Jenny. She and Jimmy ran onto the floor toward us through the crowd and hit the downbeat perfectly. I love her so very much.

Katherine and I switched places and partners with Jenny and Jimmy on my cue and we did a Viennese waltz around them in the center of the circle. The couples who were on the floor moved to the outside and gave us all the space in the world. We had just enough time to make two circles before switching partners again. Jimmy let me lead him in a waltz as Jenny and Katherine did the Bolero. We made two huge circles and the timing was perfect so that we met each time around. For the grand finale we went back to our original partners and danced a Viennese waltz. Katherine was like a feather in my arms, following my every lead. The very end has a trombone solo that seems out of place, so to make it fit I grabbed Jenny with one arm around her waist and she did the same thing with Katherine and we did a group swing until the music stopped. It sort of fit, but not really. No one seemed to notice the strange finale and when the music stopped, the crowd exploded. Even the members of the band applauded. It was a good five times longer than a normal recital dance, nevertheless we pulled it off and the choreography wasn't half bad.

After the dance, Katherine's parents found us and introduced themselves. They were all smiles and invited us to sit at their table.

"It's good to see the money I've spent on dance lessons hasn't been wasted," Mr. Kohl said with a smile. "The two of you have brought out the dancers in my son and daughter after all these years. They speak very highly of you and now I understand why. Thank you so much for coming to Katherine's graduation party."

I was glad they didn't ask what grade we were in. Jenny and I had already decided we would say we were juniors if asked.

We stayed until most of the guests left and on our way home, Katherine held my hand the whole way. We dropped Jenny off first and she got the same polite kiss from Jimmy, but on my front porch, I got a kiss that would've given the whole neighborhood something to gossip about for months if anyone had been watching. I bet Jimmy was.

He has a boyfriend?

Saturday June 3, 1944
Night

Jenny and I went shopping today. Neither of us had a birthday present for the other. There's been too much happening for us to think about it. When we got downtown, we separated and agreed to meet at Muir's Drugs in two hours. I had a card for her I got weeks ago and had no idea what else I could get. I started out at Hughes Department Store. I don't know why I started there, but I'm glad I did. It has to be the most unusual thing anyone has ever bought for a birthday present. When I saw it I knew it was what I wanted. My short visit to Katherine's bedroom must have stuck with me. When the salesman saw me looking at the canopy bed, he probably knew I couldn't afford it.

"This will be taken down tomorrow and we're selling it in pieces. The canopy fits any bed and we'll set it up for free."

That had me sold. I bought the canopy and arranged to have it delivered on her birthday. It cost me most of my savings from Florida and I didn't care. I want her to think of me when she looks up at it every night.

We met back at Muir's and had a soda with a spoonful of ice cream. That's all they would let us have. I'm so tired of this sugar rationing. Jenny handed me a box and I handed her my card. We didn't want to wait for the birthday barbecue next Saturday to exchange gifts. I opened her gift, perfectly wrapped by someone who was almost as good as Jenny. Under the wrapping was a velvet-covered box that looked like a jewelry box, and when I opened it, I didn't know at first what it was. It looked like a piece of jewelry, but when I took it out and had a good look, it was a pocketknife. It was thin and had two blades, a pair of scissors and a file. The handles are brass with the most beautiful filigree design engraved and in the middle are my initials and 1944. It was perfect. My father always carried a pocketknife and sometimes he would let me hold it. Mom keeps it in her jewelry box now. I read the stamping on the blade "Solingen Germany".

"I know we're at war with them, but it was so pretty I just had to get it for you."

"It's beautiful Jenny and only you would know me well enough to buy something like this. I'll treasure it forever. Thank you." The knife is on my nightstand now and I'm going to carry it with me every day.

She opened her card and read what I'd added at the bottom first, "Your present will be delivered on your birthday, so be at home."

She tried all afternoon to get me to give her hints. She got nothing out of me.

Monday June 5, 1944
Night

"The men from Hughes are here," Jenny yelled into the phone at ten this morning. "Is this my present? They say they have a delivery for me. You'd better come over right now."

I flew out of the house and was at the sidewalk in front of her house just as the men were getting the large box through her front door.

Mrs. Brewster, Jenny and I watched as the men tore open the box in Jenny's bedroom. They had no idea what it was even after the posts were attached to the bed. When the top frame was assembled and put in place, Jenny's eyes lit up. I thought she was going to cry as they attached the pale pink canopy. I had no idea what it would look like set up on her bed, but it was even prettier than I'd imagined. The men finished, cleaned up the mess and left. I followed them to their truck and thanked them for delivering it and setting it up. I should've brought some money for a tip.

Mrs. Brewster found her Brownie and took a picture of Jenny lying on her bed under the new canopy. It was a picture worth taking. When she left and went downstairs, I sat next to Jenny and kissed her.

"It's beautiful and something I've always wanted. You shouldn't have spent so much money."

"But there's a curse that comes with it," I said with a smile. "If you make love with anyone other than me under this canopy, it'll fall on both of you."

"That won't ever happen. I promise. Just when I think I could never love you more, I do."

Tuesday June 6, 1944
Noon

I awoke this morning to the sound of Mom praying. I got dressed and walked downstairs to find her on her knees in the kitchen. Her voice rang out for the world to hear as she asked God to watch over our soldiers. The radio was on in the living room and I caught bits and pieces of what Eric was saying. It wasn't his normal broadcast time so I knew something was up. The phone rang and it was Jenny.

"It's started—the invasion. My brother was right. We've landed on the coast of Normandy. There's a prayer service at the church at ten, bring your mom."

That's all she said. I stood there frozen and thought about the thousands of our soldiers who were fighting and dying at that very moment. It was a time to pray. I knelt at the bottom of the stairs and maybe some of my mother's gift for prayer came to me. God was in our house that morning and He surely heard us. When I'd poured my heart out, I got up and walked outside. I heard Mrs. Washington across the street and old Mrs. Beshere next door, praying. Their prayers mixed with those of my mother's into a prayer meeting that couldn't have been matched by all the saints in Heaven. It was a beautiful morning and I knew God was watching over our country and our soldiers. It was the day we had looked forward to and dreaded.

I got baby Dave up and fed him and told Mom about the prayer service at the church. We didn't bother with breakfast and were joined by dozens of others silently walking on the way. There was no organization to the meeting; everyone just prayed and afterward I found Jenny and hugged her. Sarah and her mom were there and the two of us tried our best to comfort Jenny because we knew her brother was probably in the thick of it.

"Your brother's fine," I reassured her. "A power much stronger than the Nazis is watching over him."

She buried her head in my shoulder and cried.

Friday June 9, 1944
Night

No one has missed a news report the last three days and the radio has replayed President Roosevelt's speech about a day that will live in infamy about a thousand times. We've lost a lot of men, but the Krauts are retreating and we have a solid position now. Men and equipment are flooding the beaches, Eric says, and it'll be hard for the Krauts to throw us back into the sea like they said they would. The war has to be over soon. I can't wait to read what Ernie has to say about everything in his article this weekend. I'm sure he's on the ground somewhere in France right now and sometimes he gets things past the censors that I can add to the letters the ladies in the Wives and Mothers Club give me. I've been doing that for a while now, but Ernie's been pretty tight-lipped lately and not much help. Now that the invasion's underway and so far a success, maybe he'll have more to say.

I've barely had time to notice that Jenny and I are now fifteen. One more year and we can get our licenses. The war positively has to be over by then. I want to drive across the country with her, or at least across the state from south to north. That would be a good trip. I've lived in Indiana my whole life and never even been to Indianapolis.

Sunday June 11, 1944
Night

There was a big celebration today at Burdette Park marking the laying of the 100th keel at the shipyard. I wanted the Brewsters to come with Mom, baby Dave and me, but I knew they weren't in any mood for a party so I only mentioned it once. Aunt Doris, Bob and the kids came over right after church and we rode with them to the park. I looked for Jenny and her family in the thousands of people there.

All the girls were dressed in short skirts or slacks and a huge area had been roped off as a dance floor. When the band started, I missed Jenny even more. I stood in the crowd and watched as dozens of jitter-buggers took to the floor. When I heard the first few notes of *"Sing Sing Sing"* I turned around to walk away. It's one of our favorite songs to dance to…and there she was—the prettiest girl in E'ville. Jenny was all smiles as she pulled me through the crowd onto the floor and led me in a swing I could barely keep up with. It was good to see her in a better mood.

Monday June 19, 1944
Afternoon

I got a letter today from Katherine. It was a nice surprise. She and her brother are staying with relatives in Beverly Hills and she told me all about the places they've visited and the movie stars they've seen. She sent pictures of Shirley Temple and Rita Hayworth's hand and foot prints in the cement in front of Grauman's Chinese Theater. There was nothing personal at all in the letter. She probably wrote the same thing to her mother and father. I'll write her back, but my letter will melt her cuzzy when she reads it. Then if she writes again, I'll know there's some hope. It'll be fun writing the letter anyway. I have all sorts of lines I can steal from that girlie magazine my picture was in. I probably shouldn't admit to reading it, but I did, from cover to cover. The writers never come right out and say anything, although the reader has a good idea what's happening. Everything is steaming, pulsating, or throbbing by the end of the stories.

Telegrams are bad; everyone knows that and when one is delivered now, it means someone's husband, father, or brother is missing or wounded. Telegrams aren't the worst though. When a military vehicle shows up with two

officers in formal dress uniforms, it means a loved one has
been killed. On our street two telegrams have been
delivered and on Sarah's street one young mother lost her
husband at Normandy. Every day between two and four in
the afternoon, Mom prays. That's when telegrams are
delivered and so far the Brewsters haven't gotten one. If
Jenny's brother is all right, who knows when he'll be able
to write and from where.

Friday, Mom and I went to an LST launch (LST
577), the first we've gone to since Dad died. One of Mom's
friends, Mrs. Roeder from the Mothers and Wives Club did
the christening and she begged Mom to come. Reporters
and photographers from *The Press* covered the event and
there were lots of photos in the paper yesterday. Mrs.
Roeder's daughter is in some of them. She's a salesgirl at
Peggy Hales and Jenny says she's Miss Payne's girlfriend.
I wonder if her mother knows.

Mom decided that the Brewsters needed a night out
by themselves and when she decides something, it's best
just to go along with it. She invited Jenny to spend the
night at our house Saturday night so they could see a movie
or have dinner or something, just the two of them. Mom
has a sixth sense about things like that and Mrs. Brewster
took her up on the offer. I don't know where they went or
what they did, but Mrs. Brewster had a smile on her face all
through church yesterday. It was nice having Jenny spend
the night at our house. Mom made popcorn—at least it's
not rationed—and we listened to *Hop Harrigan and The
Judy Canova Show* on the radio. I like her; she's really
funny. When a repeat of the news came on, Mom went to
bed, reminding us we had to be up for church the next
morning. Jenny found some music on WLS and we listened
for anything new. There were a couple of songs from Guy
Lombardo and Bing Crosby. Nothing you could really
dance to though. When I was sure Mom was asleep, I slid

over close to Jenny on the couch, kissed her, and held her close.

Jenny and I hadn't spent the whole night together in a long time and I think we were both a little nervous when we went up to my room. I set my alarm clock for six so Jenny could go across the hall and mess up the bed a little before breakfast. Mom wouldn't be up before then. I watched in my dresser mirror as I unbuttoned Jenny's blouse and realized again just how beautiful she is. Looking at her in profile in the mirror is like looking at one of those pin-up girl pictures, only better. I bet half of them, even Betty Grable, wouldn't look as good as Jenny if their pictures were taken without swimsuits. Jenny could see that I was watching the two of us in the mirror and she turned on the acting skills like I've seen when Mr. Evans photographs her. Soon we were playing parts in a movie that Hollywood directors would never touch. The undressing, kissing and everything else would get every actor in the movie arrested.

In bed with her, things were steaming, throbbing, pulsating... How do they write that stuff?

Tuesday June 27, 1944
Night

Still no telegram and no visit by military officers, but no letter from Jenny's brother either. The best news right now is no news and I try to explain that to her.

I heard in school last year that there are special books in the city library that you have to ask to see. They're not out on the shelf and you can only read them there. I knew Mrs. Landers would know them and she's working at the public library this summer, so today Jenny and I spent the afternoon there. When I asked about books that might answer some questions Jenny and I have about certain things, Mrs. Landers knew right away what I meant and gave me *The Human Body*, by Marie Stopes and Jenny was handed *What Every Young Girl Ought to Know*, by Mary Wood-Allen. My book was fascinating even if it did read like it was written by one of my teachers at Reitz. It described all the parts and how they worked and I learned a lot of new words. I discovered right away that girl parts are a lot more interesting and complicated than boys', maybe because they're harder to see. What I really wanted was a look at the book Jenny had, but she was taking her time, so I took mine back to Mrs. Landers and asked if there was another I could have. She gave me *Sex and the Young*, by the same author as the one I'd just looked through. Marie Stopes writes a lot like the authors in the girlie magazines; not the same words at all but she leaves too much to the imagination just like they do. I read through it and learned some things. For one, I learned that puberty can start from any age eight to sixteen in boys and girls and that it lasts for years in some before everything is fully developed. That was good news. I've always known I'm what everyone calls a "late bloomer," but if I hear that one more time, especially when there are people around, I'm going to punch someone. Jenny doesn't care that I'm not a fully grown "adult" at fifteen and neither do I. My voice is what I really hate. I still sound about eight years old. I'm tall, as tall as Jenny now, and that little bit of fuzz between my legs has grown, but nothing like hers would be if she didn't shave it off. Everything else sure seems to be taking too long for me and it's not something I like talking about even to Jenny.

I took *Sex and the Young* back to Mrs. Landers and thanked her for suggesting it. She handed me one more and smiled.

"You won't be back so soon with this one. It's not meant for someone as young as you, although you've never been as young as most of the other students."

I liked hearing that and I know Mrs. Landers could probably get into a lot of trouble for letting us have those books even though we asked for them. The first thing I noticed about the book was that it was new, just published two years ago. The second thing I noticed was that it was written by a man. The title didn't beat around the bushes either, *The Modern Sex Manual,* and the author was Polish: a man named Edward Podolsky. This man told me what I wanted to know—in sort of flowery language, but not nearly as bad as the others. I knew there were real words for some of the things I'd already experienced or at least heard about. The funniest was "hysteria" and how it was relieved in women not that long ago. Orgasm is a word that could not have been better. Just saying it sort of feels like it; maybe because it rhymes with spasm. Erection's pretty clear. I didn't know that's what it's officially called though. Vagina and penis I already knew, but clitoris was new and it was hilarious that it was just discovered a few decades ago. I wonder where they were looking all that time before they found it. Ejaculation is the real word for shooting off as some of the boys call it. I've also heard it called cuming or is it coming, or maybe cumming? It's not the kind of word you see written down so I don't have any idea. I didn't find it in the book. Masturbation—that's another word that sounds just like what it is—but my absolute favorite new word is areola. It's a beautiful sounding word and until today I didn't know what that part of the breast was called. I thought the whole thing was called a nipple. Mrs. Landers was right; I kept that book for almost two hours before returning it. Jenny was reading hers page by page instead of just looking for the good stuff like me. She wasn't half way through when we had to leave.

"I'm going to go back tomorrow and read the rest of it," Jenny said on the way home.

I suggested she ask Mrs. Landers for the Podolsky book when she finishes hers.

I have to go with Mom tomorrow to take baby Dave to the doctor for a check-up.

Tuesday July 4, 1944
Night

Jenny's gone back to the library three more times over the past week and we've had a lot to talk about. We decided we're not so terribly abnormal after all.

There was a city-wide Fourth of July celebration today and the Brewsters had something extra to celebrate—a letter came yesterday. It was heavily censored and there was no clue from the postmark where it was mailed from. Mrs. Brewster told Jenny to bring it to me to see if I could read anything between the lines. Jenny told me before I read it that some things in the letter didn't make sense.

"He wrote something specifically to me but I have no idea what he's trying to say. What does he mean by, 'remember the rhyme I taught you about our family's favorite coffee, Chase and Sanborn'? We never had Chase and Sanborn coffee at home and there was no rhyme he taught me. Mom and Dad drink Maxwell House and always have. This means something."

"Yes it does," I said with a grin. "He was headed toward Cherbourg, France when he wrote this. It sort of rhymes with Sanborn but not so close the censors would see it and he used the word 'rhyme' specifically. Your brother's very clever. Eric says we captured Cherbourg last week so it makes sense."

He also wrote, 'I can't tell you what division I'm in, but that information will be forthcoming when we're in a better place.'

"He wouldn't write like that," I told Jenny. "He wouldn't use the word 'forthcoming'. He's in the Fourth Division is what he's trying to say without saying it."

Jenny hugged me and ran home to tell her parents what I'd figured out. I hope I'm right.

Thursday July 13, 1944
Night

Today Jenny and I went to Yabroudy Amusement Park and rode the roller coaster until we were so dizzy we couldn't walk. It was a good excuse to sit close together and hold hands and when our car got to the top, no one could see us kiss. We also noticed that dropping straight down from the top is a lot like…orgasming. Is that even a word? We couldn't decide and I don't think I'll ask Mrs. Landers.

Jenny and I have been fifteen for more than a month and we haven't taken the test for our learner's permits yet. We have the booklet to study. They gave everyone in eighth grade a copy last year and we haven't looked at ours since then.

There's been lots of news this week from the Pacific. Eric says we've taken Saipan. From his description, the Japs launched a final suicide attack and lost thousands of men. Why do they keep fighting? On a map it looks like the next nearest island we'll go for is Guam, then there's nothing but ocean to Japan.

Friday July 21, 1944
Night

Eric said tonight that some of Hitler's own men tried to kill him yesterday. The war has to be over soon. If the Krauts kill Hitler and the Wops kill Mussolini, we'll take care of the Japs ourselves. The war in the Pacific will be over soon and the only thing the Japs will have left is their own little island and we can surround it and starve them if we have to. There won't be any reason to invade the place. The last two letters from Jenny's brother have been censored so much they don't make any sense even to me, but they do let the Brewsters know he's okay. I told Jenny the heavy censoring means something big is up.

Something none of us have been paying much attention to is the British and Chinese fighting the Japanese in India and Burma. I've been reading a lot more lately. The Japanese invaded Manchuria in 1937 and have marched through China all the way to Burma and if the British hadn't stepped in, they would've taken India by now. That seems a long way away from Western Europe and the Pacific where we're fighting, but it's not really. A newspaper article by Ernie last week showed how it's all connected. The Japs and Krauts have the world divided up between them. The Japs want China and maybe we would have let the Japanese and Chinese kill each other for several more years if the Germans hadn't talked the Japanese into attacking Burma, which is a British colony. We supply the British with airplanes to bomb the Japanese invaders, not so much because we want to help the British maintain control of their colonies, but because it means fewer Japs we have to fight if we have to attack Japan on the ground. It really is a world war and anything that happens affects everything else.

Friday August 4, 1944
Morning

Before I walked downstairs early this morning, I heard Mom praying. She was talking to Dad. It's been two years now. I just stood there and listened to the conversation and when she finished, I knelt beside her and hugged her. She got up and started breakfast as if she'd been talking on the phone to a neighbor.

"Did you know your father was in the CCC Camp? He joined as soon as it started in 1933 and planted trees in Utah to help support us during the depression. My favorite picture of him is from that time. I missed him so much while he was gone and he didn't get to come home very often. He was strong and handsome and every girl's dream. I fell in love with him the first time I met him in early 1922. Love at first sight does happen. His father was killed during the Great War and his mother moved southeast from Idaho, through Wyoming, Nebraska, Missouri and Illinois before running out of money near Evansville; lucky for me. His brother was left in Idaho with relatives because his mother wasn't sure she could feed him on the way. It was hard times for everyone. I was his first date with any girl and he asked me to marry him on the porch that very night. We'd gone to a dance sponsored by the Methodist Church and I knew this boy was different. I'd never even kissed him and he asked me to marry him. Maybe I was young and foolish but I knew what I wanted and said yes as soon as he got the words out of his mouth. I got pregnant with your sister on our wedding night."

Then she smiled.

"…maybe a day or two before."

I listened as she made breakfast and told me other stories about Dad I'd never heard. It's her way of making sure I never forget him.

Monday August 7, 1944
Very late

Jenny and I went roller-skating with Sarah Saturday night. We haven't seen much of her lately and it was good to catch up. She was wearing a pair of grey slacks when we got to her house. A lot of girls are wearing slacks now and not just dancing or skating. Jenny and I want to get a pair alike. The big news is that Sarah has a secret admirer, or he was a secret until a couple of weeks ago and she has fallen head over heels for him. His name is Rodney and he goes to Bosse High School. He was at the rink and she chased him down and introduced us to him. He's a handsome young man with light hair he combs back like Randolph Scott. After he and Sarah skated a couple of songs, she came back and sat down with us. We had to know everything about him. She smiled, then sort of blushed.

"His favorite color is red."

"Sarah," Jenny screamed, "what are you doing?"

"Oh, he doesn't know about that," she continued to smile, "not from me anyway. It's just a nice coincidence I thought the two of you would appreciate. We went out Saturday night and he was a perfect gentleman. His dad let him borrow the car and we went to The Grand for a movie. He held my hand and didn't even try to kiss me until we got to my house. I like him a lot."

Jenny and I skated with Sarah mostly, but a couple of young boys we didn't know came by and asked Jenny to skate with them. She turned them down, but she did it politely. We left the rink about nine and went back to Sarah's. Her parents were out somewhere and she said they wouldn't be back for a couple of hours. She turned on the radio and found some music. We sat on the couch, Sarah between Jenny and me and we talked about Rodney and everything else that's been happening.

"Remember in the spring when the two of you came over and I had really bad cramps?"

"I remember thinking you were pregnant up until then, yeah," Jenny answered.

"Thank God I wasn't, but while you were here, you both helped me with something that made the cramps go away, remember that?"

"Well, no, I don't remember that."

"Neither do I," I added. "What was it?"

Jenny and I kept Sarah going until I finally cracked up.

"The two of you are awful. You know very well what you did. It was the first and only time I ever…"

"Ever what?" Jenny added. "Took a dive off the high board? Rode the roller coaster at Yabroudy naked?"

"I'm serious," Sarah said, almost in tears. "I've tried a dozen times and nothing happens. I think there's something wrong with me."

"There's nothing wrong with you that can't be fixed," Jenny reassured her. "You're trying too hard and you give up too easy. An orgasm starts in your brain, not your cuzzy."

Apparently Jenny got a lot out of those books at the library too, however Sarah wasn't following what she was saying at all.

"If you want to learn how to please yourself, you have to learn how to please someone else first. Now kiss me, not to please yourself, to please me. If you like it too, that's well and good, but do it for me. Kissing someone is very different from being kissed. You've kissed me before, so now I want you to think about what you're doing and do it to please me. Kiss me with your whole body. It's the same with other things. You may have been fucked by Pinky Dick Rudy, but I bet you didn't fuck him back and I'm sure nobody made love to anyone. It's just as well; it would probably have scared him to death. Take my face in your hands and imagine what you're going to do, then kiss me like you would like to be kissed. Kiss me until that magnificent red cuzzy starts to tingle."

I don't know if what Jenny was saying had any effect on Sarah. It definitely had an effect on me and when Sarah did what Jenny asked and kissed her, it was so sensual. That's another new word I've learned and I know what it means. It sounds just like what it is too. Sarah made love to Jenny in that kiss and I guess if it had been anyone but Sarah kissing her like that, I would have been jealous. Watching Jenny kiss a girl, or watching a girl kiss Jenny is incredibly wizard and she knows what it does to me. Sarah got an education from both of us Saturday night she won't soon forget and I don't know how many times she had to cover her mouth to keep from screaming. Her starter button was working just fine by the time we finished. I haven't thought of that word for it in a long time. Then Jenny gave her doctor's orders.

"Now I want you to practice every night for a week and report back to me."

Both girls then turned toward me.

"Don't think we've forgotten about you," Jenny said with a sinister sort of look.

The two of them jumped on me just as the headlights of a car pulling up in the driveway shined through the window. Buttons got buttoned quickly and we were perfectly composed when Sarah's parents walked in.

She didn't mention Rodney all night. I guess that's not working out, even if he does get the car sometimes.

Sunday August 13, 1944
Night

"Doctor Brewster's" suggestion seems to have done the trick for Sarah. She says the problem has improved beyond her greatest expectations and we've heard all about it this week. Listening to her you'd think she invented peeing in the shower.

Wednesday the three of us walked to the courthouse and took the test for our learner's permits. It wasn't so hard and we all passed. Jenny got the highest score. There's no driving test until we turn sixteen and go for our licenses.

The problem now is finding someone to let us drive with them so we can learn. No one has any extra gas or tires. Well, that's not exactly true. Mom still has those two five gallon metal cans full of gas, but she says they're for an emergency and that my learning how to drive is not an emergency. We get four gallons a week. Eric says the real purpose of gas rationing is to conserve rubber. If you don't have gas to run your car, you won't wear out your tires. I guess that makes sense. Jenny's dad gets eight gallons of gas a week and that's just enough for him to get to work and back. Most dates Jenny and I hear about are walking dates.

Mom must have felt a little sorry for us because today she said we could go to church next Sunday in the car and that she would let us take turns driving. We practiced starting the car this afternoon and Mom let us back out of the driveway and pull back in. Working the clutch, brake and gas seems so easy watching someone else do it, but it's pretty hard and we killed the motor about a million times.

Thursday August 17, 1944
Very late

I was at Jenny's this afternoon when Mr. Evans called and asked to speak to Mrs. Brewster. They talked for several minutes and I could tell something big was in the works. When she hung up, she just sat there with a blank expression and didn't say anything until Jenny spoke to her.

"Oh, Mr. Evans is coming by tonight after your father wakes up to go to work. He says it's important, that he has some papers for us to sign."

She wouldn't say anything else no matter how much Jenny questioned her. We went up to Jenny's room and imagined all sorts of things. Maybe he's being sued for the pictures he sold to that girlie magazine. Jenny thought so.

"Now Dad and Mom will know about them and I'll be grounded again, this time forever. I bet he wants Dad to sign a paper saying he won't sue too. It can only be bad news if he's coming over. You have to stay until he gets here."

Jenny invited me to have dinner with her and when I called Mom, she said it would be okay. Jenny's dad was a little surprised to see me when he got up at ten to eat breakfast before going to work. Mrs. Brewster told him about Mr. Evans' call, but he didn't have much to say about it and he was still eating when the knock on the door came.

Mr. Evans was all smiles when he came into the kitchen carrying a briefcase and sat down at the table with Mr. and Mrs. Brewster. Jenny and I backed out of the kitchen, stood near the stairway and listened.

"You're not going to get my permission to take any more pictures of my daughter, Mr. Evans. Let me make that clear first. Jenny's too young to have her picture spread all over the newspaper."

"This goes way beyond a few pictures in *The Press*, Mr. Brewster. What I have here is a one-year contract with the Ray-Ban company. I sent a few photos to them I took of Jenny wearing a pair of their sunglasses and they liked what they saw. They want Jenny to help them introduce their Aviator line that will be available to the public as soon as the war's over. They've been making them for the military for the last few years and everyone will want a pair as soon as they can get hold of them. I know they'll be a great success and Jenny has the chance to be their first official model. It's the opportunity of a lifetime Mr. Brewster and I hope you'll consider letting Jenny do it."

"So everyone can see my daughter half naked in some ad for sunglasses? The answer is no, Mr. Evans."

"I can assure you that will not be the case because I'll be the photographer for every picture and I won't let anything be sent you don't approve of."

"So I get to see the pictures before they're published?"

"Absolutely, every one, and anything you don't like will be destroyed. You have my word."

Mr. Evans was sweating and I think he would have said anything at that point. Jenny was afraid to breathe.

"Will she get paid for any of this or will it be another of those 'good for her career' things you told me about when I let you take the other pictures? And I don't mean getting free clothes either or a one time payment. If this company is as big as you say, they should pay her a regular salary."

I thought the grin on Mr. Evans' face was going to split his head in two as he reached into his briefcase and took out some papers and spread them on the table.

"The Ray-Ban company is prepared to offer you and your daughter one thousand dollars to sign this contract, which is for one year beginning January 1 next year. An additional two thousand will be paid to you and her on December 31. If sales of their sunglasses are good, there is an optional one-year extension for five thousand dollars. On top of that, they're offering private sale stock options in the company if you choose to invest. Here's the thousand dollar check made out to you and Jenny. This is a real offer, Mr. Brewster, one that could set Jenny up for college or whatever else she wants to do when she graduates. They might even offer her a regular job."

"Three thousand dollars for a year's work? That's more than I make. That's more than most people in this state make."

He then turned toward us and although he couldn't see us in the shadows, he knew we were there.

"The two of you might as well come on in. I know you've been listening. Mr. Evans here seems to think this Ray-Ban company is legitimate."

"They are Daddy. I have a pair of Aviators upstairs."

"And how did you get them? I thought they weren't for sale yet?"

"I got them for her Sir, for her birthday last year," I spoke up as politely as I could manage. "I bought them from a soldier who got them on base at Camp Breckinridge."

Jenny ran upstairs and came back down wearing the sunglasses. Jenny's father examined them like he was looking over a new car. I slid the contract toward me and read it while he did that.

"Well, they are made solid and they do look good. They look like the ones MacArthur wears."

"They're exactly like the ones General MacArthur wears," Mr. Evans spoke up, "and after the war everyone will be able to buy them."

"And what, if you don't mind my asking, do you get out of all this Mr. Evans?"

He smiled and said, "I get absolutely nothing except the same stock option you and Jenny will get. I'm putting everything I have into the Ray-Ban company and within a few years, I'll be the richest man in Evansville. There are only a handful of stock owners and I intend to buy all I can and I suggest you do the same thing."

Jenny's mom had been quiet during all this, but I could tell she was dying to jump into the conversation and when she did, Mr. Brewster got his pen out of his pocket.

I don't know if Jenny and Mrs. Brewster slept that night; I sure didn't. It was late when Mr. Evans left and Jenny's dad got in their car to go to work, but Mrs. Brewster let Jenny walk me home anyway. Neither of us knew what to say so we just held hands and walked. When we got to my house, the lights were out and we kissed on my front porch. She turned to walk away and I ran after her.

"You walked me home, so I should walk you home."

When we got to her house, we stood on her front porch and kissed again. I think this night could change our lives forever.

Saturday August 26, 1944
Night

Jenny made me promise not to tell anyone about the Ray-Ban contract, not even Mom. I don't know why. It turns out that didn't matter because today in the fashion pages of *The Press* there were pictures of Jenny wearing the Ray-Bans I bought for her and an article written by Mr. Evans. Jenny didn't know he was going to do that, but it shouldn't have surprised her. It's big news and I'm glad Mr. Evans is telling everyone. We sat at Jenny's kitchen table and looked at the pictures and I read the article. He described Jenny as a soon-to-be international fashion model and I believe him.

"None of this would have happened if you hadn't bought me those sunglasses and I think you should get something out of all this too. It's not fair. If Ray-Ban extends my contract at the end of next year, I'm going to insist they hire you. Mr. Evans is good photographer, but I'm not too sure he has my best interests in mind all the time and you would."

"But what would I do?"

"For one thing you could read the contracts and make sure I get a fair deal and make sure that I fulfill all the requirements. You're good at things like that and I trust you more than anyone. We'd be partners."

"I could do that."

It was all over the radio today that Paris has been liberated. I wonder if Jenny's brother is there.

Sunday August 27, 1944
Night

Jenny and I drove Mom and Dave to church last Sunday and today. This time we went by Sarah's and picked her up and let her drive from her house. She's been practicing with her family's car and she's pretty good with the pedals. I think maybe by next June we'll be ready to take the driving test. This summer has gone by so fast; I can't believe school starts in less than three weeks.

We hadn't told Sarah about the Ray-Ban contract and she wanted to know all about it after seeing the newspaper article yesterday. Jenny made me promise not to tell anyone how much money they're going to pay her and Mr. Evans didn't mention it in the article, although he did say Jenny would be compensated. I could tell Sarah was dying to ask, but she didn't and we didn't tell her. Pastor Knott preached on the Parable of the Talents from Matthew and Luke and I thought maybe he chose that after reading about Jenny's good fortune. After church, a group of young people, mostly girls, gathered around Jenny and wanted to know if what everyone was saying was true. One boy I recognized from Reitz came right out and asked her how much money she would be making. She told him with a smile that it was more than she could make babysitting.

Thursday August 31, 1944
Night

Mr. Evans called Jenny yesterday and asked her to meet him at the pool today, that he had some new swimsuits for her that had been donated by the manager at Peggy Hale's in exchange for some photos. I told Jenny that she could do that now, but after the first of the year, Ray-Ban would have exclusive rights to all her photos. I've read the contract carefully.

"You mean that even Mom and Dad can't take pictures of me?"

"Anyone can take as many pictures of you as they want just as long as you don't get paid for them and as long as they are in good taste and not used to promote or sell anything. That's very clear in your contract. Publicity photos and photos taken by a legitimate news agency are allowed as long as they are of high quality and reflect favorably on the company."

"I never told you before…Mr. Evans has asked about taking pictures of me that don't show my face. He says he'll pay me fifty dollars for every one he takes."

"That horny old bastard just wants a look. Ray-Ban would drop you like a hot potato and I would have Mr. Evans arrested. He would go to jail for taking pictures like that of an underage girl, but I don't blame him for trying. He'd probably get away with it though, because I bet there wouldn't be any film in his camera."

"Okay, you're hired. I'm going to tell Daddy tonight that I need you and that I won't do any photos for Mr. Evans and Ray-Ban unless he agrees to pay you."

"No, you can't do that Jenny. This is too good of an opportunity to throw away. I'll watch out for you for free like I always have. I'm pretty good at it by now."

Mr. Evans and Miss Payne were already at the pool when we arrived. He had all the suits we've been looking at in the window at Peggy Hale's. Several of the major fashion houses delayed introducing new lines this spring because of the war, but now it seems everyone thinks the war's as good as over and we're seeing new swimsuits and fall fashions at the same time. It's like they're trying to catch up. At least there are some real colors available now and they're not all pale. I wonder if the hospitals have pink and blue blankets for newborns yet. One thing I noticed when looking at the new suits in the stores is that they all have removable padding, and I also noticed it had been removed from the suits Mr. Evans brought. I stood around and talked to Miss Payne while Jenny got changed. The first suit she came out wearing was a light yellow and it looked good on her. Her breasts were covered only by the thin material, but there was nothing indecent for me to object to. Mr. Evans took his photos and while I was talking to Miss Payne, I heard an uproar that sounded like it came from every male at the place. I turned around to see that Mr. Evans had talked Jenny into jumping into the pool. Her swimsuit had gone completely see-through and he was snapping pictures as fast as his fingers would work. I grabbed Jenny's robe and ran toward her, but I didn't get her covered before all the boys, and I'm sure quite a few of the girls—especially Miss Payne, got an eyeful. Jenny was right there for all to see and if she had any pubic hair, it would have been too. The thin material stuck to her like glue. She didn't realize what was going on when I wrapped her in the robe.

"You're naked," I whispered to her, "and that old man's got pictures. This could ruin you."

Mr. Evans pretended to be upset that I'd ended his shoot and he was even more upset when I told him to give me the film.

"Either give me the film or you can expect to be arrested, or worse, as soon as I tell Mr. Brewster what happened."

He opened the camera and gave me the film. I told Jenny to get dressed, that we were leaving. She didn't argue with me.

"This is why I won't do any of the photos for Ray-Ban or anyone else without you," she said on the way home.

"Ray-Ban would cancel your contract in a minute if they found out pictures like that had even been taken, whether they were ever printed or not. Now there's no proof."

Mr. Brewster called me tonight offering to pay me for accompanying Jenny on any future photo shoots and I accepted. He's going to tell Mr. Evans tomorrow. She needs me. Her father can't be with her every minute and I can. It's also the perfect excuse for me to be with her more.

Wednesday September 6, 1944
Night

Monday was Labor Day and the biggest shopping day before school starts. In every store we went into, Jenny and I were informed by the sales people that we would be given the employee discount on anything we bought. All the salesgirls knew Jenny's name and some of them even knew mine. In Peggy Hale's, Jenny was told she had a charge account and could take anything she wanted and pay for it later.

"I know this isn't going to last long," Jenny said on the way home, "so let's just enjoy it as long as it does."

When we got to my house, there was a letter to me from the Ray-Ban company. I had no idea what it could be about and Mom was anxious for me to open it. It was good news. I'm to be allowed to buy stock in the company as Jenny's manager. The letter said that Mr. Evans had recommended in a phone conversation that I be permitted to participate in the stock purchase too. He's still a lecher and he's not getting any pictures of Jenny naked, but it was nice of him to do that for me all the same. I'm going to put every bit of the money Jenny's dad pays me into Ray-Ban stock. Mom said I can do anything I want with the money and that's what I want. We're going to be rich someday.

Monday September 11, 1944
Night

I never got a reply from the letter I sent Katherine and I
didn't expect to. What I really didn't expect though was the
letter from Jimmy I got today. Jenny hasn't heard from him
all summer or she would have told me, and now he's
writing me? That didn't make any sense. When I started
reading the letter, I'm pretty certain Katherine had let him
read my red hot letter to her. He told me I was the one he'd
really been interested in all along and the more I read, the
more confused I got. He said he likes Jenny and wants to
see both of us when he gets back into town. Both of us? I
don't think I'll tell Jenny I got the letter. That's just too
weird to try to explain. Jimmy and Katherine will be back
next week according to his letter and he says he'll call me. I
hope Katherine calls. She'll be leaving for Vassar soon and
I would love to see her. I'd like to see all of her, but that's
probably not going to happen.

Eric says we've crossed over into Belgium and that
the British have taken Brussels. The Romanians have
switched sides and are now backing the Russians. I don't
think they had much choice after Russia invaded them last
month. Ernie's normally very cautious in his writing and
now he is predicting the end of the war within months.
Jenny's brother hasn't written in a while, but there hasn't
been a telegram or a visit from anyone in a military vehicle
either. In one of the letters I was asked to read from the son
of a lady in Mrs. Brewster's Wives and Mothers Club, the
young soldier mentions the good food he's had recently,
even waffles. That was easy if he really was trying to tell us
something. I told her that her son could be in Belgium, or
that maybe he wasn't trying to say anything and just had
waffles somewhere. The letters are a lot less censored now

than they were and I don't get too many requests to help figure out what they say.

Monday September 18, 1944
Night

School started today and it's back to the old salt mine. Ninth grade: my last year in junior high. This weekend was unbelievable. On Wednesday Jenny and I both got calls from Jimmy. He and Katherine arrived in E'ville the day before and he said he wanted to see us. He didn't mention the strange letter he wrote to me and neither did I. When I asked about Katherine he told me she was leaving in two days and was busy getting everything packed. That was a polite way of telling me she didn't want to see me. Jenny wanted to go out with him and I wasn't going to let her go alone so he picked both of us up Saturday night at my house. Her mother gave her permission to go after she told her I would be going too. At least he has a car, gas, and money—and we were expecting to be taken someplace nice. Jenny and I dressed as if we were going to the finest restaurant in town, but that's not exactly what he had in mind for the evening. We went straight to a motel on the outside of town and not a very nice one either. When he stopped the car in front of one of the detached cabins I couldn't believe what he had to say and he was grinning all the while.

"I thought this would give us a chance to be alone and get reacquainted, just the three of us. I have a bottle of champagne on ice in the trunk."

"You can take us home," I answered for Jenny and me.

She squeezed my hand hard.

"Give us a minute to talk, Jimmy," Jenny added.

He got out of the car and went back to the trunk for the champagne. After he disappeared inside the cabin carrying the bottle and a huge picnic basket, I exploded.

"What are you thinking? You can't possibly be considering going in there with him can you?"

And then before I thought I added, "He doesn't even like girls."

"I know. I've heard the rumors, but he might like me."

"So you're going to fuck him just to see if he likes it?"

"You think he'd like you better don't you?"

"He's not going to fuck you and he's certainly not going to fuck me. He can fuck himself. You can go in there if you want, but you're not going without me, and I promise he's not going to fuck anyone tonight. This is insane Jenny."

"I'm going."

I wasn't about to let her spend any time alone with Jimmy. He might like boys, but a girl like Jenny could change anyone's mind. One look at her naked and he'd see the light. I didn't think curing him was her responsibility though. When we walked inside the cabin, Jimmy had the contents of the picnic basket spread out on a table; the only piece of furniture in the room other than a very large bed and one uncomfortable looking chair. He hadn't just brought two bottles of champagne, there was a full meal for three and he was the perfect host. There was roast beef on a silver platter, huge buns and all the fixings to make sandwiches, fresh potato salad, baked beans, and a whole apple pie for dessert. He even brought the plates and silverware and glasses for the champagne. There was nowhere to sit but on the bed so we sat in a circle on it while we ate.

"I didn't know what you liked. I hope this is okay. It's sort of a picnic I guess, an indoor picnic. I want to hear all about what you've been doing this summer."

"And we want to hear about the movie stars you saw in California," Jenny added.

We told Jimmy about the Ray-Ban contract, which was our big news and he told us about seeing Lana Turner, Lucille Ball, and actually meeting Richard Widmark.

"Katherine and I met him in a restaurant in Beverly Hills. He and his new wife sat right next to us. I didn't know who he was, although I noticed he was getting a lot of attention from other people who came up and spoke with him. When I heard his voice, I knew I recognized it. We tried all during lunch to figure out who he was. When we finished eating and got up to leave, I guess it just came to Katherine and she yelled out 'Richard Widmark.' Mr. Widmark turned to her and said 'yes?' We were embarrassed, but he was very gracious and introduced his wife Jean to us. We told him we were big fans of *Front Page Farrell* on the radio."

Saturday September 23, 1944
Night

Yesterday was Mom's birthday. She didn't want anyone making a fuss over it, so of course we did. Aunt Doris, Bob, and I took her out to dinner at the Gerst Haus German restaurant. I'm sure Dad would not have approved. I know we're at war with Germany, but we're not at war with the Germans who've lived here for generations.

"Do you remember when I would make Mrs. Brewster's German potato cakes for your father?" Mom said when we got seated. "He loved them but if he'd known what he was eating, he wouldn't have touched a bite."

We managed to suitably embarrass Mom by having the staff sing *Happy Birthday* in German when they brought her cake to the table. It wasn't a big cake and it wasn't very sweet. It was a cake though, complete with a single candle.

Last Saturday night, Jimmy, Jenny and I had a glass of champagne with our picnic dinner and another when we finished. They were real champagne glasses, like in the movies. Jimmy then collected the plates and silverware, placed them carefully back in the basket and opened the second bottle. I wondered what his next move would be. Jenny and I sat on the bed facing him more or less and the three of us talked about nothing in particular as we sipped our champagne like we were in the finest restaurant in town. Mostly I think we looked at each other wondering if someone would make a first move. Jimmy Kohl is a very handsome young man and I can see how any girl, and maybe a few boys would fall for him. When I looked at Jenny and saw that "I'm a little drunk" look in her eyes, I knew I had to stop drinking.

"So what did you have in mind bringing us way out here, feeding us an excellent meal and then filling us full of champagne?" Jenny asked with a slur and a smile.

"Nothing, nothing really. I just thought it would be good for us to get away for a few hours and spend some time alone together. I like both of you; I really do, and would never do anything out of line."

"What if we did?"

Jenny then leaned over and kissed him. It was a kiss that would normally have made me jealous and it should have. For some reason it didn't. Maybe it was the champagne or maybe I wanted to see how far things would go with this rich handsome boy.

Thursday September 28, 1944
Night

Jenny and I have decided that sharing a boy occasionally wouldn't be so bad; if it was a boy like Jimmy Kohl. We learned a lot from him that night and I think he learned a few things from us. He's now part of our little clique. It's Jenny, Sarah, Jimmy, and me. Of course Sarah had to hear everything about our date. We didn't leave anything out and might have added a few things. She told me afterward that she thought we'd made up most of it. If she's lucky, she might find out for herself.

Jimmy has a car—and not just any car: it's a huge Cadillac and he drives it to school every day and takes Sarah, Jenny, and me home every afternoon if we want to ride instead of walk. Mom and Mrs. Brewster don't seem to object to our new friend, but Sarah's mom told her she thinks Jimmy's a little odd. Sarah said the word she used was queer, but that she didn't mean it that way, or maybe she did. Being friends with a senior definitely has its advantages at school and I think hanging around with Jenny has improved Jimmy's reputation as well. We've made it clear to him though that we don't want him introducing us to any of his boyfriends. He's taking us to a football game tomorrow night. It's our first home game and it'll be a date with both of us.

Being in ninth grade this year means that we run into the upper classmen at Reitz all the time. We even have some classes with them. Several of the boys are friendly, although the girls don't have much to do with us. Jimmy says they're all jealous of Jenny's popularity as a real model now. He told me that some of the girls say that Jenny only got the job because she'll do whatever Mr. Evans wants, and I knew what he meant by that. I convinced him that wasn't true at all, that I was with Jenny at every shoot and would be with her at every shoot in the future. I said he was invited to come along anytime he wanted. That seemed to be a big deal for him. I wouldn't mind having an extra pair of eyes watching out for Jenny whenever she's around Mr. Evans—or Miss Payne.

Sunday October 1, 1944
Night

Jenny, Sarah, and I went out with Jimmy last night. It's so nice to have a friend with a car and gas. This time we went to see a new movie at Lowe's, *Double Indemnity* with Barbara Stanwyck and Fred MacMurray. It was really good. I just love Barbara Stanwyck. She's such an elegant woman, but she can play the role of a hard villain too. Jenny and I have seen *Stella Dallas* and *The Lady Eve* three times each.

It was still early when the movie was over and none of us wanted to go home. Sarah sat next to Jimmy in the front seat and asked him what he would do on a Saturday night if we weren't along. He grinned and said that we probably wouldn't want to know. That only provoked Sarah and she kept annoying him until he told us about a private club he goes to sometime.

"Take us. We want to go."

Jenny and I let Sarah do the talking.

"Okay, but I'm warning you, it's…different."

Jimmy drove for a few minutes and it was pretty clear we were headed toward Gear Town. We parked on High Street in the business district and I didn't see a single place that looked open. There were people walking on the sidewalk, most of them were colored girls and a few were walking with soldiers. I didn't like the idea of even getting out of the car, but Jimmy assured us the area was safe and that we wouldn't be walking far. A group of white teenagers walking down High Street at night was bound to attract a few looks and we got plenty. We stopped in front of a dark storefront that looked closed, with a realtor's sign in the window.

"This is it," Jimmy said. "We have to go around to the back of the place to get in."

It was pitch dark. I held Jenny's hand, she held Sarah's and Sarah held Jimmy's. There was a single faint light bulb above the door in the back and that's where Jimmy led us. He knocked three times and a tiny door opened about the right height for someone to look out. The door opened and we walked into a dimly lit anteroom. The doorman greeted Jimmy and he introduced us as friends of his who could be trusted. I was a little scared and at the same time, it was sort of exciting. At the back of the small room, Jimmy opened a door that led to a staircase. There was light and I could hear music. We walked down into the basement of the abandoned building and it was like we'd arrived on another planet. It was huge and there were easily fifty or more people in that secret underground room; some were dancing and others were sitting close in little booths. You would expect a club this well-hidden would be for whites only, but there were as many coloreds as whites as far as I could tell. Everyone we walked past said hello to Jimmy and he tried to introduce us, although the music was so loud I don't think anyone heard him. There was a vacant booth in one corner and the four of us sat down. I noticed the 'Reserved' sign over the booth.

"You must come here pretty often to get your own table," I yelled in Jimmy's direction.

"It's worse than that," he grinned. "I own the place. I bought it a year ago because of this basement. We're twelve feet underground and no sound gets out of here. The owner was a Great War veteran who had this built as a bomb shelter. I just made it a lot bigger. We don't disturb anyone and the local police get paid every month to leave us alone. It's sort of my home away from home."

A very handsome young white man who had a bottle of something in his hand came over, sat down next to Jimmy and gave him a kiss. It wasn't a romantic kind of kiss, just a familiar kind of kiss. Then I looked around. All the couples were either both men or both women. It was a different kind of place, like Jimmy said.

"Who are your friends? You know Belinda is gonna want to meet the girls, especially that movie star sitting next to you that everyone's already noticed."

"Too bad Mickey," Jimmy answered. "She's taken, but you can tell Belinda I said she's fantastic."

"He's a little drunk," Jimmy explained to Sarah when Mickey moved on to the next table and sat down. "He and I have known each other since we were kids and he sort of runs the place for me. Let's dance."

He looked at Jenny and me as he and Sarah got up, "Don't worry, they're all harmless and wouldn't do anything to get thrown out of this place. Enjoy yourselves; you're my guests. Someone will be around to take your drink orders in a minute and order whatever you want. There won't be anyone asking how old you are."

I slid over even closer to Jenny and put my arm around her.

We got flirted with a lot and danced with total strangers; some we let have a feel, but everyone was well behaved. I wouldn't mind going back sometime but I'm not sure I could even find the place.

Thursday October 12, 1944
Early morning

Yesterday afternoon my sister showed up unexpectedly—with Stan. We haven't seen him since Mother's Day and I figured he was long gone. They brought a little present for Dave. Tomorrow's his second birthday. I could tell something was up because both of them were trying too hard to act like it was just an ordinary visit. Dave was awake and needed attention so I saw to him while Mom started making dinner, handing my sister a bowl of potatoes to peel. Mom invited them to stay even though we didn't have anything special to eat. I was in the living room with Dave and I could hear pieces of the conversation. The word "marry" was mentioned, so I listened a little closer. When I couldn't stand the suspense any longer I walked to the kitchen and stood in the doorway.

"Stan has asked your sister to marry him and he came with her here tonight to ask for my blessing. He didn't have to do that and the fact that he has makes me think he's a pretty good man. Since your father, God rest his soul, isn't here, I've told them that you would stand in for him and that they should ask for your blessing as well."

I looked straight into Stan's eyes because eyes don't lie and I think maybe I became my father for a few minutes.

"Do you love her? Do you know everything about her you will ever want to know, because after you're married, you don't get to ask questions and she doesn't have to answer. You'll be the same people; a ceremony in the church and a piece of paper won't change who you are."

Things got really quiet for a few seconds. I don't think anyone was expecting that out of me—especially me.

"I love her with all my heart and I promise to always love her. We know each other's weaknesses and we also know each other's strengths. We have accepted both. I have a good job and I'll be able to provide well for her. She and Victoria have taught me a lot about life and love and I respect their friendship as something very important to both of them. I would never do anything to try and change that. Victoria has a dozen houses already picked out for us to look at that are in our price range and she's even spoken to her family's banker about a loan. I think she's as excited about the wedding as we are."

He was talking to a fifteen year old as if he were talking to my dad and I could tell that what he said came from the heart.

With Dave in my arms, I walked over to my sister and kissed her. There were tears in her eyes and I think there might have been a tear in Stan's when I kissed him.

"Welcome to our strange family, Stan. You'll grow to love us."

I smiled at him and my sister.

"It takes a while," I added.

Plans were made and remade that night while we ate, until everyone agreed on the important things. It was late when they left, but I had to call Jenny and give her the news.

Mom stopped me on my way up to bed after I got off the phone.

"Your father would have been so proud of you tonight," she said with a single tear trying to escape her eye. "I don't know what I'd do without you."

Monday October 16, 1944
Night

The wedding will be January twentieth. That's long enough after the holidays for everyone to be back on schedule and it gives us plenty of time to get invitations sent out and the church reserved. There was no discussion as to whether it would be a church wedding or not. My sister knows she won't get Mom to come otherwise.

Saturday Jenny and I went shopping for wedding invitations. We've been put in charge of the invitations and decorations. Mom's handling the cake and church reservations. The dress will come from Peggy Hale's, with

Jenny's discount. That'll save Mom a lot of money. Stan offered to pay for everything, but Mom wouldn't have it. "The bride's family pays for the wedding" she informed him and I think he'll get used to not arguing when she's made up her mind. Victoria's the Matron of Honor and will be taking care of the party after the wedding, and I'm pretty sure she's paying for the honeymoon—none of my business. I just don't think the happy couple can afford Niagara Falls for a week on their salaries. I bet Victoria makes the down payment on their house too—also none of my business.

In the afternoon Jenny and I met Sarah and Jimmy for a late lunch, or an early dinner at the Farmer's Daughter.

"I think we should celebrate your sister's engagement," Jimmy declared after we finished our hamburgers.

"You always have a couple of bottles of champagne on ice in the trunk don't you?" I asked.

"But of course," he answered in his best British accent.

We spent the next two hours making trips to his trunk and filling our glasses. Our poor waitress had no idea what we were doing, although the tip Jimmy left her probably made up for it.

All the talk at school today was about the seniors planning a Halloween party at the Willard Library. It's supposed to be haunted and it looks creepy enough to have a few ghosts. I don't know anyone who's ever seen one though. Jimmy says that Sarah, Jenny, and I are invited and we want to go. We'll have to be in costume to get in and I don't have any ideas, but Jenny's mom can make anything. Tomorrow after school we're meeting at her house to plead for help. The only costumes available in stores are for little kids and there aren't many of them. Last year there weren't any and I don't think there were any the year before.

Wednesday October 25, 1944
Night

We'll be Robin Hood and his Merry Men; of course Jimmy gets to be Robin Hood and he already had the costume for some reason. Mrs. Brewster worked wonders with mine, Sarah's and Jenny's. Sarah will be Maid Marian. We thought that would be appropriate, and I'm to be Friar Tuck; that makes Jenny Little John. Our costumes are works of art, all in bright green from fabric Mrs. Brewster had been saving. The war's as good as over, so she thought there would be no better reason to use it. I hope she's right. Padding as needed is supplied by feather pillows, which Mrs. Brewster demands we return in good condition. We'll be dressed well enough to go on stage by the time of the party. Jimmy came by tonight in his costume and dozens of pictures were taken of us. We took our little band on the road to my house and I recognized the van parked in our driveway. Mr. Evans was there. Mom told me later that he'd called asking if Jenny and I were attending any Halloween parties. He was particularly interested when he found out that Jenny, Sarah, and I were going to the Willard Library party with Jimmy Kohl. He took about a hundred more photos, promising they would be in the fashion pages of *The Press* on Saturday. I didn't really care and I don't think Ray-Ban will either, but I made him promise he would write that three of the four costumes were made by Mrs. Brewster.

There were lots of photos in the paper this week of General MacArthur walking ashore on one of the Philippine islands. He did what he said he would do, even if it's a small step in taking back what he surrendered two years ago.

Wednesday November 1, 1944
Early morning

The party was a lot of fun and I think our costumes were the best of all. There was even a live band from Chicago. No one said anything about Jimmy inviting three ninth graders. Maybe they didn't recognize us, though they will surely remember the cleavage Sarah displayed for everyone to see. She was beautiful and put all the other damsels to shame.

After the party, Jimmy invited us back to his house. His parents were away and we would have the place to ourselves. We couldn't very well turn down an invitation like that. Sarah was taken with the place and Jimmy gave us the full tour. I didn't know they had an indoor heated pool and when we got there, Jimmy told us we were welcome to bring our suits sometime and go for a swim.

"We don't need swimsuits," Sarah said with a smile. "Let's go for a swim now."

Jenny was all for that and began taking her costume off. I think sometimes she's a little too anxious to show off her smooth hairless cuzzy, although I've always thought being shaved suited her well. She was naked and in the pool in two minutes. I'd never seen her naked in a pool before and the sight of her breasts just floating on the top of the water was a picture that would give old Mr. Evans a heart attack. Jimmy watched and I watched him watch as Sarah began undressing.

"You're in for a treat," I whispered to him just as she was getting down to her bra and panties.

"I've heard—red?"

"Very red," I answered with a smile.

Sarah turned toward Jimmy and me and took off her bra. Those fabulous nipples were definitely calling and I started undressing. Her panties were next and that furry red cuzzy had poor Jimmy lost for words. She only gave him a brief look and then jumped into the pool with Jenny. I finished undressing—with Jimmy's full attention, and joined them.

"C'mon, show us what you've got Robin Hood," Sarah yelled. "You don't get to just look."

We all watched from the pool as he undressed to Sarah and Jenny's whistles. When he got down to his underwear, it was plain to see he was more than a little excited.

"More than a pinky dick there," Sarah whispered to Jenny loud enough for me to hear.

When the underwear came off, Jimmy's perfect wang was there for everyone to stare at and we did. It was hard and bouncing around with every step he took toward the pool; a handsome wanger—if that's how wangers are described. He jumped in and swam straight for us. If he'd had four hands he still couldn't have gotten a feel of everything he was surrounded by. Sarah swam around behind Jenny and I could tell by the smile on her face she found what she was looking for. So did I, and Sarah didn't fight off mine and Jimmy's attack. The water got awfully warm.

Jimmy crawled out of the pool and lay down out of breath on a huge inflated pool mattress. He was on his back and his wang lay across his stomach. Sarah and I got out of the pool as well and lay down next to him. I didn't expect what happened next though. Sarah crawled on top of him, spread her legs and sat up on his thighs—so I could watch maybe. I must have yelled something when she slid forward, then back and Jimmy's wang disappeared.

Jenny heard the commotion and wandered over to see what the fuss was about. She was not nearly as alarmed as I was and spoke in a dead calm voice.

"Get off him, now."

Jenny pushed Sarah off him and the look she gave her said she meant business.

Jenny found Sarah's mouth and kissed her. It was a kiss that actually did make me jealous. When they separated, Jenny smiled and whispered to Sarah loud enough for me to hear:

"You owe me."

"I'm going to marry him someday."

"You're crazy; he likes boys."

Sarah just grinned. She had an answer.

"And girls. See...we already have something in common."

Tuesday November 7, 1944
Night

Jenny's been asked to ride on one of the floats in the Armistice Day parade. She wasn't too keen on the idea until I reminded her we have a lot of Great War veterans in E'ville. There was a rehearsal this afternoon after school and about fifty soldiers from Camp Breckinridge showed up in uniform. Jenny's supposed to ride on a tank wearing a short skirt, but they won't get to see her in it until the day of the parade. Mr. Evans was at the rehearsal snapping pictures and getting Jenny to pose with the soldiers. I finally remembered to thank him for recommending to Ray-Ban that I be allowed to buy stock in the company. He told me I should put every cent I have into it and encourage Mom to do the same. There's no point in talking to her about it though; she wants her money in a bank.

Sunday, Aunt Doris, Bob, and the children came over. We haven't seen much of them lately. Mike and Harry haven't changed, other than being bigger, but Millie was like a different kid. She looks so much like her mother with her thin blonde hair and green eyes. Mom's eyes are green, but mine are blue. I can't remember what color Dad's were. She's just turned three and is talking as plain as any five-year-old. She wasn't doing that even two months ago and Mom was a little worried about her. Aunt Doris said right before her birthday Millie just began talking one morning at breakfast, telling her about a friend at St. Vincent's who had gotten sick the day before.

"It was the strangest thing. She talked for half an hour about this little girl, telling me all the details of her throwing up and how that had made some of the other children throw up as well, but not her. I just sat there and listened. It's like a switch turned on in her brain or something and she hasn't shut up since."

Aunt Doris was right about that, she talked nonstop and asked millions of questions. Finally Mom suggested I take her for a walk. We put our coats on and walked to Jenny's. Mike and Harry followed us, but then kept going, saying they would stay within a couple of blocks of home. They knew where they were so I didn't worry about them. When we got to Jenny's I could hear the music as we stood on the street in front of her house. Her parents were out and she had the record player up loud enough for the whole neighborhood to hear. When we got inside, she was wearing the little outfit she's supposed to wear in the parade to check the fit. It looked like a regular WASP uniform with the white blouse, black tie and blue flight cap but the matching blue skirt was much shorter. The WASPs are the new Women Airforce Service Pilots. She looked positively gorgeous. The music playing happened to be a fast waltz and she grabbed me and danced me around the living room all to Millie's delight.

"I'm wearing absolutely nothing under this," she whispered in my ear.

She put on a swing record and Millie started to dance the way little kids do, so we taught her a few steps. She'll be a good dancer someday.

Mom told me last week that Bob is now officially Millie's father; that he has adopted her and that my ex-uncle signed the papers. I didn't know until then that he was even thinking about adoption. Millie calls Bob daddy and he just beams when she does. He's such a good man.

The war news is good. We've taken our first town inside Germany, a place called Aachen and Eric said there wasn't much fighting. Do we have to go all the way across Germany to Berlin before the Krauts give up? I bet Ernie is right there with our soldiers. We'll hear from him soon.

Monday November 13, 1944
Night

The parade was great and Jenny looked like a movie star riding on top of that tank surrounded by men in uniform. The wind kept blowing her short skirt up and the first thing I thought was whether she was wearing anything underneath. She was, and a lot of people can testify to that. I'm sure Mr. Evans got pictures, although he's not stupid enough to sell them to another girlie magazine. He can't publish them anywhere without her dad's permission, but that wouldn't keep him from sleeping with them. I bet he has dozens of pictures of girls and that he sleeps with them every night. I hate to think what else he might do with them.

After the parade a young woman in a real WASP uniform came up to Jenny and me and introduced herself. Her name was Susan and she was from Philadelphia.

"You sure look a lot better in that uniform than most of the women who wear it every day. Maybe they would get a few more volunteers if they'd let us wear our skirts that short."

Mr. Evans, who'd been following us around taking pictures, couldn't resist the opportunity of getting a picture of Jenny and Susan and he got more than he was expecting. When he posed the two of them saluting each other I thought that would make a good picture for the paper. For the next pose, Susan had her own idea though and Mr. Evans probably still has dirty dreams. Susan stood sideways next to Jenny, who was facing the camera, put her arms around Jenny's waist, stood on one foot with the other leg bent at the knee the way you see in the movies and kissed Jenny on the cheek. Jenny loved it and the two of them went crazy with poses that had Susan kissing Jenny's cheek in most of them. It was all very innocent looking or would have been if I didn't know Jenny. I finally stepped in and told Mr. Evans he'd taken enough photos for the day. He wasn't happy about that.

"What are you doing for the rest of the day?" Jenny asked Susan after Mr. Evans left.

"I don't have to be back at Breckinridge until roll call tomorrow morning."

"You want to hang out with us for a while? It's a beautiful day for November and we don't have anything we're supposed to be doing this afternoon. We can go back uptown. Someone said that Muir's has ice cream again. I know it's not exactly the right weather for ice cream, but I want some before it's gone. Who knows when we'll get more."

The two of them got a lot of attention as we walked back toward the center of town. When we got to Muir's, Susan took her cap off as we walked in. Jenny didn't know to do that and when we sat down Susan reached over and removed it for her, folded it flat and handed it to her.

"Everyone knows you're not supposed to wear a C cap indoors," Susan said with a smile.

I've heard flight caps called C caps forever but I never asked anyone why and I figured this was my chance.

"So, why are they called C caps anyway?"

Susan reached back for Jenny's cap and opened it up just a little so the folds at the top spread apart and then she stuck out her tongue and pretended to lick it from front to back.

"C is for cunt," she said with a wide grin. "You know some horny recruit made that up and I guess it just stuck. At least they call them C caps now instead of cunt caps like they used to."

I don't believe her, and I'm not going to ask anyone else either.

We sat and ate our vanilla ice cream, the only flavor they had left, and the longer we sat the cruder Susan became until she finally just asked Jenny to go to a motel with her—with me sitting right there. I would never have guessed the answer Jenny had for her.

"Twenty dollars."

Susan got up and left after using the word cunt in a way I'd never heard it used before.

Jenny burst out laughing as soon as Susan cleared the door.

"I've always wanted to do that."

"And just what would you have done if she had agreed on your price?"

"I would have told her that twenty was for both of us."

Thursday November 16, 1944
Night

The Thanksgiving dance is this Saturday night and I'm going this year. Caitlan Propst is old enough to babysit Dave if Mom wants to go too. She comes over all the time now and has already sat for several families in the neighborhood, and Dave is really no trouble.

Jenny and I spent the afternoon shopping. We rode home from school with Sarah and Jimmy and they volunteered to go with us. I think Jimmy spent the most money even though he says he hates to shop. We spent an hour in Hoffman's. I think he just likes modeling for Sarah and she thoroughly enjoyed picking out things for him to try on. She went a little far with it though and got chased out of the dressing room by a salesman. Girls are wearing men's slacks a lot now because I guess the women's fashion designers haven't yet decided that it's more than a fad. Jimmy insisted we all try on slacks and shirts while we were there. Jenny looks good in anything and when she came out of the dressing room wearing a grey pair of slacks and a pink shirt with a black tie, Jimmy decided that's what we should all wear to the dance. I didn't know they even made men's shirts in pink, but it sure looked pink to me. Maybe it's the dye they're getting. There was no way around it; we walked out with identical suits—and hats. We won't make the fashion pages of *The Press* next week.

Sunday November 19, 1944
Afternoon

I've never danced so much in my life. None of us sat out two songs in a row. When we walked in together to our table Jimmy had reserved, all eyes were on us. In the dim light not even Mom and Aunt Doris recognized us at first. As soon as we got seated, a slow waltz started playing and I got up and walked over to their table. I held out my hand and asked Mom to dance. When she saw it was me, I thought she was going to cry. I led her onto the floor and held her in my arms.

"You have no idea how much you look like your father tonight."

I managed not to cry and after the dance I walked with her back to their table only to find Aunt Doris' hand outstretched. After dancing with her, I went back to our table. No one was there; they were all on the floor. In the middle of the song I was asked to dance by Miss Payne. I barely recognized her. She was exquisite, dressed in an evening gown that must have cost Mr. Evans a bundle, although she probably paid for it at Peggy Hale's in other ways. That was a terrible thing to write. The music was Tango and I gave her the dance of her life. I squished those huge breasts of hers against me and kept my leg up her thighs as far as I could reach. If there'd been enough light to see, I'm sure her face was flushed by the time the dance was over. When I walked her back to her table, she gave me a respectable hug.

"It's too bad you're spoken for," she smiled and whispered.

Mr. Evans was just returning Jenny to our table when I arrived. I'd already guessed he was dancing with her. She didn't look too happy.

"I'm not dancing with him again. He can't dance and he can't keep his hands off my butt."

Mrs. Winston from Centennial came over and sat down with us between dances. It was good to see her again and she said she brought a troupe of boys and girls with her.

"They all know who you and Jenny are," she said to me above the music, "and I would be grateful if the two of you would dance with a few of them."

"We're here to dance, Mrs. Winston," Jenny answered. "If it hadn't been for you, we would've missed out on so much at Centennial. Send them over and we'll dance with all of them."

Of course the girls were the bravest and no sooner had Mrs. Winston got seated with her group than a tall blonde dressed in her very best came over and asked me to dance. It was a swing and she knew what she was doing. She followed my every lead without hesitation. Her name was Mary Elizabeth and she was a fifth grader. There were no fifth graders who looked like her or danced like her when I was in fifth grade. When the music stopped she walked me back to my table and thanked me for the dance.

"Can I have a waltz later? I've been practicing the Viennese waltz because I know it's your favorite dance."

"If they play a Viennese waltz, I'll find you," I said with a smile.

"Flirting with an elementary schooler are you?" Jenny said as soon as Mary Elizabeth left.

"She's in fifth grade and you know how I feel about fifth graders," I answered trying to contain the grin I had on my face.

"So I'm too old for you now? Maybe I should tell her you'll only break her heart."

Two more girls from Centennial showed up just as the music started and asked Jenny and me to dance.

"It's going to be a long night," I whispered in Jenny's ear as we were led onto the floor.

We danced with every student Mrs. Winston brought with her and I got my Viennese waltz with Mary Elizabeth. I hardly spoke to Sarah and Jimmy the whole night. We'd planned to go back to his house after the dance, but it was midnight before any of us noticed. It was just as well because we were exhausted. I slept in my clothes. I was too tired to take them off. Mom let me sleep in until it was time to get dressed for church today. The Brewsters were late arriving and Jenny said it was because she just couldn't get up. Every muscle in my body aches.

Monday November 27, 1944
Night

Mom decided that we've had Thanksgiving at the Brewster's too often and that it was high time we repaid them, so this year dinner was at our house. Jenny and Aunt Doris came over Wednesday afternoon and helped get things ready. Aunt Doris helped Mom in the kitchen and Jenny helped me clean. I didn't think the house was that messy, however Mom insisted we move all the furniture around and clean under everything and that took forever. It was after ten when I walked Jenny home.

"I loosened the bulb in the front porch light fixture before I left this afternoon," she said as we got close to her house.

"And why did you do that?"

"Because I want to kiss you when we get there— and I shaved this morning just for you."

I walked a little faster.

I held her in my arms on her front porch and didn't let her go until she was more than content. It wasn't one of those romantic moments I should even write about, but I'm sure she slept well.

I wish my sister and Stan had been here for Thanksgiving. When I invited her the first thing she asked was if Aunt Doris was coming. Aunt Doris had already asked if my sister would be coming when Mom invited her. I guess having someone steal your husband, even if he is a bastard, takes a long time to get over, although it will happen. Aunt Doris has already treated my sister a lot better than I would have.

Jenny was in the Thanksgiving parade wearing a really pretty orange blouse, dark blue skirt, and a big floppy orange hat from Peggy Hale's. She rode in a huge Lincoln convertible with Carolyn Akin, Alice Ullery, and Betty Lockyear. Carolyn and Alice are former Miss Indiana winners and as soon as we start having the contest again, I bet Betty will be the next one—and they're all from E'ville. Mr. Evans took about a million pictures of them.

Jimmy called me last night and said Katherine was home and that she wants to see me. If she wants to see me, she can call me.

Saturday December 2, 1944
Very early

Well, Katherine called Thursday night about half past nine. I hadn't expected her to, but it was good to hear her voice and I sort of melted I guess. She said she wanted to see me and that she could come by and pick me up in half an hour. She didn't say anything about Jenny coming too. I told her I wasn't allowed out after ten unless I was with someone Mom knew. It was hard for me to tell her that because I know I can sneak out anytime I want. She seemed disappointed and said she would call me again if it was all right. I didn't think she would call again last night. She said she could pick me up at the corner down from my house at ten and for some reason I said yes this time. I felt guilty as soon as the answer came out of my mouth. It would be cheating on Jenny; there was no other way of thinking about it. I know the two of us, when we first met them, joked that we would jump into bed with Jimmy and Katherine if we had the chance, but this was real and I was so nervous I wasn't thinking straight. We've had fun being together with Jimmy and neither of us ever got jealous no matter what happened. That's the way things have always been between us and anyone else. I would be alone with Katherine, without Jenny.

I waited until Mom and Dave were asleep, went up to my room and pulled on my heavy coat. It's been bitterly cold this last week and the skies were cloudy all day. I slipped out the front door at ten minutes to ten and saw snow falling in the streetlights. There were no cars and the black asphalt was just beginning to turn white. A single car with its motor running was waiting at the corner. I walked past, not knowing for certain what car Katherine would be in. When I heard a car door slam shut, I knew it was her.

"I'm so glad you came," Katherine said as she walked toward me. "Let's get in the car before we freeze."

We got in and Katherine slid over next to me and kissed me on the cheek. She'd been drinking; how much, I didn't know.

"I've been thinking about you all day," she said as we pulled away from the curb. "I just had to see you."

"You never answered my letter."

"I know and I'm sorry, but…"

"But you were afraid I might get the wrong idea and think you actually liked me?"

"I couldn't write what I wanted to say. I tried, but I'm no good with words. Everything I wrote sounded stupid. I kept your letter and I've read it a hundred times."

She pulled my letter out of her coat pocket and handed it to me. I remembered what I'd written. It was an over the top love letter I wouldn't ever want Jenny to read. Maybe I wanted Katherine to know I wasn't just some kid she happened to have kissed on a whim. In the letter I went into great detail about what else I wanted to do. There was no doubt what she expected last night.

"Where are we going?"

"Someplace where it's warm and we can be alone for a few hours. It's not the fanciest place in town. We won't be disturbed though and no one will ask any questions. I know the owner quite well."

I recognized the place when we pulled up in front of a little cabin at the same motel Jimmy had taken Jenny and me to.

"You said you know the owner. Who is it?"

"Me," she said with a grin. "When I became a senior, Daddy said I had to spend the money some uncle left me in his will and that I had to spend it on property. This was the first place I found for sale so I bought it. Business is good and I get a nice check every month after everyone who works here gets paid."

Katherine and I got out and I followed her to the trunk of the car where she took out a bucket of ice with bottles of Coca-Cola in it and a bottle of rum. Do all rich people carry liquor and ice in the trunks of their cars?

I don't know if it was the same cabin Jenny and I shared with Jimmy but it could have been. The furnishings were exactly the same; they probably all were. It was a motel after all and not an expensive one either.

Katherine dug around in the ice bucket, pulled out two glasses and made us each a drink. She downed half of hers in one gulp. I took a sip of mine and set the glass on the table. Someone had to drive us home. The room was at least warm and we found hangers for our coats in the tiny closet. When I turned around from hanging mine up, Katherine was lying on the bed shoeless with one knee up in the air so that I had a perfect view up her skirt. She was wearing hose and a blue garter. Half the women in E'ville would kill for those.

"About the things I wrote in that letter…"

"I have them all memorized."

Wednesday December 6, 1944
Night

Being with Katherine was everything I'd imagined it would be. She pulled my face to hers right away and we shared a kiss that could end the war early. The full slip she wore was a problem so I unbuttoned and slid her tight black skirt off next. I stood up, folded it and placed it on the back of the single chair in the room. She had her blouse off by the time I returned and I helped her with the slip. They were beautiful clothes that probably cost a fortune. I took the blouse and slip and hung them on hangers. It didn't matter to me that my clothes were on the floor, but I wasn't going to let hers go there. Katherine's bra didn't look like any I'd ever seen before. The fad is the padded and pointed bullet bra, but hers was light blue, thin and soft and it fit like it was made just for her. She leaned up for me to unhook it and I saw the tiny label that read Mainbocher, Paris and New York. I couldn't dare let it fall in the floor so I got up once again and draped it over her skirt. She noticed the attention I was giving to a normally insignificant piece of clothing.

"Main Rousseau Bocher. He's in New York now, next door to Tiffany's. The Nazis chased him out of Paris. Mom says that's one of the good things that has come of this war. I just love his designs."

Katherine was sitting up and I got a full view when I turned around. I've seen pictures of marble statues of women sculpted by famous artists and that's what she looked like—like that one with no arms.

"You have no idea how often I've thought about this," she whispered. We took things slowly, as if we had all night instead of a few hours. Her skin was so soft, I had to kiss or touch all of it. We might have been those ships passing in the night everyone talks about, but the time we had together made memories enough to last a lifetime. I knew I would regret what we were doing and maybe that made it all the more exciting. She knew how to make love like a real woman and I did everything I thought she'd like. I wanted her to take me home with her and keep me in her canopy bed forever. I should have felt taken advantage of, or at least sorry I'd said yes. My only thoughts were about her beautiful body next to mine.

The catnap I took after we made love was interrupted when she got up to go to the bathroom. That's when I noticed the time.

I had to help her get dressed and I drove her home. We didn't bother with the hose, garter and panties. I rolled them up together and put them in her purse. She sat with her arms around me, kissing me at every light and telling me how much she loved me. I thought of something my sister once said about Victoria, "She loves what I do for her, that's all." When we got to her house, I helped her to the front door. She was a lot drunker than I thought and I was a lot more sober than I thought.

"Katherine, I'm going to drive your car home and I'll leave it parked on the corner where you picked me up, okay? The keys will be under the mat. You can get Jimmy to drive you out tomorrow and pick it up."

I repeated that a couple of times and then opened her front door and pushed her inside. It was a little scary driving her car home. I don't have a license and it was snowing hard. I decided that if a policeman stopped me, I would just tell him the truth, that I was out with the daughter of Robert L. Kohl and she had too much to drink. When I turned down my street, I started breathing again. I parked the car on the corner and put the keys under the mat like I told her I would and walked through the six inches of snow back to my house. It was after three when I finally closed my eyes for the night.

I know what cheating is. I sold my soul for a few hours with her.

Monday December 11, 1944
Night

Katherine hasn't called. I guess I didn't expect her to. It was a one night fling and it won't ever happen again. That's probably exactly what she's thinking too.

The Brewsters got some very good news Saturday. Jenny's brother's in Paris, or he was on November second when the letter was postmarked. The letter wasn't censored at all; not a word had been cut out. They had received letters from him earlier, after the fall of Paris, but it was impossible to tell from where they'd been sent. I guess the Army has decided they don't care if the Nazis know they're in Paris now. The whole world knows. He's been assigned to guard prisoners and according to him, they don't mind being prisoners of the Americans at all. It's probably a lot better than being prisoners of the Russians. Ernie says the war in Europe will be over by New Year's, that the Nazis don't have much left to fight with or for. I hope he's right.

I was really wrong when I thought there was nothing but ocean between Guam and Japan. That's all my map shows, but there are dozens of other islands the Japs have control of that we're trying to take. There was news Friday about two major islands, Iwo Jima and Okinawa and I had to find a better map at school today to see where they are. We've been bombing them for a couple of months and we haven't landed any soldiers there yet. The Japs still hold most of the Philippine islands, although we're bombing Manila and have landed soldiers on a couple of the islands. It looks like the war against Japan is going to take a lot longer than I thought. We hear about the sinking of Japanese ships and we don't hear much about our ships the Japs sink. The last one I remember was the Liberty Ship Augustus Thomas and the only reason I remember it is because one of the sailors lost was from Evansville. We hear a lot about ships being attacked and damaged in the Pacific and Atlantic, but I guess they don't like to say if the ship was sunk. Maybe it's because they don't want to worry the families at home. When we do hear of a ship being sunk in the middle of the ocean, we automatically think everyone aboard has been lost. I know that's not always the case, but we think it anyway.

Jenny and I have been talking about Christmas presents for each other and she had the idea of exchanging professionally done photographs and I agreed. I have lots of pictures of Jenny that were done for someone else and the only one she has of me was made when we were practicing for the dance competition in fifth grade. The best part is, we can get Mr. Evans to do them—as many as we like until he gets just the shot we want—for free, or at least for the price of the film. We agreed to sit for the photos at separate times so the one each of us gets will be a surprise. That was a great idea of hers. I'd like to have a photo of Jenny taken just for me. I don't deserve it, not after what I've done.

Tomorrow I'm going to wire money to Ray-Ban for my first stock purchase. Mr. Brewster's been paying me twenty dollars a month as Jenny's manager or agent or whatever I am and I'm investing all of it in Ray-Ban stock. I'm sure Jenny and I will both be millionaires someday.

Tuesday December 19, 1944
Night

There's some terrible war news. The Krauts have launched a major attack west into Belgium, Luxembourg, and France. Thousands of Americans have been taken prisoner and it looks like the Germans are headed for the coast—Antwerp according to Eric. Where did these Krauts come from? I thought the Germans didn't have anything left to fight with. I hope Jenny's brother's still in Paris.

I had a look at the proofs Mr. Evans made last week and picked out one I like for Jenny. Now I have to find a nice frame. Maybe we'll get matching frames. Jenny talked

Mr. Evans into printing our pictures on the largest size photographic paper he has, 11 x 14 inches. The frames are going to be expensive but I don't care. Guilt is an awfully expensive thing to carry around.

There's a basketball tournament going this week at Reitz and tonight Jenny and I went. Standing in line to get in I didn't pay any attention to the couple in front of us until Katherine happened to turn around. Without blinking an eye, she hugged Jenny and me and told us how good it was to see us again. She introduced us to her date, some boy named Todd who tried his best to ignore us; a society type if I've ever seen one. After we got our tickets, she told us we four simply had to get together sometime during the holidays. I made certain we didn't sit anywhere near them, or maybe she made certain they didn't sit anywhere near us. I wonder if old stuck-up Todd can make her scream the way I did. I shouldn't be remembering things like that.

Sunday December 24, 1944
Afternoon

It's always special when Christmas or Christmas Eve is on Sunday and today the church was jammed full. You see people at church during Christmas and Easter you never see there otherwise. I thought my and Mom's seat next to the Brewster's had been taken when we first arrived and then I saw it was Sarah and Jimmy. That was a nice surprise and we squeezed in the pew with them. Jenny and I have already decided there must be something serious going on between those two and now they're in church together. Wouldn't it be perfect if they got married someday? Maybe they would invite Jenny and me to one of the Kohl's vacation homes for the weekend or at least a day of sailing on the river. I've seen pictures of Mr. Kohl's yacht in the newspaper.

Jenny and I went frame shopping Friday and yesterday and found a matching pair we like. We wanted silver but a silver frame large enough for the portrait Mr. Evans made for us costs more than either of us can afford. We did find very nice matching silver plated frames at Finke's furniture of all places. They were part of the display in the window and Jenny talked the young salesman into letting us buy them. My photo for Jenny fits perfectly and I spent a little extra time wrapping it. I also wrote something on the back of the picture I'll never tell her about. Who knows, she might find it someday and smile.

Monday December 25, 1944
Very late

Nothing was said yesterday about meeting on our bench last night. Each of us knew the other would be there and for once it was a beautiful clear night. It wasn't even that cold for Christmas I thought as I pulled my coat on and left the house. I heard footsteps behind me about halfway to the park and turned around to see Jenny gaining on me. I slowed down and she took my arm.

"You know people are going to start talking if they notice us meeting at the same place every Christmas Eve."

"Then let's give them something to talk about."

I took her in my arms and kissed her like I hadn't kissed her in a long time. We put down the bags we were carrying and wrapped our arms around each other and did it right.

"I love Jenny Brewster," I yelled at the top of my voice for the whole neighborhood to hear. A few dogs barked but no porch lights came on. Maybe those still awake think Santa Claus loves Jenny Brewster.

We sat on our bench as we had since fifth grade and it felt good to hold her just like I did then and just like then, I slipped my cold hands under her blouse.

"You know you'll lose," she said with a grin.

"I know, but I don't mind losing this game."

It was only a few seconds before I had to grab her hands and make her stop. I unwrapped her present to me first. The photo was the best of her I've ever seen. She was dressed in formal clothes I've never seen her wear. Her hair was the way she wore it years ago, curled like her mother used to do it and the plunging neckline of her dress made her look like a real movie star.

"Oh Jenny," I said with a tear she couldn't see trying to escape my eye. "I know you're beautiful, but this picture makes me want to fall in love with you all over again."

"That was the idea."

At that moment, I was glad I'd let Miss Payne help me with my photo. She picked out my clothes and did everything she could to make me look my best.

When Jenny unwrapped my present, she didn't try to hide the tears.

"It's beautiful. When I look at it, I'll always think how lucky I am to have you as my lover and best friend. I remember all our Christmases on this bench and I wouldn't take anything for them. Someday these two pictures will hang side by side in our house."

"Promise?" I said as I kissed her.

"With all my heart. I want that more than anything in the world. I want to curl up with you on our couch in front of our fireplace at Christmastime and make love with you in our bed until the sun comes up."

Someday I'm going to sneak into the park and steal that bench and put it on our front porch, when we have a front porch of our own.

Tuesday December 26, 1944
Night

On Christmas morning, Mom decorated the house while I made breakfast. My biscuits are every bit as good as hers now and I'm quite proud of that. Her blessing that morning was one I'll remember. I hope I can remember all of them. She talked to Dad a lot and told him how proud she is of me and how well the two of us and baby Dave are doing. She asked God to bless Doris and Bob and my sister and Stan—and me and Jenny. It was different hearing her refer to us as a couple like that.

I don't know where she got the pork chops but they were really good and after breakfast we exchanged gifts. I got her a pair of hose. Jenny helped me get them from Peggy Hale's and they cost me too much. It didn't matter. I knew how much something as simple as that would mean to her.

"You must have stood in line for hours. We've only had one delivery in Evansville and they were gone long before anyone I know could get a pair. They say there won't be any more until the war's over. I know it seems silly to miss something as simple as a pair of hose so much, but there's nothing better you could have gotten me. I'm going to wear them to Christmas dinner tonight."

Mom got me a card and in the card was a note that said I could have the five gallons of gas she's been saving and drive the car until it was gone. That was as good a present as she could have ever gotten me. I need the practice; after all, I have to take the test in six months.

Christmas dinner was at Aunt Doris and Bob's yesterday and Mom let me drive there. I was a little sad not being with Jenny, so I called her from the phone in the master bedroom after we ate and we promised never to spend another Christmas Day apart. Dinner was early so we could be finished in time for Doris and Bob to put the kids to bed. I missed not seeing my sister and Stan at Christmas dinner too—they weren't invited. Aunt Doris says she and Bob will come to the wedding though.

The house was decorated from front to back. Their Christmas tree touched the ceiling. Anyone could see that Aunt Doris really likes Christmas. The boys got loads of presents and they pretended to like the games Mom and I got them. I was never too excited about games for Christmas, but I liked playing with them later after all the toys were broken or lost. I still have most of them.

Since it was their house, Bob said the blessing and I was never more certain he was a good man than I was after listening to his prayer. He thanked God for his wonderful wife and children and for his in-laws like he was supposed to, but then he prayed for those who've lost loved ones in the war and for our country's leaders, mentioning a dozen of them by name, some I didn't even recognize. He asked God for a quick end to the war and the safe return of our servicemen and ended with a special prayer for all the men and women who've worked so hard in Evansville to make our country strong. It was a good prayer and we all gave an "Amen" afterward.

As soon as we got home, I called Jenny. She said her parents had just left for the hospital with a neighbor from across the street. Mrs. McCormick is the young wife of a sailor who was last home…well, about nine months ago. Mrs. Brewster has been keeping an eye on her for the last month. It was late, but it was Christmas and when I explained to Mom, with the receiver in my hand, what was going on and asked if I could go stay with Jenny until her parents got home, she said I could. I told Jenny I would be there in a few minutes.

"You might be there all night," Mom yelled as I ran up the stairs. "Take something to sleep in."

It was a dream come true finally getting to be with Jenny under the canopy of her bed. Katherine wasn't even a distant memory. Maybe guilt has a way of disappearing with time. It was a stupid thing I did and it will never happen again. I love Jenny Brewster.

Chapter Six

1945
Monday January 1, 1945
Night

Last night we had fireworks down by the river and Jenny and I went with Sarah and Jimmy. In the dark we held hands and kissed like we were back in fifth grade. I fell in love with her then and it was like I was falling in love with her all over again. Maybe it's because I'm older or maybe it's because I know what love is now, and I catch myself thinking of where we'll be in five years, ten years, and even when we're old. I want to grow old with her and live in that little house with the white picket fence everyone talks about. That's what I thought about tonight as I held her hand and watched the fireworks. All that serious thought was broken up when one of the fireworks exploded directly over us and lit up everything. Sarah was on her knees in front of Jimmy. There was a lot of hurried-up clothes rearranging going on when she stood up, but no one noticed anything except Jenny and me.

"At least she won't get pregnant that way," Jenny whispered in my ear.

On the way home Sarah sat close to Jimmy in the front seat and her head kept getting lower and lower until it disappeared. At a light, Jimmy arched back for a second then relaxed. In a few minutes Sarah sat up in the seat, turned around to us and smiled.

"Sorry, wanted to finish what I started."

My sister and Stan visited this afternoon. It was good to see both of them and it was even better to see how excited they are about the wedding.

Saturday January 6, 1945
Night

We have a wedding to finish planning. Mom reserved the church weeks ago and we sent out the invitations just before Christmas. Today my sister and Victoria met Jenny at our house to finalize everything. Mom and I helped Victoria plan the wedding party while Jenny and my sister went to Peggy Hale's to pick out a wedding dress. She wanted the party at the USO and Victoria wanted it at her house, but they both agreed to let Mom and me decide. When Victoria said it would be a lot less work for everyone if the party is at her house, we sided with her. After all, she's paying for it so she should be able to have it where she wants. It was an easy choice. There would be a live band and dancing. Sitting at our kitchen table, Victoria asked Mom if it would be all right if I danced the first dance with the bride at the party. Mom's eyes sort of watered up. I knew that dance was always reserved for the father.

"Thank you Victoria for everything you've done for this family. I can promise my daughter's father would approve. He never thought she would marry and honestly, we owe it all to you that she's still alive. I don't know what would've happened to her if you hadn't come along. I've never known how to tell you what you've meant to us, but we've slept a lot better knowing she was with you."

"She's a very special woman and I truly love her," Victoria said with a smile and then added, "but I'm willing to share her with Stan. He's a good man and I know he'll treat her right."

It was a touching kind of moment I won't forget.

We got most of the details worked out by the time my sister and Jenny got back. The dress can be picked up on Monday the fifteenth. Although they tried to describe it to us, we'll just have to wait and see it. All I remember is that it's white like a wedding dress should be. Maybe my sister's no virgin by any stretch of the imagination, but she can get married in white anyway.

Victoria said the bridesmaids are two other housekeepers from her neighborhood that my sister helped get jobs. Their dresses have already been ordered. One is a colored girl, but Mom says that won't be a problem and that the roof of the church won't fall down on us. The best man is to be Mr. Winters, Stan's boss at Sunbeam. Millie will be the flower girl and I think that's appropriate. Someday maybe she'll learn she was the flower girl at her mother's wedding, although she won't learn it from me.

It's been freezing cold this past week and Jenny talked me into going ice skating at Burdette Park tonight. I would much rather have gone roller skating at Tri-State, but every year I have to go ice skating with her a few times. She's really good and I'm really bad. My ankles aren't strong enough. I hang onto her like a four year old and I think she likes that.

Tuesday January 9, 1945
Afternoon

I am now officially a stockholder in the Ray-Ban company. The certificate arrived today and I have twelve shares. It was a pretty impressive document with my name printed in large block letters and I took it to Jenny's before dinner to show it off.

"I got something in the mail from Ray-Ban today too," she announced with a little pride, "twelve pairs of sunglasses and I'm supposed to wear a different pair every month for the entire year. I have to call Mr. Evans and tell him so he can arrange a photo shoot."

"Which pair are you going to wear to the wedding? He'll want some pictures of you there for sure."

She tried on all of them and we chose a pair with white frames that'll look great with her light blue dress.

Jenny's photo shoots begin Thursday after school. Mr. Evans told her that as soon as the contract started, there would be charge accounts set up by Ray-Ban all over town for whatever she needs. The only requirement is that anything she buys has to show up in a photo of her wearing their sunglasses for that month. We're going to see just where she can buy things tomorrow. Peggy Hale's will certainly be one place, but what about Muir's Drugs or Schear's department store, or Blackman's Florist?

Friday January 12, 1945
Night

All the stores we went into Wednesday had accounts already set up with Jenny and Mr. Evans authorized to sign for anything. The salesladies at Roger's Jewelry said they've been authorized by Mr. Rogers to take orders for items they don't have in stock and even have things made to Jenny's specifications.

Jenny and I heard salesgirls all over town say, "You have the keys to the store, Miss Brewster."

The photo shoot yesterday with the white sunglasses was pretty simple. Mr. Evans and Miss Payne met us at Reitz as soon as school was out. He brought clothes for Jenny *and* me, which was a surprise. He wanted pictures of her walking home from school with a friend. We had to change in his van and it was freezing cold even with the motor running. They brought complete outfits for both of us. Jenny was dressed all in white and I was dressed in black. Her coat and hat from Peggy Hale's were beautiful, leather and trimmed in real fur. My coat was plain cloth but nice and we got to keep everything afterward. Jenny's skirt was a lot shorter than anyone in their right mind would wear on a day like yesterday. It was only twenty degrees and light snow was falling. Mr. Evans said both were perfect for the photos he wanted. He got pictures of Jenny wearing the sunglasses, taking them off and putting them back on while we walked, and others of her holding them in a dozen ways while I looked on admiringly, and several of me putting them on her.

This afternoon after school we went by Mr. Evans' studio and had a look at the proofs. He's an excellent photographer even if he is a masher. That's a new word I've learned and I can't imagine where it comes from. The first group of photos will be sent to Ray-Ban on Monday. I hope they like them. The next group will be taken at the wedding and of course Jenny talked Mr. Evans into doing the wedding pictures for free.

Monday January 15, 1945
Night

When my sister and Victoria arrived this afternoon carrying a big box, I knew the dress had arrived. I made them wait while I ran to Jenny's to get her before opening it. Christmas couldn't have been more suspenseful. It was beautiful and my sister looked like a model from a magazine with it on. There was padding in the right places and Victoria had picked up one of those movie star bras that created cleavage where I know there is none

Everyone's getting dressed before the wedding at our house so we can help each other watch the kids. The dress was left here, in my sister's old bedroom, hanging in the closet. I have plans for that dress.

Thursday January 18, 1945

Night

This afternoon was my chance. Mom and Dave went for his checkup, so I knew they wouldn't be home after school. I told Jenny I had something special planned for her at my house and that was enough to get her to follow me home. I led her upstairs and into my sister's bedroom. When I pulled the dress out of the closet, she knew what I had in mind.

"I can't put on her wedding dress. It has to be bad luck or something. What if I rip it?"

I had her clothes off before she could think of other reasons. The dress fit like it was made for her, except for the bust, but the padding was removable.

"I just want to see what you look like wearing a wedding dress," I said as I placed the veil on her head. "I might never get to see you in one again."

When I stepped back to have a look at her, I almost choked up. She was beautiful, even more beautiful than usual. I ran to my room, got my Brownie and took a roll of pictures. Mr. Evans will develop them for me without asking questions. If there'd only been some way of getting me into the pictures with her, that would have been perfect. I stood next to her and looked at us both in the full-length mirror hanging behind the closet door. She turned, held my face in her hands and kissed me.

"Wearing this dress makes me sort of…"

"Horny?"

"You know I hate that word…and I don't get horny, although I might get in the mood sometimes."

"Like right now?"

"It's what I always think about when I hear that song. Did I ever tell you that?"

I kissed her and then carefully pulled down the top of the dress just enough.

"I can't do this standing up," was the last thing I remember her saying…but she did do it standing up, several times.

Sunday January 21, 1945
Night

The wedding was at two yesterday, but Mom and I got there a little after twelve just to make sure everything was in place. Dave was in a horrible mood for some reason and wouldn't take his bottle. He didn't stop crying until Mom sat down and breastfed him there in the church. I had my Brownie and wanted to take her picture but she wouldn't let me.

Pastor Knott showed up about half an hour later and Mom told him about one of the bridesmaids being a colored girl.

"This is a wedding, not a waltz," he said looking in my direction and smiling. "There are no rules that say what the wedding party has to look like and anyone who objects to it can leave. We're all just witnesses to the promises the couple will make to God and I'm here only to say a few words no one will remember and then sign the marriage certificate."

I've always liked Pastor Knott.

When Mom was satisfied with the flower arrangement from Blackman's that had been delivered and set up already, we left to meet everyone back at our house. Jenny and I were standing out front when Victoria and her husband arrived in a huge Lincoln Continental with my sister and the two bridesmaids. Mr. Meckler got out and opened doors for his wife and my sister and escorted them into the house. I knew from his photos in the paper who he was and when the bridesmaids got out from the back seat, they looked sort of familiar. Their dresses were bright pink and it looked like they'd just come from the hairdresser. The colored girl was about my age and the other woman was about Mom's age I guessed. They were an odd pair for bridesmaids. They introduced themselves as Maria and Amanda and I said something about maybe knowing them. Jenny was laughing by that time. She knew how I knew them.

"I'll tell you who we are, or who we were if you promise to keep it to yourself," the one who introduced herself as Maria said. I only met you once when you came to Gear Town looking for your sister. She and I were living together in a little house on Second Street."

"Annemarie?"

She nodded.

"And don't tell me... You're Mandy?"

"I sure am, or I used to be—back when your sister was Maybelline."

"But how?"

"It's a long story and one that you'll have to buy me a drink to hear," Maria answered with a huge grin.

"Let's just say your sister don't forget her friends," Amanda added. "She got us jobs as maids with the richest white families in the county and now we're the housekeepers. We're making a lot of money, with maids, cooks and gardeners working for us. I even have a boyfriend."

I hugged both of them before we went in the house and told them how glad I was to see that they're doing well. My sister's just full of surprises. Those women would still be whores in Gear Town if not for her.

Everyone was dressed and at the church by quarter to two. The bride and bridesmaids were told to wait in the rectory until everyone was in place and they heard the music.

"I want both of us to escort your sister down the aisle," Mom whispered as we sat down in the front row with Jenny next to me. They were already teary-eyed and the ceremony hadn't even started.

Mom's request wasn't really a request, so when the music started and everyone stood up, I walked with her to the back of the church; a good crowd I thought. I took one arm and Mom took the other. Like Pastor Knott said, it wasn't a waltz. At the end of the Wedding March, the groom stood in front of us and the bridesmaids took their places. Millie was supposed to stand with them, but she came over and stood next to Mom. When Pastor Knott asked the usual question, "Who gives this woman…?" both Mom and I answered, "We do". Millie loudly added her own "we do" afterward and I thought that was the perfect way to start the wedding. When we returned to our seats and sat down, I put my arm around Mom and Jenny put her arm around me. Millie crawled into Jenny's lap and did her best to keep her eyes open. It had already been a long day for her.

This was a Methodist wedding so it was over in about half an hour even with Pastor Knott's readings from the New and Old Testaments. He said no one would remember what he said, but I already knew it by heart. The first reading was from one of Paul's letters to the Corinthians. I couldn't remember the chapter and verse and looked it up when I got home.

> If I have all faith so as to move mountains, but do not have love, I am nothing. If I give away everything I own, and if I hand my body over so that I may boast but do not have love, I gain nothing. Love is patient, love is kind. It is not jealous, is not pompous, it is not inflated, it is not rude, it does not seek its own interests, it is not quick-tempered, it does not brood over injury, it does not rejoice over wrongdoing but rejoices with the truth. It bears all things, believes all things,

hopes all things, endures all things. Love never fails.

When Pastor Knott got to the "do you take" part, Millie was wide awake.

"This is where they say 'I do,'" she whispered, loud enough for Mom and me to hear.

The final reading was from the Old Testament, parts of Proverbs Chapter 31. I knew this one too.

When one finds a worthy wife, her value is far beyond pearls. Her husband, entrusting his heart to her, has an unfailing prize. She brings him good, and not evil, all the days of her life. She obtains wool and flax and makes cloth with skillful hands. She puts her hands to the distaff, and her fingers ply the spindle. She reaches out her hands to the poor, and extends her arms to the needy. Charm is deceptive and beauty fleeting; the woman who fears the Lord is to be praised. Give her a reward of her labors, and let her works praise her at the city gates.

"I now pronounce you man and wife. What God has joined, let no man put asunder."

Those words sent a chill down my spine. They always have. It's like the "ashes to ashes, dust to dust" part of a funeral. Both are final endings and in each case, it's too late to change your mind; you're either married or dead.

I hadn't gotten a good look at who was at the wedding until the crowd started filing out of the church. There were a lot of unfamiliar faces and I guess they were friends of Stan or maybe my sister. I'm glad Aunt Doris and Bob came, although it must have been a strange experience for her. When we got to the door of the church, I saw Sarah and Jimmy. They took credit for the expertly done decoration of Stan's car and the long trail of tin cans following it as they drove away.

Tuesday January 23, 1945
Night

The party after the wedding was everything I expected it to be. Rich people know how to throw a party and they love impressing us commoners with what their money can buy. It was every bit as over the top as Katherine's graduation party, and the Meckler's house was even bigger than the Kohl's. After about a dozen champagne toasts, the band started playing. It was a slow waltz as it should have been. I walked over to my sister and offered her my hand. The crowd parted and gave us the floor, which was almost as large as the dance floor at the USO. She didn't know many of the steps so I whispered them to her as we danced. Maybe it wasn't so pretty but it felt good to take my father's place. Mom finally stopped crying after her second glass of champagne.

After that first dance it was time for the all-important throwing of the bouquet. My sister stood on a chair and every girl in the place gathered around with their hands up in the air. The bouquet went over all of them and just as my mother was taking a sip of champagne, it landed in her lap. It was like someone had thrown a snake at her, but there was no passing it off to anyone else. Everyone applauded and Mom was so embarrassed I thought she would die. Maybe she will get married again someday. She's still a very attractive lady by anyone's standards. I bet she could have a date every weekend if the single men around thought she would say yes if asked. She'd kill me if she thought I started a rumor. I might do it anyway. I wonder if she'd date an undertaker. Mr. Graves' wife passed away years ago and he's a handsome man with a good business. Everyone likes him and I don't think he's too old for Mom.

Jenny and I danced with everyone who asked us, stopping only long enough to devour more crab legs. I danced with Victoria twice and she invited Jenny and me to visit her anytime we wanted. Maybe she thinks she'll be lonely when my sister moves out, although they won't miss any opportunity to be together I'm sure. It was an all-seafood buffet and I've never seen so many varieties in my life; everything from tuna to lobster and it was all delicious. The crab legs were my favorite. Jenny and I got introduced to people my sister and Stan invited and a lot of them recognized Jenny from her pictures in the newspaper. In every case I was introduced first and Jenny was introduced as my girlfriend. I like that. Jenny told me during the party that the honeymoon will be in the Florida Keys at a resort owned by the Mecklers. I thought they were going to Niagara Falls. Maybe I just imagined that. She also said the newlyweds had put down a deposit on a house on Adams Avenue. Stan doesn't make nearly enough money for them to live in that part of town, so Victoria must have a hand in that as well. I don't care. I just hope Stan realizes that while he might be my sister's husband, she's still Victoria's girlfriend.

Aunt Doris and Bob came to the party for a little while and I'm glad they did. She said Caitlan was babysitting the boys and that they didn't want to leave them for very long. I could understand that. Caitlan's only a few years older than Mike and those two boys could have her tied to a tree given enough time to plan it. Harry will do about anything Mike tells him to.

We said our goodbyes around midnight and I insisted on driving home. Mom was a little tipsy, although she'll never admit it. When I got her safely in the house, I walked Jenny home.

"I want a wedding just like that," she whispered as we walked hand in hand.

The front porch light was still out so we had a long goodnight kiss and I wanted nothing more than to go upstairs with her and crawl into that canopy bed.

Sunday January 28, 1945
Late afternoon

The newlyweds came by early this morning on their way to the airport. They've been staying at the Hotel McCurdy on Riverside, the fanciest hotel in town, and I'm sure Victoria picked up the tab for that. I keep telling myself none of that matters, but I guess it does or I wouldn't think about it.

Jenny had a photo shoot yesterday for Valentine's Day. The pair of red sunglasses Ray-Ban sent in the box earlier looked good on her, but I wasn't too pleased with the outfit Miss Payne brought along. Actually, I liked how it looked a lot, but it was much too cold outside for her to be wearing a short red skirt and a very tight V-neck short-sleeved sweater blouse. Jenny hated the bullet bra, although I thought she looked good in it. The photos were taken with Jenny walking up and down Main Street. Mr. Evans wanted Jenny in a crowd carrying a big box of candy in the shape of a heart. Everyone else had their heavy coats on and he wanted Jenny to stand out in the crowd. She did, and I bet most of the pictures show people looking at her. She ducked into a store on every block to warm up. I think she and I will be doing the clothes shopping for the next shoot. She doesn't have to wear only the things Miss Payne and Mr. Evans pick out. That's not in her contract. It just specifies the clothes are to be stylish.

The "Battle of the Bulge" as they are calling it, is over. The Krauts are in full retreat back over the German border. I feel a little guilty for not keeping up with the war news closer for the past weeks. I do know we've lost thousands of our soldiers in Belgium, Luxembourg, and Northern France trying to stop the Nazis from regaining what they've lost in the last few months. Eric says the German soldiers fought like it was the beginning of the war, with hundreds of new tanks and guns we didn't know they still had in reserve. We were caught completely by surprise and it cost us a lot of men. No one is saying how many, so that means a lot. Now we're back where we were a month ago, no closer to Berlin than we were then. Everyone's talking about us taking Berlin before the Russians. Who cares? If the Russians get there first and end this war, I won't be disappointed. Let the Russians have Hitler and the rest of his gang. If we capture them, we'll probably put them on trial in New York for a year.

The Russians have taken the big cities in Poland and Ernie has written a long article on the prison camps for Jews they found there. If half of what's being reported is true, the Nazis shouldn't even get a trial. There's a special service at the Washington Avenue Temple planned for Saturday and Mom wants to go. Several of the women in the Wives and Mothers Club are Jewish and she's become good friends with them through Mrs. Brewster.

Tuesday January 30, 1945
Night

Mr. Evans called Jenny last night and told her to have a look at *The New York Times* for Sunday. He wouldn't tell her anything else. We get the newspaper at school, in the library, but it's always a couple of days late to E'ville. The Sunday edition showed up today after lunch. We asked Mrs. Landers when we got to school today to hold the paper for us, but we didn't expect to be called out of

History class when it arrived. The expression on Mrs. Landers' face was dead serious when she walked into class and spoke with Mr. Harmon and when he announced that Jenny and I were to go with her for a special assignment, I wasn't sure what was going on. As soon as we closed the door behind us to Mr. Harmon's classroom, Mrs. Landers hugged us both. Her eyes were beaming.

"I sneaked a look before coming to get you. It's not every day that two of our students have their pictures in *The New York Times*."

It's not often you hear screams from the Reitz library, but Jenny could be heard over most of the school when she got to the page with the ad. The ad was a quarter-page and the picture Ray-Ban chose had me in it. Jenny looked so good, like a real New York model, and I didn't look half bad myself.

We went by Readmore Magazines after school and bought four copies of the newspaper, two for each of our families. When I showed the ad to Mom, she couldn't believe it was all true, that something had actually come of all the Ray-Ban talk. Seeing the picture in *The Times* made it all real for her—and me too. Jimmy called tonight and congratulated me. His father gets the paper and when he saw the ad today, he asked Jimmy if it was Jenny and me. He remembered us and told Jimmy he wanted him to invite us over soon.

Mr. Evans says that *The Press* can reproduce the ad as long as they acknowledge *The Times* and he's going to write a story about us to go along with it.

Sunday February 4, 1945
Night

Jenny called this afternoon and asked me to come over. Caitlan was there and I could tell by the tone of Jenny's voice something was up. When I got there, Jenny met me at the door and pushed me back outside. She had a deathly serious expression on her face.

"We have to talk to her and you have to talk to Doris. Something's been going on for a while and if it's not stopped right now, things would get a lot worse real fast."

"What? What are you talking about?"

"I'll let Caitlan tell you. I wanted to scream at her when she told me. I didn't know what to say so I didn't say anything and called you."

I followed Jenny in. Mr. and Mrs. Brewster were out somewhere so we sat on the living room sofa together with Caitlan. She's really growing up and is turning into a pretty young girl. We started talking about nothing in particular, school and things, until Jenny steered the conversation around to babysitting.

"So you like babysitting, huh? I know you sat for Aunt Doris and Bob so they could come to the wedding. That was awfully nice of you. Mike and Harry can be a handful, I know."

"They're no trouble," Caitlan said with a smile, "as long as you let them play doctor. I'm always the patient."

"And what do the doctors do?"

"Mostly they want to examine me. That keeps them busy for an hour and I don't really mind. They're just kids."

I tried to stay calm, not really wanting to hear where this was going.

"What grade are you in, Caitlan?" Jenny asked.

"Sixth, at Perry Heights."

"You don't go to Centennial?"

"I did until last year when Mom moved me to Perry Heights. She said Centennial was getting too crowded. I like it okay, I guess."

"Last year, did you see a movie in school called *Our Developing Bodies* or something like that? Maybe you saw it this year."

"No, I don't remember anything like that."

"Well has your mother talked to you about things, you know, like growing up and boys?"

"No, but I hear a lot at school."

"Caitlan, let me just ask you; do you know how a girl gets pregnant?"

"Sure, I know all that and I know it can't happen until the girl does it with a boy after she starts having periods. Until then she can't get pregnant. Two girls in my class have their periods already but I don't, so I can do it if I want."

I got up and went to the bathroom and stayed as long as I could without Jenny thinking I'd died. It was a very long, sometimes unpleasant, afternoon with Caitlan. When she left, Jenny and I talked until her parents came home. We told Caitlan everything and didn't hold back any of the details. That film in fifth grade was corny but I learned a lot from it and the books at the library. I had millions of questions at her age and I can't believe Caitlan's teachers or her mom haven't explained things to her. Jenny thinks I should talk to Aunt Doris right away and tell her that Caitlan shouldn't babysit the boys anymore. That's fine, but what do I say when she wants to know why?

Thursday February 8, 1945
Night

Aunt Doris is Mom's sister and if anyone can talk to her, Mom can, so I had a long talk with her tonight after dinner and told her everything. It was an awkward conversation but I got through it and afterward Mom thanked me for telling her. She said I shouldn't worry, that she'll take care of telling Aunt Doris in a way that won't upset her too much. I called Jenny and told her that Mom was taking care of everything and that I wanted us to spend a lot more time with Caitlan. She agreed. Caitlan doesn't need to be getting her information from the other kids at school. There's a basketball game this Friday night and we're going to ask her to go with us.

After our conversation, Mom had something she wanted to talk to me about.

"I had an unexpected phone call today from Mr. Graves. We talked for an hour about nothing in particular. He's a really nice man, don't you think?"

"Yes Mom, I think Mr. Graves is a very nice man," I answered with a smile.

"What would you think if I went to dinner with him sometime? It wouldn't be like a date, just dinner."

"Well Mom," I said, smiling even more, "I think Mr. Graves would be a very lucky man to spend some time with you. Of course you'd have to be home by ten on a school night, eleven on weekends, and no drinking."

I didn't spread the rumor that Mom might go out if she were asked, but I can guess who did. Sarah overheard Jenny and me talking about it a few weeks ago and I just bet she had something to do with Mr. Graves' unexpected phone call.

The Times Ray-Ban ad came out today in *The Press* and I like the article Mr. Evans wrote about Jenny and me. He called Jenny the most beautiful model he'd ever worked with.

Wednesday February 14, 1945
Very late

Mom went to dinner with Mr. Graves tonight, which meant Jenny and I had the house to ourselves on Valentine's. When I got home from school today Mom was already in a panic over what to wear. She was as nervous as a schoolgirl and it would have been funny if she weren't my mom. I told her to wear something with red in it and that was my only suggestion.

"I guess he sees enough of women in black doesn't he?"

"Yes Mom, no black."

She settled on a light brown skirt with matching jacket, a bright red belt, and a pale yellow blouse. She didn't have any shoes that matched everything else so her grey ones she wears to church had to do. I noticed she had on a little makeup as well and some lipstick, nothing obvious, just enough. Her hair was done up really nice and when I said something about it, she confessed that Mrs. Brewster had helped. I thought I saw her hand in it. Mom almost never wears her hair up, only when she's in an especially good mood and I can't remember the last time that was. It must have been before Dad died.

When the knock came on the door, she gave me a terrified look.

"Do I look all right? This was a terrible idea. I don't know why I ever said I'd go."

"Mom, you look gorgeous. Now go into the kitchen and let me answer the door. We can't have him think you were ready and waiting for him."

I noticed the splash of red Mr. Graves was wearing as soon as I opened the door and invited him in. His tie would match Mom's belt perfectly. He wasn't wearing any black either, not even his shoes. I invited him to have a seat, that Mom would be out in a minute. We sat and talked about the weather and the war. When I had just about run out of anything else to say, Mom came in. I think she was really surprised at how…what's the word…? Debonair, that's it—how debonair Mr. Graves looked. Mom turned as they left as if to say something to me, and the uncertain look on her face was almost a plea for help. I kissed her, told her to have a good time and pushed her out the door.

I called Jenny and she showed up a few minutes later wearing the short little red skirt and white sweater blouse she had worn for the photo shoot—without the bullet bra. She even brought the big heart shaped box of candy which I was sure was a prop. She was freezing and took both my hands and pushed them up her blouse before she wrapped her arms around me.

"Warm me up. It's freezing out there and I ran all the way here."

"Without a coat?"

"I put on a coat first but it spoiled the surprise so I left it home."

The box of candy wasn't a prop. She didn't know where it had come from and she kept it after the photo shoot. We ate half the box sitting on the couch underneath a wool throw after I put Dave to bed. I gave her my card, which I chose months ago because it had a single line verse in it that I really like.

Love will always find a way

That's been our story since fifth grade.

Jenny put her card to me underneath the candy and I had to dig it out. On the front were two hearts pierced by a single arrow and inside was a drawing of Cupid. Underneath the drawing Jenny had written: "Sometimes if he's lucky, he gets two with a single arrow. Think that's what happened with us?"

I gave her my best Valentine's Day kiss.

"I think it wasn't luck. His aim was perfect."

We're going to own a couch just like ours someday or maybe Mom will give ours to me when Jenny and I go to college. It has a lot of memories in it and we made another one tonight.

Thursday February 15, 1945
Night

I pestered Mom until she gave me all the details of her dinner date with Mr. Graves. I knew it went well when I heard her singing all the way from my bedroom while she made breakfast this morning. I haven't heard her sing in a long time.

"You would never believe an undertaker could be so funny! His sense of humor is something most people never get to see in his line of work, but right off, on our way to dinner, he said in a very serious tone, 'Do you know why undertakers make such good husbands?' I guess I wasn't expecting that out of him and froze for a second before responding, 'No.' He answered in the same dry serious tone, 'Because they never bring their work home with them.' I just cracked up laughing. He is such a funny, nice man and I felt completely comfortable being with him. We had a wonderful dinner at The Brown Derby out on Highway 41 and afterward he took me for ice cream at Kohn's next to the fire station. I didn't realize how much I've missed ice cream in the past few years. It was a wonderful evening and I think I might be seeing more of Mr. Graves in the future."

Friday February 18, 1945
Late

The war came to my street today.

Walking home from school today with Jenny, we saw Caitlan sitting looking out their large picture window facing the street. When she saw us she came out and invited us in. We sometimes stop by her house for a few minutes after school now, just to talk a bit. It's been painfully cold the last couple of days and we should have ridden with Jimmy, but Jenny wanted to walk. The hot cocoa Caitlan offered was just what we needed. She didn't have to ask twice.

The first thing you notice in their living room is the picture of her father in Navy dress whites with Lieutenant Commander insignia. Caitlan's hardly seen him since even before the war and he's sort of a myth to her, but she's gotten letters and her mom talks about him all the time. He'd been in the Pacific for months and it'd been six weeks since they'd heard from him. Mrs. Propst brought out the hot chocolate to us on a tray and just as she sat it down on the coffee table in the living room, I heard a car pull into their driveway. Mrs. Propst looked up, through the picture window and I've never seen such an expression of pure horror on anyone's face in my life. She took two steps toward the door and fell to her knees screaming. I recognized the Navy staff car and knew why the two officers in dress uniforms who got out of it were there. Caitlan didn't know what was happening and was frozen sitting on the couch.

When the knock came on the door, I didn't know if I should answer it or not. They knocked again and Mrs. Propst stood up and tried to walk toward the door. Jenny, Caitlan, and I grabbed her and helped her stand up. She tried to speak to Caitlan, but the words wouldn't come.

"It's about your father," I whispered to her.

The two officers were very respectful and read a letter from Mr. Propst's commanding officer and then read one from President Roosevelt. The one from the president was probably just like the one everyone who has lost someone in the war gets, but the one from Mr. Propst's commanding officer was written by someone who knew him well. I was okay until the officer said that Mr. Propst was commanding LST 577 and then the tears began streaming down my face. Mom and I went to the launching of that LST back in June of last year. It was built here. It was torpedoed on the morning of February 11 by a Jap submarine while on a supply run to Lingayen Gulf in the Philippines. There were only a few survivors and no bodies were recovered.

As soon as the officers left, I called Mom and Jenny called Mrs. Brewster. They must have stopped whatever they were doing because it seemed like they were there in minutes. After they arrived, Jenny and I took a walk with Caitlan to let the women be alone. She was in shock I guess because she wasn't crying or anything, although she understood her father was dead. It's hard to know what to say at times like that so we let Caitlan do most of the talking. She told us everything she knew about her father, which wasn't too much. It was after dark when we got back to her house. Several more women from the neighborhood were there and they all brought food.

When we were ready to leave, Jenny and I hugged Caitlan and told her we would both be there for her if she needed us for anything, and we meant it. Jenny and I sat at her house until almost ten and talked. Caitlan will need us whether she knows it now or not.

Saturday February 26, 1945
Night

The funeral for Mr. Propst was this afternoon and Caitlan asked Jenny and me to sit with her and her mother. There was no rush to have the funeral since there was no body, and a half dozen Navy officers were there. Two of them spoke and one of them had known Mr. Propst well a few years ago. The letter Mrs. Propst got from President Roosevelt was read again along with a letter from Admiral Nimitz, the commander in chief of the Pacific fleet. Pastor Knott had never met Mr. Propst, however he spoke as if he had. He knows Mrs. Propst and Caitlan and his words were meant for them anyway. After he spoke, Mayor Reichert had a few words to say. He'd never met Mr. Propst either, but he's spoken at a lot of funerals for Evansville servicemen and he conveyed the thanks and appreciation of the entire city for Mr. Propst's service. When two officers approached Mrs. Propst at the end of the service, I knew what they were delivering. It was a plaque like the one that hangs in our house.

The monument at Oak Hill was already in place and when we got there a company of soldiers representing all the services was standing guard. One of the officers read a final eulogy and *Taps* was played. Jenny and I spent the rest of the afternoon with Caitlan in her room. The house was full of guests she didn't know and she was tired of meeting them. I understood very well what she meant. When we were ready to leave, Caitlan told us something she would like to do with us.

"There's a movie playing at The Grand I would like to see sometime. Would the two of you go with me? It's *National Velvet* and I haven't seen it yet, but I hear it's really good."

"How about next Saturday afternoon?" Jenny answered for both of us.

That was fine with me. Jenny and I haven't been to the movies lately and there are lots of new ones out I want to see.

When I got home this afternoon after the funeral, I switched on the radio. Canadian and British troops have reached the Rhine River in Germany. I got out my map to see where that is. It's still a long way to Berlin, but we're deep inside Germany now. The Brewsters haven't gotten a letter lately, which probably means Jenny's brother's not in Paris anymore.

Saturday March 4, 1945
Night

We saw *National Velvet* this afternoon with Caitlan. Since it was a matinée, there were lots of kids there with their parents. We sat in the back and before the movie started, Caitlan grinned and told us it would be all right if we wanted to kiss during it.

"I've seen you kiss before, remember? The two of you were babysitting me—or the three of us were babysitting Millie and Dave. It was the first time I ever saw two people kiss in real life. I promised I wouldn't tell and I never did. Do you remember that?

"Oh yes, I remember that," I answered with a smile toward Jenny, "but I bet she doesn't."

"I do too," Jenny answered, "but I didn't know we had an audience."

When the movie started, I reached for Jenny's hand and when Velvet rode The Piebald over the first jump in the Grand National, Caitlan reached for my other hand and squeezed it. It was a good movie and Angela Lansbury might be my newest favorite actress. The young girl who played Velvet was someone I'd never heard of, Elizabeth Taylor, but I bet she'll be a famous actress when she grows up. I've heard that she was only twelve when the movie was made and I know a lot of boys will be seeing the movie just to get a look at her. She sure didn't look twelve. She was beautiful.

After the movie, we walked back to Caitlan's. Her mom wasn't home and had left a note saying she wouldn't be home until four. Caitlan begged us to stay with her until then and we had nothing else to do so we agreed. The first thing I noticed when we came in the front door was that the picture of Caitlan's father was gone. I didn't ask about that. People deal with death in different ways I guess. We sat on the sofa and listened to the radio. Caitlan knows all the latest songs and the best stations. There's a new song by the Andrews Sisters called *Rum and Coca-Cola*. Jenny and I both like it even if we can't figure out what to dance to the beat. We've made it fit a Rumba, Cha-Cha combination that sort of works. I've heard it called Calypso, but not even Mrs. Brewster knows the dance. When the song came on the radio, Caitlan talked us into dancing it for her, and toward the end, she joined us. It was fun trying to figure out the steps that fit the music. Maybe dancing wasn't exactly appropriate under the circumstances. We didn't care. It was what she wanted.

Caitlan made us peanut butter sandwiches and we sat around the kitchen table talking.

"Was Jenny your first real kiss?" she asked me out of the blue.

I almost didn't get that bite down. We talked about a lot of things after that and when we moved back onto the living room sofa, I found out the real reason for her questions.

"There's this boy at school," she finally admitted—there's always a boy, "and I like him and I think he likes me. He asked me to go to the movies with him sometime and I'd like to go, but what if he wants to kiss me? I've never kissed anyone before and I don't want to look stupid."

"It's easy," Jenny answered, "just watch me."

She leaned over and kissed me. It was like a classroom kiss that didn't have much behind it, so I took over.

"No," I said with a grin, "it's more like this."

I took Jenny's face in my hands and gave her my best 'I haven't seen you in a month' kiss that she wasn't expecting.

"If he kisses you like that," Jenny said with a grin, "slap his face and walk home."

Caitlan laughed, even though she knew Jenny was giving her some good advice.

"So what's an ordinary kiss? Do I keep my mouth closed or do I open it and what if he tries to stick his tongue in my mouth? I think I'd gag."

"Just close your eyes and pretend I'm Mr. Loverboy for a minute."

Jenny kissed her and if she hadn't been doing it in the line of duty, I might've been a little jealous because it wasn't another classroom kiss. She held Caitlan's face in her hands the way I had held hers and I saw Caitlan's arms go around Jenny's waist. It was definitely not a simple lesson in kissing. Caitlan's face was flushed when they separated.

"Now that was a respectable good-night kiss, not a kiss any girl would give her brother and not one a girl would give her favorite lover either."

"My very first kiss and it was with a girl," Caitlan grinned.

"Girls are just better kissers," Jenny said with just as big a grin.

"The second kiss is always better," I interrupted.

I pulled her up off the couch and took her in my arms. That kiss was intended to make Jenny as jealous as she'd made me. When I opened my mouth slightly and touched Caitlan's lips with my tongue, her mouth opened and I slipped my tongue inside just far enough to touch hers.

I don't know how far things would have gone if her mother hadn't come back when she did.

Thursday March 9, 1945
Night

We're getting war news from Europe almost as soon as it happens. I guess some of the radio censors think the war there is as good as over too. The news from the Pacific is still scarce and we only hear about things a week or longer after they happen. The big news today was the crossing of the Rhine River yesterday by our 9th Armored Division— on a bridge no less. The Canadians and British might have gotten to the Rhine first, but we were the first to cross it. Eric says there are other crossings planned and that this crossing will really shake up Berlin since we did it across a bridge they were throwing in everything they had to try and blow it up. Not even their great V-2 rockets we hear so much about could stop us.

The Russians have captured Budapest and that's on my map. Most of the cities in the East I can't find. The river in the East that's as important as the Rhine is the Oder and the Russians got there sometime last month. Eric says they're within eighty miles of Berlin now. The Krauts have to give up or the Russians will destroy everything in their path, just like the Germans did when they were going east. Is Hitler going to let that happen? Does he care so little what happens to his own country?

The Brewsters finally got a letter, even though it was so heavily censored this time I couldn't make anything of it. Jenny's brother definitely isn't in Paris anymore.

Sunday March 19, 1945
Late afternoon

Jenny's March photo shoot was yesterday and she wore an outfit we picked out together. When we walked into Bon

Marché on Main Street last week we were greeted by the store manager as if she were expecting us. It's the finest women's clothing store in E'ville and the most expensive.

"Miss Brewster, I can't tell you how pleased I am to have you in our store. My name is Mrs. Laurent. An account has already been set up in yours and Mr. Evans' names and I'll be glad to order anything we don't have in stock. With the war winding down, we've been told we'll be the first store in the state to start receiving fashions from Paris again. In the meantime, we can have anything from New York in two days."

Jenny introduced me as her manager and fashion consultant.

"I will of course add your name to the account and anything you need for Miss Brewster only requires your signature."

Jenny brought the green-framed sunglasses with her, sort of a spring color, and I told Mrs. Laurent we would be looking for an outfit that matched them.

"I realize it's an odd request, that usually sunglasses are bought to match an outfit, not the other way around, but that is what we require." I tried to sound like I knew what I was talking about.

"I like a challenge," Mrs. Laurent replied with a smile.

Two hours later we walked out with a complete outfit that did not include a bullet bra or a short skirt. Mr. Evans got a well-dressed sophisticated woman out for an early afternoon on the town as the subject of his photo shoot. Jenny looked gorgeous. We may never go back to Peggy Hale's unless of course Ray-Ban complains about the two hundred dollars worth of clothes we signed for at Bon Marché.

Our next stop was Kruckemeyer and Cohn Jewelers where Jenny got a pair of silver bracelets with colored stones in them that matched the outfit. They were thirty dollars each and were ours for a signature.

Mr. Evans had scheduled the shoot for just outside the USO Club and when we arrived, Jenny told him the location had been changed to just outside Lowe's Theater. He complained but when he saw how Jenny was dressed, he couldn't very well argue. He took photos of her going into and coming out of about every door in the place and walking down the sidewalk in front. The manager at Lowe's was a little curious until I explained what we were doing and that Lowe's would appear in the Ray-Ban ad. He was very cooperative after that and we left with a handful of free tickets. On the way home Jenny told me she's been asked to the prom by a senior. I asked her who but she wouldn't tell me. She said she didn't want to go, that last year's prom was boring and that she'd rather go out with me. That got her two kisses—and I didn't tell her she should go to the prom anyway.

We heard last week about the first major bombing of Tokyo. It happened on March 9 and 10 and Eric says this is only the beginning. If we're close enough to bomb their capital whenever we want, how can they continue the war? It's going to be all over in Europe soon and the Japs will be on their own against the Allies.

Tuesday March 28, 1945
Night

Jenny went out with Edward Meier last Friday night. He's a senior at Bosse and the grandson of one of the Jewish ladies in the Wives and Mothers Club. Mrs. Brewster sort of arranged the whole thing and Jenny went along with it. They saw *Jane Eyre* at Lowe's. It's a great movie. Jenny and I have seen it already but she went anyway. When I saw her Sunday at church she smiled when I asked her how her date had gone.

"It was a very respectable good-night kiss and that's all, no tongue."

Exactly what I wanted to hear.

Caitlan came over Sunday afternoon and we listened to records and worked on our Calypso. It's still not very good. She wanted to know about our week and we asked about hers.

"And how is it going with the boy who likes you?" Jenny asked with a grin. "Have you gone to the movies with him yet and did he kiss you?"

Caitlan hung her head and mumbled something that I caught.

"I made up that story."

I knew it. I didn't think she kissed Jenny and me the way she would have if she was just trying to learn how.

"I made it all up," she repeated for Jenny as a single tear wound its way down her cheek. "There's no boy. I wanted to kiss you. You're so beautiful. I tricked you because I was too afraid of what you might think."

She then turned toward me.

"And then you kissed me and I really didn't know what to do. If you don't want me coming around anymore, I won't."

"It's not the first time I've been tricked into a kiss, although it was the best," Jenny said as she wiped the tear from Caitlan's cheek and smiled.

Tuesday April 3, 1945
Night

Sunday was Easter, on April fool's day. It was beautiful weather and there was a huge turnout for the parade on Saturday. Jenny and I went and took Caitlan. Sarah and

Jimmy met us there. Now this was an Easter parade like before the war. There were more floats than I ever remember and not a military one in the bunch. I think we're tired of olive drab.

Bright yellow-framed sunglasses are what Jenny picked for the photo shoot next weekend. We're going shopping tomorrow for something yellow for her to wear. She looks so good in yellow and she doesn't wear it nearly enough. The weather forecast is for rain, which isn't too good for a photo shoot that's supposed to feature sunglasses.

I've written nothing about school in a while; maybe because there've been so many other things going on in my life. There weren't nearly as many new students this year as in the past few years, but one new girl stands out. She was only at Reitz for the first half of the school year, although she made a lasting impression on a lot of people and I should write about her. Her name was Ellen and she was from Georgia. Everyone made fun of the way she talked, but Jenny and I liked her, and with her height, she became our star volleyball player. We had a winning Junior High girls' volleyball team at Reitz this year for the first time and they were always in the newspaper. Even the parents came to watch. Mostly it was mothers because the games are usually in the afternoons before the fathers get home from work.

Sometime after the beginning of volleyball season, Jenny asked me on the way home from school if it would be all right if she invited Ellen to come over and hang out with us.

"She seems nice and she calls me almost every night and I wanted to ask you before inviting her. Do you want to know what she told me? She said that I could be the next Margie Stewart, you know, the army pin-up girl. Did you know she's from Indiana?"

I didn't know Ellen called her almost every night. She never called me and I didn't know Margie Stewart was from Indiana, although I do know who she is because her picture's everywhere. I told Jenny it would be fine with me if Ellen wanted to come over. What else could I say? Ellen was a pretty girl; more than pretty, she was beautiful. All the boys knew who she was already and I heard that even some seniors asked her out the first week of school. So why would she want to hang around Jenny and me?

When I got to Jenny's that afternoon Ellen was already there. They were helping Mrs. Brewster make something in the kitchen.

"Ellen brought a recipe with her and we're going to try to make it today," Jenny announced when she saw me. "We've made the dough and now we have to roll it out really thin and cut it into little circles, then bake them until they're brown. That's just half the recipe though."

"Yeah," Ellen added, "the easy half, but I've watched my mother and grandmother make banana puddings since I was a little girl and I finally wrote down the recipe from memory last night. I hope I got it right."

I rolled out the dough and we cut out about a hundred of the inch and a half cookies and put them on a greased baking tin. When they were brown, Mrs. Brewster took them out and we each had one. They had a nice vanilla flavor.

Ellen then took charge. She measured out flour and cornstarch and some of Mrs. Brewster's precious sugar and mixed them in a bowl. She then poured some sweet milk into a sauce pan and put it on the stove at low heat. When it was right, she poured some of it into another bowl containing egg yolks Jenny had prepared. I stirred a while and then Ellen started slowly adding the sugar, flour, and cornstarch mixture and finally the rest of the hot milk from the stove. She then poured the whole thing back into the sauce pan on the stove and stirred it herself.

"This is the hard part. It has to cook just long enough, but not too long. If it scorches we have to start over."

After a few minutes, she declared it done and took it off the stove. She stirred in some butter and vanilla until everything was smooth. Jenny and I were in charge of the next step and we lined the bottom of a deep baking pan with the vanilla cookies we'd just made and then made a layer of banana slices. Ellen poured some of the mixture over it and we put on another layer of the cookies and bananas. We did this until the pan was almost full and we had used all the mixture. I was put in charge of beating the egg whites and it took all three of us taking turns to make a really fluffy pan of the meringue. Ellen spooned it over the pudding mixture and made little peaks in the egg white. Into the oven it went until the meringue was just turning brown. We managed to save a little for Mr. Brewster. I think we could have eaten the whole thing. It was that good. I wanted to take some home to Mom, but there wasn't enough left.

After we ate and cleaned up the kitchen, Jenny, Ellen, and I sat around listening to the radio. When Glenn Miller's *In the Mood* came on, Ellen spoke up.

"Everyone at school says the two of you are really good dancers."

That was all it took; well, that and Jenny turning the radio up to full volume. She already had that "please ask me to dance" look on her face she gets whenever that song comes on. We put on a show for Ellen, doing every swing move we know. It felt so good to hold her in my arms again, even if it was a swing and there isn't much holding in swing dancing. We were exhausted when the song ended and collapsed on the sofa next to Ellen.

"Everyone was right. The two of you are good."

Then—the words I knew were coming—came out of Jenny's mouth.

"We can teach you."

I didn't want to teach Ellen to dance. That's something Jenny and I do together. Maybe she was just being nice to her guest and Ellen wasted no time accepting her offer. I soon figured out Ellen didn't want *us* to teach her how to dance; she wanted Jenny to teach her. She was either the fastest learner in history or she already knew how to dance, because in no time she was following Jenny's every lead. When a slow waltz came on, they danced much too close. She didn't get that close to me when Jenny suggested I dance with her. The two of them looked beautiful together, too beautiful, and the longer they danced, the more jealous I got.

"She likes you," I said to Jenny as soon as Ellen left that day.

"I like her too. She's really nice, but I think she knows a little more about dancing than she let on."

"No, I mean she really likes you—the way I like you. If I hadn't been here, I believe she would have kissed you."

"You're imagining things. She was just being nice and I'm sure the touching while we danced was accidental."

"Okay, but I know what I saw."

I left and came home. I'm used to boys, even teachers, flirting with her and she's always put them in their place or I have, but Ellen was a girl and a very pretty girl who I could tell really liked Jenny. I didn't exactly know what to do and tortured myself with thoughts that Ellen would be payback for Katherine.

Jenny had to have known Ellen was flirting with her and whenever I brought it up, she said I was just overreacting, that Ellen wanted nothing more than to be a friend to both of us. Well, if that were true, why didn't she ever call me? She wasn't interested in being *my* friend. This drove me crazy. I hated to seem so horribly jealous. I was though, more than I ever was of Mr. Mattox. Every morning on our way to school I asked Jenny if Ellen had called the night before and what they talked about. I called Jenny too, a lot, and when the line was busy, I imagined it was because she was talking to Ellen. I thought the girl needed a boyfriend, or a girlfriend, just not Jenny. She even walked home with us and Sarah, although she lived in the opposite direction from school. She was with us every minute at school and if I wanted to talk to Jenny about anything, I had to call her on the phone after I got home.

Then she started showing up at church and of course she sat with us. Everyone thought it was just great that Jenny and I had a new friend. After the banana pudding party, Mrs. Brewster made a point of inviting her back anytime and she showed up Saturday afternoons like clockwork. She practically invited herself to the movies with Jenny and me and made sure Jenny sat between us. I was waiting for the other shoe to drop.

Then someone at school who knows someone who knew Ellen from the Louisville school she used to go to, spread rumors that she had to leave school because she was caught half naked and kissing another girl in the janitor's closet. Of course then everyone thought Jenny was Ellen's new girlfriend. At the time I sort of wished I'd thought of that, but I could never have done that to her, not even to get rid of Ellen. Jenny came over to my house one night after the rumors died down a few days later and we talked a long time sitting in the swing on our front porch.

"Maybe you were right about Ellen. I didn't want to tell you, but there are some things you should know. She came over to my house last Sunday night and we went up to my room and listened to the radio for a while. We were just sitting on my bed facing each other and talking and then she leaned over and kissed me—without any warning. Maybe I was paralyzed or something because I couldn't move, but when she tried to put her hand up my blouse, I managed to back away and say something. I don't know what I said."

At that point I had to leave. I got up, walked inside and closed the door. With Fat-head Mattox it was different. I knew he was so creepy I would eventually win—Ellen was beautiful and tall...and did I mention beautiful? She really did make me look plain as a jam sandwich and I think Jenny fell for her. Thank goodness Ellen's family found a house close to Central High School just before Christmas and she transferred. Jenny and I have seen her a few times since then and she still calls Jenny occasionally. Maybe she has a new girlfriend by now.

Friday April 13, 1945
Night

Terrible horrible news today and I can hardly write for crying; President Roosevelt died yesterday. We heard on the radio that he's been sick, but it didn't sound like anything serious. Mom and I had just finished dinner and she was feeding baby Dave. I switched on the radio for the news and heard Eric's voice as usual, although it sounded different and in a few minutes I knew why. The news hit Mom like a shot, nevertheless she kept feeding Dave while tears flowed down her cheeks. When she finished, she changed him and put him in his bassinet. I walked outside on the porch and heard her begin to pray from the kitchen. I came back in, knelt down beside her on the floor and prayed with her. It's a complete shock, here at the end of the war, that he won't be alive to see the end of the long fight. We went to school today and were sent home after homeroom. Flags flew at half-mast and there was a gloomy sadness over the whole city. All day there were news reports and tonight there was a prayer meeting at church. It wasn't arranged and people just showed up. The funeral's tomorrow and he'll be buried Sunday at Hyde Park in New York.

Vice President Harry Truman has already been sworn in as the new president. I don't know much about him other than he's from Missouri. He spoke on the radio and I was glad to hear he doesn't intend to change any of President Roosevelt's plans for after the war. His voice isn't as strong as President Roosevelt's was and maybe I shouldn't care, but President Roosevelt's voice made us feel safe, that things were going to be okay. I guess vice presidents don't get a lot of opportunity to speak.

The 9th US Army crossed the Elbe River yesterday and that's only fifty miles from Berlin. The Russians are even closer on the east side of the city and it looks like there's a race on as to which side will get there first. Jenny got a letter from her brother this week. He's guarding prisoners again, this time at a camp on the Rhine River. The letter wasn't censored and he had some pretty terrible things to say about how the prisoners are being treated. I don't understand that. The war is as good as over.

Thursday April 19, 1945
Night

More bad news; Ernie Pyle has been killed in a car accident in the Philippines. I just read an article he wrote in the newspaper this last Sunday. He and Eric have been our eyes and ears throughout this war and I feel like I've lost an old friend. From the London blitz to North Africa to Europe and the Pacific, he lived with our soldiers day in and day out. It was the closest any of us could get to knowing what it was like. He once said that if you go without a bath long enough, even the fleas will leave you alone. That's how close he was. I've saved some of his articles in a scrapbook and a couple of lines caught my eye tonight when I re-read them. "Someday when peace has returned to this odd world I want to come to London again and stand on a certain balcony on a moonlit night and look down upon the peaceful silver curve of the Thames with its dark bridges."

He won't get to do that, but my favorite quote, and one I'll always remember is: "War makes strange giant creatures out of us little routine men who inhabit the Earth."

He also had a way of reminding us of the real sacrifices our soldiers have made, especially when we at home get to be a little too proud of our Army-Navy E Awards. "The front-line soldier wants it to be got over, by the physical process of his destroying enough Germans to end it. He is truly at war. The rest of us, no matter how hard we work, are not."

I can't believe he's gone. I want this month and this war to be over. This is not how people are supposed to live. This is not how children are supposed to grow up, in a world where thousands of people killed in a single day becomes ordinary news. I just want to go to sleep and not wake up until it's all over.

Sunday April 29, 1945
Night

There are reports on the radio that Mussolini's dead, killed by Italian partisans under orders from the Italian Communist Party leadership. If this doesn't convince Hitler to give up, nothing will, or the same thing's going to happen to him. The whole country's holding its breath just waiting for the next something to happen, whatever it is. Thirty thousand servicemen from Indiana have been killed in this war so far, almost four hundred from Vanderburgh County alone. We've paid more than our share.

Mr. Graves just happened to be at church today, although he's Catholic, and he just happened to sit with us. Let the gossip begin.

Tuesday May 1, 1945
Night

It's all over the news; Hitler's dead. There aren't any details, just what the German radio said and the American news agencies are being cautious about reading too much into it right now. Eric says the new leader of Germany is a Navy admiral named Donitz. If that's true, then surely he'll end the war now since he must know the real military situation. The BBC is reporting Hitler's death as fact so maybe they have more to go on than just the announcement from Germany.

The Germans also surrendered all their forces in Italy today. That barely made the news with everything else going on and I thought they'd already surrendered anyway. Everyone's on pins and needles hoping the surrender of the rest of the German military will be announced. I'm so tired of being glued to the radio. When Jenny called and invited me to the movies, I jumped at the chance; anything to get away for a while. *A Tree Grows in Brooklyn* is playing at The Grand and we both wanted to see it. It was a school night, but Mom said it would be all right. I think she's as on-edge as everyone else. It was good to spend some time with Jenny and the theater was practically empty. Everyone was home listening to their radios. Joan Blondell was great, playing the crazy aunt who'd already been married twice and was about to marry again. I've seen pictures of her naked in a girlie magazine Jenny has that she stole from Mr. Evans' studio. The article said it was her anyway and it really did look like her. What I remember were those big breasts and areolas. I keep forgetting that word. In the photos her cuzzy was shaved and Jenny thinks all movie stars probably do that.

Maybe I was thinking about Joan Blondell's breasts when I slipped my hand under Jenny's blouse after the movie started.

Tuesday May 8, 1945
Night

It's finally come. The war in Europe is over and Hitler really is dead. The official surrender was signed last night and Eric, who's always somber and chooses his words carefully, got downright excited when telling us about it this morning. The radio was on when I got up and when I heard Mom scream, I knew it wasn't a bad scream. I ran down the stairs in my pajamas and she grabbed me and hugged me. The phone was ringing; it was Jenny. School was cancelled, but if it hadn't been, no one would've showed up. School's almost over for the year anyway. There were guns firing and bells ringing all day and they only stopped when the president came on the radio. I remember exactly what President Truman said in the opening of his speech to the nation. "This is a solemn but a glorious hour. I only wish that Franklin Roosevelt had lived to witness this day. General Eisenhower informs me that the forces of Germany have surrendered to the United Nations. The flags of freedom fly over all Europe." The guns fired again and the bells started ringing again so loud I didn't hear the rest of his speech.

I ran down the street toward Jenny's and she met me halfway. I don't care who saw that kiss.

Monday May 14, 1945
Night

There are graduations to go to next Saturday and parties to attend. Jenny, Sarah, and I graduate junior high and Jimmy graduates high school. Yesterday was an official day of prayer declared by President Truman and Pastor Knott outdid himself. It was a prayer service, but it was also a celebration and after church there was a barbeque on the church grounds. Mr. Brewster was in charge and everyone had a good time. We know, as President Truman reminds us, the war is only half over, but surely the Japanese will surrender now that their two allies have been beaten. They're all alone on their island and we're getting closer every day.

Jenny's photo shoot for May was Saturday and she decided the sky-blue framed Ray-Bans were perfect. We didn't have time to do any serious shopping so we just took something off the rack at Schear's and some cheap jewelry from Neisner's. Next month though, we're going to Dunhill's and Salm's. I've been in both with Jenny and they have accounts set up for her already. Their windows are filled with the most beautiful women's clothes I've ever seen and Jenny would look fabulous in any of them. We're going to spend a day in each store as soon as school and graduation things are done. The outfit Jenny chose from Schear's was nice and we found a salesgirl who helped us pick out something that matched the color of the sunglasses perfectly.

We decided the underlying theme would be dance so the short blue skirt and the tied above the waist white blouse we found worked out well. Jenny refused to wear a bra saying that she would never be able to jitterbug wearing a bullet bra and that's the only style we could find in the amount of time we had to look. I think Mr. Evans has a sixth sense when it comes to Jenny's breasts and I'm sure there will be some photos that I'll have to veto. In the bright sunshine, when she turned just the right way, and

Mr. Evans made sure she turned that way often, you could see right through the thin material. The shoot was done at the shipyard with all the construction equipment in the background. We weren't really supposed to be inside the gate, but Mr. Evans got special permission, he said. A couple of guards watched us while we were there, although I'm sure they were just watching Jenny.

Sunday May 20, 1945
Night

Both graduations were yesterday, the junior high was first, followed by the high school, but most people came late, just for the high school ceremony. Our graduation was pretty short and we didn't get to wear caps and gowns. It was nice anyway and as soon as it was over, we got reserved seats down front for the high school graduation. I never knew Jimmy's full name was James Robert Lawrence Kohl, Junior. Mr. Evans was the official photographer of the graduation. He's told me he hates doing them but that they pay well. I talked him into getting several pictures of Jimmy, Sarah, Jenny, and me.

There were two parties, one at Jenny's and one at the Kohls'. The one at Jenny's was small, just the families really and a few friends, including Mr. Graves. It was nice that my sister, Stan, and Victoria showed up for the graduation and party. Aunt Doris even got me a graduation present, a sterling silver necklace with 1945 on the pendant, and of course Mr. Brewster had barbeque going in the back yard. It was a nice afternoon and as soon as everyone left, Sarah called Jimmy and he came and got us for the party at his house. It had been going on for some time and it didn't seem as large as the one Mr. Kohl threw for Katherine last year. She was there, although Jimmy wasn't sure she would be. She brought a friend from school and the girl was drop dead gorgeous. Jimmy didn't have to tell me they were more than just friends. I could tell by the way Katherine danced with her. Jenny and I were introduced by Jimmy and I immediately asked Katherine to dance. It was a slow waltz and I kept a respectable distance.

"Eleanor knows who you are," she whispered as she pulled me just a bit closer. "I've told her all about you and we think the three of us should get together sometime this summer."

"Well, I haven't told Jenny all about you…and I'd like to keep it that way."

"What your girlfriend doesn't know won't hurt you. Is that what you mean?"

"That's what I mean."

"I think that if you can find time for Eleanor and me once, I could keep your little secret."

The song ended with that offer, which sounded a lot like blackmail, and it wasn't hard to guess what she had in mind. A thousand consequences went through my mind. Why hadn't I kept my mouth shut? If I didn't agree to what she wanted, she would tell Jenny or she would tell Jimmy and he would tell Sarah who would just have to tell Jenny. If I did agree to what she wanted, she would have even more to tell. I was screwed either way. I went back to where Jenny was sitting and asked her to dance. Thankfully it was another slow waltz.

"Would you do it with Katherine Kohl?" I just asked outright.

"In a minute and so would you," she answered with a smile I knew all too well.

I didn't know when the call would come from Katherine but I knew it would come, and she would get more than she and her pretty little girlfriend bargained for.

Jimmy took us all home a little drunk sometime after midnight. I got out at Jenny's so I could kiss her good night, but the porch light was on. Someone had fixed it. I guess we were just drunk enough it didn't matter.

Thursday May 31, 1945
Morning

Yesterday was Memorial Day and I went with Mom and Dave to put flowers on Dad's grave and while we were there, we put flowers on Mr. Propst's too. We didn't know him but that didn't matter. As we were leaving, Mrs. Propst and Caitlan were just arriving. We talked with them for a few minutes and Mom invited them to dinner at our house. I was a little surprised when Mrs. Propst accepted. On the way home, Mom told me that she talks to Mrs. Propst often on the phone and that she's invited her to our house several times, although she always finds an excuse not to accept. Mom won't let anyone drown in depression if she knows about it. She would've made a great headshrinker. Before they arrived, Mom asked me if, after dinner, I would mind finding something to do with Caitlan so she could talk to Mrs. Propst alone.

"Mom, if you want me to get lost, I can do that," I said with a grin.

"Well, I didn't want to say it quite like that, but I would like some time with Mrs. Propst. Maybe you could take Caitlan up to your room and the two of you could play records or something for an hour."

I assured her that I would be glad to entertain Caitlan while she and Mrs. Propst talked and that she could just yell for me when their conversation was over.

Mom didn't make anything special for dinner, but Caitlan and her mom seemed to be thankful to eat someone else's cooking for a change. After dinner, I dutifully invited Caitlan up to my room to listen to records and her mom said it would be all right. I bought two new records last week and hadn't listened to either of them. They're both by Les Brown with Doris Day singing. The first one we listened to was "*My Dreams are Getting Better* All *the Time*" and it was fun dancing to because it starts off as a waltz and then you can turn it into a slow swing. Caitlan caught on to my leads. We played it about a dozen times. Then when I put on the next record, I knew I'd found something special. "*Sentimental Journey*" is the name and it's my favorite song now. After listening to it once, I played it again and took Caitlan in my arms. It's the most beautiful song I've heard in a long time. The lyrics are so romantic and the music is to foxtrot what "*In the Mood*" is to swing. I don't even like foxtrot, though the music fits so well, it's hard not to do it. My room's too small for a foxtrot, so I opened the door and we used the hallway down to the bathroom and back. After dancing to it a half dozen times, Caitlan and I had the steps down perfectly and I think we can keep up with the best of them now. She's a good follower.

To cool down, I put on some Mills Brothers and Dinah Shore. We sat on my bed, because I only have one chair in my room and neither of us wanted to sit in it. Caitlan looked so sweet. I took her face in my hands and kissed her. I don't know why I did that and it wasn't that kind of kiss either. It just seemed the right thing to do at the time and I knew she wouldn't object.

The music stopped, but I didn't want to stop what I was doing and change the record. That's when I heard Mom yell that Mrs. Propst was leaving. Caitlan had a pained look on her face before I kissed her once more and promised we would take up where we left off another time. When I heard footsteps coming up the stairs I raced for the record player. I was just putting another record on when Mom walked in. Caitlan was sitting on the bed and I hope Mom didn't notice how flushed her face was.

Today I'll tell Jenny everything that happened. She wasn't there, but this wasn't cheating. Caitlan's one of us.

Saturday June 2, 1945
Night

Jenny and I went shopping for birthday presents today. We'll be sixteen this coming week and the next week we're going for our driver's licenses. We've practiced as often as we could with the rationing we've had to live with and I think we'll pass. I hope at least one of us does.

A week ago I'd decided what I wanted to get Jenny and went straight for Bon Marché's. I wanted something French. Since the liberation of Paris, there have been some shipments of women's fashions to the States and Bon Marché has been able to grab a few of them. Mrs. Laurent calls me when she has new arrivals and I usually have a look. Nothing really caught my eye until a week ago when a shipment of evening wear arrived that I was allowed to help unpack. It was like Christmas. There was this dress, this little black dress. The tag said Nina Ricci, Paris and I knew the name, but had no idea her fashion house had survived the war. Maybe she was one of the, what the French are calling, *les collaborateurs horizontales*, and it's not hard to figure out what that means—a horizontal collaborator. I've read that Coco Chanel's hiding out somewhere in Switzerland because of the rumors she was a collaborator.

The little black dress was perfect and it was in Jenny's size so I bought it. Mrs. Laurent held it for me until today and even offered to put it on the Ray-Ban account, but it won't be used for a photo shoot and I don't want to do anything to mess up that arrangement. So far they haven't questioned anything Jenny and I have bought and every item has appeared in a photo. Mrs. Laurent did let me have the dress at a nice discount and she's letting me pay it off over time. She knows Jenny and I will be back. Even with the discount, it was still over a hundred dollars. I don't care. Jenny's going to look like a movie star in it.

Thursday June 7, 1945
Night

It feels good being sixteen. Our official party will be Saturday night and Mrs. Brewster has reserved one of the big rooms at the USO, although Jenny and I drew the line at having a live band. That would just be too expensive and besides, they wouldn't know all the latest songs anyway. We would rather have records and food. The USO has two expensive record players hooked up to microphones and speakers and the management allows local radio disk jockeys to operate them for special events. That'll be fine. Jenny, Sarah, and I can even provide the records. Neither Jenny nor I are too crazy about a big party, however Mrs. Brewster made it clear that we'll only be sixteen once and that she would have a daughter turning sixteen only once in her life, and for that we would have a party. There was no arguing with her, like with my mom when she makes up her mind. We have a photo shoot Saturday morning and Jenny says that Mr. Evans told her it will be somewhere out of town this time. As long as we're back in time for our party, I don't care where it is.

It's been such nice weather, Jenny and I decided to meet at the lake in the park yesterday afternoon to exchange gifts. The shorts she wore were too tight and too short. I didn't complain. We were carrying boxes about the same size, but this time I knew for sure we hadn't gotten each other the same thing. The warm sunshine brought out all the children and their parents, even on a Wednesday, and several of the youngest ones saw that Jenny and I had brightly wrapped presents for each other. They stood around, clearly wanting to watch us open them. There was no point in arguing with Jenny when she said I had to open her present first. As usual she had outdone me with the wrapping and I admitted defeat. She says she wraps my presents herself. I don't believe her. The bow on the front was in the shape of a car and the card she made looked like a driver's license. She's so creative when it comes to things like that and I kept the card. I could smell the present before I got the box open…something leather and it was from Hoffman's, the men's store. I had no idea.

The thin black leather briefcase with brass hardware looked like it could be carried by the finest New York lawyer. I was speechless. I'd never seen anything that nice up close before.

"If you're going to be my manager, you have to look like one. You can keep all the contracts and paperwork in there and records of our photo shoots. It can be like your office you take with you, and it'll go with anything you wear."

I've been keeping everything in a brown paper bag I carry with me when we do photo shoots or meet with Mr. Evans and I guess she must have noticed. I have records of every correspondence with Ray-Ban and prints of most of the photos in there too. It's an unorganized mess. It was the perfect gift and one I'll cherish forever.

Jenny pretended not to notice the tag on the little black dress when she took it out of the box, but I saw her take a peek.

"I have to put it on right now. It's like the little black dress you see in the movies. They say every woman should have one and now I do. It's beautiful and I really do have to put it on right now. I can't wait until I get home."

For anyone else this would have been a problem, but not for Jenny. She calmly instructed all the children to turn around for a moment and then she waited until no one close was looking in our direction. She knelt down a little behind them and had her blouse off and the dress over her head in seconds. Thank goodness she was wearing a bra, like it would have mattered. She slipped her shorts off as she pulled the dress down and it was done except for the buttons in back and I helped with them. She looked ready to walk into the finest restaurant or theater in New York. The dress fit her perfectly. I know her size in both English and European clothes. After doing a few runway walks for the children, we started for home. Jenny got a lot of looks on the way.

Saturday June 9, 1945
Late afternoon

The photo shoot today was way downriver in Union County, Kentucky on a gravel road near a farmhouse. It looked abandoned, but there were cows in the pasture behind a fence. Mr. Evans wanted to get Jenny walking down the road with just a little wind and dust in the air. Miss Payne picked out the dress this time. Jenny and I were going to do that but there just hasn't been time. It was a nice summer print dress with a lot of pink in it and we both approved. The pink-framed sunglasses Jenny chose and the big floppy white hat Miss Payne brought worked well with the dress. She helped Jenny change in the middle of the road and I made sure Mr. Evans kept his back turned. The bright sunlight went straight through the material and that wouldn't work. Thank goodness the print mostly hid how naked Jenny was under that dress and I'll definitely have to take a look at the photos before they go to Ray-Ban. I think most of them will be all right.

The news organizations are reporting that Jap Kamikaze bombers sank seventeen Allied ships (mostly ours I bet) in twenty-four hours on May 4 off the island of

Okinawa, just three hundred fifty miles from Japan. Since we're only being told about it now, it means a lot of men were lost. The closer we get, the more of these Kamikaze attacks we can expect and according to Eric, it's hard to defend against them. They come in at full speed because the pilot isn't concerned about being able to pull up after the attack. If the soldiers on the Japanese mainland are as fanatical as the Kamikaze pilots, it'll take us a year to defeat them. I hope we don't have to go from one end of the island to the other before they give up.

Sunday June 9, 1945
Very late

Maybe there is something special about a sixteenth birthday. I do feel different and I guess the party last night made me realize how grown up Jenny and I have become since fifth grade. That seems so long ago now. The ballroom was filled with people. Mom and Mrs. Brewster had announced that anyone was welcome and that there would be food. That brought out a lot of people we didn't even know and it turned into a party for anyone turning sixteen this summer. Most were from my class at Reitz, but there were a good number of high school students there as well. Jimmy said he invited everyone he ran into, including his sister and she showed up with Eleanor. The disk jockey from WMLL brought lots of records with him and he played a good mix of music that everyone could dance to. I think he played *Sentimental Journey* about a dozen times. We didn't get tired of listening or dancing to it though. When I danced with Katherine, she mentioned again that she hoped I'd be free sometime soon to spend time with Eleanor and her. If I'm going to be her prostitute, shouldn't I get paid up front or something? Isn't that the way it's done? I didn't let Katherine spoil the party for me and I only danced with her once. She'll get her date—on my terms. She won't be too quick to play her only ace and tell Jenny about my cheating. I have time.

The two punchbowls were spiked early and Jimmy brought a bottle of rum, so we had rum and Coca-Cola. When Sarah saw Jenny in that little black dress, I thought she was going to rip it off her.

"I wanted a dress like that for graduation. That was the only thing I specifically asked my parents for and I didn't get it. Mom says I'm too young and I hate it when she says things like that. Daddy just goes along with her when it comes to clothes, but even he told me I'd look beautiful in a dress like that. I don't understand. It's just a little black dress and I have skirts that I wear skating that are shorter. Promise me I can wear it sometime, Jenny. I'll take good care of it."

Jenny looked at me and I nodded. She was going to say yes anyway and I really didn't mind if Sarah wore the dress. It won't fit her very well, but if it makes her happy then I don't see the harm.

After the party, I rode home with Mom, Mrs. Brewster, and Jenny in our car. Mr. Brewster left the party early to go to work. I got out with Jenny and Mrs. Brewster at their house and told Mom I'd walk home a little later. Jenny's mom told us good night as soon as we were inside and went straight to bed. Jenny and I made ourselves peanut butter sandwiches and walked back toward the living room.

"I'm going to make her promise not to do anything with Jimmy while she's wearing my dress," she whispered. "She'll do it anyway. I saw the way he was looking at me tonight and that's what she wants. He would have pushed this little dress up to my navel and had his way with me right there on the dance floor if he thought he could have gotten away with it."

I put down my sandwich and milk on the coffee table and did the same with hers. I held her in my arms and kissed her, then reached down for the bottom of the dress and pushed it up above her waist.

"You mean like this?"

Our house was quiet when I walked up the stairs to my bedroom. I could probably have stayed the night at Jenny's. Sarah might make love with Jimmy while wearing that little black dress, but she won't be the first.

Monday June 18, 1945
Night

The streets in Evansville, Indiana aren't nearly as safe today as they were yesterday. There are two new drivers on the road. We passed. The test wasn't very hard and when I saw the short skirt Jenny was wearing when Mom and I stopped to pick her up, I had to say something.

"You know that's cheating," I said with a smile. "No policeman's going to fail you wearing that skirt."

"They might," Mom added, "just so she has to come back."

"I never thought of that," Jenny answered with a pained expression on her face.

Her plan didn't work anyway. It was a female officer who did the road test with us and I'm pretty sure she wasn't interested at all in what Jenny was wearing.

Mom says I'll be able to drive only during the day and Jenny's parents told her the same thing. That's okay because there are lots of places we can go and still be home before dark.

Friday June 29, 1945
Night

Jenny got a package from Ray-Ban today. It was a rolled up poster, three feet wide by four feet tall and she came over to show it to me. It was a blow-up of one of the pictures from the last photo shoot. If I didn't know how pretty Jenny was before today, I do now. That little print dress covered just enough and Mr. Evans caught her at the moment a gust of wind took the big floppy hat off her head. She was stretching up for it, which pulled her dress up high, and the sunglasses had slipped down on her nose. The dress was just transparent enough and the print covered the fact she wasn't wearing anything underneath it. It's no doubt the best photo of her Mr. Evans has taken for Ray-Ban so far. In a separate letter inside the package, the manager of Ray-Ban's advertising department enclosed a snapshot of the poster being displayed at their Bausch and Lomb corporate headquarters in Rochester, New York. We took the poster down to Mr. Evan's studio to show him and when we got there he was just putting one up in his window. They sent him one too. In the letter Ray-Ban sent him, they said that the posters will be for sale and that he and Jenny will get a commission for each one sold. Mr. Evans said he's placing an order for a hundred to sell in his studio for three dollars each. Pretty soon every horny high school boy in E'ville will be able to look up at Jenny from their beds. I'm not sure how I feel about that.

The Brewsters had something to celebrate yesterday. They got a letter finally; their first since the Krauts surrendered and it wasn't censored at all. Jenny's brother's safe and still guarding prisoners on the Rhine. He doesn't know if he'll be one of the lucky ones who gets to come home or if he'll be stationed in Germany for a while, or possibly even transferred to the Pacific. Surely they wouldn't do that to him. The war news from the Pacific isn't good. Japan vows to fight on without allies and defend their island against all invasions. Eric says the Japs know exactly where we'll land, that there aren't many choices. They'll be waiting for us and most think we'll lose more servicemen in the invasion than we've lost in the entire Pacific war so far. There's no doubt we'll eventually win, but at what price? The Japs have no regard for human life, even the lives of their own citizens.

Tuesday July 3, 1945
Night

The photo shoot for July will be done tomorrow during the Fourth of July parade. Jenny's in it and will be riding on a float sponsored by *The Press*. We found a swimsuit at Salm's that has red, white, and blue in it. The suit is white with wide red and blue stripes running diagonally across her bust and stomach. The material is thin, very thin, but the suit comes with removable bra inserts that we tried. They're clearly visible through the suit and look terrible. The problem was solved with wide white adhesive tape made right here in E'ville by Mead Johnson. It came in a first aid kit distributed to all the students at Reitz. I cut out circles that just covered her nipples and areolas so that nothing could be seen through the material. It worked perfectly.

It wasn't hard to figure out which sunglasses to wear. I think they were put in the shipment for the Fourth of July because the frames are red, white, and blue striped. When she put everything on this afternoon and I had a look at her, she looked sort of ridiculous, but that's expected for a Fourth of July parade. At least she didn't have to dress as the Statue of Liberty. Mr. Evans has arranged for Jenny to get her hair done early tomorrow morning at the Benson Beauty Salon even though they're closed for the Fourth and she wants me to go with her. I want it done up in a Lana Turner style, even though she'll have to get it cut a bit before that'll work and she hates getting her hair cut. She's never worn her hair short, but I think she'd like it and I know it would look good on her.

Wednesday July 4, 1945
Very late

The whole town turned out for the parade today. Jenny looked beautiful as always and Mr. Evans took hundreds of pictures for Ray-Ban. There was only one problem I found out about after we got back to Jenny's late this afternoon. I was waiting downstairs in the kitchen with Mrs. Brewster while Jenny changed when she yelled from her room for me to come up and help her with something. When I got there she was almost in tears.

"This damn tape was your idea and now it won't come off."

Her breasts were red where she'd been trying to peel the tape off. I tried and it was stuck to her skin like a thick layer of paint, and then I had an idea. I went to her bathroom and found some fingernail polish remover and cotton swabs. After a few minutes I had the tape off and left her nipples in place. I'm glad Mrs. Brewster didn't ask what the emergency was.

Jenny and I then walked up to my house. I really like her hair shorter. Mom was out with Mr. Graves and I had plans to spend some time alone with Jenny. The phone was ringing when we got inside. It was Katherine and she wanted to know if I was free to go out with Eleanor and her tonight. I put her off but said I'd call her back in a few minutes and hung up the phone.

"Remember when I asked if you would do it with Katherine Kohl? What if I was serious and what if I told you that was her on the phone and that she's expecting me to call her back."

"She called you, not me."

"Well I'm not going if you don't go with me."

"What about her girlfriend?"

"She'll be coming too."

"She is kinda cute, but I'll be with Katherine, right?"

"Right."

"Okay, I'll go. We'll be a couple of expensive prostitutes tonight. You think they'll pay us?"

I smiled and reminded her that the last time she asked for money, the girl turned her down and called her a cunt.

I called Katherine back and told to pick me up at the corner where she'd waited before. I also told her I had to be home by midnight. That was one of the new rules for Jenny and me since our birthdays. We get to stay out till midnight. We've never been able to do that before except on special occasions or if I was out with Jenny and asked permission first. I left Mom a note and Jenny called her mom and told her she and I were going out for a while and that she would be home by midnight.

Katherine wasn't expecting both of us, but there was nothing she could say when Jenny and I walked up to her car. Eleanor was in the back seat and I slid in next to her as Jenny got in the front with Katherine. Nothing was said about the extra guest as we headed east out of our neighborhood. I knew where we were going, but I was wrong, so wrong. When we pulled up in front of Lowe's, I had no idea what Katherine had in mind. We followed her into the Hotel Sonntag next door. She didn't bother stopping at the desk and by that I knew she already had a room waiting. While standing at the elevator, Katherine leaned over and kissed me. It was a little embarrassing because there were others waiting with us. They politely pretended not to notice. Our room was elegant and a couple of bottles of wine in an ice bucket had already been delivered. Maybe Katherine was trying to impress Eleanor because this was a far cry from the cheap motel she'd taken me to. The two beds were huge, so big there was hardly any room between them, and the bathroom had a tub big enough for the four of us. I whispered to Jenny that at least we were being treated like high class prostitutes.

Saturday July 7, 1945
Afternoon

Katherine poured each of us a glass of the wine and when Eleanor sat down on one of the beds, I sat with her. Jenny would get her wish and I would have to be with a total stranger. After the second glass, Eleanor switched off the lights.

"No, leave them on." The smile on her face told me Katherine had a plan. She wanted me to watch—punishment for bringing Jenny along. Eleanor picked up on the idea right away and pushed me off the bed, threw back the covers, then pulled me down to her so that we were both on our sides, her behind me, facing the other bed.

"Your girlfriend's in for the time of her life," Eleanor whispered in my ear. "Katherine's the best." I know how good she is and wanted to close my eyes but I couldn't—and I hardly felt my buttons being undone. It was like the two of us were watching a movie together sitting on the front row, except for the strange hands all over me and the tears streaming down my face neither of the actors would notice. This was all so wrong and I was already worried knowing Eleanor and I would be expected to perform for them later. Poor Jenny had no idea what any of this was really all about.

Katherine got what she wanted, torturing me; Jenny got what she wanted, playing prostitute for an evening— and I got what I deserved—payback. Everyone's even now

I guess. Katherine has no reason to talk and she'll be able to brag someday to the other social climbers in her world about making love with a real model before she was famous, and she has a witness. I'll never be able to forget what I saw and heard and did; that's a lifetime of punishment for my cheating. This wasn't us having fun with Sarah or even Jimmy. These people are not our friends and will never be our friends.

Maybe the night didn't turn out exactly as Katherine had planned, but we gave her and her girlfriend what they wanted and then we were taken home, well before midnight. It won't be one of those nights Jenny and I talk about when we're eighty.

Sunday July 15, 1945
Night

Katherine and Eleanor left last week going to Florida and then they're going north to visit Katherine's Aunt Eileen in Maine, although Katherine's father doesn't know it. Jimmy told Sarah and Sarah told Jenny and Jenny told me. They'll get back right before they have to leave for school in the fall. I don't think Katherine told Jimmy anything about our date on the Fourth of July. He's too much of a gentleman to bring it up even if she did. Besides, the two of them know too much on each other.

It was in the paper last week that General MacArthur has announced that the liberation of the Philippine islands from the Japs is complete. I know that doesn't mean our sailors and soldiers are safe now, and maybe that's why Eric hasn't mentioned it. The Japs still have lots of ships in the area and they can fire on any of the islands from them.

Tuesday July 24, 1945

Night

Jenny and I spent the day at the pool. It's almost the end of July and we haven't been to the pool at all until today. I remember when we would have gone every day after the last day of school. When Caitlan called last night and suggested we all go, I volunteered to bring sandwiches and iced tea for a little picnic. We haven't seen much of Caitlan in the last month and when she arrived, I knew why. She introduced us to Teresa Kay who was her age and just as pretty.

"She and her mom moved in across the street a few weeks ago and I've been showing her around."

"Caitlan has told me so much about the two of you," Teresa spoke up. "It's like I already know you."

There were enough sandwiches for all of us, but Caitlan and her new friend had to share a glass of iced tea and I could tell they didn't mind. There was something special between them already. We were all in swimsuits and they sat close enough at the picnic table for their bare legs to touch; the way Jenny and I always sat at the same table at the same pool when we were their age.

"I was wondering," Caitlan said with a smile, "if maybe sometime the four of us could go to a movie or something. Teresa and I aren't allowed to be out late at night, but I know our moms would let us go with the two of you."

Jenny answered for both of us but I wasn't expecting what she said.

"Well I don't know. Would there be hand holding and kissing?"

"No, I promise," Teresa answered quickly. "Not if you don't want us to."

"She's just kidding you, Theresa," Caitlan added. "I told them the first time I went to the movies with them that it would be okay if they kissed. I saw them kiss when I was ten and never forgot it. It was the first kiss I ever saw in real life."

Then it was my turn.

"You also promised never to tell anyone as I remember, and now you have." Then I winked at Caitlan and added, "she must be something special."

On our walk home, Jenny asked me if Caitlan and Teresa reminded me of anyone. I thought about that when we got to her house—during the kiss I gave her on the front porch in broad daylight.

When I got home, there was a cake on the kitchen table with candles on it. During the blessing at dinner, Mom said a special prayer for Amelia Earhart.

Sunday July 29, 1945
Afternoon

Jenny and I took Caitlan and Teresa to see *Laura* with Gene Tierney and Dana Andrews last night at The Grand. Jenny and I liked it, but I think our guests were much more interested in each other than the movie. I tried not to spy, but watching them hold hands and kiss reminded me so much of the hours Jenny and I spent together in that theater doing the same thing when we were their age. After the movie we went to Muir's for ice cream and sat at the same table Jenny and I always sat at. I remember Mr. Muir's tablecloths because they hang down far enough no one could see us hold hands. Caitlan and Teresa figured that out pretty quick too.

Thursday August 2, 1945
Night

The USS Indianapolis has been torpedoed near Tinian in the Philippines. I've been following that ship for a long time because of its name. I don't know anyone aboard and Eric didn't have any details about whether the ship sank or not. Usually, when they don't release any information, it means the ship was sunk.

The photo shoot for August is tomorrow and today Jenny and I spent over a hundred dollars of Ray-Ban's money on her outfit at Dunhill's, then we had dinner at the Spaghetti Bowl. I like that place and the owner's nice. Max always comes out and talks to us when we eat there. He's a real Italian and tonight he told Jenny he had a favor to ask of her. He left and returned a few minutes later with four of the Ray-Ban posters. He bought them from Mr. Evans who had told him that Jenny would sign them if he asked. Jenny signed one to each of Max's sons, but we knew he only had three sons. When Jenny asked who the fourth poster should be signed to, Max dropped his head and sort of mumbled something that was probably Italian.

"To Gina if you wouldn't mind," he repeated. "My ten year old daughter thinks you're the most beautiful woman in the world."

Jenny wrote "Hugs and kisses for my Gina" and then drew kissy lips on the poster before signing her name.

The free Ricotta cheesecake Max brought us after our meal was delicious. Being out with a celebrity has its benefits.

Saturday August 4, 1945
Night

It's been three years now and when I look at Mom's favorite picture of him from the CCC Camp, I have trouble remembering what Dad looked like the last time I saw him.

She prayed tonight at dinner and thanked God for the years they had together. She talked much more than usual while we ate and she fed Dave. It seemed she was trying to get around to something important but just couldn't figure out how. She gave me an extra glass of milk and a shortbread cookie after we finished. That meant it was serious.

"You know I think the world of Jenny and Mrs. Brewster thinks the world of you, and maybe she and I are poking our noses in where they don't belong, but we see how fond you are of each other and you're our children and…"

"I love her."

"And I love her too. She's like a member of the family, but…"

"No, I mean I really do love her, the way you loved Dad and the way your mother loved your father, the way Romeo loved Juliet, the way…"

"But dear, they were all…"

"Yes, and Jenny and I aren't, but that doesn't mean I don't love her."

"Do you know what you're saying? Are you sure? Are you really sure, because…"

"I'm as sure as I can be. It's hard to explain; she's all I think about. You told me Dad's mom was only thirteen when she got married and maybe I know how she felt. This isn't exactly what you would have planned for me, I know, but Jenny and I have been in love since we were in fifth grade. You must have seen it. It just happened and we would never do anything to…"

"You've always been my hope, and you were your father's too. It's the way I raised you. I never wanted you to depend on anyone for anything and I guess I made you grow up too fast and didn't pay attention to some things I should have. I wanted a child I could sit at the table and talk with, just like we're doing right now, and someone I could depend on if I ever needed to and I've depended on you since you were old enough to walk. Lord knows I tried with your sister but she was never like me, or your father. You've known from the beginning Millie was her daughter and you never brought it up. I realized how mature you were even then, so if you tell me now that you love Virginia, then I have to believe you and that's just the way it is."

"I love you Mom and I'll always be your kid, regardless of what happens with Jenny and me. We're a family, maybe an unusual family, but we do love each other and that's all that matters."

She kissed me and started clearing the table as if we had been talking about the weather. So now everyone I care about knows.

Tuesday August 7, 1945
Night

Big news tonight on the radio; Eric says we dropped an atom bomb on Japan yesterday—whatever that is—and that this bomb is more powerful than any ever made. I have no idea what he was talking about, although according to him, this might just end the war. How can a single bomb end the war when the thousands we've already dropped on Japan haven't?

The atom bomb wasn't the only bomb that got dropped. After dinner tonight Mom dropped a bomb of her own. While we were doing the dishes, she told me Mr. Graves had something important he wanted to discuss with me.

"You told me something Saturday that was hard for you and now I have something to tell you. He's asked me to marry him. I told him right quick I wouldn't even discuss it until he talked with you and I thought that would put him off a while, but he agreed on the spot. Even if he gets your blessing, I'm not going to marry him right away."

"Do you love him, Mom?"

"Not like I loved your father from the time we first met, but I don't think it's fair to Mr. Graves that I compare how I feel now to how I felt then. That was a long time ago and I was a lot younger. Mr. Graves and I are happy when we're with each other and I know he's a good man. He would treat you and Dave well. Nevertheless I can't make this kind of a decision without your support. You live here too and you have every right to an opinion. If you tell me that you want whatever makes me happy, I'll strangle you. I'm happy now. I don't need a man to make me happy."

"Sometimes it's about want instead of need. If you want a man to make you happy, then Mr. Graves is as good as any and better than most."

"Would it be all right if I asked him to dinner Saturday night?"

Saturday August 10, 1945
Night

We dropped another atom bomb on Japan yesterday and they're saying the one we dropped Monday killed tens of thousands and destroyed an entire city. We don't know how much damage this one caused. Everyone has been holding their breath since last Tuesday, hoping the Japs will surrender.

The Russians have declared war on Japan and I guess that's important, although Eric doesn't seem to think they'll be committing any troops to the fighting if the invasion comes. Maybe they're a little late in declaring war because we were a little late in landing at Normandy.

Mom and I had our dinner with Mr. Graves tonight and he was a perfect gentleman as always. There was never any doubt in my mind that I would approve of their marriage. Mom might not need a man to be happy, but she deserves one if she wants one. I began the conversation very serious-like after Mom and I cleared the table.

"I understand you have asked Mom to marry you, Mr. Graves and that you would like my blessing. My mother is a very special woman and she deserves a good man who will stand by her and one who will always consider her feelings in any important decision. You will also be called on to be a father to my little brother and we expect you to treat him as your own. It's not just my mother you'll be marrying either; you'll be marrying her family as well, including me and my sister. Before you agree to that, you should know something important about me. I don't know how much Mom has told you, but I have a girlfriend and the two of us are very much in love. Her name is Virginia Brewster and she'll be a part of this family as well. I hope you'll love her as much as the rest of us, however you'll be expected to treat her well even if you don't. You're taking on a lot, Mr. Graves, however I believe you're a good honest man and that you'll weigh everything before committing to this marriage. If you love my mother and are willing to accept all our family's shortcomings, then I would be proud to have you join us. If not, neither my mother nor I will think any less of you." I had written down and rehearsed what I wanted to say and I covered about everything.

"I do love your mother and I promise to take care of her and Dave to the best of my ability. Your mother has told me some things about your sister and you. I also know the Brewsters well and I know Virginia. They're a fine family, one of the most respected in Evansville. If Virginia's a part of this family, then she's a part of this family and that's all there is to it. If you and your mom love her, then I'll make every effort to love her too."

He's so much like Mom it's scary. After that I had to give my blessing and, just as I'd done with my sister and Stan, I kissed them both. In a funny way, I was being Dad again.

Tuesday August 14, 1945
Night

It's all over! The war is over! The Japanese have surrendered. President Truman announced the surrender on the radio at six tonight. It won't be official until things are formally signed but no one cares. People ran out onto the streets; fireworks or maybe it was gunfire started even before the end of his speech—as soon as the word surrender was spoken. Mom and I hugged each other and we walked down the crowded sidewalk toward the Brewster's. About halfway, I spotted Jenny and her mom walking toward us and ran for her. She was crying and laughing when I took her in my arms. With Mom and Mrs. Brewster and anyone else who cared to be watching, I kissed her like I've never kissed her. I squeezed her tight, lifting her up off the ground and swinging her around like a rag doll.

"I love you Jenny B.," I yelled above the noise.
"And I love you, Katie R."

She calls me that sometimes.

Chapter Seven

Afterword

January 2018

Only Jenny ever called me Katie or Katie R. I was always Kathleen to Mom and Dad, and Kathy to everyone else.

For decades I had no idea what had become of my journal. I searched occasionally after I got older and finally gave up looking. It took me a full year to transcribe the first draft of my diary after I found it in October 2008, and it was several more years before I could add the last lines and ask someone else to read excerpts from it.

When I sat down and wrote the foreword to this manuscript, I had plans to keep writing the story as long as I lived and maybe that's what has kept me alive this long. I never gave a thought of how to end it. When I first started, it helped with the writing for me to think that the story was about someone else. The writing began as me simply transcribing a diary I'd supposedly found in an old house, and now I rather like that bit of deception. It took months to become that eleven year old again and once I did, I didn't want the story to end. This hasn't just been a temporary escape from reality however; it's been the reliving of a reality that once was. Not many have that opportunity.

I took with me only what I needed when I sold this house after Mom died in 1980 and I left most of her things where they were. I was a very young fifty-one year old widow at the time and anxious to move back to Chicago to be near Jenny. The tin on the mantle was just a cookie tin I kept things in, like my diary. I guess Mom found it and put it on the mantle, probably because she liked the way it looked there. I've often wondered if she read it or even looked inside the box. When I left this house in 1980 it had already been more than thirty years since I carefully wrapped my diary in waxed paper and put it in that tin, and somehow in that time span, I simply forgot what I'd done with it. I don't know when Mom put it on the mantle, but I don't ever remember seeing it there. I'm fortunate in that the ladies who lived here after Mom died liked it just where she'd put it, or maybe one of them found it and put it there. There's no way of knowing. When I bought the house back in 2008 and moved in permanently, the tin was the first thing I noticed and all the memories came back when I opened it and began to read what I'd written so long ago.

Sometime after I started transcribing this diary, I re-read what I'd written and realized I hadn't identified myself, not by name or even gender. That was just how I wrote back then, which sort of made sense; it was a diary and not ever intended to be read by anyone but me. It became a sort of game to see if I could keep up the charade and the longer it went on, the harder it would have been to stop, so I never identified myself in the transcription either. My mother, whose name was Helen, was Mom, my father, whose name was Donald, was Dad, and my sister Olivia was my sister. Considering the content of the diary, I was also a little concerned from the beginning about others being identified if it fell into the wrong hands. I changed everyone's name just to be safe. Things were very different in 1940 and when I finished transcribing my diary almost a decade ago, I was still a little hesitant about revealing real names. Being ninety however does give one the courage to do things that wouldn't be considered at eighty, so I've given everyone their true names back in the final version. A few of the people mentioned are still living and those who aren't have children and grandchildren who might be surprised to learn that grandma was quite a character in her day. It was indeed a very different time.

Jenny and I graduated high school in May of 1949 and in the fall we became roommates at Indiana University in Bloomington. It was close enough to Evansville, but also far enough away. When we were high school seniors we started corresponding with two soldiers from Indiana who were stationed in Germany, Raymond Sparks and Charles Dover. Every girl in class was encouraged by our teachers to write to a soldier and Jenny and I enjoyed doing it. They were both officers and had been in the Army since before Pearl Harbor. They volunteered to stay in Germany after the war and intended to make a career of it—until they met Jenny and me when they were on leave at Christmastime in 1948. We started getting marriage proposals as soon as they were back in Germany. We married those two wonderful men, in a double ceremony of course, on October 20, 1950 and moved to Chicago with them when they got out of the Army in the spring of 1952. We even bought houses on the same street and finished our degrees together at IU by mail. Ray and Charlie knew about Jenny and me—they must have—but neither ever brought it up. We saw each other every day and went on long weekend trips together whenever we could. Our husbands were almost ten years older than us but we were happy. Jenny and I had our children together. I had one son, Paul, and Jenny had one daughter, Josie, and they were born within a few days of each other in 1953. That might not have happened if Mom hadn't become concerned about me when I turned sixteen. I still hadn't had a period. Over Christmas break in 1945 she took me to a doctor who gave me an injection of some sort and my periods started. I didn't think I'd been missing anything.

Neither Jenny nor I ever used the word lesbian to describe ourselves. We weren't lesbians. We were two women who happened to love each other and that was it. Jenny always described us as lovers to anyone who got too nosy, and that was explanation enough. She was right; we had husbands and children we loved, but she and I were lovers and that was different.

My Raymond died in 1972 of a heart attack—he was only fifty-two—and Jenny was there for me as always. I continued to live in our Chicago house until I moved back to Evansville temporarily to take care of Mom. I didn't sell it because I had a feeling I might be coming back soon. Mom wasn't in good health and I didn't want to permanently live that far away from Jenny. After Mom died, I returned to Chicago and had another twenty-eight wonderful years with her. I was there for her when her Charlie died in 1991 and then the two of us were able to do something we'd always dreamed of. We sold our houses, bought a smaller one and slept together every night. We lived together as a couple of sixty-two year old widows and did as we pleased for the next seventeen years. There have been so many best times of my life with Jenny, but those years were the best of the best.

Jenny modeled for Ray-Ban until we went away to IU and both of us invested every spare nickel we had in stock. When Bausch and Lomb sold Ray-Ban to an Italian company in 1999, we made enough money to live another lifetime. Mr. Evans had even more stock than we did, but he died before the sale and I don't know what happened to it. Soon after he died, Miss Payne delivered a package to us and avowed with a big smile on her face that she didn't know any details about the contents, but that she recognized very well who should get it. It had been a long time since I'd seen Jenny blush so I knew she suspected what we would find. I handed the box to her and she handed it back to me. When I opened it, dozens of nude photos of Jenny fell out.

"I knew that old bastard would make prints for himself. He told me he hadn't and I made him give me the negatives, but I never trusted him. I have no idea what became of my copies or the negatives. Maybe Charles found them and tore them up. Mine were supposed to be the only prints made."

There were pictures of Jenny when she couldn't have been more than thirteen, all the way up to just before we graduated high school.

"He made the photos because I asked him to. At first I just wanted to see what I looked like naked in a photo—like those in the girlie magazines. Later I wanted them done so I could look back and remember what I looked like when I was young. You know how vain I am."

I kissed her and the two of us spent an entire evening looking through the photos. Mr. Evans might have been a bastard, but he'll never know what a favor he did us by making those prints. The memories they brought back were priceless and someday I might just show them to Jenny's grandchildren...probably not.

Our children married and they had children and we enjoyed having them visit their quirky grandmothers. Paul married a girl he met in college who was from a wealthy family in Southern California and Josie married a hometown Chicago boy. They both married well and were happy by all indications. Paul and his wife, Cynthia lived in Evansville near the house I grew up in, and live in now, so they were pleased (or Paul was anyway) when I decided to move back here after Jenny died. I got to see a lot more of them and my two grandsons who had grown into fine young men by that time.

Early this year, Paul and Cynthia unexpectedly moved to Southern California and I was devastated. It was only after my youngest grandson told me his mother is terminally ill that I knew why. Cynthia and I have never been really close, and I understand her wanting to be near her relatives during her last days. Paul's house is up for sale, but it won't sell in this market and I'm sure that after Cynthia passes, he'll move back. It's hard to stay away from this town for very long. Josie and her husband Ed still live in Chicago and we used to see a lot of their daughter, Christine before she went away to school in Virginia.

Sarah married Jimmy, much to the consternation of his father. It's impossible not to like Sarah though and she soon became a part of the Kohl family. I think maybe Katherine's becoming a professional lesbian had something to do with it as well. Professional lesbians are what Jenny used to call those lesbians who are always in the news or on television shows. Katherine and her lover moved to Maine, I think it was, after she graduated college, to be near her aunt, and Sarah sort of took her place as the young woman of the family. In 2004, as soon as the law was passed in Massachusetts, Jimmy told us that Katherine and her girlfriend at the time went there and got married. She'd been written out of the will long before that and all the Kohl holdings went to Jimmy when his parents died. Jimmy and Sarah are still living and are in reasonably good health. They visit often and we've gone on several trips together.

My sister, Olivia, and Stan lived in their house on Adams Avenue until Victoria died of cancer in 1979. Her husband died a few years before her. I don't know how much Victoria left Olivia, but she and Stan lived very well the rest of their lives in a huge house near the one they moved from. By that time the area was becoming the Riverside Historic District. Olivia died soon after my Jenny. It was sudden and I think Stan just didn't want to live anymore. He died a year later leaving Millie everything. Olivia may have told him she was her daughter, but it was never mentioned in public by either of them. Millie and her husband now live in the house and they're good to visit me. She never asked why Olivia left her everything. Maybe she still doesn't know she was her mother and I see no reason to tell her. She and her husband have two children and I see them occasionally. Aunt Doris and Bob are both gone now and I miss them every day.

Mike and Harry grew up and joined the Navy. They made a career of it and settled somewhere on the west coast with their families after retiring.

My brother Dave never got to grow up. His was one of the last cases of polio in the country. It was so bad that when he was only five, Mom had to put him in a care facility in Owensboro. We visited him every weekend and he kept getting worse. He was only eight when he died and I miss him still. Mom married Mr. Graves in the fall of 1946 and he was what got Mom through the pain of losing Dave. We were right about Mr. Graves. He was a good man and he and Mom were happy for the twenty years they had together. Mom's buried between him and Dad at Oak Hill. Jenny's brother, Sammy made it home from the war without a scratch. He arrived on Christmas Eve 1945 and brought a very pretty English girl named Audra with him. He was transferred back to England right after the war and the two of them got married. She was the girl in the picture he sent, I think in 1940. It was a surprise for the family, but Audra and Jenny became friends almost overnight and that spread to the rest of the Brewsters. Sammy took a job in Chicago in 1946 and he and Audra moved there, but they visited regularly. They had twin girls, Annette and Janet, who live with their husbands on opposite ends of the country now. Sammy died in 1978 after a car accident and Audra moved to Boston to live with Janet and her family. I sort of lost track of her after that.

I don't know how much Jenny's mom ever told her dad about the two of us, but he was by far the happiest man at our weddings to Raymond and Charles. Jenny's parents lived alone for several years after everyone moved out and they died within a few days of each other in a retirement home here in Evansville in the mid 1980s. Caitlan Propst and her mom moved in the summer of 1946 to somewhere in South Carolina. Mrs. Propst never got over the death of her husband and I guess she thought moving away from

Evansville would help. Jenny and I got a few letters from Caitlan after they moved but they eventually stopped. I should try to find out whatever happened to her. She was an interesting girl.

Jenny died in my arms right after New Year's in 2008. We both had the normal aches and pains that come with getting old, however Jenny developed late onset diabetes in 2000 and almost died before it was diagnosed. It eventually killed her. Thankfully she was coherent right up to the end. The truth is…she was a little drunk. Her passing wasn't a surprise. Our doctor told us how it would come and for a month before she died, we knew it could be at any time. She'd become so weak I had to help her walk and she couldn't sit up for very long. That Friday after New Year's though, she felt pretty strong so I talked her into going to the local senior center in the afternoon. After we lost three hands straight at gin, we decided we would rather drink gin than play gin. As a toast with the first martini, we promised each other that neither of us would ever drag the other to that damn senior center again. We'd made that promise before, but this time we meant it. We started going because our doctor said they needed a dance instructor there. He was wrong. What they needed was a reason to dance and Jenny and I couldn't provide that. When it was well past our bedtime, I stood up and reached down to help her.

"Just sit with me a few more minutes, Katie," were her last words.

When she closed her eyes, I sat down, kissed her and held her in my arms. I closed my eyes and didn't care if I ever opened them again. All the beautiful women were gone.

The pictures Jenny and I gave each other for Christmas in 1944 hang together in our bedroom and for some reason a week after she died I thought of the note I wrote to her on the back of mine and wondered if she ever found it. In the middle of the night, I got up and took my picture down and out of its frame. I remembered what I'd written.

"HVNTKCMSSQZCDNMDLNQDXDZQVHSGXNTEN QZGTMCQDCVHSGNTSXNT"

Underneath was written in her handwriting:

"HCSQZCDZKKLXXDRSDQCZXRENQITRSNMDLNQ DSNLNQQNVVHSGXNT"

Letting her go was the hardest thing I've ever had to do and ending this story is like having to let her go again.

Please…just one more dance and one more kiss. I love you Jenny B.

Coming soon from d.a. gregory and Solstice Publishing:

Bring the Curious Midwife

Curious once had a different sort of meaning in the South; it meant peculiar—not in a bad way necessarily. "That girl's just curious," was how folks who knew her often described Otha May St. Clair, even before she was old enough to go to school. In the small rural North Alabama community where her family lived, most everyone knew full well what made Otha May curious and most everyone also thought it to be none of their business.

It's the early 1940s; the country's at war and Otha May has come to accept that finding anyone else like her, especially in the South, might take forever, but a new family moving into the community and a real job working for the only midwife in the county turn her life around. A respectable job and someone to love mean the world to her and she finds both, but the wedding she wants more than anything can't be had for love nor money. That would cost her much more.